VAMPIRE
RESURRECTION

Vic Brown

High Tide Publications, Inc.
Deltaville, Virginia

High Tide Publications, Inc.
1000 Bland Point Road
Deltaville, Virginia 23043
www.HighTidePublications.com

Publisher's Note: This is a work of fiction. Names, characters, places, and incidents are a product of the author's imagination. Locales and public names are sometimes used for atmospheric purposes. Any resemblance to actual people, living or dead, or to businesses, companies, events, institutions, or locales is completely coincidental.

Ordering Information:

Quantity sales. Special discounts are available on quantity purchases by corporations, associations, and others. For details, contact the "Special Sales Department" at the address above.

Vampire Resurrection by Vic Brown, 1st edition

Printed in the United States of America

ISBN 978-0692379134

Vampire Resurrection is dedicated
to Jenny Lindberg Brown,
the beacon of my life.

1

Apocalypse Revealed
November 25, 2011

"The greatest trick the Devil ever pulled was convincing
the world he didn't exist."

Charles Baudelaire,
The Generous Gambler, 1864

L ungs heaving, Lamar leaned his forehead against the brick wall, willing the dizziness away. His hands ached from the cold. "Where's my trench coat?" he mumbled, unable to see much in the dark alley. As his breathing slowed, he began to retch. The stench of urine, garbage and vomit was overpowering. He tasted iron and touched his right cheek, which was burning.

Blood dripped from his chin. I've been cut. Or clawed?

He found his handkerchief and gently daubed his face, then frowned, not sure what to do with it. Lamar looked down. It took a moment for him to recognize the peculiar shape at his feet: a cat. Dead. *Mutilated.* He bent over. The cat was still warm.

What could have done this? He heard footsteps running toward him. I need a weapon. Something. Anything. He spotted a broken whiskey bottle and reached for it but lost his balance and fell against the wall.

"Mr. Bradford. Are you all right? Here, let me—" the man's voice trailed off as he looked down. "Oh, God. It's started. Sir, put your arm around me." He pulled Lamar upright. The street lamp at one end of the alley cast grotesque shadows that reached for them with long bony fingers.

"Robert?"

"Here, sir. Lean back against the wall for a moment." Robert produced a handkerchief and began wiping Lamar's face, patting his right cheek. "We'll get you home and sorted out." Robert took Lamar's bloody monogrammed handkerchief, balled it with his own, and looked around, then jammed them into his topcoat pocket. "Can you walk now, sir?"

"Yes, yes, I'm sure I can." His voice sounded hollow, and his mouth tasted foul.

As the two stumbled through the alley, Robert found Lamar's trench coat and wrapped it around the shivering younger man. Within minutes they were in the warm backseat of an Ambassador cab.

"The Jaguar."

"I'll collect it in the morning," Robert said.

"Robert, did you see the dead cat that was at my feet?"

"Cat, sir? I don't seem to recall one, no. Wouldn't surprise me though. The way that alley smelled, all manner of vermin must have crawled in there and died."

Lamar took a deep breath and exhaled. So much for seeing *The Hound of the Baskervilles,* he thought. He remembered Robert dropping him in front of the Cambridge Central Square Theater, a favorite with Harvard students, and driving off to park the Jag, then that strange sensation, almost like falling. It reminded him of the seizures he used to have as a schoolboy. Then nothing until the cold bricks against his forehead. He felt exhausted but with a strange sense of exhilaration. His head sagged, and his chin rested on the knot of his tie, which Robert had pulled down. It was shredded.

Oh, God. It's started. Lamar bounded out of bed, trembling. Robert's voice echoed like the fading chime of the ponderous clock downstairs.

"What's started?" The large, opulent room swallowed Lamar's voice; all the rooms in Coleson Manor were opulent. One of seven colonial mansions in the heart of West Cambridge's Brattle Street District, the homes were still referred to by some as "Tory Row," 230 years after the Revolution.

Why couldn't he remember what happened in that alley? Damn and blast. A burning sensation on his right cheek reminded him of the scratches from last night, and he touched the gauze pad and bandage. The recollection made him dizzy.

Lamar never thought of himself as handsome. Everything about him was average, even his age—thirty-seven. At five-ten, one-sixty-two, trim and in fair shape from his twice-weekly visits to Harvard's Malkin Athletic Center, he looked reasonably good. In an average sort of way. A few gray hairs announced the fading bloom of youth. In a few more years he'd be totally gray, like his father had been at forty-two.

His pale blue eyes—this morning they were red, with puffy eyelids—turned almost black when he was angry. Or frightened. At least that's what his mother had said. With perfect white teeth he could make a TV commercial for Aquafresh, but this morning his mouth tasted like the stink from the alley, and he reached for his toothbrush and the Listerine.

Still somewhat dazed, Lamar felt a chill draft and wandered into the bedroom to shut the window. A mocking bird was blasting through its entire repertoire on the limb of a nearby white birch. "Damn stupid bird," he shouted, slamming the window. Neither shouting nor slamming was recommended, Lamar discovered. His scalp tingled, reminding him of Robert bending him over the sink, scrubbing for God knows how long to get the blood out of his hair.

His stomach rumbled.

He glanced at his wrist. No watch. Nor was it on the bedside table. Where the hell's my watch? Maybe Robert took it off when he was scrubbing me. He could have left it beside the bed, damn him. And why is my clock radio unplugged? Whatever time it is, he's overdue with my morning coffee.

Gripping the banister he slowly descended the staircase. When he reached the landing that joined the two flights of stairs, he called, "Robert! It is way past coffee time." Nothing. The house was silent save for the ticking of the eighteenth century English longcase clock in the hall.

Strange. As he reached the first floor he noticed a card, folded like a tent, on the Queen Anne handkerchief table next to the clock.

4

Mr. Bradford,

    I am off collecting the XKR. It needs an oil change according to the Jag maintenance manual, and I've booked it for next Thursday. Your watch took a beating, and I shall drop it off at the Swiss Watchmaker on Church Street. A pot of coffee with two croissants and honey await you in the kitchen, along with two Advil, which I suggest you take. The Times and Globe are in the library. I also plan to stop at Formaggio's to replenish the wine cellar a bit.

    Do rest easy until I return. I'll fix your favorite Eggs Benedict and champagne brunch. By the end of the day you will be back to being a regular old sod.

    Robert

Lamar read the note a second time and shook his head.

Good old Robert. A peculiar man. As much a part of my life as my shoes. Put them on in the morning and never think about them the rest of the day. I get up, put on Robert, and don't much think about him either.

Indispensable yet rather intrusive. Extremely helpful but to a fault. Doesn't seem to have any vices. Doesn't have a life other than looking after me and this cavernous old haunt. In spite of a slight paunch, he seems unusually agile for a man his age. Maybe sixty? I ought to ask. And quick-witted. Bloody man insists I dress for dinner as if we were part of a large, turn-of-the-century Victorian family, and there's only the two of us.

He grew up in England, but I don't even know where for sure. No family apparently.

Butler, valet, chef, nurse, tutor, estate manager—the man does everything but pee for me. Faithful as an old hound dog, but I don't even know if he likes me. Watches me like a mother hen, even more so of late. Especially last night. Can't imagine what would have become of me….

Wonder what my father's trust fund pays him? Couldn't fire the man if I wanted to, not that I would. Besides, he's the only person in the world I can talk to.

Ah, Robert Diamond, you are a world-class chamberlain. It might behoove me to find out—crap, I'm even using words like 'behoove.'

Lamar scowled and walked into the kitchen, poured a cup of coffee, and swept the two Advil into the disposal. Ignoring the croissants, he headed for the library.

Robert had made a fire. Lamar added a couple pieces of apple wood from the neatly quartered and stacked logs in the brick arch next to the fireplace. Dull gray light from the windows cast a pall throughout the dark, wood-paneled room, and Lamar turned on the electrified candle stand lamp, settled into his favorite leather wingback chair with matching footstool, opened the *Globe*, and read the weather forecast. Hope Robert gets back before it starts snowing.

Almost an hour later he spotted an article about the annual Dedham antique car rally to be held in July. Antique cars had been a secret passion of his since early boyhood, and he recalled pouring over the 1911 edition of the *Encyclopedia Britannica* and marveling at the Stanley Steamer, the Baker Electric, the Reo Runabout and other early automobiles. He had always longed to own an antique car. His all-time favorite was the 1929 Stutz

Bearcat two-tone, dual-cowl phaeton with the LeBaron chassis. A hot car during Prohibition, it could outrun the Feds any day of the week. He'd even seen one once that had a bullet hole in a back fender. Ah, for the Roaring Twenties. He sipped some coffee and smiled, wondering if he could find the Stanley and the Baker again.

The bottom shelf of the floor-to-ceiling bookcase held a long row of thick, gray-green volumes, covered with a light film of dust, notwithstanding the cleaning crew that came once a week. He would mention that to Robert. That'll wilt the starch in his collar.

Crouching down, he extracted volume A. As he did, the longcase clock began striking, and, as he had all his life, he counted the number of chimes. Twelve? It can't be noon. Lamar looked at his wrist, grimaced, and then peered at the library mantle clock, which showed ten forty-four. "What's wrong with you, old friend?" He recalled it had only been a couple of months since the guy from the Swiss Watchmaker serviced it. "Damn and blast."

Gathering volume A, he was about to return to the wingback when he noticed another book lying behind the row of encyclopedia. Pulling out two more volumes, he retrieved an obviously old, leather-bound book almost two feet long, nine inches wide, and a couple inches thick, with gilt-edged pages.

He walked to the kneehole desk that had been his father's and placed the strange book, with its dark green leather spine and thick covers, on the desktop. He switched on the desk lamp, pulled open the lower left drawer and retrieved a half-full bottle of twenty-five-year-old Chivas Regal and an eighteenth century tavern glass, both left there by his late father. He poured the scotch and sniffed it, then took a sip. Drinking in the morning. What's to become of me?

In the top center drawer, he found his father's 1940 Yello Bole pipe along with an amber glass pipe holder from India, a half-full, zippered leather tobacco pouch, and pipe tamper. His father's pipe lighter was ten-carat gold plated and monogrammed: *Coleson B. Bradford.* The pipe had a well-chewed yellow stem, which set off the rich brown patina of the shank and apple-shaped bowl. These were the only artifacts of his father's Lamar had been able to salvage.

A month after his father's death, his mother, Allison, was discovered at the Saugus landfill burying all of her husband's worldly possessions. His mother was nude. She died six weeks later in Mt. Auburn Hospital; she hadn't known her son when he visited. That was 1996, the year Lamar graduated from Harvard.

Lamar didn't like the taste of scotch at first, nor did he enjoy smoking a pipe, but now he smiled as he produced a cloud of smoke that hovered over the desk. The vanilla aroma of Billy Budd blended nicely with the mellow flavor of the Chivas. As usual, they strengthened his sense of place—of belonging. Few things did. He studied the leather-bound book.

A large opal in the center of the front cover was surrounded by what appeared to be gilded Celtic scrollwork. The opal seemed to fire off green and gold sparks, picking up the colors of the cover and the raised letters. Lamar puffed on the pipe, adding to the fragrant cloud, and reached for the volume, but hesitated, feeling a tremor in his hand. He squeezed his right hand into a tight fist before finally opening the cover. The faint licorice scent of Absinthe mingled with the Billy Budd.

Odd.

He was stunned by the extraordinarily intricate and colorful image that graced the first page. A monk in a black robe sat hunched over a desk in a monastery scriptorium, copying a manuscript, sunlight shining through narrow, leaded windows. A cat, perched on the windowsill, watched the scribe. Under the rich tableau was the inscription *Codex Damnatus.* MCCXCII (1292). He puzzled over the Latin. Book of the Dead? Book of the Damned? My Latin is rusty, he thought. He'd have to get Professor Dorrel in the history department to translate it.

An envelope was wedged between the binding and the second page, addressed to him and sealed with dark red wax, imprinted with his father's Masonic ring. Holding his breath he pried up the dry seal with a silver letter opener, being careful not to crack or break it.

> *11 May 1994*
>
> *My Son,*
>
> *If you are reading this I am surely gone to my just reward, although I don't care to contemplate the nature of the justice that lies ahead. For I have taken the coward's path with you, alas. The contents of this codex will reveal the shocking and terrible truth from which I have shrunk, unwilling to tell you in person.*
>
> *Lamar, you are third generation in a familial line whose every third generation bairn have been cursed down through the ages. Your mother knew, but she, too, kept an icy, silent vigil. We had agreed to have a childless marriage and were shocked to discover Allison was with child not long before her forty-third birthday. You were a "change-of-life" baby, as they are called. The change in all our lives was total. And devastating.*
>
> *You no doubt felt our rejection, our distancing. I regret with all my heart that we*

*did not find the fortitude to overcome our fear
and revulsion. From your early childhood we
looked for the signs. Soon after you entered
grade school, they began. Your petite "seizures,"
the headaches, bouts of depression, your peculiar
pets, your estranged, friendless childhood, your
unusual eating habits and at times, your
insatiable thirst. All fit the description passed to
me by my father, Annison, along with this
codex, just before he died.*

*Your Great Grandfather Misner was a
third-generation Bradford, one of those
unfortunates scourged by the curse. Grandfather
Annison had but one brother, at a time when
most families were blessed with many siblings.
Annison's father and brother were killed,
violently, his mother driven insane. Annison ran
away to escape a terrible fate at the hands of the
venomous, fear-ravaged demons the townspeople
had become. Later, he made his fortune in the
gold fields of California but was extremely
secretive, preferring a common, anonymous life,
never calling attention to himself. He left me a
fortune in gold bullion hidden away in a bank
vault. In turn, I have made certain financial
arrangements, including two annuities.*

*By now, no doubt, you have been
privileged to receive the legacy from the annuity
that should keep you in exceptional comfort for
as long as may be. Our Robert will acquaint you*

with the particulars in the fullness of time, may the gods keep him sound in mind and body.

If you can find it in your heart to forgive me, and your mother, it will ease, if but slightly, the tortured existence that—may Heaven find another path—lies before you. In the name of all that is decent, Lamar, you must try with all your heart.

Your Wretched Father,

Coleson

Lamar finished reading the letter for the third time. He shuddered with a violent chill, as if he'd been thrown into an icy pond. A meteor shower of tiny bursting lights all but blinded him, and he gasped for air. He bent over, lowering his head until it almost touched the floor and began to recite Hamlet. "To be or not to be: that is the question: Whether 'tis nobler in the mind to suffer the slings and arrows of outrageous fortune—"

It took a while before his heart slowed and he stopped gasping. The shower of incandescent pinpoints abated, and he took four deep breaths, holding the last one as long as he could.

Mother of God. What secret about me was so monstrous that it consumed both of them?

Lamar finished the rest of the scotch in his glass and relit the pipe. He looked around the library. It hadn't changed, but somehow he had. A new door was opening unto some formless evil. He forced himself to turn to the first page in the codex. As he did, the paper made a crinkling sound like dried leaves rattling in the wind, and he hoped the pages wouldn't disintegrate. A badly faded, brownish, spidery script seemed to echo down the centuries.

Unconsciously, Lamar held his breath as he began to read.

The Year of Our Lord, Creator
and Master of All Souls
1661

In each human form there liveth the sacred tree of life, its branches supplying the compound and structure of each corpuscle of the body. Whilst the sacred tree takes form in each body, it will sometimes suffer the rare few to become no less than the Devil's spawn.

The hidden wisdom of the ages reveals that whilst the clockworks of creation have operated in an almost flawless manner throughout the birth-to-death cycle of mankind, there remains a most vexatious exception in the nature of the errant formation of blood spores, one of monstrous import, for it singles out in every third generation from each contaminated lineage which contains the errant spores, a marked (that is to say) flawed issue, and in so doing, doth continue the ancient—and evil—error of creation.

There be no known remedy, though many have been tried throughout the dim mists beyond recorded time. Fear hath led the peasant class to unspeakable acts against those thought to be carriers of the flawed spore. Men of science, who have *approached this subject with no little trepidation, have sought an answer to the effects of the corruption of the single, transcendent spore believed to link the body, and its power to reason, with the soul. Though they claim to have found said spore lodged at or near the apex of the sacred tree, they fared no better than to bear witness to, and factually describe, the ghastly results when said spore was found to be flawed. Some have said that it represents a grave threat to the continuation of the human species. They hypothesize that this 'sinister pox,' left unchecked, will one day change—yea destroy—the benevolent nature of mankind. Further, they hold that only through the transfiguration of final death of the afflicted can we hope to rid the world of this menace.*

____But therein lyeth the grand canard, for if those so afflicted are not truly of this life, how, then, can they be deprived of it?

Father Joshua

Lamar jumped up, almost knocking over the chair, and strode to the fireplace, staring deeply into the growing conflagration. I've known I was different, he thought, but this! Coleson cannot be referring—No, I will not accept that. My father's letter is the product of a disturbed mind. My mother died from insanity—an acute mental collapse. My father's mental decline was more subtle, progressing more slowly. Something he must have contracted in the Pacific during the war. Some rare disease that slowly eats at the mind, causing it to create monstrous illusions, like this, this third generation fable.

The codex reads like a version of the Spanish Inquisition. Prelates trying to find and kill heretics, using mobs of hysterical peasants. That outrage is long dead, well and truly buried in the dustbin of history. But my parents apparently believed in curses and fables. That's the stuff of a B-grade Hollywood script.

The scent of Absinthe grew stronger, and a cat howled from somewhere. He sank to his knees.

It was dark, cold, his face dripping blood. Lamar leaned his forehead against the coarse brick.

The fire snapped as a log shifted, sending a shower of sparks onto the wide, polished brick hearth. Lamar opened his eyes. He felt as though he might burst into flames and spiral like sparks up the chimney.

"Mr. Bradford. Are you all right? Here, let me help you to the chair." Robert's topcoat was dusted with snow.

Lamar allowed Robert to help him to the wingback and sank into it with a groan. "I'll get some hot coffee with a dollop of cognac. You had a nasty fall last night."

Fall? Lamar watched him as he turned toward the library door. Robert paused only a moment as he passed the desk—just long enough to glance at the codex and the letter lying on the ancient manuscript.

Lamar stared out of the library windows, pressing his lips tight. Wind was blowing waves of fine sleet against the panes, making an intermittent hissing sound. The storm had made the room darker in spite of the fire and two lamps.

Robert prepared a splendid roast pork for dinner. The wine he'd selected, Cakebread Cellars, a fifteen-year-old Cabernet Sauvignon, was exceptional.

"Rather a bit extravagant, Robert." Lamar remarked, nodding toward the decanter on the Queen Anne sideboard, as Robert finished lighting all five candles in the antique sterling silver candelabra.

"I thought you needed a bit of a boost, sir. If I may suggest, let the wine rest a few moments longer in your glass. A really good cab needs to breathe more than most other reds."

I do need a boost, Lamar thought. He couldn't remember passing the hours before dinner and rubbed his temples in frustration. What he needed was Houdini to get him out of this miasma. He studied Robert's face. The man looks somehow timeless. The fine lines around his eyes, the salt and pepper hair, and his sallow, care-worn face give him away, but he has unbounded energy. Lamar yawned. Dammit to hell, all I've done since last evening is yawn.

There's no reason for me being so tired. And yet somehow I feel so alive. He sipped his wine. Robert, standing in the shadows, watched him.

Lamar ate little but enjoyed a second glass of the Cakebread, then accepted a third glass before wandering back to the library. The walls pressed in on him. Peculiar; wine had never affected him like that before.

The codex was gone. And the letter. The half-smoked pipe sat in its holder, the tamper, tobacco pouch, lighter, and letter opener were scattered about the desk top.

A faint aroma of Absinthe clung to the library like the scent of a funeral parlor.

2

Old Salem
November 27

"O Christian Martyr Who for Truth could die
"When all about thee Owned the hideous lie!
The world, redeemed from superstition's sway,
Is breathing freer for thy sake today."

John Greenleaf Whittier
Bartlett's Familiar Quotations, 17th ed.,
2002

Morgan Summers admired her image, turning left and right before the full-length mirror.

Dr. Chandless had done an extraordinary job, but for nearly twenty thousand she deserved no less. She pulled her ash-blonde hair back and slipped an elastic band around it, fashioning a loose ponytail. Leaning forward, she studied her eyes.

They turned dark when she was angry or frightened. The eyebrows he'd tattooed were slightly darker than her hair and had a certain "lilt" to them, as if she possessed some arcane secrets. Morgan smiled. She did, in fact.

The implants exceeded her highest expectations. First, he'd given her a touch more uplift, though that hadn't been much of a problem, and filled them out a bit—she would need to buy C-cups now—but best of all, he'd made the slightly smaller one equal in size to its sister. She squeezed them. They felt just as they had; not a hint of the implants. And the nipples were as sensitive as they had been. Not that that mattered. At least not for an age.

She couldn't even find where that mole on her chest had been, couldn't even find a suture scar. Nice. She sighed with delight.

Next she inspected her abdomen, and the scar from a World War II shrapnel wound, stitched up at a forward-deployed field surgical unit. Dr. Chandless had repaired the ugly purple scar, and it was already lighter.

"In a year it will take a magnifying glass to find it," Dr. Chandless had said.

A year? Piece of cake. Morgan grimaced at the cost of having the doctor's medical secretary "accidentally" delete all of her pre-op blood work. There went another five hundred. She flashed her image a grand smile, admiring the bright, freshly cleaned and polished caps. That had set her back another couple of thou, after having two teeth straightened. Half the dentist bill had been based on a one-time barter arrangement. She grimaced again. God she hated having to do that, but her bank account looked like a classroom one day after the start of summer break.

Marta Sorrel's dull pewter cross hung on its fine silver chain almost to Morgan's cleavage. She touched it, felt its uncanny warmth, and looked at the crude initials: "MS." It had been her mother's—the only item of hers Morgan had—and she'd worn it since the night they killed her mum.

She had been no more than six, but the horror of that night had become part of her soul, her DNA. Morgan vividly recalled her mother's execution.

The Salem Village witch trials began in the summer of 1692. Samuel Parris, the village minister, could have stopped the madness. He didn't even try. His daughter, Betty, had supposedly been the first to be attacked by witches. Absurd. The "attacks" spread to Ann Putnam, Mary Lewis and Mary Walcott, and what a colorful tableau they created. When Dr. William Griggs couldn't cure them, he claimed the symptoms were supernatural in origin. "The devil's hand was on them," he'd pronounced.

All knew that witches did the devil's work. Most of the villagers became obsessed with the mortal danger to their souls posed by the witches among them, many of whom—conveniently— happened to owe them money, were adulterers, or had stopped attending church. First the fearful villagers turned on Tituba, the Indian slave woman. Then Sarah Good and Sarah Osborn. The trials began, and soon the gaol was overflowing with the accused and condemned. The hangings followed. For four months processions escorting the convicted ended on Gallows Hill, a barren slope not far from the village. Nineteen were hung before the obsession ended. Not all the convicted were hung, however: six died while awaiting their trials; the villagers even put two dogs to death.

Giles Corey, eighty years old, was the first to adamantly refuse to go before the court magistrates. He was found guilty nonetheless and "pressed" with heavy stones, laid one at a time over him until his ribs cracked and punctured his lungs, stilling his pitiful cries. Marta Sorrel was the only other accused to refuse to stand trial. She was convicted in absentia, like Giles, and sentenced to be pressed.

The morning of her execution, Marta Sorrel told her daughter where she had buried her simple pewter cross, telling her it might protect her from "the curse."

Morgan smelled the rancid fat from the torches, heard the whispered chant from the Salem Village crones: witch, witch, witch. They came to the gaol for her mum, who showed no emotion, would not look at her only child, her daughter, just turned six, held tightly by two old shrews. One had a handful of Morgan's long hair, the other a numbing grip on one wrist. Marta Sorrel, convicted witch, would soon join the nineteen who had been hung, not counting Giles Corey.

The shrews pushed the child in front of the circle of villagers so she could see the four stakes driven into the ground and the pile of stones laid by. Two men tore the ragged dress from Marta, exposing her body to all who had gathered. Several of the women pointed to the blood that ran down Marta's leg and murmured and nodded and spat. Other men tied old barnacled fishing rope to her wrists and ankles and played it out to the four posts.

Reverend Samuel Parris, his voice like an echo from a rain barrel, beseeched her to recant her sins and call upon Jesus for forgiveness before it was too late. He began to shake his fists at Marta, alternately clasping his hands in a prayerful gesture and finally slapped the convicted witch. Marta watched him and finally laughed, undulating her hips at him, causing the village women to moan and reach for their crosses. One of the men pushed her down on the frozen ground, and four others pulled the lines taut, fastening them around the stakes, leaving Marta on her back, arms and legs secured to the posts. Reverend Parris knelt beside her and opened his bible and began reciting a passage from memory, until Marta spit at him.

"Damn you, witch. May you burn in the eternal flames of hell," he screamed. He reached down, found a dirt clod, and hurled it at her but missed. Others began hurling clods at Marta until she was nearly covered.

"Mum, Mum," Morgan cried. "Tell them to let you go."

"Be silent, you witch's get," said the crone who held her wrist, "or we'll throw you in your mum's grave and cover you with dirt."

Tears streaked the young girl's dirty face, and she wiped her running nose on her sleeve. She knew her mum wasn't a witch. How could she be? Why are they hurting her? "No!" she screamed. The other crone yanked her hair and slapped her bottom hard.

One of the village elders stood, looking down at the stoic woman, and asked if she had ought to say, and all fell silent. Gray breath extruded from the crowd as they watched and waited. The silence was broken only by a barking dog somewhere in the village, and a yowling babe. Bunched clouds permitted intermittent glimpses of the sickle moon and timeless stars.

"Your sins weigh far more than the stone you will soon bear, witch. Don't expect God to be merciful to a handmaid of Lucifer." The village elder nodded and one man carefully placed a large, flat stone on Marta's stomach. Then another and another and yet one more. Her breath hissed, eyes tight shut, lips pursed.

"Mum, get up, get up," Morgan screamed. The bigger crone, who was holding Morgan's hair, yanked the child off her feet, causing the young girl to cry out.

Another stone. And another. Marta's breath wretched. The village women began to hum as the men started a second pile over Marta's breasts. Slowly, they added more stones. Marta's breathing etched the cold night air like fingernails on slate. Finally the closest villagers could hear her ribs crack, hear the rasping breath turn to gurgling . . . and then stop.

As they drifted away, Blind Gretta walked to Morgan and, using her walking staff, banished the two crones who still held her. "You will come with me, child. I will take you home."

"Let her go," the bigger woman said. "They deserve one another. A miserable clatch be Blind Gretta, her mangy cat, and the witch's daughter. Best if they starve or freeze this winter—all of 'em."

Calvin, who was black and white and not the least mangy, followed them back to Gretta's two-room thatched hovel behind the Gaol, where they could hear the coughing and moaning and screaming from the accused, the confessed, and the condemned.

Marta was left on the village green for two days, then thrown in a pauper's pit near the remains of Giles Corey.

Morgan became Gretta's eyes, and Gretta became Morgan's heart.

She looked at herself in the mirror again. Her different colored eyes, one brown, one green, always had a startling effect on people. Unfortunately, it made her hard to forget. One eye had turned brown a few days after she had fled from Salem Village. The villagers had often told Morgan she was cursed, and her life would be dark and dreadful.

By 1703, at nineteen, she had become a street-smart, hardened young woman, living by her wits and the purses she expropriated around the cafes and salons of Paris. Only when desperate and hungry did she use her body.

Morgan thought of Pythia, the crusty old gnome who claimed to be a direct descendant of the Oracle of Delphi. She'd given Morgan a reading.

"You will find no respite till you meet the keeper of the key that will unlock the curse laid upon you. Then you must overpower him and take it. Kill him if you must, but use your cunning, and he will surrender the key willingly." Pythia spat into her palm and pressed it to Morgan's forehead. "You will find him methinks, but you must wait for the start of the next thousand years." She refused to take Marta Sorel's cross, the last thing of value Morgan possessed, as payment for the reading.

No reference to the trial of Marta Sorrel had been placed into the court records, and in but a short time the memory of the twenty-first condemned witch of Salem faded, then disappeared.

She would be ready for him, the bearer of the key, she thought, studying her reflection. "Tools of the trade," she murmured.

She observed her thick forest of pubic hair. That needs serious trimming. Morgan laughed, then sighed and shook her head. Why bother? Who's going to see the freshly trimmed me? I will. That's enough. For now, anyway. She stared at her image. I'll do my nails, too. Why not have a glass of champagne to celebrate? Put some Herb Alpert on the stereo. And some caviar. I'm no Jackie Kennedy by any stretch, but I have a quiet, introspective face, with depth. I'll get a new hairstyle next week, she thought. Two of the girls at the Citizens Bank where she worked as a teller told her to go to Zina's Hair Salon. I'll try a different color. Maybe auburn. That should go with my green eye anyway.

She walked resolutely into the bathroom and stood on the scales: 125 pounds. Her goal was 129. Most women would kill to be five-feet-six and 125 pounds. But most women didn't have her problems with eating. She needed four or five more pounds for insurance against another starving time. Starving times could lead to complete loss of control, and then the hunting. Morgan pursed her lips and shook her head. Maybe a starving time wouldn't occur till her next period. Let's see, that would be another, ummm, four months.

Locking the door on the way out of her Porter Square studio apartment, she turned left on Summer Street, intent on collecting the champagne, caviar, bath oil, some new lipstick—Revlon's *Wine With Everything*. Morgan laughed aloud with an all too rare, if momentary, feeling of joy. The studio apartment suited her, as it had been recently renovated, just like her body. And with any luck she would soon be a Harvard employee.

She stopped to watch some young girls playing hopscotch and, on impulse, she hopped through the numbered chalk squares. At ten she turned around and winked at the three young girls who watched her. They winked back.

No. She began to walk briskly, not wanting to draw attention to herself. She still wasn't known in the neighborhood and wanted to keep it that way.

Excuse me, Morgan, but didn't you almost drain your savings account dry on a total makeover? You think that won't attract attention?

I merely added some tools-of-the-trade, she replied, entering fully into her self-dialogue.

And how do you propose to use these new tools?

I'll need to be able to get close to the man who has the key that will unlock—

Well, and who is that man?

I'll know him if I see him.

If?

She didn't see the man following her, didn't sense his eyes, and couldn't hear the silent tread of his rubber-soled shoes. But he was there.

Behind her.

Herb Alpert and the Tijuana Brass were playing Tijuana Taxi, the sound filling her apartment, the bathroom door ajar, inviting the sounds to fill her, body, mind and...? The ice-cold champagne tasted great. The caviar too. And the swirling hot water was soothing, as was the fragrance of the bath gel. Damn, it's been too long since my last workout. Maybe I can sneak into the university fitness center after the job interview. She surveyed the petite electric razor she'd purchased that afternoon, and the new pair of scissors and lotion assembled on the shelf built into one corner of the Jacuzzi tub. Should I shave it all off? Probably not.

The bathroom door slowly opened. For a second Morgan froze in terror. Then she laughed as Calvin, her primeval orange tabby, who had once belonged to Gretta the Blind, padded in and put his front paws up on the side of the tub, meowed and sniffed.

"Come on in, you old fossil. Why do I bother talking to you? You're deaf as a post." She reached over the side of the tub and scratched behind his ears, wetting him down but eliciting a loud purr.

When the door opened further, Morgan's eyes widened, and she tried to scream but could make no sound.

The man wore a black ski mask. He bent over her, a dagger raised above his head.

He was purring.

3

The Codex
November 27

"The condition of mankind is exemplified
by"…continual fear, and danger of violent death;
and the life of man is solitary, poor, nasty,
brutish, and short."

Thomas Hobbes, 1651

Y ou rang, sir?" Robert arched his eyebrows.

The man has become insufferable. "I didn't ring, I yelled." Lamar gritted his teeth and pointed to the desk.

"Ah." Robert reached the desk in three quick strides, leaned down, and pulled open a lower drawer. He removed the codex and placed it gently on top of the desk. "May I bring you some fresh coffee?"

Lamar drew a deep breath, held it, and nodded slightly. When Robert closed the library door, Lamar's breath exploded. "Damn and blast," he muttered, sinking onto the red leather swivel chair that matched the desk. He opened the front cover. His father's letter was there. He wished it had vanished, along with the codex. Taking another sip of the Cakebread he set the glass aside, opening the codex to the entry dated 1661. He shook his head, trying to clear it.

Somebody remind me not to mix scotch and wine, he thought. He reached for the reamer and loosened the burnt tobacco in the bottom of the Yello-Bole, then tipped the pipe over the ashtray. After refilling the pipe, he tamped it and used his father's Colibri—now his—to light up, satisfied with the cloud of smoke that drifted toward the bookshelves.

Robert is taking damnably long to bring that coffee.

The thought had scarcely crossed his mind when the door opened, and Robert wheeled in a silver tray with a small coffee pot, cup and saucer, spoon, and small dish of assorted chocolates. He had also included the Cakebread decanter.

"Chocolates. You really know how to play to my weakness, Robert."

"Wine, coffee, and chocolate. You only lack for one ingredient, Mr. Bradford."

He's like a dog retrieving a favorite bone.

"A new family has moved into Tory Row, I believe." Robert stroked his chin. "I understand their daughter—in her late twenties if I'm not mistaken—has moved in with her parents while she works on a PhD at Harvard. If you'd like, we could invite them over for an aperitif. Word has it that she possesses a rather well-turned ankle." Robert arched his eyebrows, the hint of a smile gracing his usually somber features.

Lamar's face colored, and he looked down. Where does he come up with those ancient expressions like a "well-turned ankle"?

"Ummm. I'll think about it." He'd never really had a date, discounting a couple of painful blind dates during his undergrad years. He liked women; he just didn't know how to act with one. And thirty-seven years old was way too late to figure them out. He'd visited two professional ladies of the evening—for some reason he detested the word "prostitute," and "whore" was even worse. The older of the two had taught him how "it" was done. She said he'd come a long way, but then he had been a generous tipper. Lamar grimaced. The other, much younger, had dressed as an underhouse parlor maid. Lamar was unaware of the warm smile that suffused his whole being as he thought about them and was startled when Robert strained his throat, interrupting his reverie.

"As you wish." Robert turned to go.

"Robert, what did you mean when you said, 'Oh God, it's started.'"

Robert flinched but immediately regained his composure. "When you have finished studying the codex, I suggest we have a long talk, sometime at your leisure."

"You've read it, then?" Lamar's eyes widened, and he stiffened. He felt a strange pulsing, and the air seemed to quicken, as if it were swirling into a black hole. The two men stared into one another's eyes. The older man's face darkened. Lamar stood abruptly. "I asked you a question."

"Your father told me of its existence. *Sir.*"

"He told you—"

"If that will be all, Mr. Bradford." Robert bowed slightly, turned and departed, closing the door without making a sound.

Lamar withered and sank into the chair, glancing around the library. That smell again. "Damn and blast." He swallowed most of the remaining Cakebread, relit the pipe, and opened the codex. He hadn't dismissed the man, he'd just left. A tremor of panic coursed up from his gut.

"What is wrong with me?" He choked and looked down at his hands, which had curled into fists.

And what had happened to his library—his womb? The books were no longer orderly. The fireplace tools were jumbled. A crow was pecking at the window glass—a terrible sign, his mother always said. Was his mother's despicable old cane rocker, the one he'd placed in the darkest corner, rocking? He'd been intending to get rid of it ever since she died. His pipe rolled over, spreading ash on the desktop. Strange. He hadn't touched it.

Acid churned in his stomach as he envisioned himself torching the room and then calmly sitting at the desk, watching it, and himself, consumed in an agony of purification.

He placed the pipe in its holder, then leaned over and propped his head in his palms, covering his eyes. His breathing slowed, and he sighed.

Warm fur slid across his hands and forehead. Lamar hurled himself backward. "What—Oxnard, you damned old, miserable, rotten cat." Lamar shook his head and grabbed the white and ginger tabby, settled it into his lap and began stroking it. You're the first normal thing that's happened to me all day, he thought, as Oxnard purred loudly. But it took only a few moments for the tabby to send Lamar reeling back to that dark alley and the grotesque carcass of a savaged cat.

Lamar's grip tightened unconsciously. Oxnard howled and sprang from Lamar's lap, leaving his master to massage the scratches in his upper thighs. "I hate cats," he shouted. The library absorbed his oath in the folds of its burgundy draperies, thousands of dry pages, and thick Persian carpet. The cat vanished. Probably behind the *Britannicas.*

He poured some coffee and gulped it, burning his mouth. He relit the pipe and turned to the end of the 1661 inscription. An oblong inkblot obscured the last paragraph and most likely the author's name. Lamar's forehead furrowed as he ran a finger over the inkblot. He would have to get that analyzed. Maybe someone at the university could read through the blot. He turned the page and was surprised to find a note written by his father in the right margin, dated 13 September 1980:

> *Better the afflicted ones be sequestered, kept in secret places known only to the Keepers, those guardians of the denizens of the dark, till one day the secret is revealed, and the hapless bearers of the ancient stigmata be returned to mortal life.*
>
> *May God strike down the OVFS.*
>
> *CBB*

A tic began in his right eyelid, along with a tremor in his chest. The afflicted ones? Sequestered by Keepers? Returned to mortal life? And who or what is the OVFS? Lamar spread his arms and gripped the sides of the desk.

Oh God, it has started.

"What has started?" Lamar cried aloud. Again the library engulfed his words, shrouding them in reverberating silence. A volume of Britannica on the bottom shelf slumped over. It must surely be Oxnard. Go and see, he chided himself. But he didn't. Instead, he turned the page.

Though unsigned, the neat script was obviously his father's. Lamar began to read:

> *13 February 1958*
>
> *Dr. Gene Claude Vompre (1859-?) collaborated extensively with Dr. Sir Archibald E. Garrod, KCMG, FRS (1857-1936), a prominent physician at St. Bartholomew's Hospital in London, an early pioneer in advancing the new science of biochemistry and the emerging discipline of genetics. From the turn of the twentieth century the two men exchanged considerable technical correspondence, and Vompre was known to have visited Garrod on two, possibly three, occasions. Jean Claude agreed with Garrod that genetic defects caused not only pathologic disease, but also cellular transmutation, which Garrod called "metabolic disruption."*

The last available correspondence between the two men discussed several experimental approaches to the question of whether the fundamental nature of man could be genetically altered to form a "new kind of man." Garrod warned in the strongest terms that Jean Claude's proposed experiments should be studied carefully before being attempted on a human, stating that they embodied inherent severe risks.

Vompre's notes on the isolation of a "morbid blood spore," and his attempts to find a compound that might render it inert, were cryptic, often employing an encipherment scheme to protect his findings. A portion of the unencrypted notes, however, referred to the possibility of arresting the 'disease' and preventing its transmission through sexual congress or any manner of contact with corrupted blood secretions.

Near the end of Vompre's notes were vague references to experiments upon himself, but his untimely disappearance—and the outbreak of the Great War—brought sudden closure to a promising inquiry into the subject. His notes were placed in the British Museum where they remained until sometime during the inter-war years, when they mysteriously disappeared. Apparently no credible effort was made by the museum to search them out.

My father was forty-two when he wrote that, Lamar mused. He squinted at another tiny notation in the margin and fished his reading glasses out of the inside pocket of his smoking jacket.

> *From the turn of the century, Gene Claude Vompre's name has been inextricably linked with the creatures so darkly afflicted, their condition referred to as Vampirism.*

Vampirism! Lamar grimaced as he swept the glasses off his face. This has to be some gigantic hoax. Someone—Robert?—is trying to drive me insane, like my parents. And probably Great Grandfather Misner. Insane I can handle. But Vampirism?

He wiped his forehead with the handkerchief Robert always placed in his top left breast pocket and snatched the Chivas and tavern glass out of the desk drawer, pouring the glass half full. He swallowed twice and coughed. Then he tamped the Yello-Bole and soon had a cloud of Billy Budd drifting around the desk. Scotch and pipe smoking were becoming a ritual, but at least they occupied his hands and, for brief moments, refocused his mind.

Lamar recalled the day after he'd graduated from Harvard in 1996. Wanting to do something rather pointedly masculine—he felt those traits were singularly lacking from his makeup—he'd walked into an Air Force recruiting office, rather certain that the Air Force recruiter would see right away that he didn't have "the right stuff" and turn him away. He could then announce to himself and a few faculty members that he had tried to serve his country in the military but would now seek out other ways to serve. He might even undertake a PhD. It began as a good plan.

But the recruiter said that "Harvard Boy" would likely make a good intelligence officer.

Thank God Captain Wilkinson, an Air Force flight surgeon, thought otherwise.

"You have a most, uh, bizarre blood chemistry," he had said to Lamar. "Your first red cell count suggested severe anemia. So severe that you couldn't possibly have walked in for the test." The doctor paused and studied Lamar. "So I had more tests run. The results varied wildly each time. And you appear to have no platelets at all, although that's impossible. I've never seen nor heard the likes of your blood profile. Are you taking any meds or drugs you haven't told us about?"

"No." Lamar's face felt like cement.

"Humm. I've shown your results to two other doctors, and they're as baffled as I am, Mr. Bradford. I've recommended you be classified medically unfit for military service. You should consult your personal physician as soon as possible."

Wilkinson looked around as if to ensure no one was listening, then leaned closer to Lamar and lowered his voice. "I will be happy to send your doctor all the results of our tests. In fact, I'd like to consult on your case, if you're okay with that. Off the record, so to speak. No extra cost to you."

Lamar, a strong proponent of the concept, "If it ain't broke, don't fix it," mumbled his thanks, gathered his forms and left. He felt okay. Normal—whatever that felt like. But the whispering fear that he was different, which plagued him almost like tinnitus— always there, always in the background, usually easy to ignore— had become more than a babbling brook as he listened to Captain Wilkinson. Normally, whenever the brook threatened to overflow its banks, Lamar would bury himself in a complex technical paper he was editing at work. Or sometimes Haig & Haig Pinch. He saved the Chivas 25 for special occasions and the odd crisis. The two strategies worked, after a fashion.

He had to stay away from that brook. If he were ever to face the reason why he was so different, he was certain he'd drown in it.

As he resumed reading the codex he became aware of the rush of fearful whispering and a burning cold sensation in his gut. Finishing the glass, he poured two fingers more and wished Robert had brought some ice cubes instead of chocolates.

Lamar possessed a phenomenal memory, but for years he had stored most memories in compartments that were all but impenetrable. One contained the early episodes of his "seizures" at school. He'd long lost track of how many tests he'd been subjected to. Another compartment housed his obsession with blood. He was almost maniacal about avoiding the sight of blood, yet compelled to read about it, listen to stories that were bloody, look at pictures and attend movies, especially war and horror movies, the more graphic the better. The sight of actual blood, however, caused him, on occasion, to experience terrible visions of ancient atrocities. Men tied to trees and disemboweled, their entrails falling to the ground, steaming in the cold, others stretched on the rack, bones cracking, their screams stifled.

But the compartment that caused him the most acute distress was marked "Relationships." Very large. Very deeply buried. So many events stuffed where they would never come to the surface except in his dreams and nightmares. The more important the event, the worse the fears that oozed out from the chained trunk in his mental attic.

Something had changed in the past two days. It felt like the lids to his mental compartments had been pried open, leaving him exposed, vulnerable—terrified. Lamar's head snapped up. Oxnard sat on the desk, his tail wrapped around him, licking one paw and cleaning the side of his face, acting as if he could read Lamar's thoughts. Lamar noticed the discarded handkerchief on the desktop. It was splotched with fresh blood.

"Dear God." He sat, transfixed. His back spasmed and his fingers curled. The pain in his stomach became acute. He doubled over until his forehead rested on the codex, dimly aware of Oxnard purring.

The smell was putrid, chocking him, and the hissing grew louder. He was on his hands and knees, but where? The alley? Yes. His suit coat was shredded and hung in tatters. He tried to get up, but the dark sludge held him fast. Oh God, it was drying blood. He had to get up.

To his horror he saw short, fat, squiggly things—worms!—crawling up his arms, and he tore off his suit coat, what was left of it. Clawing desperately at the worms, he couldn't get them all off. Some reached his arm pits and started sucking his blood.

He screamed. The hot breath on his face smelled like dead fish, and he looked up into huge incandescent yellow eyes.

The cat was almost too large to fit in the alley.

"Sir! Mr. Bradford. Wake up." He eased the younger man into a sitting position. Lamar retched as the black aura around him began to dissipate.

A medieval torture device was crushing his head. He would die momentarily—of that he was certain.

"Here. Drink this. Steady on. There's a good chap."

"Robert?" His voice was weak, plaintive.

"Right here, sir. One more swallow, there's a good lad."

The liquid burned all the way down. Brandy. His muscles gradually relaxed, and the pain subsided, leaving him woozy and scattered.

"Can you tell me what happened?" Robert asked.

"Must have fallen asleep. Had a devilishly bad nightmare. What brought you into the library?"

"You were crying out in a most desperate manner."

Lamar felt hot. A sheen of sweat covered his brow and upper lip. He groped for his handkerchief. Robert snatched it off the desk and handed it to him. Lamar flinched, staring at the handkerchief.

It was spotless.

4

Calvin's Revenge
November 27

As Morgan's assailant leaned over, knife raised to strike, he crushed Calvin against the side of the tub. Calvin twisted and affixed himself to the intruder's groin, claws and teeth fully engaged. The knife-wielder grunted and hunched over. Using his free hand he wrenched Calvin off and hurled him against the wall. The cat dropped to the floor, motionless, but Calvin had given Morgan a momentary opening. Her vice-like grip encircled the assailant's wrist above her, the snapping of small bones audible. She caught the falling knife with her other hand, reversed its arc and plunged it upward through the man's stomach, burying it to the hilt.

He grunted and staggered back, then sank to his knees. With both hands he pulled out the knife and looked up at Morgan, eyes already becoming opaque as he gasped: "You—will—die."

Morgan stood, dripping, her breathing fast and shallow. "Not bloody likely."

The knife slipped from the man's fingers and fell onto the bathroom throw rug. In slow motion he sagged forward, face first onto the black and white floor tile.

She stepped around the body and knelt beside Calvin, stroking him, feeling for any injuries. When he began to purr, she smiled. "I owe you a whole bag of fish treats my feline Ninja." She set him down, and he padded over to the body, sniffed it, then turned and stalked out, his tail pointing straight up.

Rolling him onto his back, Morgan bent over the man and pulled off the ski mask. Late forties, close-cropped black hair, probably a two-day growth of beard. She regarded his right hand, which was splayed out at an awkward angle, and wondered what he'd been paid to kill her. She pulled up the heavy black sweater, unbuttoned his shirt, and pulled up his dirty, blood-soaked undershirt. Where his nipples should have been she saw two patches of scar tissue. "I knew it," she murmured. *Opus Dei Lamia Eradico.* The work of God to eradicate vampires—the mission statement for the Order of the Vampire Final Solution. The OVFS.

The first time she'd seen a member of the OVFS shirtless had been at a field hospital in France in 1944 while working on a wounded soldier. His nipples had been carved off. First Lieutenant Sandra Morgan, U.S. Army nurse, had only a few seconds to contemplate his past membership in the OVFS before he died, and she quickly moved on to the next wounded man.

Morgan stood and toweled dry. Glancing down at the knife, she scowled and picked it up. The knife was made of wood. "Aspen." Known by the Druid priests for its special properties. A stake through the heart, usually followed by cremation. Decapitation first, if they adhered to the old European tradition. She shuddered. How many close calls do I get? She wondered. Nine maybe? If so, I am well over the limit.

She bit her lower lip at the difficult task ahead. How to get rid of this offal. She dressed hurriedly, strapping on her fanny pack with its quick-release holster housing a Beretta .25 caliber semi-automatic with a ten-shot clip. It was loaded, with a round in the chamber, but she checked it anyway, making sure the safety was on. The OVFS almost always worked in pairs. A second "footman" (agent) waited to verify the outcome of an operation. The OVFS had been formed in the mid-1920s, and they were highly skilled. She would have to act quickly.

Disguised as a bag lady, Morgan slipped past the OVFS stakeout, then changed into a red mini-skirt, white blouse with plunging neckline, and spiked high heels. She approached two husky young men, both juniors at the university, and convinced them to skip their afternoon classes the following day to help a charming lady in need. Especially one offering a hundred bucks apiece. All they had to do was haul a rather heavy box from her fourth floor apartment down to the street level, load it into a U-Haul, drive with her to the Saugus landfill, about twelve miles from campus, and offload the box.

Two bulldozers rumbled and belched exhaust as they covered the latest mound of debris. Her contribution to the landfill was interred by one long scoop. The college boys offered to buy "Julie" lunch at the John Harvard, a popular undergrad suds and sandwiches emporium, but she had to get back to work, she told them. Lingering hugs, the cash, and a promise to meet them in two days mollified her helpers. As she drove off to the U-Haul drop lot, a blue Chevy Cobalt followed her. She wiggled and felt the outline of the Beretta against the small of her back. "Damn." Now she would have to find a new apartment. She wondered if she could find one across the street from the Cambridge Police Headquarters.

The next day Morgan hired Oscar's Moving Company to pick up her few possessions and deliver them to an address in Boston. Once again disguised as the bag lady, Calvin under one arm, she left the apartment after midnight, and walked four blocks to an old, dark green Dodge minivan. The former owner had agreed to leave it with a full tank of gas, unlocked, the key under the mat. Placing Calvin in the front passenger seat she began a nightlong circuitous drive through Cambridge and Somerville. It would have taken a skilled surveillance team, including at least three cars, to follow her. Four hours later she ended up back in her original apartment. With luck, the OVFS would be deceived. Where better to hide from them? She would change her phone number as soon as the phone company opened.

Morgan applied for a new credit card in Boston, obtained a library card for the Boston Public Library, applied for a passport, purchased an airline ticket from Logan to Toronto Pearson International and ordered some cookware to be delivered to her new address. Would that be enough to fool the Vatican thugs?

She groaned. Now she absolutely had to get the position at Harvard. She was nearly broke, and the balances on both credit cards had spiked. Hopefully the "move" to Boston would keep the OVFS busy for a while.

She twisted her head to loosen her neck muscles. By all the demons in Hell she felt like she'd been on the run for centuries. In fact, she had.

"Yes, yes, her tradecraft is excellent, but no match for ours." Number Three tightened his grip on the phone. He hated calls from the OVFS Director, code named Number Two. "One of our informants has located her. Our terminator obviously underestimated her. No doubt she killed him and smuggled his body out of the apartment in a large box. What? No, not one that went with the moving van. We think two boys—

"Yes, of course I'll submit a new plan, but now she knows we're still after her and will take every precaution—I understand. I'll send you a lock of her hair for your collection, as usual.

"This phone? The encryption is the very latest. We've run some dummy operations and never found evidence of any law enforcement—

"All right. All arrangements will be made by couriers. I— shit." Number Three scowled at the phone, his lips pursed white. He snapped the phone together and shoved it in an overcoat pocket. Number Two is an asshole. I need coffee and danish before starting on a new plan, he thought. It will have to be my best one yet. He wondered if the Summers woman had any supernatural mental powers to go along with her physical strength. How like Number Two to bring up the expenses. Somebody at the Vatican ought to know what it cost to chase vampires.

They'd had eighty-six years to get it right. Did Number Two think the OVFS could rid the world of vampires on a shoestring?

Fluffy snowflakes stuck to his shabby gray and black checked topcoat. Cold weather always made his chest ache where his nipples had been. He pulled his Navy knit cap down over his eyebrows, plunged his hands into his coat pockets, hunched his shoulders and trudged toward his favorite coffee shop, careful not to make eye contact with anyone.

Morgan placed a bowl of fresh water on the floor, poured some kibble into the dish next to it and added three teaspoons of Fancy Feast. Calvin brushed against her ankles and purred. That cat eats a hell of a lot better than I do, she thought. Several times during her last starvation cycle she had cast a predator's eye on Calvin. Once she'd even locked him in a closet and mailed the key to herself.

She'd learned her lesson too many times. When a vampire went too long without hunting for blood, she sunk into a "starvation cycle," a prolonged period of blood hunting.

The fridge was pretty bare, save a two-week supply of Fancy Feast. Maybe that would taste good on crackers. Morgan cringed and grabbed her default Brie and stale French bread along with a half-full bottle of wine. She had to start eating more. The times when she'd let herself go inevitably led to episodes of "hunting." She hated those. Loathed and despised herself, even though she had no control over her actions by the end of a starvation cycle. She had followed the prescribed esoteric rituals of penance for killing an animal, along with the one called absolution in earlier centuries, for the remission of sin. No ritual could expunge the guilt, though.

"Absolve me Father, for I have sinned," she said aloud, her voice filled with disdain. Just who in hell provides absolution for vampires, anyway? Still, she clung to at least some of the old ways. She had little left to cling to.

Her mind wandered to a gypsy camp in 1750 or 51. She had not meant to kill the man, but he had a knife and was drunk, and he intended to rape her. It was the only time she'd killed a human and the only time she had ever drunk human blood. For more than three months she had run before finally losing her pursuers. Morgan shuddered, and her vision misted. If only she could forget. But, may the gods weep, she had never felt so alive after killing that man. Colors were brighter, smells more pungent, her food tasted better than she could ever remember, and her sexual appetite bubbled up like untended broth over a cook fire.

She had seduced a young Jesuit priest three times after killing the drunken gypsy and drinking his blood. I'd give a lot to enjoy sex like that again, she admitted. Over the years since, she had developed stainless steel willpower. Sex was a weapon or a service to barter but almost never joyful, or loving. She had come close during World War II, but "her pilot" had been shot down and killed six weeks after they first had sex. She still had seven of his V-Mail letters. Ironic, she hadn't looked this good in over three hundred years—or felt so sexless.

The cheese tasted like rubber, the bread like cardboard. Together they smelled like the inside of an old lunch box. At least the wine was a little better. She forced herself to finish the Spartan meal. If she allowed herself to lapse into a starving cycle, she would lose weight, become seriously depressed, and then go on a hunt.

Morgan was jarred when her phone rang. She let it ring. She hadn't given the number to anyone. After four rings the recorder clicked on. She caught one word: "Shit."

A wrong number? Her intuition said no, it wasn't. She finished the wine, tossed the last piece of cheese into Calvin's dish, and deposited the end of the loaf into the garbage canister. Time to review her escape plans.

Morgan owned a ten-year-old Toyota Corolla, registered to the deceased Harriet Rankin. She garaged it three blocks away at the home of an elderly spinster, Miss Lillian, who rented out four of her rooms and half of a large, two-car garage.

Morgan had stocked the car with her getaway package, which included a cat box, litter and cat food, a snub-nose Detective Special .38 revolver and box of ammunition, a small duffle filled with a few clothes, a case of bottled water, a bottle of wine, a night vision device, and some flashbang grenades she had obtained from an arms trafficker in exchange for a roll in the hay. Out of necessity she had become an escape artist and kept her plans current and well-rehearsed. She had owned a Taser since they had first become commercially available. A second one was tucked away in a side table by the front door. She'd practiced escaping across the roof and down the old iron fire escape into a back alley. She'd even made a cat sling for Calvin. On several practice runs Calvin had voiced his concerns about being slung over her back but had gotten used to such handling after several trial runs.

Time to check for surveillance. Putting on a dark brown wig, she dressed in a jogging suit, complete with a Patriots stocking cap, tight-fitting driving gloves, and her New Balance shoes. She strapped on her fanny pack with its arsenal: the Beretta, two spare magazines and two flashbang grenades. "Ready on the right, ready on the left, all ready on the firing line," she intoned.

The pounding on her door sounded like cannon fire.

5

The Shower
December 1

"The problem with being dead is that it's for the rest of
your life."

Source and Date Uncertain

L amar enjoyed being a technical editor at Harvard. The dry
monographs, journal articles, international publications,
books, and occasional editorials that filled his inbox were
intellectually absorbing. His reputation for "finding the fatal flaw"
had increased of late. While he did not hold an advanced degree,
he was a Harvard graduate and a closet scientist, with specialties
in blood and the English language. The income was irrelevant, as
his father had left him a wealthy man.

But it was a way to be productive and, just as important, a
way to escape the cloistered Tory Row residence ... and Robert.

He hadn't become used to hanging his coat on the antique coat-tree in his new corner office in University Hall, with windows overlooking the Yard. Jennifer Marsh came in with his morning pot of coffee.

"Good morning, Mr. Bradford. Umm, I like that tie. It must be new."

Robert always overdresses me, Lamar thought. Silk tie, pin-striped three-piece suit, black wing-tip shoes, and the damn suspenders. Each morning there they were, and each morning Lamar hung them in an obscure part of his closet. It had become ritual. Always the damn suspenders.

"Good morning, Ms. Marsh." He reached for the pot.

"Let me pour," Jennifer said, filling his mug. She never failed to bring danish along with cream and sugar, though he seldom touched either unless the coffee was too strong. She moved his briefcase to its usual place on top of the safe next to his desk. Jennifer was his "administrative assistant" according to her job description. Tall, slender, and quite nicely made, a brunette with brown eyes and long bangs. She dressed professionally and smiled a lot. Altogether disconcerting. On several occasions she had accidentally pushed her breasts against his arm.

Yeah, right, Lamar thought. Some accidents. Why does she do that?

Lamar's face reddened, as it usually did when he first saw her in the morning. He'd been awarded the new office and his own administrative assistant only two months ago. "Ah. Thanks. How are we coming on the Gibson monograph?"

"Almost finished." She glanced at the replica London Paddington Station clock over the door. "I should have it on your desk by nine-thirty if we don't have another fire drill." They both smiled. "Fire drill" was code for a crash project.

On the way out Jennifer leaned over to arrange some fresh-cut flowers in a vase on the coffee table. He grabbed a document from his inbox and pretended to read it. Jennifer obviously wasn't wearing a bra. His face crimsoned. Why did she do that?

The efficient Ms. Marsh had arranged his inbox, as she did each morning, based on her assessment of his priorities—she was usually right—and he had retrieved Dr. James R. Heller's draft on the latest gene splicing techniques. Wouldn't Heller have a field day with my platelets—or lack thereof—Lamar mused. Heller's research might lead to a cure for hemophilia, lupus, or maybe even AIDS. Dr. Heller wore two hats: Dean of the Faculty of Arts and Sciences and Director of Harvard's Genetics Laboratory. Everybody called it the lab, or more often the GenLab.

Lamar smiled, recalling Heller's reaction when he and his boss visited Dr. Heller to show him a major technical mistake Lamar had found—he thought of it as a "gaffe"—in Heller's research, one that would have proven irredeemably embarrassing, very likely producing a serious setback to Heller's career, and possibly even reducing the lab's funding. Lamar's lifelong fascination and study of blood had, without his having any preconceived goal, led to his becoming a closet "hemoglobin" expert.

Heller was shocked, almost desperately appreciative, and quite generous. Lamar was moved into a new office on the third floor of University Hall, given a personal assistant, and awarded a handsome year-end bonus several months early. Further, Heller had made arrangements for Lamar to edit all of his technical writing thereafter. Lamar thought about his Jaguar XKR, three stories below, in his newly acquired reserved parking space on Oxford Street.

If someone didn't know any better—and only Robert did—he would think that Lamar B. Bradford had everything life could offer. Great job in the heart of academia, elegant office, personal assistant with looks and brains, a magnificent driving machine, an estate on Tory Row, inherited wealth, and all that by age thirty-seven. So why was he falling apart?

Lamar called, and in a moment Jennifer appeared.

"I need another fifteen minutes, boss. Hope you're not going to announce one of your fire drills." Her smile reminded Lamar of Marilyn Monroe. So did certain other features.

"No. I need to book about twenty minutes with Dr. Heller. Could you call his assistant and fix that? Any time that is convenient for him is good."

"Right. Do you need that cushion for your back? It's on the sofa. I can—"

"No. Thanks, though." She looked like she was about to say something more, and Lamar raised his eyebrows. She nodded and left.

She looks younger than I do. His face reddened as he thought of his call to the HR department.

"Good morning, this is Mr. Bradford in Tech Editing. I need some personnel information on one of my people." He didn't mention he only had one "people."

"Yes, Mr. Bradford. And your justification?"

"I, uh, I plan to submit her for a special clearance for compartmented information."

"I see. Well, if you would have your admin assistant prepare a brief memo to that effect, I'll see that your request is evaluated."

"Evaluated?"

"After those hackers got into our database, the rules tightened up quite a bit. I know it's inconvenient, but I don't have any input to policy matters."

"Ah. Well. Thank you." He hung up. Pretty soon a mother will have to submit a bloody requisition to see her newborn babe, he thought. The following day he'd casually asked his boss how old Jennifer was.

"Forty-one, I think. Why?"

"Oh, I don't know. Sometimes she acts like my mother." Both men laughed.

So she's four years older than I am, Lamar thought. Damn. She could pass for five years younger. And here I thought vampires weren't supposed to age. A cold chill swept through him. How can I joke about vampires? he chided himself, pulling Heller's manuscript forward and reading aloud, a technique that sharpened his critical faculties.

"Development of artificial platelets has its antecedents in the development of blood plasma during the 1940s. Manmade platelets, super-infused with calcium, vitamin K and fibrinogen, inserted under pressure and vectored to the target site with a yet-to-be-developed microminiaturized laser transporter device—" Totally absorbed, he jerked when he became aware of Jennifer standing in front of the desk.

"Yes?" he asked, his voice too loud.

She smiled and handed him the finished copy of Dr. Gibson's monograph, along with a note providing the date and time of his appointment with Dr. Heller. "Anything else I can do for you before I head out to pick up the new batch of drafts?"

"Uh, can't think of anything at the moment." Impulsively he added, "You must work out to stay in shape for all the circuit riding you do. This is a rather large building." Lamar, you really are a world-class dork, he thought, coughing to cover his discomfort.

"I try to make it over to Malkin three times a week, but it's not as good as some of the other fitness centers in Cambridge. The price is right, though. Do you work out, too?"

"Nowhere near enough."

"Maybe we could exercise together sometime. I think that would be fun."

"Uh, maybe. If I can ever get to the bottom of that inbox."

"Well, all work and no workouts, as they say."

"Can't argue that one." He checked the Paddington, and she flashed another Marilyn Monroe smile and was gone. Why the hell did I make it sound like I'd be willing to go to the fitness center with her? I am definitely losing it. Tighten up, Bradford. This is the worst possible time—

His intercom buzzed. "Mr. Bradford, Dr. Gibson's administrative assistant just called. He wants the monograph back today."

"Tell her it will be in his hands late this afternoon." There goes lunch.

"I can stay late and insert any final changes. And I'll bring you some lunch."

"Thanks. I may have to ask you to do both."

"I'll have to cancel my date with Brad Pitt."

"Ooohkay. Who is Brad Pitt?" He heard her giggle before the intercom clicked off. Damn. That wasn't very professional.

At five-thirty a bleary-eyed Lamar walked the edited monograph down to Dr. Gibson's second-floor office. His administrative assistant was shrugging into her raincoat.

"Oh, Mr. Bradford. I, that is we, weren't expecting you."

"Really? Your boss asked for this by close of business today, and I promised to get it to him." Lamar checked his watch. "There are a few points I need to go over with him."

"Uh, I'm afraid Dr. Gibson got called home a bit early."

"Nothing too serious, I hope." Lamar's raised eyebrows betrayed his skepticism.

"No, his son's soccer practice, uh, I mean he had promised his son, you know, and forgot. His wife was sort of upset. You know how that goes."

"No, I can't say that I do. Here." Before he handed it to her he wrote the date and time on it and signed it. "Have him call me at his convenience."

She looked irked as she put down her umbrella and rain hat, took the document and deposited it in her desk.

"I suspect your boss would want that secured," Lamar remarked dryly, as he turned to go.

When he got back to his office, Jennifer was waiting with his raincoat, leather fedora, and umbrella. "I think we ought to take a rain check on working out tonight," she said. "I'm exhausted. But I know a wicked cool wine bar—as the locals say. You up for a quick one on the way home?"

When did I agree to—wicked cool?

"They're featuring a Nouveau Beaujolais. I've tried it, and I'm sure you'd like it, too."

"Are you that determined to make a wino out of me, Jennifer?" Lamar couldn't help chuckling. "Okay, but just one. I'm bushed, too. What I need is some sack time."

"Me, too."

Lamar bit his lower lip and flushed, but she was hidden behind the raincoat she held out to him. "It's raining cats and more cats, so I'll drive you to your car. Mine's probably closer to the front door," Lamar said.

"Uh, that's kind. Actually, my car is in the fixit shop. I had to bum a ride in this morning, so I'll grab a cab after our drink."

"No, Ms. Marsh, you will definitely not grab a cab."

"Thank you, sir."

"*Sir?*" Lamar shook his head but couldn't suppress a smile as he buttoned his raincoat.

The Sylphon Nymph was packed, but they managed to find a booth in the back. Lamar had to admit, the Nouveau Beaujolais was surprisingly good. He noted that the crowd was younger, and several people spoke to Jennifer or waved. Everybody was talking, and he found it difficult to hear her. Both had to continually repeat what they said and finally laughed in frustration.

"Why don't we take the rest of the bottle to my place? It's quiet there."

Lamar nodded his assent a split second before the ramifications of her invitation grabbed him by the throat.

"Uhhh." He couldn't think of a suitable way to backtrack.

"Come on, Mr. Bradford. I won't bite."

Lamar gripped the tabletop for a moment. "You might not bite, but I might."

"Umm, that sounds interesting." Her smile faded. "Lamar, you really do need to unwind. I don't want to help carry you out of the office feet first one of these days."

That's the first time she's ever called me Lamar. He could feel the heat rising, his face becoming oven warm. He really hated that.

The drive to Jennifer's condo turned into a total scrum: slanting rain, snarled traffic, a symphony of honking horns, an accident requiring them to detour, and at times the wipers couldn't keep up.

"If you have to be stuck in traffic I can't think of a nicer car to be stuck in, or a nicer driver," Jennifer said. Lamar switched on the CD that was already loaded. He'd always loved Debussy's *Prelude to the Afternoon of a Faun.*

"Um, nice," she murmured. "I hope we don't get there too soon."

Lamar realized he was holding his breath and exhaled. "Damn traffic."

She patted his hand. "We'll get there okay." She pulled the seatbelt out and arched her back.

"Do you like the Impressionistic Period?" he asked, his voice strained.

"I haven't heard that much of it, but I like that," she said, nodding at the sound system. "In two blocks, turn right on Fayette, then go two blocks, and I'm on the left. I have a reserved spot where you can park."

"I'm not sure—"

"Mr. Bradford, give yourself permission to relax. We'll have a glass of wine, listen to some music, enjoy a few hors d'oeuvres, and look at my baby pictures."

"And look at what—"

"Just checking to see if you were paying attention. Left," she pointed. "And don't expect too much. My pad is not exactly an estate on Tory Row. See where that driveway is past the streetlight? Turn into it. Our private garage is in the back."

The lighting in her condo was subdued, and he detected a mild floral scent. She put the umbrellas in a stand by the door, hung their raincoats on the backs of two hall chairs and then started a CD: Louie Armstrong playing *Mack the Knife.*

"Do you like traditional jazz?"

"I haven't heard that much of it, but I like that," Lamar answered, smiling.

Jennifer laughed. "Great. We're both going to learn something new, I guess. Uh, about music. Sit on the sofa or look around, whichever. I'll turn on the fireplace and get to work on the goodies. We should be dry in a jiff. Oh, and take off your coat and tie. Can you believe we left the Beaujolais in your car? I have a nice Pinot Noir at cellar temperature. Will that be okay?"

"Okay." Thank God I'm not wearing those suspenders Robert keeps laying out. Lamar began wandering around. Modern art left him cold, but the reproduction Persian carpets were of good quality. How does she afford a place like this on her salary? She must be working two jobs, or maybe she has wealthy parents.

Scanning the bookcases on either side of the fireplace mantle, he was stricken by two Anne Rice novels: *Interview with the Vampire* and *The Vampire Lestat.* He grabbed the mantle with both hands, knuckles whitening. An Audubon bird clock in her kitchen, its song sparrow chirping the hour rather raucously, interrupted his terror, and he heard the faint pop of an extracted cork. He took several deep breaths and pushed off from the mantle.

Lamar flinched at the tiny meow from a small black and white fluff-ball kitten on the staircase behind him. It sat, tail switching, and watched him.

"Oh, that's Cricket. She won't bite either. The wine is poured. Snacks in a mo," she called. "Come into the kitchen. You can help me carry them into the living room."

Lamar took a couple of deep breaths and walked into the kitchen. She handed him a glass of wine. "Cheers," they both said, clinking glasses. "The wine will improve after it breathes some more." Jennifer smiled. "Here, take the Brie in while I slice the French bread. You do like Brie? Almost everybody does."

"Oh, sure. Brie is fine with Pinot."

She chuckled and grabbed a bowl of red grapes out of the fridge. "If you'll carry the grapes and wine into the living room, I'll slice the bread; won't take a sec."

Mr. Armstrong and company were into their signature version of *Hello Dolly.* "I may become a fan of traditional jazz before the evening is out," Lamar said, placing their wine on the coffee table.

"Ahhh, dammit!" The knife clattered to the floor, and Jennifer bent over as Lamar rushed back into the kitchen. Blood dripped rapidly from her left forefinger onto the cutting board. "I'll run upstairs for some Cortisone cream and a bandage." She held her finger under the cold water, and then wrapped it in a paper towel and headed for the stairs. "Sorry. Back in a flash."

Lamar's face whitened, and he stepped back, aware of a queer taste in his mouth and, the cloying scent of Absinthe. He began to hyperventilate and slumped down, back to the refrigerator, head between his legs. The overhead kitchen light undulated, and the blood in his veins began to roar. His face flushed a cold damp. Drops of blood marched from the sink across the counter and down the side of the island, then across the floor, over his shoes and through the living room to the staircase. The drops began to jump up and down, finally joining into a figure. With a face. That howled. Like a ravaged cat. Lamar got up and stalked the bleeder.

"Oh Lord. You startled me. I didn't hear you—What's the matter, Lamar? You look so, so strange."

The look on his face was more than strange. It was hideous. His mouth kept opening and closing, his eyes riveted on the red-stained water in the sink. His hair, always perfectly brushed, hung disheveled over his forehead. His fingertips were bloodstained, the front of his white shirt smeared. Lamar yanked a hand towel off the rack and began furiously buffing his bloodstained shoes.

"Are you all right?" Jennifer's voice was taut. One hand covered her mouth as she watched Lamar working on his shoes, humming tunelessly from deep within his diaphragm.

"I have something that will get the blood off your shoes. Here, take them off, and give them to me," Jennifer said.

Lamar straightened. He shook, and a tic began in one eye. Cricket meowed and rubbed against his ankle.

"No! Get it away from me."

Jennifer snatched Cricket and fled downstairs, pitching the cat into the laundry room and slamming the door. She ran back upstairs. The bathroom was empty except for Lamar's shoes. Her finger began to bleed again, and Jennifer quickly smeared it with salve, then, with shaking hands, managed to get a bandage around the wound. She heard a sound. It came from her bedroom. A sob?

The bedroom was dark. Switching on the hall light she saw him, face down on her bed.

He sobbed again.

"Lamar. What is it?" She began to massage his shoulders. Slowly, he rolled over, his face tear-stained.

"Oh, God. It really has started."

"What has? What's started?"

He reached up and pulled her onto him, his arms vice-like.

"It's okay, you just had a bad reaction. Let's lie here and relax for a bit. The wine will get to breathe longer that way." She wiped his face with the end of the pillowcase.

Lamar's breathing finally slowed, and his muscles relaxed. "I'm sorry. So sorry," he said, his voice barely audible.

"Hey, I rather like this. Let's lie here a little longer. When you've relaxed a bit more I intend to hurl you into the shower." They lay motionless for a long time as Jennifer gently rubbed his temples. They finally sat up on the edge of the bed.

"I'll run your shirt through the laundry and clean your shoes, right after we have a couple glasses of wine. Or would you like something stronger? I have a bottle of scotch for emergencies like this. So here's the plan. You get out of your clothes, and put on my bathrobe. We drink some well-earned scotch, then you take a long hot shower while I get your clothes and shoes processed."

Lamar was dazed.

While Lamar was in the shower, Jennifer tiptoed up to her bedroom and completely undressed.

"Oh my God," Lamar murmured when she stepped into the shower.

"Don't   worry,   Lamar.   I'm   not   going   to   bite."

6

OVFS Fire Drill
November 30

"Hell hath no fury like a vampire scorned."

From the 1697 play, *The Morning Bride*,
by William Congreve—as amended.

The pounding thundered through Morgan's apartment. "Who is it? What do you want?" she yelled, snatching her fanny pack and cat satchel off a hook near the door. The fire alarm bell began to clang, and she could hear muffled voices and people yelling.

"Fire department. The apartment's on fire. You've got to get out. Open up."

"What fire company are you from?"

There was a long pause. "Lady, we don't have time for twenty questions, open the damn door."

"Coming," she called. She stuffed Calvin in his satchel and fastened it over one shoulder, then yanked open the small entrance table drawer and pulled out the Advanced Taser M26C, inserted ear plugs, pulled the pin on a flash-bang grenade, unlocked the door and stepped to one side.

A man dressed in a fireman's uniform hurtled through, swinging a fire axe.

"Here," Morgan said, rather casually, as she tossed him the grenade and dove behind the door, closing her eyes against the brilliant flash. The concussion was deafening. She felt woozy as she looked out in time to see a second "fireman" reach for a weapon from a holster under his open slicker. The blast from the Taser, pre-set for maximum impact, threw him backward into an elderly couple emerging from the apartment across the cramped stairwell. The three fell in a jumble, the fireman convulsing.

Morgan screamed "Fire" and kept screaming as she bounded down the stairs. She paused in the entrance hallway to allow a small crowd of highly agitated apartment dwellers to burst through the front door and then blended in with them. Flashlight beams arced all over the front of the building as frantic adults yelled for their spouses and children to assemble. At least two police sirens wailed as they drew nearer, along with the distant sound of a fire siren. As residents fought their way outside, hordes of people from nearby apartments flocked to the scene. Dogs barked frantically, more sirens wailed, and someone with a loudspeaker began exhorting everyone to stay calm, creating a scene Dante would have been proud of.

Morgan easily made her way to Miss Lillian's and around back to her rented garage. She unlocked the roll-down garage door as quietly as possible. The door squealed, but the noise from three blocks away drowned out the sound. Morgan made a quick check of the intrusion indicators. No one had entered her car. She gave Calvin a handful of kibble on the front seat and petted him for a minute, allowing her heart rate to slow. She started the Toyota— Ole Gnarly Head she'd named it—and edged forward enough to close the garage door.

As she was about to get in the car the porch light came on. Miss Lillian stood on the side porch, arms folded across her chest. Morgan froze.

"I guess this is good-bye, then," the older woman said, her voice thin.

"Uh, I have to get scarce for a while till all the crap that's hitting the fan down there blows away. You've been a good friend, Lillian. I have no right to ask anything more of you, but if you are questioned, you've never heard of me. Can you do that?"

"Hell, if it's all the same, I'd as soon go with you."

"Go with me—you're kidding, right?"

"You think I wasn't your age once? I got a police record, you know." Lillian leaned forward bracing herself against the porch railing. "I used to entertain some of the more important gentlemen in this town. One or two of them would go my bail even yet. Now you get going. I'll send the bloodhounds into the New Jersey swamp. But on one condition. You got to let me know you are all right? Do you need any money? I have a .38 revolver that might come in handy, too."

Tears filled Morgan's eyes, and she stepped up onto the porch and hugged Lillian. "I will never forget you. And I *will* contact you. Who knows, I may need to use your garage again."

"Yours for the askin', Julie."

"Morgan. My real name is Morgan."

"Nice name. I used to have a gentleman friend named Morgan. Really sweet, except for those damned cigars. But you get going before the fuzz gets itself organized."

Morgan hugged and kissed Lillian, jumped in the car, and eased it out onto the street, driving a block before turning on her headlights.

Why was it always like this? She had made so few friends during her cursed life... and left them all.

It was hard to see where she was going. Everything was so blurry.

7

The Interview
December 2

"All that we see or seem is but a dream within a
dream."

Edgar Allen Poe, 1827

G ood morning. May I help you?" The stiff woman with black hair pulled back into a bun, thin to emaciation, studied Morgan as if she might be a terrorist.

"Good morning. I'm Morgan Summers. Here to interview with Dr. Senger. For the research assistant position." Morgan's smile was forced. She placed her well-worn leather pocketbook with the long straps, circa 1944, on the sofa.

"Ah, yes. Here it is," she said, leaning toward her computer. "You are a bit early. Would you like some coffee? I'll tell the Director of Human Resources you're here." She pushed a button on an electronic device beside her computer.

"Thank you. Yes, please. It takes several cups to get my heart started in the morning."

"I'm Ms. Bundaeker, *Executive* Counselor to the Director." She marched over to the coffee mess as if she were the senior drill sergeant on a parade ground.

Executive *Counselor?* Morgan gave herself at best a fifty-fifty chance to be hired. She couldn't list a lot of her experience on her résumé—too much of it was in the past, way past her stated age of thirty-two. Just getting an interview required all the planets to line up, she thought. If it wasn't for Dr. Miles Lamdeth's superb recommendation, she wouldn't be waiting to see Harvard's Director of HR. Morgan had helped him through his wife's long fight with cancer. Her extensive computer background, fluency in French, Italian, and Spanish, and her writing and editing skills helped, no doubt, but Harvard only took the best of the best. She wondered how many others were interviewing for this position.

The coffee was outstanding, and as Morgan breathed in the aroma she responded with an "ummm." The mug had Harvard's logo on it—a red shield with the word *Veritas* surrounded by a crown of golden leaves, with the word *Harvard* at the bottom. The other side read: ASPIRE Recruitment Management System.

"That's Jamaica Blue Mountain Organic Coffee Blend," Ms. Bundaeker said. "Dr. Senger's favorite." She lifted her chin as she spoke.

"It's marvelous. I haven't tasted it since I was last in a little coffee shop in Basseterre." *In 1885.* Morgan smiled sweetly, receiving a look of disapproval in return.

"Please have a seat and enjoy your coffee. I should think Dr. Senger—"

Morgan nodded at the green light flashing on Ms. Bundaeker's electronic device.

"Well. It seems you can go in now." Her face was pinched as she opened the door.

Morgan grabbed her pocketbook, set the coffee mug on Frau Bundaeker's desk, and entered Dr. Senger's office.

"Ms. Summers. Do come in. I'm Florence Senger. You're welcome to call me Flossie, almost everyone does." She smiled and walked around the desk, holding out her hand for a hearty handshake. "Let's sit over here. More comfortable. Did Judeland offer you some coffee?"

"Yes, and it was outstanding. I didn't realize Blue Mountain was being exported." *Wow.* She's taller than Judeland and almost as lean. Padded shoulders and beautifully coiffured hair—gray with a tinge of blue. Bright red lipstick and matching nail polish. She's a throwback like my pocketbook. Really impressive.

"It is, thanks to the coffee gods. I'll ask Judeland to bring us some fresh." She got up as the door opened and the executive counselor marched in with two Harvard mugs.

"Thanks, Judeland," Morgan said, smiling. Judeland compressed her lips, nodded almost imperceptibly, and closed the door as she exited. The two women were silent as Morgan sat in the upholstered leather sofa and Florence sat facing her in a leather wingback chair, both sipping their Blue Mountain.

"Are you called Morgan, or do you have a nickname?"

"Nobody ever gave me one, so it's just Morgan." She adjusted the skirt of her beige suit, with matching wide belt, hemline at half calf, nylons and elegant dark brown crocodile heels.

She wore no jewelry or perfume, just her new Revlon Wine With Everything lipstick.

"My, where did you get that pocketbook? I love it. Reminds me of Casa Blanca. Uh, Morgan, do you mind if I smoke? I'm down to three per day, but it's devilishly hard to get to none. Do

---

---

you smoke?" Both women glanced at the monogrammed sterling silver cigarette holder and matching lighter on the desk. Morgan noted a small stack of folders in Dr. Senger's inbox—probably résumés.

"I've managed to give it up. At least seventeen times," Morgan replied. They both laughed. Florence lit her morning cigarette and inhaled deeply. "When Harvard went smoke free, they grandmothered me in," she said and chuckled. "Dr. Heller got grandfathered in for his pipe, too. We're the only two I can think of, though."

Morgan would kill for a cigarette. She'd begun smoking during World War II as an Army nurse. Everybody smoked during the war, but every article about interviews warned not to light up. Maybe she's testing me, Morgan thought. Wonder what she'd think if I told her I got the pocketbook during the war? Or that I once made a living in Gay Pariee as a Parlee?

"So, Morgan, why do you want to work at Harvard?"

Morgan had rehearsed for that one. "When I was six, my mother died of cancer, and I was sort of handed around. I saw too many sick kids that didn't get much medical attention. A long time ago I decided I wanted to help find some answers to the big health issues: TB, cancer, AIDS, that sort of thing. Being a research officer with Harvard's Faculty of Arts and Sciences would be like catching the brass ring."

"Your father didn't raise you?" Florence flicked ashes into an old fashioned tall ash tray standing beside her chair.

"No. I sort of lost track of him. Or he of me. I have no idea where he is, or even if he's still living."

"Any kids of your own?"

"Just Calvin, my cat."

Florence got up and went to her desk, returning with a folder, which she opened. "You have a strong and eclectic résumé, but it's a bit spacey on details."

"Dr. Senger, I'm not much into writing about my past."

"That could be a serious liability during a job search. I've read the monograph you submitted with your résumé and your writing is excellent. Top two percent. But your keyword search recommendation hooked me, and I'd like to talk to you about that later.

"And it was rather audacious of you to recommend a bit of reorganization when you haven't spent a day on the job, but I like audacious." Dr. Senger casually dropped Morgan's résumé on the rug beside her chair and sipped her coffee.

Morgan wondered if she or the résumé was being dismissed "Dr. Senger—"

"Call me Flossie, unless it makes you uncomfortable."

Morgan paused and smiled. "Flossie, may I ask you to judge me on my merits and not on the 'spacey' résumé, as you put it? I can recite your entire organization and name the heads of every department. I have become familiar with Harvard's Aspire software. I am studied in the ethical principles of human subject research," she continued, almost quoting from the job description. "My social, organizational, and management skills are exceptional, as are my research skills. I'm prepared to offer my services for a week at no pay as a demonstration of my talents."

"Much of our work is proprietary, and we have recently ramped up our security program. It's even tighter of late with all the concern about cyber security. Part of your duties likely would include functioning as a security officer. Another major area would be beta-testing genetics software. How does that strike you?"

"Frankly, it sounds exciting. As I was being handed around in my early years, I learned to keep my mouth shut. You can sense by my résumé that I am a rather private person by nature. And the software work is a challenge I would welcome."

"Umm." Flossie stubbed out her cigarette and sipped her coffee. The silence lengthened. The Chief of Human Resources seemed to be studying a reproduction impressionist painting—a Monet landscape (1878) on the wall over Morgan's head. "I have always trusted my intuition, Morgan. I won't accept your offer to work for a week off the clock—Lord knows, I don't think we have any forms that fit that situation—but I will put you on probation for a month, maybe longer. The position is funded by grant money, which gives me certain leeway to bypass the standard selection committee interviews. You will have to be approved by Dr. Heller, of course, but he hasn't turned down anyone I've sent him so far, and he needs to fill the vacancy quickly.

"Dr. Heller and his colleagues in the Genetics Lab are working on DNA mapping, molecular gene splicing, cloning technology, even some paleontological studies of ancient genetic materials. Does that sound interesting to you?"

Morgan was sitting ramrod straight, all but quivering. Her lips were slightly parted, eyes glistening. The man with the key was nearby. She could feel it.

"Dr. Senger, uh Flossie, the job sounds too good to be true."

"I think you will fit in, Morgan."

"We are having a hail and farewell gathering in the Harvard Faculty Club tomorrow about six. I'd like you to attend. Can you make it? It would be a great opportunity to meet the people you will be working with. By the way, when could you start?" Flossie picked up the résumé and put on her glasses.

Right after lunch, Morgan almost blurted out. She adjusted her skirt again. Why did it feel like it was wrapped around her throat? "Dr., uh, Flossie, since this is Thursday, how about Monday morning? And yes, of course, I'll attend the hail and farewell party tomorrow evening. Thanks for inviting me. Uh, will I need a parking permit or anything?"

"Judeland will fix you up with an ID and a parking sticker. And start your file. You might want to get it right with her. She's someone you'll need in your corner. I'll chat with Jamie about your pay scale. I'm sure we can meet your needs. I wouldn't worry about that." Florence stood, smiled, and extended her hand. "I wish we could talk longer, but I have a full inbox, and I have to get ready for a job fair. You'll have your own inbox pile like mine in a few days, I trust. Very nice to meet you." She handed the résumé to Morgan. "Would you give this to Jude?"

As the door closed behind her, Morgan let out a long whoosh. Forty-eight minutes ago she was unemployed. Now she worked for the Faculty of Arts and Science at Harvard. She hadn't felt this good since the Army promoted her to captain in 1945.

Morgan and Judeland handled the processing paperwork quickly, and Morgan left.

As the door closed Judeland wrote "Watch List" on the inside cover of her new HR folder.

8

Murmurings of Death
December 3

"It was nothing personal. I didn't really want to harm her. I thought she was very nice. Soft spoken. I thought so right up to the moment I bit her on the neck."

Paraphrased from Truman Capote,
In Cold Blood, 1966

T he stairs creaked when he was half way up the second flight, and he froze, listening. It gave him a chance to catch his wheezing breath. A single light bulb over the stairwell caused the shadows to ebb and flow like a boat wake. No more than forty watt, he thought. The motherless bastard could have rented a room for the day in a hotel with an elevator. And some light. He snugged his left arm again the bulge of his nine-millimeter Sig Sauer in its shoulder holster. He missed his old Colt .45, now retired. His breathing still labored, he resumed his climb.

He bitterly resented having to fly from Rome to the U.S. because of one man's incompetence.

Cardinal Alfonso Loconis, known within the OVFS as "Number Two," detested dressing like a homeless man, but it was a necessary disguise. The founder of the Final Solution served for forty-one years and had never visited his "footmen," had never left the Vatican. At his death the title "Number One" had been permanently—and reverently—retired. The organization had flourished under Number One and his successor, Number Two. Alfonso succeeded as Number Two but had not enjoyed the success of his two predecessors, a fact that tormented the new OVFS Director.

His arthritic knee ached, making the climb to the third floor an even more arduous trial. He hammered on the door of number 309, his mood as frayed as his badly worn black topcoat. Silence. He listened intently and surveyed the hall.

A chained door opened a crack behind him. The wheezing man whirled and dropped to one knee in a long-practiced motion, his hand inside his overcoat pulling the Sig. The chain swung free, and the door opened wide enough to admit Number Two. Number Three's face was yellowed and gnarled, like dry, exposed roots, as he watched the Sig being returned to its holster.

"Welcome to my humble abode," Number Three said, his smile a carnival face painting.

Number Two looked around, tempted to spit on the floor. "You're living in a pigsty—as usual."

"Maybe it's all Bob Cratchit can afford." Number Three's chuckle sounded like an old hand-push lawnmower.

"Where's the coffee?" He looked around at the threadbare furniture, what there was of it. The apartment smelled like a French armpit. Cigarette butts were heaped in ashtrays on the sink, on a lamp table next to a splitting, overstuffed chair, and on the breakfast nook table. He scowled at the chipped mug. The coffee tasted rusty. "Where do you buy your coffee beans, off a tramp steamer?" He pulled out a pack of English Dunhills and an ancient Zippo. He waved the cloud of smoke in the direction of Number Three, who had slumped down on the chair opposite him.

Number Three pulled out a pack of Turkish Fatimas, lit up, and waved the smoke back at Number Two. Three sipped his coffee and sighed, as if contented, then cracked his knuckles.

Number Two glared at him. "Well, you have failed twice, Number Three. I want to hear your latest plan, and it had better be a good one. A perfect one. If we are to rid the world of vampires, we can't continue to squander opportunities like this. And while you may think the Vatican grows money on olive trees, it doesn't. Every time a dolt like you fails it makes it that much harder for me to maintain our funding."

Number Two flicked ashes on the faded circular throw rug under the table. He was startled by a low-pitched growl. A cat stalked out from under the table.

"Jesus, Mary, and Joseph. You have a cat? Do I have to read you the OVFS regulations after all these years?" Number Two kicked at the cat. The cat raced behind the sofa, hissing. "I've a mind to put that stupid creature out of its misery, but a shot would likely bring this firetrap down around my ears. So, how will you take her out?"

Number Three called to the cat in Russian, and the cat stopped its complaining. It slunk out from behind the sofa and sat licking its paws and cleaning behind its ears, ignoring the two men.

"The target will be attending a party they call a 'Hail and Farewell' at the Harvard Faculty Club on Friday evening. She will eat an hors d'oeuvre that will induce a coma. I have two men on staff at the Club. They will see that she gets one that is laced. When the 911 vehicle arrives, it will be driven by my people. We have made arrangements to transport her to Mount Auburn Cemetery in Cambridge, where a grave has been dug for a funeral on Saturday. We will lay her body in that grave and cover her. The head, of course, will be flown to Vatican City to join the others in the vault. We will take the before and after pictures at the cemetery."

"That's too complex. Too many failure points. I disapprove the plan. Give me your alternative plan." Number Two dropped his cigarette on the rug and stomped it out.

Number Three lit another Fatima with the stub of his previous one and squinted through the smoke, plucking a piece of tobacco off of his tongue with thumb and forefinger. "That will take more time. Another week, more like two."

"I give you three days. My patience is running out. You should have had a contingency plan ready in case I disapproved your primary one. You are slipping, Number Three. Don't slip. The OVFS retirement plan is short for failures. Very short."

Number Three grunted and stood. Number Two was already putting on his topcoat. He paused at the door. "Three days. Don't forget my lock of her hair. And get rid of that God-rotted cat." He slammed the door.

"We will see whose retirement comes first," Number Three mumbled to the cat. In Russian.

9

Mayhem at the Harvard Faculty Club
December 9

"You will be dead so long as you refuse to die."

George Macdonald,
What's Mine's Mine,
1886

H arvard Faculty Club on Quincy Street," Morgan told the cabbie. She had decided not to drive as neither Old Gnarly Head nor the minivan would pass for elegant, and she needed to make a good first impression.

"I know it," the cabbie said, his voice heavily accented and angry. It would be a short ride to the club.

I'll bet you don't have a green card. Morgan opened her purse and pulled out a mirror to check her lipstick and make sure the wind hadn't rearranged her hair. She was pleased with her new hair stylist and had given her an extra-large tip. But her appointment had taken longer than expected, and now she was running late. Her second credit card was almost red-lined after the hair styling and the new clothes and accessories purchased for the Hail and Farewell, especially the fur cape. That first paycheck can't get here too soon. Still, Flossie told me not to worry about the money. If she could see my credit card balances she wouldn't be so quick to say that.

Morgan, who normally was instinctively aware of her surroundings and alert for anything unusual, hadn't looked out of the cab windows. Had she turned around, she would have seen a blue Chevrolet Cobalt, one she'd seen before on the way out to the landfill. She knew it wouldn't take long for the OVFS to realize the move to Boston was a ruse, but at least it bought her some time. She was mortally tired of running. They turned onto Mass. Avenue. Nearly there; shouldn't be more than fifteen minutes late.

The cab's brakes squeaked as it stopped in front of the wrought-iron double gated entrance, flanked by ornate marble pillars. The front of the club was impressive. Elegant, stately, almost somber, except for the bright red door. Old world brick work surrounded massive windows set geometrically along the first and second floors; a row of dormers above them accentuated the third floor. On either side two large bow-front windows jutted out. Dentil molding graced the eaves of the roof, and three stately brick chimneys reached upward from the center and both ends of the building.

Morgan paused at the stairs leading to the front door and took three deep breaths. She touched her Greek Key gold necklace and matching earrings and glanced down at the matching gold ring on the index finger of her left hand. The spiked high heels matched her dress perfectly, as did her purse and Greek key designer watch.

An icy ripple coursed down her back. I'm way out of my league, she thought. She would have to eat something, and that would be a trial. What she really wanted was a martini, or at least a large scotch on the rocks. As she reached for the door handle, an eighteenth century brass box lock and knob, the door opened. A pale elderly gentleman in livery and white gloves, looking like a funeral director, bade her enter. He took the cape from her shoulders and disappeared.

Morgan cupped her hands and blew on them as she surveyed the ornate threshold.

More than forty people were droning, laughing, and clinking glasses in obviously high spirits. The formal room was warmly appointed. She noted the crystal chandelier, antique longcase clock on one side, dark, fluted columns, winding staircase and two large red banners with white lettering: "Hail Newcomers" and "Farewell Wayfarers."

She jumped at the hand on her elbow. Ms. Bundaeker.

"Forgive me Ms. Summers, I didn't mean to startle you. Please follow me, and I will make the first introduction. After that you are expected to mingle and introduce yourself." Flossie's counselor looked as if she were about to add "If you dare." As they threaded their way through the crowd, about equally divided between men and women, Morgan brushed past a man, probably middle thirties, and received a jolt that stopped her in mid-step. For a long moment, she stared at him. The trace of Absinthe was unmistakable. He stared back, still and intense.

"I, uh, excuse me," he finally mumbled.

"My fault," she mumbled back.

"If you will come this way, Ms. Summers, I'm sure Dr. Heller would like to meet you." Judeland glared at the two of them, her words clipped.

"Yes. Coming. Sorry."

They stopped at a circle of men, all of whom looked at Morgan.

"Dr. Heller, may I present Ms. Morgan Summers. She will join the staff as of Monday morning. I trust Dr. Senger spoke to you about Ms. Summers." Judeland thrust out her chin like a schoolmarm in a B-grade silent movie.

"She did indeed," Dr. Heller said, beaming. "Where is Flossie, I wonder?" Judeland pointed to the opposite corner of the room. "Ah, good." He turned back to Morgan and extended his hand. "Ms. Summers, I am looking forward to showing you around my lab and talking you into joining us. May I call you Morgan?"

"Yes, of course." The other four gentlemen smiled. Dr. Heller introduced her to them, including a gentle barb for each. All seemed friendly, if a bit reserved. Judeland disappeared. "But where are my manners," Heller said. "We must get you a beverage. What would you like?"

"Would martinis be on the menu?"

"My dear, may Harvard crumble if it ever comes to pass that we can't produce one of the best martinis in academia." He waved to one of the liveried waiters and placed the order: Tanqueray, dry, shaken, ice cold, extra olives.

"You must have ESP, Dr. Heller. That is exactly how I would have ordered it." Not quite, she thought. But no one will notice that I didn't eat the olives. In fact, she couldn't recall her last real meal and winced at the thought of another starving time. I have to eat.

"Well, I figured that if you didn't drink your martinis that way, now would be a good time for some on-the-job training." The others laughed in an obligatory manner. Morgan appraised Dr. Heller but not in the way he was appraising her, something she was long used to. He wore a three-piece vested black pinstriped suit, white shirt, bold red tie, and gleaming black Florsheims. His wedding band was overpowered by a large diamond set in a companion gold band, looking like an engagement ring. Heller was telling Morgan about the lab protocols when her martini was delivered.

"A toast. To Ms. Morgan Summers, newest member of the Faculty of Arts and Science. May you and the department prosper for as long as Harvard will have us."

The toast was followed by a reasonably hearty "Here, here!" from the group. While Heller was relaxed and in his element, the others seemed to be a bit tense. She guessed their boss was not a particularly tolerant or forgiving man.

"So, what do you think of our Flossie?" he asked.

Before Morgan could respond, a bell rang, and all turned to the podium, which had been wheeled in. A gentleman moved quickly to the podium and tapped on the microphone.

"Welcome all to our quarterly Hail and Farewell. My job is to introduce the one person on campus who needs absolutely no introduction, the President of Harvard University, Dr. Glenn Ellen Martin. Dr. Martin." The applause was prolonged as she walked to the podium.

"Thanks, Ben. You've no idea how refreshing it is not to have to listen to introducers drone through my history back to the sixth grade." The group laughed with genuine appreciation. "Not far away from the Yard flows the Charles River," she began. "And like that river, we who serve the College flow into the Yard and finally out of it. It is fitting as we begin the celebrations commemorating our three hundred seventy-fifth anniversary, that we welcome the new and bid a sad farewell to. . . ."

The kitchen was hot and steamy. The chef, sous chef, and three line cooks were working at a frantic pace to finish the entrees, while one other cook prepared a final round of hors d' oeuvres.

The Head Chef strained his throat as he conspicuously tapped his watch. "You must make haste, everyone." His French accent was pronounced. Ah, for the days when kitchen staff knew what they were supposed to do and when to do it. "David, if I have to ask you one more time to refrain from sampling the hors d' oeuvres, you shall lose your position." David mumbled something and hustled out with his tray.

Paula was about to take her tray out when she was intercepted by the new line cook. "Here, take these. They are a special surprise for Ms. Morgan Summers," he pointed, "the lady in the blue dress standing with Dr. Heller. Serve her *only*, and return immediately. Now hurry." He turned and strode back into the kitchen.

Paula looked at the new tray she'd been handed. No one was watching. She snitched one of the goose liver pâtés in a tiny pie crust. It tasted rather strange, but then she had never tasted one before. As she started forward, she suddenly felt cold and began to shake. Her lips and tongue felt swollen. Her breathing became rapid and shallow. Everything turned gray. The tray pitched forward and crashed, startling the nearby guests. Paula flailed for the staircase railing, missed and plunged head first into it, gashing her forehead. Blood spread rapidly around her head as she lay face down at the bottom of the staircase, and her limbs began to convulse.

For a long moment nobody moved. Then several of the guests began yelling for someone to call 911. Morgan sprinted across the floor and knelt by the stricken girl, gently rolling her over. She accepted a large white table napkin and made it into a compress, which she held on the wound.

"Quick, I need a belt," she commanded. Someone handed her one, and she tied it around Paula's head to secure the compress. While doing this Morgan unobtrusively palmed one of the pâtés lying nearby and managed to scoop it into her purse. Morgan's hands were covered with blood, and splotches of it had seeped into her nylons and dress. Even her face was blood stained. Her vision clouded, and sound became hollow and distant. She clenched her teeth. *Not now.*

Shuddering, she looked up into the eyes of the man she had bumped into earlier. She could smell the Absinthe again, but there was no time to dwell on that.

"Help me carry her to the front door," Morgan said, her voice raw. A chorus of guests objected loudly, telling them not to move the girl and that they should wait for the emergency responders. "On three," Morgan said. They could hear a siren. "Quickly." Both seemed to possess uncanny strength as they carried Paula to the front door.

"Will somebody *please* open the damn door?" Morgan shouted. Someone did. They carried her outside as the rescue squad vehicle back doors flew open.

"Lower her onto the gurney," one of the responders said.

Morgan pivoted and ran back inside, with Lamar right behind her.

Flossie watched one of the first responders struggle with one of the straps. "Where are you taking her?" she asked one of the responders.

"Mount Auburn's," he replied, getting in behind the wheel. Turning on the siren and flashing lights, the rescue vehicle quickly pulled away. Flossie looked at the license plate and memorized the number, then went inside to find paper and pen. As the rescue vehicle left, a second one wheeled into the front of the club.

Morgan looked at herself in the women's room mirror. Her hair had come undone, and she was covered with sticky blood. She leered at her image as she slowly licked her fingers. The taste was Champaign, cherry and Absinthe. She moaned and could no longer face the woman in the glass. Energy surged through her. Her sense of smell sharpened, which helped her find the purse. Opening it she smelled the pâté. "Calcium oxalate crystals." she breathed.

This has to be an OVFS operation. I was supposed to eat one of these. Then fake rescue squad guys hustle me off somewhere, do the old stake-through-the-heart bit, off with my head, and that's the end of one more vampire. Maybe it would have been a blessing if they'd succeeded. What will they do with that poor young woman who ate the one she was supposed to give me if they think they have a vampire? Morgan shuttered.

"There you are, Morgan. My God, are you all right? I mean all that blood is from the waitress I trust." Flossie tried to put her arm around Morgan, but was shrugged off.

"I need to go home," Morgan blurted. She was shaking.

A sharp rapping startled both women. "Yard Security. I'm coming in." A short, rotund, bleached blonde in uniform burst in. "I need to interview, uh, her," she pointed at the blood-spattered Morgan. "Maybe the both of you."

"Why don't we go upstairs," Flossie suggested. "Do you know where the library is?"

"Of course. I've been employed here for three years. Who are you?"

"Good. You go up, while I get Ms. Summers cleaned up. We'll be with you in a couple minutes."

"I'm not sure—"

"Just give her a few minutes to regain her composure and clean up, officer. We will be up directly." Flossie gently pushed the campus security officer out of the restroom. "Morgan, would you like to spend the night with me? I have a pretty swanky guest bedroom, and I can get your dress cleaned overnight."

"Thank you, Dr., uh, Flossie, but I really need some time alone now."

"Well, at least let me get you a cab."

"Flossie, you take care of the Yard security woman, and I'll see you Monday morning. I'll be happy to give an interview to campus security early tomorrow."

Flossie peeked out of the door, didn't see the officer, and motioned Morgan to get going.

She watched Morgan stride quickly through the stunned crowd. Nobody tried to stop her, but one man—Flossie had hired him a year or two ago—followed her out. In a bleak mood, Flossie headed to the library. The night was a shambles. She wondered what more could go wrong.

Lamar sprinted to catch up to Morgan before she could order a cab from the doorman. "Uh, Ms. Summers, I just wanted to say, uh, that you did a great job in there. Would you let me drive you home? I know we haven't met properly. I'm Lamar Bradford, Chief of the Tech Editing Division. Flossie could vouch for me."

"Mr. Bradford—"

"Lamar. Please."

"*Lamar*, I am a flaming wreck and badly strung out. I would be wretched company, even for a short ride. For all you know I could be a vampire." She watched for his reaction.

"You, too?" Lamar's laugh was weak. "Oh, and here's your cape." He tipped the doorman. "It's rather brisk out, and it will cover up some of the, uh, damage to your gown. Give me a sec to retrieve my topcoat, and I'll walk us to my car. Or rather, I'll swing around and pick you up."

Is this guy for real? she wondered. Still, I can't go back to it tonight. The OVFS may have my place under surveillance. "Lamar, go get your coat. I'll wait, and then we can walk to your car. I need a good, brisk walk."

"Nice," Morgan said. "I've never ridden in one of these. Could we have a little more heat? I seem to be a wimp tonight." She was shaking.

"Sure. You know, I could use a double scotch on the rocks. Could I buy you one on the way to your place?"

He's not handsome—kind of straightforward-looking. And he's not professionally smooth. Definitely not cool. Maybe a drink would help. I only had a couple sips of martini. And something light, like a dead cat. She almost choked at her own sardonic humor.

"Not a bad idea. You know a good spot, one that's on the quiet side, kind of out of the way, and one that wouldn't mind serving a blood-soaked lady?"

"I know just the place." He turned on some classical music.

Why does this guy remind me of that Jesuit I seduced back in seventeen something or other? She could feel her body responding, like it had with the priest. What is wrong with me? They drove in silence for a few minutes.

"Excuse me, Lamar, but this doesn't look like a neighborhood where we could find a bar. If I'm not mistaken we are cruising up Tory Row." She squeezed her purse enough to confirm it still contained her mini Taser.

"To find an out-of-the-way place, quiet and secluded, requires a slight adjustment to our original plan. Trust me, you'll like this place."

"I hardly know you, Lamar, and you're asking me to trust you." Morgan shook her head. "This has been one bizarre night." In for a dime, she thought.

Lamar chuckled. "Well, we can flip for who's taking the bigger risk. If I'm not mistaken, you said you were a vampire."

"I told you, we haven't had anyone by that name admitted from anywhere, never mind the Yard. Have you tried Cambridge Hospital?"

"Yes, I called them after I called you the first time," Flossie said.

"Well, we don't have her at Mount Auburn. Good luck, and have a nice night," he said, with equal parts finality and sarcasm.

She was wasted, her ash tray heaped, and her nerves were doing a caffeine kabuki dance. She'd been up half the night talking to President Martin, campus security, the Cambridge police, hospitals, and morgues, while intermittently trying to reach Morgan. Where had Morgan gone after she left with what's-his-name? She looked through her notes. Lamar Bradford. Dr. Heller saw them drive off in Lamar's Jag. Probably took her for a drink.

She propped her head up with both hands. Where is the waitress? And what's happened to her? Her mouth and throat tasted like the inside of a damp fireplace. Damn, she hadn't even begun to prepare for the job fair that would begin in about thirty-two hours. I need to find my leftover amphetamine. Having a bout of depression was at least good for something: leftover pills.

Flossie poured another cup of coffee; it tasted stale. She added some sugar and cream, a rare departure. She'd weaned herself off those years ago. Time to wean myself off these coffin nails. She cleared her throat and stubbed out another cigarette. Way past time, so when these are gone I won't buy anymore. God, how many times have I said that? She suddenly had an idea and wondered why it hadn't occurred to her before. Third stage exhaustion, that's why. What time is it? What the hell, blood-soaked people don't just disappear out of the Faculty Club every week. She reached for the phone.

The rusty padlock dropped to the ground, and a man dressed in black handed the bolt cutters to another man, also dressed in black, who stowed the tool in the back of an old, windowless panel truck. It only took a moment to unwind the chain and push the wrought-iron gates open.

The squeak caused them to hesitate. The one called "Driver"—the OVFS called all operational team leaders "Driver"—motioned to the other. The older man drove the truck through, while his accomplice closed the gates and pocketed the pieces of the lock after wrapping the chain around both halves of the gate to make it look secure.   Driving without headlights, they inched forward.

The back gate to Mount Auburn Cemetery, off Grove Street, was rarely used.

Fortunately for the two, the roving security patrol ended at midnight, there were no night lights in the cemetery, and with the heavy cloud cover it was dark as a tomb. Perfect for what they planned.

"How the shit are we supposed to find the right grave in the pitch black?"

"Shut up, I'm counting. At the fourth driveway we turn right. That was the third. We're looking for Bluebell Path. Would you keep the damn flashlight on the road." The panel truck moved forward slowly.

"Man, what a creepy place. Look at that gigantic flower pot."

"That's an urn, you dork. There. That's Bluebell. Now look for the tent."

"Yeah, right." They inched forward for several minutes.

"Is that the tent?" the second one asked.

"Has to be." Driver stopped the truck. "Go take a look. Name on the headstone is Fronheizer." His accomplice was back in a couple minutes.

"It's Fronheizer."

"Will you stop waving that flashlight all over Cambridge. Turn it off, for Chrissake, and let's get it done. We dig first."

"How 'bout we kill the damn vampire first? What if it wakes up and decides to drink our blood?"

"I'm really getting tired of all your shit. The knockout stuff they gave the vampire works for over twelve hours. Jesus, if you worked as hard as you complain we'd be done by now. Get the damn shovels."

They crept over to the fresh-dug grave. "Help me pull this tarp off the hole. We'll dig about two feet down, throw the body in, cover it up, and nobody'll know."

"Man, I really don't want to crawl down in a damn grave."

"Well, do you happen to have a shovel with an eight foot handle? Jump down. I'll hand you the shovels." The earth was filled with rocks, making the job harder. It took forty-five minutes of furious effort to finish the digging. Both men were breathing hard and sweating in spite of the cold.

"We're taking too long. This is deep enough. Time to carry her over to the grave, finish her there and dump her in." Both men walked back to the truck, opened the back doors and slid the gurney out, pausing to look at the inert woman strapped to it.

"She don't look like a vampire to me."

"You think they all look like they do in the movies?"

The wheels clattered over the gravel until the gurney was on the grass. Driver started unfastening the straps.

"Why don't we whack her while she's still strapped to the gurney?"

"God's death, man, you were at the very end of the line when they passed out brains. Do you really want to clean all her blood and crap off the gurney? Undo the straps around her legs, and hurry. Next thing we know a cop car drives up, and the officer casually asks what the hell we're doing."

They dropped the woman on the grass beside the open grave and pushed the gurney back to the truck and loaded it inside. "Grab the tool bag," Driver said. He walked behind the bag carrier until he collided with him.

"*Kee—riste on a crutch!* She's gone." The terrified man's voice cracked.

Driver pushed him out of the way and looked. No body. A spasm of fear gripped him as he shined the flashlight around frantically. Then he peered into the grave. "We must have put her too close to the edge." Driver couldn't keep a tremor out of his voice. They hadn't put her too close; she'd been a good foot and a half from the edge. Maybe the knockout stuff was wearing off. He touched the automatic in its holster. "We better get this over with and fast."

"Get in the hole, and I'll hand you the tool bag. We'll have to whack her down there."

"You think I'm gettin' in a grave with a live vampire you can kiss my ass."

"Goddamit, I'll get in, and you hand me the bag. We don't have time to draw straws.

You take the pictures when I tell you." He jumped down, careful not to disturb the body.

Driver unzipped the bag, pulled out the camera and handed it up. The vampire was on her back. At least he wouldn't have to roll her over. "Take two photos before, and then two with the stake in her." He reached for the stake and hand maul, then laid them aside. Driver unbuttoned her blouse and unhooked her bra, shining his flashlight on her chest.

"Nice tits, don't you think? Stand up good even when she's laying on her back."

"Jesus, man, you are one weird asshole. Hold the flashlight steady." He looked at the ghoulish face peering down. The bastards weren't paying him enough for this kind of job, he thought. He positioned the stake over her heart, took a deep breath and raised the maul. For some reason he glanced at her face.

Her eyes were open. She was staring at him. And she blinked.

The maul drove the spike half way through her chest. Blood spurted into his face, and the body hunched as if doing a sit-up.

"Ahhh." Driver lunged back against the side of the grave, frantically wiping his face with the sleeve of his jacket. Her mouth hung open and blood trickled from both corners. She slowly relaxed as if lying down for a nap. But the eyes remained open. With one more blow Driver buried the stake all the way into her chest. The body spasmed once, then lay still.

"I need to go find a rag. Get down there and finish the job. You don't have to worry, the vampire is dead. I drove the stake right through her heart."

"Man, I ain't goin' down there and cut off its head."

Driver pulled his automatic and pointed it at the other man. "You have two choices, asshole. You either cut off its head or you join her, and I bury the both of you. Who knows, maybe you could spend eternity screwing a vampire. You do know how a vampire does it, don't you?"

"Put the fuckin' gun away, man. I'm goin'. I thought I was supposed to be the lookout or some fucking thing." He jumped down and stood, shaking, his back against the hard-packed dirt, until Driver came back, wiping his face.

"Do I pull my gun again, or are you going to get it done?"

The other man mumbled some obscenities and pulled out the saw and a waterproof, zippered freezer container. Shaking his head, he continued to mumble. It took ten minutes to get her head off and zipped inside its carrying case. Driver took several more photos while his partner worked. As Driver was packing the camera, the footman slipped a gold band off the left little finger of the corpse and put it in his pocket.

"Hand me the head," Driver said.

The two men resumed shoveling till the body was completely covered and the earth tamped down. They rolled the tarp back over the grave, picked up the carrying case and their tool bag and started for the truck. After stowing their gear, they drove to the gate.

"Stop wiping yourself and open the damn gate," Driver said. "And close it after the truck gets through, then wrap the chain like we found it. First chance you get, throw the pieces of the lock in the river."

The truck pulled away from Mount Auburn Cemetery. It had taken over two hours to dispose of the vampire, but Driver was pleased with the job. They would have to get rid of the gurney and tools, wipe down the stolen truck, dump it on the outskirts of Boston and then deliver the vampire's head to Number Three, along with the photos. Who knows, after this gig they might give me a number, Driver thought. Number Six sounds good. This numbskull next to me ought to become shark bait, though.

Mount Auburn Cemetery was quiet. Dead quiet. Driver thought about the container and began to hum.

"I'm hungry," his accomplice said.

"Here? This is it? It looks like the Grand Hotel." Morgan had once spent a weekend at the Grand during World War II, having just completed nurses training. I wonder if Lamar was a Jesuit priest in a former life? Morgan grinned.

"You like it?" Lamar asked, studying her.

"Sir, I will reserve judgment till I see the inside."

"Right." He pushed the button to raise the garage door. A bank of outside floodlights lit up the front of Coleson Manor.

"Yuk. You light up the neighborhood for night baseball or something?"

"They go out when the garage door closes." Lamar hustled around to open the car door for her, then keyed in a code on the pad at the garage door, and walked them to an elevator. Morgan whistled over her lower teeth. The ride upstairs was awkward. He stopped it on the first floor.

"Follow me, fair vampire." Morgan's smile faded abruptly. They had just entered the library when both were startled by the sound of a throat being cleared.

"Ah, Robert. May I present my new friend, Morgan Summers. Morgan, this is Robert Diamond. He actually runs the place. Gives me a handsome allowance, though."

Robert stared at the bloody, disheveled woman who held out her hand, smiling at his discomfort. His face was stiff as he bowed slightly, shook her hand and murmured something about it being his pleasure, then turned an inquiring gaze on Lamar.

"Robert, bring us one of our best reds, same for white, and a bottle of our oldest scotch. Add a few snacks on the side. Seems we didn't get to have dinner tonight. But don't go to too much trouble. We don't want to keep you up."

"As you wish, *sir*. Perhaps your friend would like to freshen up before your repast?" Robert shut the door quietly, a moment after straining his throat again.

Morgan laughed. "How many others are there in this house monster, Lamar?"

"Just three of us. And the cat. Cozy, yes?"

"*Cozy?* Lamar, I've stayed in places that would fit in one corner of this library.

"Where can I wash up?"

"Oh. Sorry. I'll show you."

When she returned, he motioned her to sit by the fireplace. He had added a couple of logs. "Give me your purse and cape," Lamar said.

"The cape you can have. A woman is never without her purse."

"I don't suppose you keep a .357 magnum in that purse?" Lamar grinned.

"Wrong caliber. This library is beautiful, in a way. Mysterious, too. I love the fireplace."

Robert knocked and rolled in a tray containing the two bottles of wine, the scotch, ice and assorted canapés, reminding Morgan of the one in her purse. Probably crushed by now, she thought.

"So, Miss Morgan—I trust it is 'Miss'—what will be your pleasure?" Lamar asked, after Robert retired.

"Yes to the miss. Scotch on the stones will do nicely."

The first scotch revived them. The second made them quite mellow. They stared into the fire, their conversation having lapsed. Lamar finally roused himself.

"Morgan, I could drive you home or, if you prefer, call you a cab, but I've got a better idea. Besides, you would scare the cabby half to death like that." He motioned to her dress, shoes, and stockings. "Coleson Manor has several colossal guest bedrooms. You can do a long tub soak, don a bathrobe until the laundry returns your gown, and sample some of Robert's superb breakfast cuisine. When you are exhausted with my hospitality, I'll drive you home. How does that sound?"

Morgan stretched. "Too good to be true. Can we go upstairs now? I'm exhausted." That wasn't true; she'd rarely felt so alive.

She knew why and hated it—the blood. But, as the twenty-somethings say, "It is what it is."

As they climbed the stairs, she wondered how Lamar would be in bed.

She sat in the tub, all traces of blood long gone. Lamar had taken her clothes down in a laundry bag for Robert to take care of in the morning. She heard a soft knock on the door. "Yes?"

"Is there anything else you need?"

"Well, yes, there is. But I don't propose to yell at you through the door. Come in." The expression on Lamar's face was worth the wait. "Hand me that towel, please."

She stood, water dripping from her scrubbed and bath-oiled body. She smiled at the "Kodak moment." Obviously Lamar was not a ladies' man. He was flustered, but couldn't keep his eyes from devouring her "pieces-parts," as she called them. She was glad she had given herself a major trim, but she hadn't shaved it all off.

"What"—his voice broke, and he started over— "What can I do for you?" He still wasn't looking into her eyes.

"You can take that towel and dry me off before I get cold." Lamar began his task eagerly. When he was done not a single drop of water remained. "How did I do?"

"I don't know. Ask me later." A very dry Morgan led Lamar to the bed.

He has a lot to learn, but what a willing student, she thought, much later. I shall make a project out of him. Us. Ha! I'm satisfied, he's exhausted, but at least he's still smiling. Later she became vaguely aware of a phone ringing somewhere.

As she drifted back to sleep she breathed in the faint aroma of Absinthe and sighed.

She would sort that out later.

10

The Abyss
December 10

"Whoever fights monsters should see to it that in the process he does not become a monster. And when you look long into an abyss, the abyss also looks into you."

Fredrich Wilhelm Nietzsche
Beyond Good and Evil, IV, page 146

T wo thumps, followed by one, then two more. The chained door opened a crack. Dull gray pallor from the skylight made the threadbare hotel corridor look even more dismal.

"Ya?" The voice was guttural. Stale cigarette smoke extruded through the door to join with other smells: mold, cat urine, garlic.

"Special delivery." Driver looked at his partner, who carried the insulated container with its grisly souvenir. He hated Number Three, but he wasn't paid to like anybody. He had one friend, and that was enough. Monty was a good car mechanic, and he could provide cars without VIN numbers. Best kind of friend to have given his "profession"—killing vampires.

Monty had told him where to find the kind of truck they needed for this job, his fourteenth. He wondered how many vampires were left. An OVFS footman for almost five years, he'd been promoted to driver a year ago. Soon he hoped to be given a number and begin planning and directing operations.

The fiasco at that vampire's apartment hadn't been his fault. Damn bitch had used a Taser on him. The other footman was still recovering from the flashbang she handed him. Well, the bitch wasn't smiling now. In a few hours she would be lying under Mr. Fronheizer. Except for her head. The door opened just wide enough for the two footmen to squeeze through.

Number Three motioned for them to put the container on the table. "Any problems?"

"No. The Summers vampire will lie under Mr. Fronheizer, whose funeral is this afternoon."

Number Three studied the two with obvious distaste. "Anybody see you go in or come out? You dumped the tools in the river, sanitized and got rid of the truck according to your instructions?"

Driver nodded. The footman grinned, eliciting a disdainful look from Number Three. "Where are the license plates and the camera?"

"In the river with the tools." Driver's response was too quick, too loud, and he glanced at his partner who had also recovered quickly. They'd forgotten to take the plates off the truck.

Number Three squinted at the two. "Where's the lock of hair?"

Driver's eyes widened. "You didn't tell us to cut a lock of her hair off."

"Do it now."

Driver wiped the sweat off his upper lip with the back of his hand, which was trembling. *I'd like to shove a handful of vampire hair up his ass.* He walked slowly over to the container and opened his switchblade. Unzipping the bag, he held his breath and quickly chopped off a handful of hair. He closed and pocketed the switchblade, zippered up the container and turned. He had only taken two steps toward Number Three when the latter blurted, "What 's that?"

Driver's eyes widened. "Huh?"

Number Three dashed to the container, unzipped it and raised the head. Paula's eyes met his. Several drops of blood fell from the ravaged neck.

"May you rot in Hell!" Number Three screamed, in his native Hungarian, dropping Paula's head. "You fart-brained excrement. You have killed the wrong woman," he bellowed. Three reached beneath his suit coat and dropped to one knee.

Driver launched himself behind his accomplice while drawing his own automatic.

Number Three's first shot caught Driver's partner in the chest and hurled him back into Driver, causing his shot to miss Three's head. An envelope fell from the footman's lifeless fingers.

Three's second shot missed Driver, but Driver's second shot grazed Three's left shoulder. Three squeezed off a carefully aimed shot and hit Driver in the forehead, blowing brain matter all over his accomplice. In his death spasm Driver fired one more round, but that shot buried itself in the wall behind the table.

Number Three stood, dazed, muttering a stream of oaths in Hungarian. He had to get out fast. All that shooting would bring the police. He stuffed Paula's head into its carrying case and zipped it closed, snatched his overcoat, muffler, hat and the container, and headed for the door but stopped. Going back, he bent over the two dead men. Moving the footman over with his boot, he reached for the blood and brain-spattered envelop. The cat cried piteously. Number Three frowned and shook his head as he locked the door behind him. "Sorry old cat, I'll miss you," he said, in Russian. As he hurried down the stairwell a door opened, and a bent-over, graying, woman in hair curlers and a shabby bathrobe appeared.

"What happened? What's going on?" she croaked, a cigarette wedged between her lips.

"Two burglars tried to rob me. Quick, get out. *Get Out!*" Number Three vaulted down two flights of stairs as several more doors opened a crack. He raced past the vacant concierge desk and through the front door. Pausing briefly on the sidewalk to don his overcoat, muffler and hat, he hurried to the corner. Probably should have shot the cat, he thought.

His left shoulder began to hurt more as the shock wore off. The cold air didn't help.

Neither did the light drizzle. And, as usual with cold air, his chest ached where his nipples had once been. He hailed a cab and gave the cabbie an address about four blocks from his emergency safe house. He felt for the two envelopes in his suit coat. They contained the cash he was going to pay the two idiots that had, once again, botched the job. At least it would be their last botched job. His last one, too, no doubt. He had put his plan to kill the Summers vampire into effect against the direct orders of Number Two. Now, he was dead meat on the hoof unless he acted quickly. Number Two would issue a contract on him using one of the hit men they kept under retainer. His mind raced as he hurriedly walked to another shabby apartment over a mom and pop grocery store near the Mission Hill Playground, his alternate safe house, one known only to him, he devoutly hoped.

First, he checked his markers to see if anyone had broken into the double locked closet where he kept his operational gear. It had not been disturbed. He opened it, found a box of cartridges, and reloaded his Sig Sauer P220. Then he loaded ten rounds apiece into two empty magazines and pocketed them. Along with the two payments for the footmen, and his emergency thousand, he had $3500 plus the fifty or so in his wallet. Not much, especially since he'd have to buy a two-way ticket to somewhere. A one-way ticket overseas could set off alarm bells within airline security.

Three decided to ship the wrong girl's head through the Vatican Diplomatic Courier Service to his boss, Number Two. With a lot of luck his "mistake" wouldn't be discovered until Number Two opened the container in the OVFS secret chamber. He would need some dry ice. And he needed something for his shoulder. It was only a flesh wound, but he couldn't afford for it to become infected. He would have to hustle to get the head into the courier service before Number Two found out something was wrong. Fortunately he kept both of his apartments clean. He had no fingerprints—part of his OVFS "induction." There were the cigarette butts, though. Turkish Fatimas were uncommon in the U.S., but his supply had been shipped into the country in a diplomatic pouch. The cops might get some DNA off of the stubs, but they wouldn't be able to match it to anyone. He wondered where he could get the left shoulder of his suit coat repaired.

"Imre Sandar." He pronounced his real name aloud. I'm no longer Number Three, he thought. Stuffing all the cash in a suit pocket, he placed his three passports in another pocket and patted the Sig. The envelope was propped up against the coffee pot, still damp with the footman's blood. The photos showed a close-up of an aspen stake driven into the woman's chest, which wasn't disturbing—he'd seen many such pictures. Nor did Driver standing in the grave and holding up her head make any impression. Only the hair. Black. Not blonde. His shoulder reminded him to get going.

Former Number Three grabbed the head carrier, hurriedly looked around and locked the door on his way out. He would buy some Neosporin, an analgesic, and bandages, make one last trip to his favorite deli, and then stop at Acme Dry Ice on Kirtland Street. Oh, what he'd give to see the look on Number Two's face when he pulled the head out of the container, opened the envelope with the pictures, and found a lock of *black* hair.

Maybe Switzerland, he mused and took a large bite out of his corned beef on rye. No, too obvious.

Chief of Detectives Cordell Peyton perched on the corner of his desk at Cambridge Police Headquarters. Two of his subordinates, Detective Sergeants Jim Larkin and Blanton McConnell, were standing in front of an ancient pull down map of the city. "Okay, let's go over it again. Jim, start from the top."

"Friday, a little after six p.m., at the Harvard Faculty Club, one of the waitresses, Paula Bernard, fell and bashed her head on a banister, causing enough of a gash to lose a fair amount of blood. The 911 call came in at," he consulted his notes, "6:36. I can play you the recording if you want."

"Nope, keep going." Cordell locked his fingers behind his head and yawned.

"A rescue unit arrives at 6:42. A woman at the club copied the license plate number. The S-2 Paramedic Response Unit vehicle that answered the call belongs to Cambridge Squad Number Two. It was stolen probably around 5:45 the afternoon of the Faculty Club party.

"Somebody in uniform said he had to take it to the garage to fix an oil leak or something, and simply drove it off. Can you believe that?"

"Anyway, two people at the club carried out the unconscious victim and even loaded her on the gurney. The stolen rescue vehicle arrives just as the two guests get her to the front door. As soon as the stolen one left with the Bernard woman, another one showed up. Talk about timing."

"The two who carried Bernard out were Morgan Summers and Lamar Bradford," Blanton said.

"One of the guests," Jim checked his notes again, "Ms. Florence Senger, the one who copied the license plate, asked where they were taking the victim. They said they were taking her to Mount Auburn. Later, when Ms. Senger called Mount Auburn, they had no record of admitting a Paula Bernard. The rescue vehicle was found early this morning in a driveway on the other side of the river. Swept clean. Had to be somebody that knew how to do that. So far, there are no reports of the victim's whereabouts. We've checked all the morgues and hospitals— Cambridge, Mass

General, and Brigham. Nothing. Paula's parents say she had no enemies. Her boyfriend, a Marine sergeant, was killed in Afghanistan. As far as they know, she was perfectly healthy. So maybe she tripped, but then what the hell happened to her? The parents haven't received any kind of ransom call. They're lower middle class, a ridiculous pick for a ransom job anyway." Jim stopped and swallowed some cold coffee. "Ugh. Gimme a sec to get some hot. Either of you want another cup?" They did.

Cordell rubbed the back of his neck, then his eyes, and sighed. Jim came back in with the coffee and slumped into a chair. "Somebody went to a hell of a lot of trouble to take out this Paula whoever, and yet it doesn't make sense," Cordell said. "How could they know she was gonna take a dive at the club? The timing is just too perfect. We need to talk to Summers and Bradford. Jim, line that up."

"Maybe somebody spiked her Kool-Aid," Blanton said. "But it's probably way too late to try to do any food and beverage analysis. A place like that would get cleaned up in a hurry. Especially after a bloody accident. If it was an accident. Wouldn't hurt to go talk to their kitchen staff, I guess." Blanton got up and stretched.

"I'd bet on a mob hit," Jim said. "She saw something, and they decided to take her out."

"It can't be ransom, and she had no known enemies, so it has to be tied to something else," Cordell said, wearily. "Anything interesting on the blotter?"

"We had a shootout Saturday at a fleabag hotel, the Brookstone off Atlantic Avenue," Blanton said. "Left two guys dead and probably a third wounded based on analysis of the blood spatter and positions of the shell casings. We've asked for DNA matches. Might get something tomorrow if we really push. We found a few drops of blood in an area that don't match up with the other three shooters, so likely a fourth person was involved and got nicked. The lab guys are gonna call with the results."

"There were at least five shots fired," Jim said. "Nothing yet to indicate what caused the shooting. Might have been a drug buy gone bad, but that's pure speculation." Jim finished his coffee, pulled his tie down and unfastened the top button. "Ballistics will take another day or two."

"Anybody see any possible tie-in with the missing waitress case?" Cordell looked at his two subordinates.

Neither did.

11

Vampire Awakening
December 12

"Stare at the monster: remark how difficult it is to
define just what amounts to monstrosity in that very
ordinary appearance."

Edward J. Hughes, Poet, 1957

Morgan took a deep breath, held it, then exhaled an audible sigh. She sat in an ergonomic chair in front of her ponderous oak desk, whose patina was marred by a thousand scratches and two cigarette burns. The office was surprisingly large, had a window overlooking the Yard and several large color photographs of campus scenes hanging on the walls. She crossed the frayed Persian carpet to the window, enjoying the casual, elegant—if well worn—feel. She pulled the Venetian blinds all the way up and looked out. The sky was Harvard gray. As usual the oaks were desperately hanging onto their leaves in a futile attempt to deny winter. The maples made no such attempt.

Wispy flakes settled on the window sill, paused, and then blew off to find a better perch.

Morgan switched on one of the lamps and looked at the two old coffee table books: *Pleasure of Ruins* by Rose Macaulay, 1964, and Ansel Adams's *Yosemite and the Range of Light,* 1979.

What was I doing in 1979? Back in Paris I guess. I'm sort of like an oak leaf in winter, she thought, sighing again.

Morgan considered her inbox, which already had a few items in it. A memo on a forthcoming fire drill, a faxed bill from an office decorator, something from the campus police chief, and a memo from IT about her new account. Morgan opened her Mac, using her password, *Vampire1686.* Her contact data was already in the online phone book, but she only had one email, and that was from Flossie suggesting they do lunch on Tuesday.

She pulled out the two bottom desk drawers and found a staple gun, a 2011 calendar and a Harvard coffee mug. She was about to look in the other drawers when she heard a light knock a second before the door swung open, and Dr. Heller walked in. He smiled and waved at the room.

"Will this do ya?"

"A very handsome office, thank you," Morgan said, standing.

"Come sit." He sat on the sofa and patted the seat beside him. Morgan chose one of the chairs and did not cross her legs.

"Just came by to see if you were settling in okay. Before I forget, you're on the painter's schedule for Wednesday to get your name put on the door. And I've ordered you a coffee mess and a fridge. Tell the guys where you want them placed. Maybe under that picture of the Faculty Club? Damn shame about that waitress bashing her head like that. I have to admit I—we all—were shocked to see you playing nurse and then carrying her out. Are you going to be able to get the blood out of that elegant dress?" Before she could answer, he continued.

"Do you know the guy that helped you carry the waitress out to the rescue squad?"

"Yes. Well, I can't say I *know* him. He gave me a ride home from the club. Lamar Maxwell. Uh, no, that's not it. Bradford. Lamar Bradford. Nice guy. First time I've ever ridden in a Jag. Said he works on staff." Morgan never broke eye contact with Heller, who seemed to be studying her. She was adept at lying, with over three centuries of practice.

Heller looked down. "Does some work for me, actually. He's a tech editor and a damn good one. You might see him at one or two of my staff meetings. If I hadn't coaxed you into accepting this position I might have gone after his secretary. He's lucky to have her. Best he keep his head screwed on straight, though. I think she's a climber. That's confidential. A lot of what I say will be. It's best not to share any of the confidences you hear or observe around the Genetics Lab, comprende?"

"Yes, certainly. A slip of the lip will sink a ship." Morgan shifted slightly to tug on her skirt.

"Well. You must be quite a student of history. Haven't heard that one since the war ended in 1945. What did you think of the lab tour this morning?"

"Very impressive. It looks like the perfect place for some ground-breaking discoveries."

Heller gave her a thumbs up. "Astute observation." He reached into his suit pocket and pulled out a pipe. From the other side he produced a tobacco pouch, lighter, and tamper. "Hope you don't mind?"

"I love the smell of a pipe. Not much for cigars, though. Guess I'll have to scrounge up an ash tray," she said, looking around the office.

"No problem. I'll have one sent around." In a few moments a cloud of smoke drifted up and hung below the high ceiling. "I smoke a cherry blend. I think you'll come to like it."

Morgan smiled as she sat back almost imperceptibly.

"Tomorrow I plan to submit the forms to get you cleared for compartmented access. Some of what we do in the lab is cutting edge and proprietary; some of it relates to the Department of Defense. I trust a young woman like you doesn't have any skeletons in her closet that would come tumbling out during a background investigation?" He grinned.

Morgan pursed her lips.

"Oh, you don't have to worry about the pot you did in your teens; we all did that. But we've outgrown that sort of thing, right? My drugs of choice now are this," he held up his pipe, "the occasional martini and, well, man can't live by bread alone, right?" Heller smirked.

Morgan's smile remained fixed. First day and the boss is already hitting on me. I am going to have to tread carefully. Very carefully. "I hope all the skeletons in my closet are rather old."

"I'm sure you have nothing to worry about, Morgan. Ever taken a polygraph?" Morgan inhaled sharply and looked down.

"Ah, not to worry. They're a bit scary at first, but it won't be a problem. Trust me. By the way, Flossie and I discussed your salary. She suggested a generous figure, but I have a certain leeway with the grant money we have in the till. I plan to sweeten the pot for you based on my assessment of your future value to the lab. That's not to say you'll be driving a Jag any time soon, but I think you will find that I'm a generous man. I believe in rewarding team players." He smiled and stood, as did Morgan.

"Thanks for all this," she said, indicating the office. "I'll work extra hard to deserve it. As you know I have to attend the two-day orientation program starting Wednesday. And tomorrow I'll be filling out a lot of paperwork with Ms. Bundaeker. Maybe on Friday you, or someone you designate, can give me a more detailed understanding of my responsibilities."

"Leave that to me, little lady. I'm right down the hall, and my door is always open. Well, almost always." He laughed, patted her on the shoulder and left.

Little lady. Good grief. Better get used to the patting, too. I've got to become indispensable, and fast. When lover boy wants to collect for all his generosity, I'm going to have to become the world's greatest "go-away-closer" artist. How the bloody hell am I going to make it through a background investigation? Or worse, a polygraph? He had to be testing me with that question about Lamar. Hopefully I can get a few insights about Heller from Flossie at lunch tomorrow. Her thoughts continued bounding like a pin ball.

Wonder why Flossie is so taken with me? Maybe I'm the daughter she never had. If she only knew, she'd get down on her knees and thank her god that I wasn't her daughter. I wonder if the OVFS has figured out I'm not living in Boston yet? I need to stock up on notebooks, printer paper, some ring binders, and the few other items Dr. Heller overlooked. He hadn't overlooked much, including selecting her office location, only three doors down from his. He wants me to be convenient. Wonder who he kicked out of this office to make room for me?

When the day was finally over, and Morgan was about to lock the desk, she realized she didn't know the combination to her safe. Searching for a notepad, she pulled a sheet of paper out of the top long drawer. The raggedly torn piece of yellow, lined notebook paper contained a message:

"Beware, you are being closely watched."

It was unsigned and undated. Morgan stiffened. The words were formed by cutting letters out of magazines and pasting them on the page. Has the OVFS already penetrated the lab? Or do I have some competitor trying to rattle me? A joke of some kind? Something left over from the former owner of this desk? She checked the room for possible hiding places for a surveillance camera or voice-activated audio recorder. Tomorrow she would make a thorough but discreet search.

I wonder what Mr. "Maxwell" will be doing tonight at Coleson Manor. Maybe he'll call me. We shall see if I made a sufficient impression on him.

As she was locking her door the phone rang. Other than Flossie, who knows my number? she wondered, sprinting to the phone. "Hello?"

"Morgan? Glad I caught you. Look, if you don't have a better offer I was hoping we could get together and, uh, talk."

"*Talk,* Lamar?"

"Uh, the offer includes some good wine and dinner, of course, in an out-of-the-way place that has great ambience, one where we could, uh, talk without being disturbed."

"Would this place happen to be on Tory Row?"

"Mmm hmm. Unless you can think of a better place."

"No, I can't. Tee Row is great. It has really nice ambience, I mean." Morgan giggled.

"Right. I'll meet you at the front door in about twenty. I have a reserved parking place on Oxford Street. "

"I'll be watching for you." She could feel her heart thudding. Ah, another evening of 'ambience,' she thought, walking toward the stairs. It had been three days since she'd tasted the waitress's blood. Obviously, the effects hadn't worn off yet. Her mind wandered as she walked, unaware of her smile or her surroundings. I haven't heard anything more about the waitress. I'll ask Flossie at lunch tomorrow.

Almost everyone was gone. A pair of high heels clicked in the corridor behind her. As she turned around, a figure darted into an office. That looked like Ms. Bundaeker. I wonder what she's doing around here this late? She saw Lamar and started for the door. Fortunately, he had a large umbrella as it was sleeting. It will be a cold walk to the car but a nice night to snuggle, she thought, carefully picking her way down the steps. Lamar kissed her. Good start.

Morgan kissed him back and laughed as he blushed.

Sleet covered the roads, and Lamar drove slowly, trying not to pay any attention to Morgan as she rubbed the inside of his right thigh. That didn't work.

Lamar didn't see the other car until it had run the red light and was halfway through the intersection. He instinctively jerked the steering wheel hard left. The Jag slewed into a sickening half-revolution, jumped the curb and jolted to a stop with two wheels up on the sidewalk, facing the wrong way.

"Jesus," Lamar breathed. Morgan gasped. For a few moments they sat, stunned and silent, before they heard it. A cat—screaming. They looked at each other without a word, unbuckled their seat belts and got out. Waves of sleet beat down on them in the early gloom, while distant thunder grumbled, adding to the sound of swaying trees and crunching tires. A passing driver flashed his headlights but kept going. Lamar dived back into the Jag and retrieved a flashlight and an umbrella, which he handed to Morgan, who opened and held it over both of them. Sleet bouncing off the umbrella made a muffled drumming sound.

They both saw the blood beside the car. A few feet away lay a large, black and white cat, its ribcage crushed, its hind legs thrusting feebly, its cries becoming piteous. Lamar's body spasmed and he lurched forward, almost pitching over.

"Lamar?" Lamar's cry was inhuman. He bent low and began to circle the stricken animal, which blinked rapidly as the sleet stung its face. Lamar's eyes blazed with red luminescence, hands curled, fingers spread wide.

"Lamar!"

He pounced on the cat, twisting its head until he heard a crack, then bit into its crushed flank. The thunder grew, and the sleet hissed as if to provide a dreadful harmony. Lamar hunched over the lifeless creature, his face a bloody, garish mask.

And then there were two vampires—smeared, garish, ripping, howling. Blue with cold but oblivious to it. And the wind. And the sleet. And the thunder. And the roaring in their veins.

Time and reality drifted out of reach. Finally, they stumbled into the Jag and sat, numb. "Start the car," Morgan said, her voice harsh. They drove the last two blocks and fishtailed into the garage.

Their breathing created faint traces of vapor. Morgan finally stirred, pulling down the visor and opening the lighted mirror. She choked at the sight she beheld. Finding a rag under the seat, she got out and scooped some slush off the hood to wet the rag, then rubbed her face in a vicious effort to clean it. Finally, she opened the driver side door and began to scrub Lamar.

He jerked and opened his eyes. "What are you doing? Morgan? Stop it." He grabbed her, and she moaned. He suddenly felt like laughing, felt like he stood atop the highest peak in the world, arms lifted wide, wind caressing him, his face warmed by the sun.

A noise intruded on his mountain top reverie. A cat. Crying out desperately. And he began to cry with it, hot tears flowing unlike any he'd ever shed. "Oh, God. It's started," he choked.

In darkness, they groped for the door, the elevator—their sanity. He recognized the elevator's voice. Functional. Strange, he didn't recall punching in the code. "I never punched in the code," he said.

The hot, steaming shower made similar sounds, the kind that were grounding. Water was always grounding. He was finally connecting back to . . . back to what? She had a scrub brush and a bar of scented soap and was trying to skin him. It didn't matter. Nothing did. The codex was right. Welcome to the third generation, Lamar B. Bradford.

He opened his eyes. She of the brown and green eyes was staring into his soul, or at least the cavity where it had once been. It felt good, and he wanted more. More of her.

Lamar watched his last shred of hope gurgle down the drain beneath his feet. He convulsed with shame, remorse, self-loathing, and finally, devastating loss. She held him as he wept and trembled, remembering her own devastation when she first understood the curse—with its unholy immortality. She thought of Anna Marie in Paris during the late nineteenth century and how she had helped her to reconcile to a life in eternal shadow. Now it was Lamar's turn to awaken unto his darkness. Now they were fully joined in the brotherhood of vampirism. At least they would share the road less traveled.

From the depths of a deep and frantic longing, they joined their bodies in the shower, wanting—needing—to fill their voids. The water warmed them, cleansed their skin, and gentled them. They dried each other with tenderness, and fell, exhausted, into bed, their bodies entwined like the ivy that climbed to the very gunwales of Coleson Manor. Awakening in the night, they reached for one another, again releasing the animal passion that surged through them, their mingled energies creating a dull glow in the darkened bedroom.

Oxnard howled plaintively from the garage.

After making love again, they slept like the dead.

12

The Secret Chamber
December 13

"I like to find what's not found at once, but lies within
something of another nature in repose, distinct."

Denise Levestov,
Pleasures, 1959

Lieutenant Colonel Johann Selento, Deputy Commander of
the Pontifical Swiss Guard, marched, stiff-necked, through
Saint Peter's Basilica en route to the Vatican's necropolis,
two stories below the Papal Altar. Long inured to its grandeur—
massive dome, world-class art, dazzling colors and endless gilt
work, the product of master craftsmanship, often highlighted by
brilliant sun streaming through high windows in the dome,
blessing the magnificence of God on Earth—he resented being sent
on such a menial task. The suitcase he carried was heavy and

banged against his leg, making the long walk a penance. If the contents of this suitcase are so important, why didn't the commander carry it? He had waited too long for promotion to colonel and command of the Guard.

Tall, skeletally lean, the colonel's hollow cheeks accented his sunken face, and his permanent frown had dug ski trails across his forehead. Dark eyes, too close together, were divided by a classical Roman nose; stiletto black eyebrows and mustache made him look like villainy going somewhere to happen. He rather liked the effect: the perpetual bearer of bad news.

He descended the stairs leading two stories below, "down through over eighteen centuries of history to ancient Rome," as the tour guides were fond of saying, to meet the President of the Fabbrica, Cardinal Alfonso Loconis. Managing the necropolis, the Vatican's hallowed tombs, required a special organization and a special person to govern the dead.

He took a deep breath before entering the airless corridors. The brick work had probably been done by slaves, the lower portions anyway, and the flagstone walkway glistened in the faint light that illumined its ancient patina. A clammy place, it signified the third part of the holy trinity: birth, life, death. He hadn't been in the wretched necropolis in over ten years and devoutly hoped it would be another decade before he entered it again. Using his flashlight, he searched for Mausoleum C.

"Here, my son."

The voice startled him, and the beam of his flashlight zigzagged.

"You may turn that off now. You have found your way, may God continue to be of such benefice in your life." The cardinal produced his own flashlight and smiled at the tight-lipped officer. "You may hand over your burden, and return to your normal duties with my heartfelt thanks. We could not entrust the task to a lesser servant." Alfonso reached for the suitcase and almost dropped it.

"If you wish, I can carry it all the way to its destination," Johann said.

"You are generous, but that won't be necessary." The cardinal fixed the Swiss Guard with a prefabricated smile.

"At your service, Cardinal Loconis." Johann saluted and began to retrace his steps.

The cardinal waited till he could no longer hear the deputy commander's footsteps before picking up the suitcase and walking through the gloomy corridor. He was half way between Mausoleums C and D when he stopped, carefully placing the suitcase between his legs. He listened. Nothing. This long after visiting hours there should be no one left in the necropolis. And there wasn't. Apparently. He shined his flashlight up and down the corridor and then into the alcove to his right. It looked like someone had decided to dig a corridor but abandoned the effort about seven feet into the earth. The walls and ceiling of the indention had been bricked and then abandoned. Broken and chipped bricks lay in a haphazard pile in the center of the alcove. On the left side of the pile the cardinal began counting the rows of bricks that buttressed the wall. He murmured: ". . . thirteen, fourteen, fifteen, sixteen." In the sixteenth row above the earth floor, one brick was offset about an inch. He pushed the brick flush with the rest, and a door opened. The scraping noise caused the cardinal to tense and look back, before quickly grabbing the suitcase and stepping through the opening into the OVFS's secret chamber. From inside he pushed the brick back to its former position, and the door swung shut with another protest.

The chamber had been carved out of solid rock and was about eighteen feet long and almost thirteen feet wide with a vaulted ceiling. He found one of the kerosene lanterns and lit it, causing undulating shadows to probe the chamber. Alfonso absently wondered how a draft could penetrate the chamber and why it felt more humid than the rest of the necropolis.

He took off his red skull cap and mopped his brow with a large handkerchief. Ceiling to floor wooden shelves lined three walls, all except the wall that housed the door. He would make the usual inventory—he always did—but why it should be necessary eluded him, as it had for the past thirty-nine years. He arched his back and groaned. Ah, well. We live by ritual, he thought.

He started with cylinder number one. The fluid had darkened over the decades, and it was harder, year by year, to see the detail in the faces of the OVFS's early conquests. As he walked past them, he thought of what their expressions revealed: surprise, fear, desperation, resignation, sadness, hatred. Every human emotion was registered, the irony being that these heads had not perched on the necks of humans. All their headless bodies lay pinioned with an aspen stake through their hearts. Their heads, however, were in God's hands for eternal safekeeping. The OVFS had been rather successful over the course of its eighty-six year crusade to rid the world of vampires. He walked past the fifty-seventh head, added a mere three months earlier. Nice catch, that one. He wondered how many more heads they might have had but for the eight year suspension caused by World War II.

Alfonso reached up for one of the new, empty cylinders. Not empty, really, for it contained the host solution, a preservative that dated back to the time of the pharaohs, its formula lost to the rest of the world for millennia but preserved, like so many other secrets, by the Church. He placed it on the long workbench in the center of the chamber. Alfonso opened the bound volume he'd retrieved from an ancient trunk and ran his hands over the leather cover, the magnificent result of half a lifetime of some monk who labored in a scriptorium during the Middle Ages. He opened it to the bookmark and began reading the description of number fifty-eight. Blonde, one green eye/one brown, exceptionally curvaceous, she had been high on the OVFS target list for years. "Splendid," Alfonso murmured. "A true handmaiden of Satan." No mere vampire, this fey creature. We have finally rid the world of one of its most dangerous scourges, a vampire leader. Ah, for the days of the Inquisition. She would have burned at the stake, and with her extra fat she would have burned greasily. But would even that have brought cleansing? How can a soul be cleansed if it has taken leave of the body, or become so putrefied as to be beyond redemption?

He dallied, practicing delayed gratification. It gave him an all-too-rare sexual thrill.

I shall have to send the blessings of Saint Peter to Number Three, along with a special bonus to his Swiss bank account, Alfonso thought, as he hoisted the suitcase up onto the bench. He pulled out a gold chain from under his collar and inserted the key into the lock on each side in turn. The odor made him gag and brought tears to his eyes. He snatched the sealed envelope from in front of the cylinder and slammed the lid. My God, the cylinder used for transport must have leaked. Grabbing the lantern, he walked to the far end of the bench before slitting open the envelope.

He moved the lantern closer to the envelope and again peered inside. "What is this?" A lock of black hair glistened in the light. Alfonso moved quickly to the OVFS volume and reread the description of Morgan Summers. "*Blonde!*" The word exploded through the secret chamber. With shaking hands the cardinal extracted the dripping cooler from the suitcase and placed it on the bench. He snatched his handkerchief and tied it around his nose and mouth, unzipped the carrying case, pulled the cylinder out, and placed it on the bench.

"Mein Gott im Himmel," he cried out in despair. The face that looked back at him was contorted with terror, eyes open, staring, mouth open, trying to scream. Blood had mixed with the host solution, what there was left of it, turning it an oily brown. Shining black hair floated on top, moving gracefully with the undulations caused by moving the cylinder with too much haste. Alfonso frantically looked around the chamber, desperately searching for a rag, his hands dripping with the ancient solution mixed with yesterday's innocent blood.

Retching, his heart pounding, the cardinal staggered toward the entrance and pushed on the offset brick. The door scraped loudly as it swung open. On the other side he punched the brick again, then turned and raced up the corridor.

The door screeched as it jammed before closing all the way allowing lantern light to seep out into the corridor. The fragrance of Egyptian mummy fluid mixed with the blood of a freshly severed head, ebbed into the corridor. The Swiss lieutenant colonel pressed behind a pillar at the end of the corridor... and watched.

As the cardinal ran from the vault, fifty-eight voices cried a hideous lament across the sweep of nine decades.

13

The First Day of One
of Your Lives
December 13

"You'll try to reveal what should remain hidden, you'll
try to incite people to learn from the past and rebel,
but they will refuse to believe you. They will not listen
to you. You'll possess the truth, you already do; but it's
the truth of a madman."

Elie Wiesal,
A Beggar in Jerusalem, The Truth of a Madman,
1970

D r. Heller closed the file folder as Lamar tapped on his
door and walked into the office. "Nice of you to make
time for me," he said, motioning Lamar to the
conference table as he shut the door. "I know the boys are keeping
you nailed to your desk with all the editing jobs they send you."

He planted his best warm smile on Lamar. "How is Jennifer working out, by the way?"

"She is most efficient, Dr. Heller. I've come to depend on her. Thanks for assigning her to the editing staff." Both men smiled, aware that the staff consisted of Lamar and Jennifer.

"Well. Care to join me for a cup of java?"

"Who could turn down a cup of Blue Mountain?" Lamar smiled and shook his head.

In a few moments Dr. Heller's administrative assistant was placing Harvard mugs in front of them.

"Black, right?" Heller asked.

"Right." Lamar spotted his personnel folder on the conference table. He realized he was holding his breath and exhaled.

"Let's see, you've been with us almost a year now, right?" Not waiting for an answer, he continued. "And you've certainly proven your worth." Heller leaned back, seeming to appraise his subordinate.

"I think we can use you in the lab, my boy. I've ordered Security to begin a background check on you—we do that on all our candidates for the Genetics Lab, so don't get your walnuts in an uproar."

Lamar coughed and studied his coffee mug.

Heller laughed and reached for the file. "If that pans out, and I have every reason to believe it will as I can't imagine you Tory Row people have anything to hide, we will follow that with a polygraph. Once we get all that out of the way, we can indoctrinate you for some of the more esoteric stuff we do here. Might even find you a place to sit in the lab. Do you think Jennifer could cover for you?"

Lamar carefully placed his mug on the table and looked at a wall chart showing the status of various projects, including one of his. "That's a little hard to answer, as I'm not sure how good a writer or editor she is. I could try her on a few tracts and let you know in a week or two. I'd hate to have to guess."

"Ummm." Heller opened the folder. "It says here you are unusually well versed in the properties of hemoglobin." In fact, Heller was looking at a note from Flossie's assistant, Ms. Bundaeker.

'RE: LBB List of peculiarities observed to date:

A blood specialist, he reacts almost with terror when confronted with real blood. Failed an Air Force physical based on a severely atypical blood profile. The flight surgeon who performed the physical, now a civilian in private practice, wants to "consult on his case."

Subject and his admin asst. were seen at the Sylphon Nymph, a twenty-something hangout. Their deportment may have exceeded university standards (?)

Recently, the Chief of HR hired a woman, Ms. Morgan Summers, after no more than a cursory review of her background. I have a source that confirms that she and the subject have spent several nights at Coleson Manor, subject's abode on Tory Row, beginning the night of the last Hail and Farewell party.

The standard psychological profile that subject filled out raised some unanswered *questions with our staff psychologist that might be pursued, at your discretion. I will continue to monitor both subjects. JB*

"Hemoglobin was the subject of my honors thesis," Lamar said. "It was an outgrowth of an undergraduate history paper I wrote on the development of blood plasma during World War Two."

Heller retrieved his pipe from his desk, tamped the remaining tobacco and lit it with a pipe lighter. "Oh, smoke 'em if you got 'em. We may be in the middle of a smoke-free campus, but I have a special dispensation." He chuckled as he sat down and picked up the folder again. "Lamar, I shouldn't tell you this till after you go through the security screening, but we are doing some really cutting edge research on blood properties, and I think there is a place for you in that activity. How does that sound?"

"To quote from Spock, *fascinating*."

"Ah ha. You're a Trekkie, too. See what you can do to clean out your inbox over the next couple weeks, and give Jennifer a try on a few items. I'll put an expedite on the security processing, and then we can get down to the good stuff." As he spoke Dr. Heller stood, puffed his pipe back into full vigor, and opened the door. "Let's do lunch soon. It's been too long since I took time to go over to the Faculty Club for their special Oysters Rockefeller and pecan and mandarin orange salad. I'll ask Lenore to book a date for us next week. That work for you?"

"It would be an honor, Dr. Heller."

"Well, you know what they say: all work and no sandwiches." The Lab Director's laugh filled the outer office.

James Heller sat at his desk and relit his pipe. Bradford's a smart egg but a bit off. Goes beyond being an introvert. Works hard but doesn't need the money. A genuine blue blood with a peculiar background, almost as opaque as our fair Ms. Summers. He probably ought to talk to Flossie about them. Flossie's still really upset about the disappearance of that waitress the night of the Hail and Farewell. Glenn Martin's memo said the police are still baffled. Their best guess is that Ms., uh, what's her-name, had witnessed some crime, and the bad guys took her out. Probably like Jimmie Hoffa, they'll never find her.

It's going to be interesting watching Lamar and Morgan. My intuition says they will have important roles to play in our next round of gene splicing experiments. God, I'd give a lot to know what went wrong with our first resurrection attempt. Tears glistened in his eyes as he pictured the first two candidates—before and after. He'd have to figure out a way to get rid of them, and quickly. Like the founding fathers, he'd committed his life, his fortune and his sacred honor to Project Vampire Resurrection—the return of immortal entities to this mortal coil as restored souls. He pulled his glasses off and wiped them, then wiped his eyes. His sigh—like a venting compressor—filled the room.

Heller's path had been filled with boulders and chasms. His son, James Junior—everyone called him "JJ"—was in permanent lockdown in Heller basement in West Cambridge. JJ, one of the cursed third generation, was now fully aware of the meaning of that. He had books, his dog and parakeet, exercise equipment, TV, and a computer without Internet access. He used the computer to journal and write poetry and had become an expert chess player. A live-in elderly couple from Norway was his only real family, ever since Martha had killed herself. His wife had always been frail in mind, body, and spirit, James thought, and the world was the better for her departure. She couldn't live knowing her son was a vampire.

For the past two years after her suicide, JJ had been confined. Waiting. Waiting for his father to discover the process of genetic resurrection for the victims of vampirism. Hang on, Junior. We are so close, so very close.

He thought of Morgan. It had been too long since he'd had his horns trimmed, and she could grace a *Playboy* centerfold. That one won't be easy, though. She gives off mixed signals. He thought of Jennifer. She wasn't above granting special favors for the right kind of rewards, the kind he was able to grant, such as a handsome salary increase. No doubt Mr. Bradford has already made that discovery—or soon will.

James stretched and walked over to the project status board. We need to crank out some articles on Hemophilia and Lupus. Got to keep our cover story current. If anybody outside the lab ever suspects we're working on the cure for Vampirism, we'd be visited one night by a horde of peasants with flaming torches.

Lamar fell into his chair, his hands shaking. What was that all about? I'm not a PhD. Why does he want me in the lab? He knows something. I can smell it. A security background investigation could ruin everything. I can just see me biting the polygraph operator. With the back of his hand Lamar wiped sweat off his forehead. Maybe Morgan can give me some—

"Heller must have put you through the wringer."

Lamar almost jumped out of the chair. "Jesus. You scared the scales off me." He slumped back in the chair and took a deep breath.

"Scales? Wow, you're wound tighter than Big Ben's mainspring. But I have the perfect solution for us. I brought my workout togs, and you, sir, are in one super need of a trip to the athletic center. After a good sweat I know where we could do some damage to a bottle of Dewar's 12."

Lamar's shoulders slumped. For the past twenty-four years he couldn't get the time of day from a female. Had to pay for it. Now he had two really sharp ladies lusting after him.

Lord, I'm even starting to think like a twenty-something. Damn nice, though. Yesterday Morgan moved all of her clothes into a guest bedroom in Coleson Manor. We got a cackle at the look on Robert's face when she dumped Calvin in the front hall, and the two cats started a meowing contest. My batman didn't even wait to collect our hats and coats, he just stomped off. Robert disapproves, but to bloody hell with him. He'd better start getting used to Morgan and Calvin. I have.

"Look, Jennifer, we have to talk."

14

Vampire Bodies Lie A-Moldering in Their Graves (or should)
December 14

"She is older than the rocks among which she sits; like the vampire, she has been dead many times, and learned the secrets of the grave."

Studies in the History of the Renaissance,
Walter Pater, 1873

You understand everything, number Four? Success has eluded us for too long. You will ensure that our agent identifies the subject without even the remotest possibility of error. We will dispense with the usual custom of sending a souvenir back to the Vatican. Have the accomplice record the deed with a long range telephoto camera. Upon receipt of the photos, the final payment is to be made. Are we clear? Good. I will expect a report in three days." The cardinal hung up the secure scrambler phone.

Cardinal Alfonso summoned Colonel Solento, newly promoted and appointed Commander of the Pontifical Swiss Guard, whose predecessor gracefully retired with a generous pension. "You have completed the tasks I placed in your charge?" Alfonso hated the arrogant man who stood at attention, his uniform immaculate with its four rows of medals, especially after his veiled threat to expose the OVFS. Well, Colonel, we shall see if we have a canister large enough to fit your head. I will not abide his shadow crossing my path every— His thoughts were interrupted.

"All is in order in the chamber, Your Eminence. I personally replaced the mechanism that operates the door and tested it several times. I cleaned up the spill, placing the, umm, unfortunate *souvenir* into a new canister and refilled it with the sacred solution, as you directed."

"I would appreciate you lowering your voice." Alfonso said, glaring at the colonel. "And where did you place that vessel?"

"In the storage chest beside the door. Here is the key."

It resembled the key to a medieval dungeon. The cardinal's smile looked like cracked plaster about to fall from a crumbling wall. "You have done well, my son. Continue to do so and your life will be one of milk and honey. But take care not to step out of line. Those desirous of replacing you are numerous." That wasn't true, and they both knew it.

The colonel rendered a crisp salute, executed an about face, and marched out of the cardinal's office. He failed to bow, however.

The Jag turned onto Porter Square and stopped a block from where Old Gnarly Head was parked. "I still think I should go with you, Morgan. They're probably watching your room."

"If I spot any surveillance I'll meet you at the alternate place. If I don't show up in ten minutes you—"

Morgan leaned forward and shaded her eyes against the street light. "Would you look at that bloody bugger breaking into Old Gnarly." She unbuckled her seat belt and opened her door.

Lamar grabbed her arm and pulled her back into the car. "You don't go confronting some crazy at night who no doubt has a gun and is hopped up on something. I'll call 911." Lamar reached for his cell phone.

"He's inside now." Morgan squinted. "That motherless bastard is going to hot wire Old Gnar—"

A bright, searing flash preceded the ear-crushing concussion. Car parts flew in every direction, some of them slamming into the Jag, as a brilliant yellow-orange fireball vaulted fifty feet into the air. Lamar and Morgan instinctively ducked. They could feel the heat as they crouched, stunned, blinking, ears ringing. Something thumped on the hood. It was a man's hand. The conflagration grew as two cars, one parked in front of, the other behind the wreckage, burst into flames.

"Gods of all ages." Morgan's voice shook. She tasted blood from her bitten lip and thought of the burning P-47 fighter that crashed at Duxford airfield in England during the war. Sobbing, she had watched them pull the charred pilot out of the crumpled cockpit. He lived for ten horrible minutes.

Lamar opened his door. At least a half dozen car horns were blaring. Making a quick inspection of the Jag he found a blizzard of dents, scratches, and gouges. The front grill was caved in, but the tires had survived. A red, slimy substance was smeared over the windshield, now spider webbed with cracks. And the outside rearview mirror on the driver's side was missing.

"I'll try to start this thing," Lamar said.

Morgan sat, rigid, the burning hulk that moments before had been Old Gnarly Head painting her face with flickering yellow light. It had nearly been her coffin. "If you hadn't grabbed me—" Her voice broke.

The engine started but clattered as the fan blade made contact with the radiator. Lamar shifted into reverse and slowly backed to the intersection.

"Where are we going?"

"As far away as we can get before the police and fire guys show up." In a block, he stopped.

"Now what?"

"That." Lamar pointed to the hand on the hood. He fished out a towel from under his seat, wrapped the hand and put it in the trunk.

Lamar's thoughts were jumbled, and his jaw was clamped so tight his teeth hurt. *If I hadn't grabbed Morgan, or if I'd run after her. . . . By all the saints that was close. No doubt vampires can be killed by blowing them into tiny bits. We need to stay as far away from the police investigation as we can get. It was dark; maybe no one saw us. The poor slob who was trying to hot wire Old Gnarly Head had probably waited until nobody was around, so there's a fair chance we weren't seen. Except by the OVFS guys.* Lamar's thoughts accelerated.

Morgan said they always have a surveillance guy as a backup on their operations. He probably copied my license plate.

"That bomb was meant for you, Morgan." His voice sounded raw. A new thought rocked him. The serving woman who fell and bashed her head and was taken away by a phony rescue squad crew. That was supposed to be Morgan, too. Jesus, Joseph and—

"What, Lamar? Talk to me. You've been talking to yourself long enough."

"I'd bet my vampire wings on the OVFS having a couple of guys nearby to confirm you getting blown up. They would have seen and probably photographed the Jag, which means they have the tag number and can trace us back to Coleson Manor." He decided to wait for a while before mentioning his theory about the missing waitress. "We better get back and man the battlements."

"Robert, sit down."

He looked at Lamar and Morgan and sat, stiffly, on the edge of one of the library chairs. Lamar poured scotch into three lowball glasses, added some ice, and passed one each to Morgan and Robert.

"Sir, I really wish you would let me—"

Lamar cut him off with a gesture. He filled his pipe and lit it. "Robert, it's time we get all the cards on the table face up. Long past time, actually. I know about my Third Generation history; I've read the codex. You've known all along, haven't you?"

After a long pause Robert, his face impassive, looked at Morgan. "Are you sure this is the right time for this?"

"Morgan not only knows my family history, she is a Third Gen, too. We have formed a partnership. Robert, do you recall my father mentioning the OVFS in the codex?"

"Yes."

"Well, they're on Morgan's trail. Have been for years. And tonight they tried to kill her by planting a bomb in her car. Someone else accidentally set it off as we were driving over to collect it. Now it, along with the idiot who was trying to steal it, are in small pieces spread all over Porter Square. The Jag took some shrapnel in the grill, the driver's door, the roof, and probably the hood. I think it has some human viscera on it as well. We need to get it repaired and cleaned, but not at the dealership. I want you to find a reliable guy to do the work, one that can keep his mouth shut. Pay him double the going rate. Got that?"

Robert's eyebrows arched and he sucked in his breath.

"Do you know anybody like that?" Lamar asked.

"Monty's Auto Repair and Body Shop. I once had your dad's Bentley fixed there after a small, shall we say, private altercation."

"Good. Make that your first priority tomorrow. We need to decide on our story in case the police find a witness who saw the Jag and, in the worst case, copied the license. And of equal importance, we need a game plan for the OVFS. Maybe we need to hire some guys from one of the local protective services."

"Sir, above all, we need to shield you from anyone discovering your, uh, special nature. Yours as well, madam."

"Cut the madam, Bob. My name is Morgan. Morgan Summers. And I was born in 1686. And so was my cat, Calvin." They looked at Lamar's desk. Both cats were sleeping on top of it within touching distance.

Vic Brown

"I see. Morgan." Robert pulled at his collar and sighed, after an unsuccessful attempt to rearrange his countenance back to its formal state.

"Here's the way I see our situation, but I need you two to buy into this, and I'm open to your suggestions," Lamar began.

15

Old Vampires Never Die, They Just...
December 15

"Things always seem darkest just before they become
pitch black."

Author, Source, Date Unknown

P hones rang, people yelled, doors slammed, coins tinkled in a vending machine. It was the usual morning scrum at precinct headquarters. Cordell looked at the name plate on his desk: "Cordell Peyton Chief of Detectives." The nameplate was cheap—there wasn't room enough to include Cambridge PD. I should buy a good one.

"You know, this used to be a nice, clean, sleepy little town," Cordell said. "All we did was chase the dope peddlers off campus and round up the drunks. Now we have a kidnapping, a hotel shootout, and a car bombing murder. All we need to hit the quadrafecta is a nice, hairy terrorist attack. The press is having a field day at our expense. So what have you two got for me since yesterday?"

"Boss, that fourth bloodstain matched Paula Bernard, the waitress at the Faculty Club," Blanton began. "Five shots were fired. Two killed, one wounded. Paula was apparently still bleeding from her head wound at the club, because her blood was way out of the line of fire." Blanton looked at his notes and continued.

"The rescue squad vehicle had only been driven eighteen miles from the time it was stolen till when it was recovered. And, as you would predict, wiped clean."

"Odds are good the perps transferred Paula to another vehicle nearby so they could ditch the highly conspicuous rescue squad vehicle," Cordell said. "Which means we don't know if Paula is alive or where they might have taken the body if they killed her." He wished he had a cigarette. Hadn't had one for two years the middle of next month, and he was proud of that, but he wondered how he was going to get through today.

"Another factoid, boss," Blanton said. "The car bomber used C-4, which you can get readily enough. And he used a lot of it. Totaled the cars parked in front and behind. Even blew out some windows across the street.

"The problem is, he blew himself up. At least that's what Jim and I think. Probably an amateur. We found one shoe and not enough human particulate to fill a matchbox. I wouldn't bait your breath that the Bureau comes up with an ID on the bomber. Missing Persons didn't have anything for us. Likely the bomber wasn't a local. Not likely the shoe will be of any use, and as far as I know, they didn't recover even a trace of the detonator."

"Why use an amateur bomber?" Cordell asked. The other two shrugged.

"We got some beat cops going door-to-door around Porter Square. Maybe somebody saw something, but I doubt it. Even if they did they wouldn't want to get mixed up with the bomber."

Jim pulled down the map. He had highlighted the Harvard Faculty Club, the Cambridge Fire Department Squad Number Two, and the location of the abandoned rescue squad vehicle. "Did you guys study the morgue photos of the two guys killed in the shootout?" The other two shook their heads. "Funny thing, one of them looked like he'd had his tits amputated. Maybe the Bureau could run a check using their gangbanger database. Could be some outfit requires nipplectomies to be a member."

"Jesus," Blanton whistled. "Are the pics in the file?"

Jim pulled the file and tossed it on the small conference table adjacent to Cordell's desk. The three men bent over the two that showed the corpse with no nipples. "Man, that's got to be a first," Blanton said.

Cordell leaned back against his desk. "We need to move out smartly. This is Harvard. Any minute that phone is going to ring, and it's going to be Governor Wilder wanting to know if we are on vacation or have we assigned anybody to figure out what the hell's going on in Cambridge. As a recently re-elected governor he has to show he's tough on crime. And rumor control says he doesn't much like cops. We're lucky he hasn't called yet."

Cordell's phone rang.

"Hey, Charlie. What's up?" Cordell asked, his relief obvious. He yanked a small, badly worn leather notebook out of his jacket, pulled a pen from his shirt pocket and leaned over the desk. "Harriet Rankin. Where's she— Deceased? When? We got a graveyard registration then. Drill down as far as you can on the late Ms. Rankin. See if we can tie her to the person who used her name. By yesterday, Sarge. I owe you one. Thanks." Cordell hung up.

"The boys got a VIN number. The car was registered to a woman who died in 2001. Okay, where were we?" Cordell rocked back in his chair.

"I think the bomber was dropped off at the target vehicle," Jim said. "He wouldn't want his car near the blast, nor would he want to carry a load of C-4 and the detonator for several blocks through a strange neighborhood at night. My guess is he was going to be met and driven away. Wish we had some traffic cameras around Porter Square."

"Can I come in?" Sergeant Charlie Poston walked in without waiting for an invitation. "Got something you'll want to see. An anonymous tip, hot off the press." He handed a scratch sheet to Cordell, who read it aloud.

"A dark-colored Jag drove up close to the bombed car moments before it detonated. It was probably damaged, but managed to drive off after the blast. And there's a license plate number. Charlie could you—"

"Already done that, detective. The owner is Lamar Bradford, who works for the university. Even has his own private parking place, number twenty-three. The make, model, year, and VIN number of the Jag are on the other side of that note."

"Charlie, I'm gonna have to get you promoted," Cordell said, smiling and punching the sergeant's shoulder.

"Hey, boss, he has to get in line. You promised me—" The laughter could be heard out in the hall as Charlie left.

"Time to pay Mr. Bradford a visit," Cordell said. "Jim, would you man the fort?" Jim pursed his lips and looked down. "I want you to obtain arrest warrants for Lamar Bradford and Morgan Summers. Might as well obtain a search warrant for the GenLab while you're at it. Call it in, and tell 'em it's priority one. Who knows, maybe they're makin' some bombs."

"They're all priority ones." Larkin slammed his pen on Cordell's desk as the other two headed for the parking garage.

Cordell and Blanton took one of the unmarked sedans. "You know, I'm getting that prickly feeling down the back of my neck, and it's telling me that all the crap that's hit the fan in the past few days is tied together somehow. In this town it defies the laws of average for all this kind of shit to go down boom, boom, boom. It's just gotta be related." Cordell rubbed the back of his neck.

"How does this scenario sound, Blanton? The bad guys are trying to off somebody, but they hired the keystone cops for the hit. What if the Bernard woman was the wrong one? Or, maybe they needed to take out more than one person. What if the shootout was a result of the keystoners screwing up? The cartel doesn't suffer fools gladly. So they bring in a new hit man who wires a bomb in the Rankin car for another try at the target. Maybe he got their man, or maybe, like you two think, he blew himself up. How does that sound?"

"Lot of ifs built into your scenario, Cordell, but it sounds at least plausible."

Neither detective noticed the blue Chevy Cobalt following them.

"Yes?" Cardinal Alfonso's implacable face could have been carved from granite. He detected a nervous twitch in the colonel's left eye, something he'd not noticed before. More bad news; he'd bet his biretta on it. "Out with it," he all but shouted.

"Your Eminence, the agent hired from our list wired the subject's car with a powerful explosive. While our observer watched from a second story window across the street, a hoodlum, a car thief, tried to steal the car. The observer was about to intervene when another car drove up and stopped fairly close to the one your agent had armed. He was able to read the license plate number using night vision equipment." Colonel Solento paused.

"Am I to sit here until the second coming while you babble about night vision equipment? Finish your report."

"The hoodlum set off the charge, utterly destroying the car, himself, and damaging the vehicle that had parked close to it. That vehicle may have contained our target, who might have been about to retrieve her car."

Alfonso groaned and looked down, clenching and unclenching his fists. "May have been, might have been, I can see your promotion has done nothing to improve your efficiency. Idiot. I am served by a pack of idiots."

"Your Eminence, I contracted one of your two top agents for this task. It is he who—"

"Where is he now?"

The colonel brushed an imaginary piece of lint off his braided cuff. "He seems to have disappeared. Neither his OVFS control nor the observer can account for his sudden disappearance."

He took half our payment and vanished rather than risk standing before an OVFS trial, Alfonso thought. "Find him. And bring back our payment. He hasn't earned anything but an OVFS trial. Have you any leads on the whereabouts of that swine, Number Three?"

"No, Your Eminence, but I have a friend who works for Interpol, and he thinks he may have a lead."

The cardinal sighed. "Every other word out of your mouth is either 'may' or 'might.' Come back and tell me where he *is,* colonel. Have you completed the anonymous donation to the parents of the unfortunate woman who was the victim of Number Three's incompetence?"

"Yes, and your instructions were carried out precisely. The parents know that if they say anything to anyone, the monthly payments will stop."

"One small victory for a man," Alfonso muttered, as he waved the colonel out of his chambers. "Wait. Have you tracked down the owner of the car that was damaged?"

"We have. It is registered to a Mr. Lamar Bradford of Cambridge, Massachusetts. He is an employee of Harvard."

"Find out all you can about this man, and report back to me no later than tomorrow afternoon."

As he departed, the colonel thought how fortunate the OVFS was to have a source inside Harvard's Human Resources Department. And our ongoing cooperation with Interpol's Tactical Intelligence Unit and its Command and Coordination Center has proven most useful. Johann was proud of his long service as the Vatican's Interpol liaison officer.

Lamar paced as he talked, hands behind his back, looking and sounding a bit like General Patton, or so he thought.

"We have to assume that the OVFS has run a make on the Jag, which means they know we're holed up here. We need an old clunker to drive back and forth to work. Can you obtain one, Robert?"

"Surely."

"Pay cash, and buy it from an individual. Wear a bit of a disguise, and get some fake ID." He stared into the fire. "Let's check out the family arsenal. It wouldn't hurt for us to have some ready fire power. Robert, I would like you to ensure they are all in proper operating condition. Check the ammo supply, too. Now the question is, where do we stay? If we stay here, let's hire some muscle. Have them dress as gardeners, and let's start a big project, maybe installing a patio out back with a pergola. And a fishpond with a fountain. Morgan, where is your minivan?"

"Hmmm. If the FBI can identify Old Gnarly Head and trace it back to the late Harriet Rankin, they'll ID the minivan and impound it. A few people around Cambridge can link me to the minivan, and then the police will come looking for me. It might be a race between the cops and the OVFS as to which ones get here first. I happen to have a one-way ticket to Toronto. Maybe I should use it."

"No, Morgan, we are not going to split up. We win this one together or—"

"We go underground," Morgan finished for him.

"Sir, speaking of underground, it is time for you to learn one of the old Coleson Manor secrets. It could prove useful, especially now. If you will follow me." Robert stood, pointing toward the library door.

In the hall he opened the glass front door covering the longcase clockworks and pulled a small lever on the right side of the clock face. A humming sound preceded the inward swing of a panel, partially hidden behind the clock.

"I recently replaced the mechanism. The old one had begun to malfunction, causing the clock to chime twelve times at odd intervals." Retrieving a flashlight, Robert crouched to walk through the small opening. The other two joined him. When he pressed a recessed button, the panel swung back into place. A widely spaced row of 25-watt bulbs produced barely enough light to follow a short passage to a narrow staircase. At the bottom of the staircase Robert used a cipher keypad, hidden behind a distressed wooden door frame that might have once been an outside wall when the house was originally built. The second door opened into what appeared to be an eighteenth century office, complete with desk, three chairs, a single bed, small wardrobe, large hook rug, two kerosene lanterns, a few vintage books in a small bookcase next to the desk, some folded blankets, and a pillow.

Robert lit one of the lanterns. "Welcome to Coleson's secret chamber. It has housed a wounded officer and spy who served on General Washington's staff, several runaway slaves, and a young bride who had been badly abused by her husband. In that crate you will find a stash of canned goods, which I have kept up to date, and a case of drinking water. The, umm, necessarium is located behind the door in the corner. You will find it well stocked with paper products, even some female necessities. It sits above a drain that leads to an underground stream. Most convenient. The room is soundproof as far as I know. There are two pistols in the desk. One, however, is a nineteenth century Derringer. The other is a contemporary semi-automatic. Both loaded."

Lamar whistled over his lower teeth. "Robert, why am I only now learning about this underground citadel?"

"I was saving it."

"Meaning?"

"Should your behavior require your temporary sequestration." Lamar and Morgan looked at one another, then back at Robert.

"Well, Robert, you've kept the place in good working order. Thank you. We may need it now as much as all of its former, uh, guests. How does one know if it is safe to leave this place?"

"There is a rather high-tech peeping device—at least that's what I call it—which I'll show you. It is built into the crown molding. On our way out I'll demonstrate the system. But there is one more secret to unveil."

Robert moved the desk aside, as well as the small rug it sat on, revealing a trap door. "The trap door is an entrance to a short passage leading to the garage, formerly the livery stable."

"My heavens, Robert. You've thought of everything. This is rather like a medieval priest hole."

"While I would much enjoy taking credit for all this, I must defer to the original owners of Coleson's Manor. Your father discovered this quite by accident when you were but a young lad. The two of us added some of the more modern features, the cipher lock and the surveillance 'periscope'—you'll find them in any reputable spy novel—and I stocked the place with some C-rations and water, but most of the credit belongs to your ancestors."

"Robert, your credits are multiplying like the national debt," Lamar said. Robert managed a smile, obviously pleased.

Morgan shook her head. "Who would have ever guessed that buried deep inside Coleson Manor was a vampire hole?"

16

Genesis and Exodus
December 16

"No doubt I have died myself a thousand times before"

Leaves of Grass, Walt Whitman

Heller leaned his head against the wall of his office in University Hall. The day was unraveling. Maybe the future as well. His future and, worst of all, maybe his son's. He groped for his pipe, patting both pockets in his jacket before seeing it in the amber glass ashtray on his desk. He puffed as if trying to lay down a smoke screen.

Damn that man. Cordell something-or-other and his lackey demanding to interview Lamar and Morgan. I've got to get those two in here and find out what in hell is going on before the police come back, tomorrow at eight o' clock. He walked out and found

Lenore, his administrative assistant, hammering away at her computer. When she looked up he beckoned for her to come into his office.

"My word, Dr. Heller, you're going to set off the fire alarm."

He waved off her comment. "Lenore, I need to talk to Lamar Bradford and Morgan Summers as fast as you can get them here. But do it quietly. I don't want to alarm anybody."

"Quietly. Okay. Do you need their personnel files?"

"I still have them, thanks."

In twenty minutes the two were sitting on Heller's couch, coffee mugs in hand, looking apprehensive. Dr. Heller never sat down; he paced.

"What kind of trouble are you in? I got a visit from a couple of detectives from precinct headquarters. They just left. I told them you weren't available, but they'll be back tomorrow morning. My background investigations on you two are just getting started. What do I have to worry about?" He stopped pacing and fixed them with a hard look.

Lamar and Morgan exchanged glances. They had prepared for this moment. "Can you tell us anything they said or asked that might bear on their inquiry?" Lamar asked.

"Nothing beyond a sense of urgency. And they warned me to keep a watchful eye on both of you, and that it would be extremely unwise if you were to decide to leave Cambridge."

"As you know, we are linked to the disappearance of the waitress that cracked her head open at the hail and farewell party," Lamar said. "But that linkage is only because the two of us rendered first aid and carried her out to the rescue squad vehicle. They may think that the act of carrying her out indicates we were part of the kidnapping plot. But there's more. Night before last Morgan's car exploded as we were driving up to it. Morgan was going to take it back to Coleson Manor. Did you read about it in the *Globe*?" Lamar blew on his coffee.

"Yes. Someone was killed. The papers said it might have been the bomber who made a mistake when he was setting the timer. Go on."

"We were witnesses to the explosion. Had it gone off thirty seconds later we would probably both have been killed," Lamar said.

"Let me guess. You got the hell out of Dodge, and you failed to report the incident to the police, am I right?" Heller stroked his chin.

Both nodded.

"Why did you leave the scene of a crime?"

"We're convinced someone is trying to kill Morgan. And that's why we beat feet back to Coleson Manor. That, and we were in shock."

"Who the hell wants to kill you, Morgan, and why?" Heller was pacing again. They looked at each other, and Morgan began.

"We strongly suspect the missing waitress was poisoned. She was supposed to bring me the fatal hors d'oeuvres, but she probably sampled one on the way. That's not uncommon among wait staff. Her body is likely at the bottom of the Charles."

"Who are those bastards, and why are they after you, Morgan?"

Morgan took a deep breath. "An organization called the OVFS is after me. Probably they are after Lamar now, too, for helping me escape. OVFS stands for the *Order of the Vampire Final Solution.*" Morgan sat back, her eyes never leaving Heller's.

He opened his mouth but said nothing as he slowly laid his pipe on the conference table and leaned forward. "Did you say 'vampire solution'?" Again Lamar and Morgan looked at one another.

"They search for and kill vampires all over the world," she said. "Founded in about 1925, they are a secret order of the Roman Catholic Church. Much more secret than Opus Dei. And a pretty effective one, though almost no one is aware of their existence, much less their success rate at killing vampires."

Heller slumped into a chair, his teeth clenched so hard his jaw muscles rippled. "Morgan, are you trying to tell me *you* are a vampire?" Heller's voice sounded plaintive. "Lamar, how long have you been aware of her condition?"

"Ever since she helped convince me that I am one, too."

"Jesus H. Christ on a rubber crutch!" Heller exploded, leaping from his chair. He grabbed his pipe and burned his hand lighting it. "I can't believe this. This is too big a coincidence to be a coincidence. The Universe is moving the pieces around so fast, and all I can do is try to keep up."

"What does that mean?" Lamar asked, frowning.

Heller walked to the door, listened, then yanked it open and looked out at Lenore, who was standing a few feet away with Flossie's assistant.

"Dr. Heller, this is Judeland Bundaeker, Dr. Florence Senger's—"

"We've met." Heller's voice was icy. "What can I do for you, Ms. Bundaeker?"

She cleared her throat and looked around. "I'm afraid it is rather confidential." She leaned to one side permitting her a glance inside Heller's office before he stepped forward, blocking her view.

"My secretary can make an appointment for you, Ms. Bundaeker." Heller turned and went back into his office, closing and locking the door. "Now, you two are going to tell me the whole nine yards."

Dr. Heller sat, breathing as if he'd just finished a marathon. He pulled down his tie and unbuttoned his top shirt button and rolled up his sleeves—something he never did—refilled his pipe, drained his coffee mug, and shook his head repeatedly during the revelations. When Lamar and Morgan finished, the three sat in a quivering silence. Morgan left the office and returned with a coffee pot and refilled all three mugs. She lit a cigarette and offered one to Lamar, who refused.

"I'm going to call off the security investigation on both of you," Heller began. "And no polygraph, either." His voice caught, and he struggled to regain his composure. "First thing in the morning I will have the security oaths for you to read and sign. You will become a vital part of the DNA and gene-splicing experiments in the lab. Before you do all that, there are some things you need to know. While three of our lab guys are actually working on diabetes, lupus, hemophilia, and related diseases, the bulk of our work is devoted—and this is Top Secret—to a project called *Vampire Resurrection,* the thrust of which is to turn vampires back into mortal humans, to promote the restoration of their souls, and to enlist them in the search for other vampires who wish to be restored. So you see, we are in direct competition with the Catholic group that is out to rid the world of vampires by eliminating them with extreme prejudice."

This time it was Morgan and Lamar who sat, stunned, unable to speak. Tears streaked Morgan's cheeks, and she began to shake.

They were matched by those coursing down Dr. Heller's cheeks as he told them about his son.

"We need you working on the VR Program, not sitting in a jail cell." He didn't bother to ask if they were innocent of any crime. "Be here at 6 a.m. tomorrow to sign the oaths and begin your indoctrination into the program. Use the rest of today to wind up anything important in your inboxes. This will be a real test for Jennifer. I'll let you break that news to her, Lamar. That's it for now. We have a lot to do before the detectives come back, starting with figuring out what we're going to tell them."

At 6 a.m. Friday morning, the sixteenth of December, the sun would not break the horizon in Cambridge for another hour and twelve minutes. In the faint pre-dawn a few birds called to their mates, and two squirrels scampered from tree to tree. A security guard walked past the Science Center. But none of that registered on the four people in Dr. Heller's office. Two of them had their right hands raised as Heller administered the oath. Lenore handed out the forms and they were quickly signed, dated, and witnessed. A minute later Lenore supplied mugs of Blue Mountain and some danish and closed the door as she left. Heller locked it.

"Sit, please. Leaving out most of the history and technical details, what follows are the bones of Vampire Resurrection. As the name implies, our intention is to turn existing vampires who want to return to mortal life back into normal human beings. We are convinced that vampirism results from a genetic mutation. Vampires begin life as relatively normal human beings. But they carry a latent, mutant gene that, when triggered, causes them to

150

evolve into a vampire. We haven't yet discovered what activates the vampirism gene—how the trigger mechanism works. Some individuals undergo a rapid transformation, while others take quite some time to evolve. Contrary to all the Hollywood cinema, it is not contagious. You can't contract vampirism by being bitten on the neck, as the movies have long depicted. Our studies show that exposure to vampire-tainted blood won't spread the condition, either. The only known method of transference is through genetic inheritance. But when a vampire breeds with a non-vampire, there is a statistically significant opportunity for the offspring to inherit a latent vampire gene.

"We are trying to identify and isolate that gene, remove it and, in its place, splice in a genetically engineered inert gene, grown from stem cell cultures, that will reverse and/or prevent the development of vampirism. Ideally, we will find a method to test humans for the presence of the latent 'vamgene,' which is what we call it for short, allowing us to splice out that gene before it can be triggered. Better yet, we hope to confirm what triggers the latent vamgene and find a substance that blocks its activation. Any questions so far?"

Lamar was stroking his chin. "Not a question but a comment. I have been bequeathed a late thirteenth century manuscript, a codex, and it may contain some valuable information for your research. It speaks to the periodicity of vampirism in an 'infected' family tree, so to speak. Apparently the gene stays latent in first and second generations but is eventually activated in every third generation carrier. I am a 'thirdgen' member of my family, and I'd guess that Morgan must be as well. Her mother was executed as a witch during the Salem witch trials. Before she died, she hinted to Morgan that she was 'cursed' and should wear a handed-down family cross for protection. Of course the cross couldn't really protect her."

"The Salem witch trials?" Heller's mouth hung open as he stared at Morgan.

Morgan pulled the cross from under her blouse to show Heller. He fished out his glasses and peered at it.

"Lamar, can you bring me the codex?"

"I'd rather you come and see it in my library. It is very delicate."

"All right, when?"

"This weekend would work. What day would suit you?" Lamar asked.

"Sunday morning around ten. That okay?"

"Right. Plan to join us for brunch. My 'batman,' Robert, makes a mean Eggs Benedict."

"Done. Now, I wish my story ended with what I've told you so far, but it doesn't."

Heller paused to fill his pipe and light it. Morgan reached for another cigarette, but changed her mind.

"Our first attempt at vampire conversion failed, and that failure breaks my heart as a human being and as a scientist. As with many scientific breakthroughs, there is danger involved. How many men lost their lives during the early days of aviation? We will pay a price—we already have—before we can claim success against vampirism. This OVFS gang can't fix the genetic problem by killing vampires. Killing doesn't stamp out the flawed gene, nor interrupt the continued birth of contaminated individuals, most of whom likely don't know they are destined for vampirism until that gene has been triggered. And, as I've said, we're not yet sure what the trigger mechanism is, or how it operates, unfortunately. Once vampirism has been triggered we think the victims stop aging. As

I've said, when vampires mate, they can pass their genetic flaw on to following generations." He tasted his coffee, but it was cold.

"Before you volunteer for the next round of gene splicing, I am compelled to show you something." He stood, put his pipe in its holder, and opened the door.

Judeland Bundaeker stood outside the door, briefcase in hand, still wearing her black trench coat, earmuffs and gloves.

17

The Splice of Life
December 17

When she saw the two vampires she scowled and
stepped back. "Let the past bury its living."

Source/Date
Unknown

The room was all but totally dark, with faint reddish light emanating from behind the crown and baseboard molding. The three of them looked like indistinct dark shapes. Morgan shivered and tucked her hands under her armpits. The smell, almost a stench, was a combination of bleach, air freshener and decomposition. She felt Lamar's arm around her waist, a gesture that felt oddly protective, a feeling she hadn't experienced since Gretta the Blind back in Old Salem.

"This, obviously, is our cold room," Dr. Heller said. His voice sounded flat and clipped, due in part to the sound absorption material in walls and ceiling. The floor was carpeted cement. "I want you to see something. Two somethings, actually." He led them to the far end of the room where two gurneys were pushed against a wall. Sheets covered whatever lay under them. Morgan felt an emotional tide surge through her. Dr. Heller grasped one end of a sheet and slowly pulled it down.

"By all the gods," Lamar breathed.

Morgan squinted and forced herself not to step back. The body appeared to be translucent. Internal organs jutted through a tissue-like web of what once must have been skin. A mask of horror out of Madame Tussaud's Wax Museum leered, imperceptibly animated, with cheeks and lips drawn back to reveal encrusted teeth and sunken eyes that looked ready to roll out of their sockets. Fat veins bulged and pulsed from beneath what little tissue remained. His—or its?—tongue lolled over the lower teeth. The jaw, having been dislocated, rested on its neck. The figure's hair had grown into a thatch of black kudzu that crept down over its eyebrows.

Morgan stiffened. "Lamar, do you smell it?"

"Yes." His voice was thick. "Absinthe."

"Do you want to see the other one—a woman?" Heller asked.

"No, we've seen enough." Lamar turned to go, as did Dr. Heller.

Before Morgan could turn away, the eyes, which had been staring at the ceiling, turned to her, and the figure grunted like a pig, raising its right hand about two inches, revealing grotesque fingernails. Morgan stood, transfixed.

The three sat in Lamar's cramped office, Morgan sobbing, a somber Lamar rubbing her back and neck. Dr. Heller, head in hands, elbows on knees, lost in anguish.

"Something went terribly wrong, and we—I—don't know what. We went over all our calculations countless times, both before the operations and after. The genes we used to replace the ones that control vampirism must have become corrupt somehow, causing the onset of massive and rapid degeneration—a 'radical unwinding' as we call the condition. What you just saw is probably not the end state of that, either."

Morgan sat up abruptly and wiped her eyes on her shirt sleeves. Both men handed her handkerchiefs. "We have to kill it. Them," she said, her voice resolute. "He asked me to do it. You two had already started for the door. Dr. Heller, we have to release them from this misery. Those clicking and grunting sounds they make are cries for help ... and I intend to help them. I will perform the Rites of Charna tonight."

"Rites? Are you telling me that vampires have some sort of death rites? I thought vampires were immortal. Or almost. And loners." Heller stood, his lips pursed.

"The rites are short and simple. I've done them twice before, in nineteenth century Paris. A few of our kind seek release through voluntary death. Some of us have been taught the rites. I'll provide that for them. And the decapitation."

"Decap—you make it sound like the whole program is—"

"Dr. Heller." Morgan stood and put her arms around him. He was shaking. After a few moments she released him and stood back. "Several possibilities occur to me about your program. First, it isn't destroyed by the failure of the first two you tried. Second, if I may suggest, we need a program to prepare candidates before you do the gene-splicing technique.

"And finally, the failure of the inert gene might not have been an anomaly; someone may have sabotaged the experiment. Someone who is on your team or at least has access to this facility. The OVFS has power, influence, money, and a lot of agents that they call 'footmen.' They also have good intelligence and may already have your lab under surveillance. Or, as I said, it may have already been penetrated." Morgan looked at her watch.

"I suggest you go deal with the detectives and Ms. Bundaeker. I'll perform the vampire rites with Lamar's help. You must make special arrangements to inter the remains, since we can't risk sending them to a crematorium. I'll need to use some equipment you probably have in the GenLab."

Both men looked at her as if she were a shooting star arcing across the heavens. Finally Heller clenched his jaw, shook his head and extended his hand. He had just made a deal with a vampire.

The day hadn't dawned at all. Instead, a dome of dark clouds had settled over Rome, lashing all the faithful, as well as those who sold them souvenirs and sandwiches, with cold, gusting rain, yanking umbrellas from the hands of old ladies and blowing off hats, while providing pontifical puddles for kids to jump into and slosh about in. None but the sequestered and the sublime could see the light on a day like this, and that did not include His Eminence, Cardinal Alfonso Loconis. He gingerly rubbed his right knee. The weather always provided a test of his faith, and he often failed that test miserably. He would visit his angst upon any hapless occupant of the Vatican, sometimes including visitors. On this day he was waiting, with growing impatience, for the arrival of Colonel of the Swiss Guard Solento, with the latest news from North America. No doubt the series of disasters had to come to an end. Didn't everything?

Cardinal Alfonso's secretary timidly announced the arrival of the colonel.

"Ah, the esteemed Colonel, newest pontiff of the OVFS, come to explain how the entire pusillanimous organization can be brought to its knees by one hapless female. You have brought me a finger, perhaps? A lock of singed hair, may Saint Lucifer welcome her to his fiery domain."

"I trust the weather has not brought with it a pox upon your knee, Your Eminence." The colonel tried valiantly not to smile, and he almost pulled it off.

"Do enjoy yours while they last, my Prussian friend. So, what tale of woe have you to brighten this day?" Alfonso noted that Colonel Solento's eyes were downcast, not quite masking the tic in one eye. The colonel began speaking as he opened his attaché case.

"The associate we sent to wire the vampire's car apparently gave or sold his watch to some unsuspecting street person. When we traced the watch via GPS, we found a vagrant with an expensive watch."

"Have you managed to find the bomb maker and kill him?" The cardinal's voice was harsh.

"Alas, he remains among the quick, Your Eminence. Our operative bought the OVFS watch from the vagrant."

"How thoughtful of him. I doubt you have the slightest clue as to the whereabouts of your bomb-making Bolshevik who pocketed half the payment for a job he botched? Not to mention the whereabouts of that wretch, Number Three?"

"No, Your Eminence. We have focused our attention on not one, but two vampires. The Summers woman and one Lamar Bradford who is now cohabitating with her. They live in Cambridge, Massachusetts, near Harvard University. I think you will find this—a transcript of a meeting in the office of Dr. James R. Heller, a PhD who is Dean of the Faculty of Arts and Sciences and, more importantly, Director of Harvard's Genetics Laboratory—interesting. The transcript was prepared by a trusted OVFS asset, I think the 007 spy novels would refer to our asset as a 'mole.'" Colonel Solento handed it to the cardinal.

"Was this 'mole' present at the meeting?"

"No, she surreptitiously recorded it, however, and then prepared the transcript which you now hold."

"What level crypt system was used to transmit this document?"

"I believe it was level three. I can confirm that if you wish."

"Do so." Alfonso began to read the multipage document. He hadn't invited the colonel to sit and was irritated when the man pulled up a chair and made himself at ease. "You forget yourself, colonel."

"Oh, no, Your Eminence. That's one thing I never do. I am prepared to accept any instructions you may wish to relay to Number Four." He smiled and inclined his head slightly while sitting, one leg crossed over the other, showing the bottom of his boot to the cardinal.

Alfonso tried to ignore the slight. Extraordinary, he thought. I have read about genetic mutation and DNA. Could these American scientists manipulate the genetic structure of a vampire and convert it into a mortal human being? Dr. Heller thinks they are getting close. And should he succeed, would the OVFS cease to function? If it did, I would revert to being no more than the Vatican's President of the Fabbrica, little more than director of housecleaning and keeper of old bones. Still, Fabbrica provides an excellent cover for my real mission as Director of the OVFS. In that capacity I report to no one.

Well, there is Cardinal Manlocara, the Vatican's Financial Information Authority, whose primary activity is guarding against money laundering. Who better to launder the OVFS operational funding? Thanks to a generous God, Manlocara is a true believer in our work. And thanks to that same God, Number Two died, leaving me to command the OVFS. We retired the number one after our founder died.

While the Holy Father is unaware of our anti-vampire organization, it is devilishly hard to keep a secret in this place. He looked up at the fidgeting colonel.

"The failure of Dr. Heller's first genetic alteration was a singular success for the OVFS. That operation proceeded flawlessly. Our future depends on how well we can replicate that. We have lost Number Three along with four of our footmen, one an experienced terminator.

"I am looking at you, Johann, for an increased role in our field operations. You have been Number Three in an 'acting' capacity of late. Do my bidding successfully, and you could earn that ranking permanently, along with its remuneration. The key word, Johann, is 'successfully.' You have the opportunity to help rid the world of the scourge of vampirism.

"Vampires are known to destroy souls—their own and those of others. Our job is to protect and guide souls. Dr. Heller, so aptly named, is a threat to our mission. He seeks to preserve and strengthen vampirism—a blasphemy against God. He must be stopped, but with a deft hand. Violence and bloodshed must be reserved for vampires and their mentors and protectors, like Heller and his people, not for others, if at all possible. We deeply regret what happened to that waitress. Do you understand all that I have said to you, Johann?"

The colonel rose to his feet and stood at attention, with no trace of levity or intended slight. He saluted and then bowed. "Your Eminence, I am yours to command. I shall prove worthy of your trust."

"Have your mole keep close watch on the Heller Laboratory. Ask your mole for recommendations on how to subtly intervene again, such that Heller's future experimentation is unsuccessful as well."

The colonel gently closed the door to the cardinal's chamber.

Alfonso pulled on his right earlobe and scowled. That man is an egomaniac and an ass, but Number Four is no more than a plodder. Until I can train a new man with the talents that Number Three had, I'll have to live with that Prussian fop. He is not a true believer, and that could prove dangerous. He is motivated by money and power, period. I shall have to create a contingency plan to have Agent Dante provide for the colonel's eternal rest when the time comes. And I need to recruit replacements for the other late and missing bunglers. Cardinal Manlocara was outraged that we lost a quarter of a million dollars to our former bomb maker. He wasn't the least interested in hearing about the car thief that blew up the car before the vampires arrived. One more fiasco like that, and our laundry will stop sending us clean shirts.

The cardinal groaned loudly as he stood and limped across the richly-appointed room to a replica oil portrait of the Mona Lisa. It had hung in the same position on the wall since about 1520 after it had been completed by one of Leonardo's long-forgotten students. Alfonso had no idea how it came to the Church, nor when one of his long-dead predecessors had installed a safe behind it. But Alfonso had converted the safe from an old tumbler combination lock to a contemporary cipher pad.

Mona must be gaining weight, he thought, grunting as he lifted the painting down. I shall have hinges installed. He punched five double-digit numbers and smiled as he heard the faint click, then opened the cylindrical cover and reached into the safe, quickly finding what he wanted. He closed the safe and re-hung the portrait, retrieved a prayer book from a shelf filled with books, including many first editions. One he particularly liked was a signed first edition of *The Black Chamber* by Herbert O. Yardley, the man considered by some to be the Father of American Cryptology.

He untied the two gold ribbons from the tightly curled papers, folded them out, and pressed them in the heavy prayer book to flatten them. Glancing at the London Museum's accession number in the upper left hand corner of page one, he smiled. It was time for him to read again the history of Dr. Archibald E. Garrod, the Father of Chemical Genetics. And especially the works of Dr. Gene Claude Vompre who claimed to have found the "morbid blood spore" that was the root cause of vampirism.

Some of their correspondence was enciphered in a simple, probably home-made, double alphabetic substitution system, which had posed only a moderate challenge, if that. The enciphered text revealed that Vompre planned to inject himself with this so-called morbid spore. His last letter to Garrod was virtually incomprehensible, and his misuse of the code had provided key cribs to its deciphering. Had he found a way to *become* a vampire?

I wonder if any copies were made of this correspondence before the OVFS managed to borrow the documents from the

British Museum in 1928, and if yes, who held them? Why did Dr. Garrod place these documents in the museum eight years before he died? Was he afraid of something or someone? Vompre perhaps? He pulled on an earlobe and looked at the title of the first article in the package: *Metabolic Disruption in the Genetic Structure of Mankind.*

As he began to read, his mind detoured. Somehow he needed to "borrow" Mr. Bradford's codex.

Judeland waited for Dr. Heller in the lounge downstairs. She surveyed a pile of magazines, all current issues: *The Harvard Crimson, Harvard Business Review,* a monograph entitled, *The Genetic History of Hemophilia, Scientific American,* and others. Nearby a young man was drinking coffee and reading the *Wall Street Journal.* A mother was quietly coaching her teenage son in the art of the interview. Judeland detested the lab, detested Dr. Heller, and had come to detest Morgan Summers and, of late, Lamar Bradford. She knew who they really were and what they were doing.

Heller had been a womanizer from his youth, from when he and Judeland's mother were Harvard undergrads. That bastard should have been castrated at birth. She didn't need to look at a copy of an old photograph of the two of them, having a picnic under a tree in the Yard. It was seared into her memory. They were smiling. Happy.

Until he got my mother pregnant. And then he bolted. Left my mom to fend for herself.

She was kicked out of school, and her parents disowned her. She ended up in a home for battered women. After I was born she signed the papers and put me up for adoption. But nobody wanted a sick baby, one with TB and some other mysterious blood disorder the doctors could never diagnose, and I was handed around like some old used car. Once again, Judeland tasted her mental bile.

Her fourth foster home was the worst, she recalled. She'd been raped and threatened with her life by his *wife* if she ever said a word about it. Judeland remembered the miscarriage almost three months after she was raped. She had wept with joy that day, wept through the pain, the degradation, the blood. But her life had crashed like the flaming wreckage from 9/11 with the arrival of her mother's letter, so many years after her suicide.

In spite of her fierce attempt to control her emotions, Judeland's eyes welled up, remembering the day she received a special delivery from the law firm of Gilman, McLaughlin and Hanrahan. The cover letter advised her that her mother had written a letter to Judeland to be delivered on her twenty-first birthday. It was enclosed and dated the day before she committed suicide. The letter had told her about the love affair she had with Jamie Heller when they were freshmen, and that he was Judeland's father. She had signed away all rights, even to naming her daughter, to ensure her baby would have a chance to make good in life. Get a good education, her mother wrote. And stay away from men.

Judeland tore the hundred dollar bill into tiny shreds and flushed it down the toilet in her dorm room. She was working two jobs and had a reasonably good scholarship. That was enough to get by. She went to class, studied, worked, and dreamed of graduating. Judeland followed her mother's recommendations about getting an education and especially the one about staying away from men. Most were disgusting, but none more than James Heller. She would find a way to get to him, to poison him slowly, anonymously. Her bile ducts opened every morning as she fantasized, plotted, and planned. It had taken years, but it was worth the wait.

"Dr. Heller will see you now. Would you care for some coffee, Ms. Bundaeker?" Judeland was jolted out of her bile duct journey, a trip she had taken countless times.

"Uh, yes, that would be nice. Just black." Black suited her like fur-lined gloves.

The colonel grabbed the scrambler phone on its first ring. "Is this Father Christmas?"

"No, it is Father Time. What have you to report?" the colonel asked.

"Our assets are in position near the target. They report that the target has hired a professional security organization to provide surveillance and possibly some personal guards. Watts Security of Cambridge. Good reputation. They handle mostly business organizations but have been known to take on private individuals if the price is right. We plan to send in the woman for a neighborly visit to see if she can assess what the security detail has set up inside the house. They are using Cambridge Landscape as cover for the security guys, and it is likely they have already installed a counter- surveillance capability, so we have to move more carefully from now on. They are planning to build a pergola in the back, lots of flagstone, new plants, and a fish pond with a fountain.

That will take quite a while to complete. They think it provides excellent cover for their security detail.

"Our source says that targets number one and two have moved into offices inside the lab. Source has a meeting scheduled with the Prime Contractor. We should know more after she debriefs to Santa's Helper. Copy all that?"

"Copy all. Is our lab penetration still in place and reliable? Make him another payment.

"Ask source to work that, but warn her to be exceedingly careful. We don't want anyone involved in the lab to know they are under surveillance or have been penetrated. And find out how far the local police have gotten in solving the waitress case, the shootings, and the car bombing. But again, tread lightly. Use this scrambler when you have anything to report.

" The Director of Santa Enterprises grows more agitated by the day because of all the botched operations. In addition, the mission has expanded substantially. Targets one and two must be terminated, as both are infected. And, the work of the GenLab must be permanently neutralized. Understood?"

"Understood. We may soon need some additional associates and a financial transfusion."

"I'll work that. Send me your estimates as soon as you can. Out." The colonel took a deep breath and cradled the receiver. He replaced the unit in its steel box, closed the top, spun the combination and opened the trap door under the footwell of his desk. He placed the unit in its hidden compartment and pulled the throw rug back over it.

Then he made a few cryptic notes—in Latin.

18

Vampire Warning
December 19

"The graveyards are full of indispensable men."

An old saying from Ralph Keyes's
The Quote Verifier, page 84

D r. Heller, unsmiling, stood behind his desk as Lenore escorted Judeland into his office. He did not indicate that his visitor should sit, and when Lenore returned with two full coffee mugs she found both still standing. She gave Dr. Heller a questioning look, and he finally pointed to a seat, sat down, and took a sip of his coffee. His voice was flat and uninviting. "What is the subject of your visit, Ms. Bundaeker?"

"I know you are busy, Dr. Heller, so I will be brief. I have come with a warning."

Heller reached for his pipe, filled, tamped, and lit it before looking up at Judeland, who sat like a piece of statuary, hands folded in her lap. He blew smoke in her direction as his eyes narrowed. "A warning you say?"

"Yes. I believe that one of your employees is a plant, one hired to neutralize your DNA experiments. That person has reason to sabotage our stem cell culturing and gene-splicing capabilities."

"*Our*, Ms. Bundaeker?"

"I should have said 'your.'"

"You must have a very credible source to make such an allegation. May I ask you to reveal that source?"

Judeland looked around the office.

"I can assure you we are not being recorded. I have the lab swept frequently and would know immediately if a recording device had been found. Our security team is quite skilled at finding and tracking such things." His smile was perfunctory.

"A distant cousin, with whom I am close, works at the Vatican. Many years ago a few cardinals began to study the question of the reality of vampirism. They concluded that the condition is a reality, and that it represents a serious and growing threat to mankind. He wouldn't have told me this—it is known to very few—except that he is dying and wanted someone outside the inner circle to know the truth." Judeland drank some of her coffee as she tried to relax.

"I don't mind telling you, Ms. Bundaeker, that I find your tale incredulous. I am, and have long been, a man of science. Nowhere, to my knowledge, is there any credible scientific data to support the existence of vampirism. Is it possible that this brother-in-law of yours is suffering from some cognitive dysfunction as well as from cancer?"

"I believe him to be of sound mind, Dr. Heller."

"Did he provide any supporting documentation, any data that supports this premise?"

"Yes. He is in possession of an authenticated history of one particular vampire. And that vile entity is in your employ."

"And her name is?"

"Morgan Summers."

"Morgan? I find that all but impossible to credit." He pulled over a pad and began writing some notes, smoke curling from his pipe. "But I will make some discreet enquiries, Ms. Bundaeker, and I appreciate your concern for the lab and its mission. We can't be too careful. There are no few 'entities,' as you called them, who would dearly love to obtain the details of our research findings over these past few years."

"I would be most happy to assist you in this investigation, sir." Judeland leaned forward, placing her hands on the edge of his desk.

"Thank you, Ms. Bundaeker. I shall consider your offer. By the way, does Dr. Senger know of your concerns or of this visit?"

Judeland's face flushed. "I thought it best not to burden her with my concerns until we had talked. Was that the correct decision?"

"Under the circumstances I think it was. I may call upon you to brief my security team, and you can be sure that we will keep a watchful eye on Ms. Summers, starting today." He stood and smiled.

Judeland stood and extended her hand, and they shook.

"Thank you for bringing me this extraordinary, uh, revelation. We will be in touch and soon."

As the door closed, he murmured, "She's lying like a rug."

In the outer office Lenore smiled and started to say something to Judeland, but the latter's stone face as she brushed past silenced her farewell greeting.

As Judeland walked across the Yard she smiled—a brittle smile. "Father Dearest, I shall soon have your balls," she said, softly.

Heller reached for the phone and dialed the chief of the campus police. "Hal, this is Jamie Heller. Good to hear your voice, too. How 'bout I treat you to lunch at the club? I need to talk to you about a rather sensitive matter. Any chance you could clear your decks for an hour today? Twelve-thirty? Great. I'll meet you in the lounge." He called Lenore into his office.

"I made a lunch date with Hal Stone for today at twelve-thirty. We'll be at the club. You have my new cell number?" She nodded. "Good. Keep it handy. We may be in for a visit from a Detective Cordell Peyton. He couldn't make it this morning but said he'd be here today by mid-afternoon. Wherever I am, round me up as soon as he arrives. Make him comfortable. After lunch I'll probably be in the lab."

"Hi, old sod. You must be doing a great job. We haven't had a panty raid in a quarter century," Jamie said.

"You're in a cheery mood for an old codger. You ready for another whipping on the handball court?" Hal grinned at his old handball nemesis.

"Boy, do I need the exercise. All work and no trips to the gym make Jamie a flabby boy." They were seated promptly.

"So, what's the agenda?" Harold was a poster person for how to age with dignity and grace. Full head of gray hair, tall, trim, impeccably dressed, and on top of his game.

"I am seriously concerned about an employee that works in HR. She has been making unwarranted inquiries into our work in the GenLab. And she sounds like she has an informant on the inside, it pains me to admit. In short, she knows too much." They paused to order. As usual, Heller ordered the house specialty: Oysters Rockefeller from the Yard. Harold ordered a seafood medley.

"Would her initials be 'JB'?" Hal maintained eye contact as he sipped his coffee.

Jamie's eyes widened. "How did you know?"

"She's been doing some odd things of late. While trying to be crafty she's actually been a tad ham-handed."

"Like what things?" Jamie leaned forward.

"Asking for certain personnel records for one."

"Well, hell, she works in HR. It doesn't seem out of line that she—"

"After we got hacked so badly two years ago, we made a lot of changes to the computer system, building in some covert safeguards. Don't repeat this, but we have red-flagged a bunch of records, both personnel and projects, including Dr. Martin, you, me, Flossie, other top-tier faculty, staff, board of directors, a few select contractors and advisors, and all of the GenLab.

"When you query those records it triggers our system, causing us to take a look into what's going on. Same with attempts to get into proprietary or classified files. In a few cases we've had to look into a person of interest's computer. Surprising what we have found. And we don't care a jot about porn."

"Can you go into any detail on what you've found out about JB?" Heller looked around, but the nearest tables were empty.

"Will you tell me why you need to know?"

"Judeland came to my office this morning to warn me about a member of my staff, one that I have come to trust and depend on. She was wired tighter then the E-string on a violin. Although she seemed to have prepared carefully, she made a lot of mistakes. Kind of tipped her hand. I think she wants to ingratiate herself with me and work her way into the GenLab.

"She knew too much about our work. Spun out this cockamamie story about a dying relative in the Vatican telling her about some secret Catholic organization that was trying to eliminate certain afflicted people and that this group posed a direct threat to the lab and those of us who work in it. Judeland hadn't informed Flossie about her concerns, by the way. And I tripped her up several times as I questioned her." Heller pushed his salad aside and continued.

"I played her into thinking I had taken her warning seriously and planned to investigate, even implying I would include her as a party to the investigation. So my agenda, old buddy, is to convince you to watch her, with a great deal of stealth, and let me know what you find out. Do you have any more details based on your investigation to date?"

"One. And all this is really close hold, James. If it were anybody else, I'd be doing all the listening." Heller nodded.

"JB has a deeply covert relationship with an outside organization, one we haven't been able to get a handle on. Don't even know its name. Our best guess is that it is some kind of security organization, probably international, with a lot of resources. Some of their communications are encrypted; I'd have to get NSA to break into them."

Heller whistled. "Good Lord, Hal, you sound like you never left the Bureau."

"Well, they can debrief you—take away all your clearances— but they can't degauss a lifetime of experience." Hal had spent thirty-three years in the FBI's National Security Branch and its predecessors, most of it in counterintelligence. The Bureau had bestowed the Medal for Meritorious Achievement for his work on uncovering the most notorious spy in FBI history. But he was especially proud of his contributions to the development of Harvard's intelligence and security curricula. His two mobile intercept vans had proven their worth as training platforms while contributing to the overall Intelligence Community mission.

"As far as JB is concerned, will you watch her and keep me up to speed on every detail, no matter how unimportant it may seem to you?" Jamie asked. "I'll reciprocate. And we will have to walk softly; I don't want to spook her contacts. I want to find out who they are and what they're after. And just as important, how many of them work here. Do we have a deal?" Jamie extended his hand.

They did.

Cordell and Blanton parked in number twenty-three. The blue Cobalt glided into a space a hundred feet away. Both detectives were watched as they walked into the Science Center, which housed the GenLab.

One of the men in the blue Chevy got out and walked slowly toward the sedan parked in slot twenty-three. When he was right behind it he stopped and kneeled down to retie his shoe laces. He glanced back and saw the driver of the Cobalt give him a thumbs up signal. He reached inside his coat pocket, pulled out a device, pressed an activation button, and reached under the car where he stuck it to the undercarriage. He resumed walking, ending up in a deli several blocks away. In ten minutes he was joined by another man. They ate in silence.

"Detectives Peyton and McConnell. You are expected. May I see some identification?" Lenore asked.

They showed Lenore their badges. "And a driver's license please."

The two detectives looked bored but produced their licenses.

"Please have a seat. Would you like some coffee? Dr. Heller will be out shortly."

They had just finished their first swallow when a distinguished man, one just beginning to become a bit portly, walked into the lounge, a commercial smile in place, hand extended. "Cordell and Blanton? Ah, good. I'm James Heller. How can I help you?"

"I don't think our discussion should be conducted here," Cordell said, glancing around.

"Of course not. Please, follow me. Lenore, hold my calls, there's a love."

"I suggest you hang your coats over there." He indicated a coat tree outside his office.

Neither man took off his sport jacket. When they were seated, Dr. Heller began. "How can Harvard's Dean of Arts and Sciences cooperate with our men in blue?"

The two detectives glanced at each other. Cordell cleared his throat. "As we said earlier, we need to interview two of your employees: Morgan Summers and Lamar Bradford."

"I see. And the subject is?"

"I trust you read about our little car bombing, professor?"

Heller's eyes narrowed. "Of course."

"We would like to ask them some questions that might help our investigation. Could you call them to your office for us?" Cordell kept his voice neutral but not his thoughts. *I already don't like this pompous egghead.*

"I can't imagine either of them could contribute anything useful on the car that exploded. We do a good job vetting—"

"Sir, we're not asking you to imagine anything. We simply want to talk to two of your people. Will you help us with that, or shall we go look for them?"

"I'm afraid that would be impossible. We have quite a few classified projects in process." Heller reached for his phone and punched double zero. Lenore answered immediately. "Would you ask Ms. Summers and Mr. Bradford to pop in to see me? Tell them I have guests that want to meet them. Thanks." He turned back to the detectives. "They should be here in a couple of minutes. More coffee?" The two detectives watched Dean Heller relight his pipe and sit back in his chair.

Lamar and Morgan knocked and then entered. Introductions were minimal.

Cordell turned to Heller. "I like your office, but we could conduct this interview in some place that won't inconvenience you."

"This is as good as it gets," Heller replied, sweeping the room with a gesture.

"Our investigation requires confidentiality. I'm sure you understand the nature of police work, professor." The level of testosterone continued its upward sweep.

"Detective Sergeant or Sergeant Detective, are you suggesting–"

"It's lieutenant," Cordell said.

Lamar interrupted. "Not a problem, *Dr.* Heller. My office will do, and it will give me a chance to show our guests some of the lab's geography. Right this way, gentlemen." Lamar led the other three out of Heller's office. Heller stood rigid, face flushed, hands on his hips.

They walked for a couple minutes in silence. Lamar said, "Here we are." Lamar opened the door to a rather cramped office that might once have been a storage site. "Sorry about the chairs."

"We would like to start with you, Ms. Summers. Mr. Bradford, if you would be so kind as to wait outside." Cordell motioned toward the door.

Lamar scowled. "I'll go check on one of my programs in the lab." He closed the door hard and walked off but ducked into an adjoining men's room where he could hear the detectives and Morgan through the thin wall that separated the two rooms.

"Thank you for seeing us on such short notice," Cordell began, his eyes belying the cordial words. "For the record let me get your full name, address, including email, and phone numbers, including cell, date and place of birth. Go slowly as Blanton will be jotting down your info."

Morgan sat, stiffly, looking at an old black and white photo titled *The Yard in Winter, 1979*, the only adornment on Lamar's office walls. She flushed at the next question.

"And how long have you lived at Coleson Manor?" Blanton asked.

"Just long enough."

"Come, Ms. Summers, it's a simple question." Cordell stared at her. "How long have you lived with Lamar?"

"I never said I lived with him. I live in the same house."

"All right then, how long have you lived in the same house?" Cordell rubbed the back of his neck.

"You began by stating that you needed to gather our contact information, which I am perfectly willing to provide."

"Then why are you not willing to answer the question? Did you skate out of your apartment in Porter Square without giving the landlord any notice or paying the final rent due?" Cordell's face had become rigid.

Morgan smiled at him. She crossed her legs, causing her mini-skirt to rise alarmingly. Both detectives looked away. She smiled again and reached into her pocketbook for a pack of cigarettes, extracted one, found a pack of matches, and lit the cigarette.

"This is a no-smoking area, Ms. Summers," Blanton said.

"So, are you going to arrest me for smoking?"

"You watch too many old movies," Cordell growled, waving the smoke away from his face. He glared at McConnell, who was looking at the ceiling, desperately trying not to laugh.

"Do you intend to pay your back rent?" Cordell demanded.

"If you are as good a detective as the salary Cambridge is paying you suggests, you would have found out that I pay several months' rent in advance."

Cordell looked down, grinding his teeth. His partner looked up at the ceiling again, where cigarette smoke was collecting in the absence of an air handler. "You hesitated when Detective McConnell asked about your date and place of birth. Why?" Cordell's voice was brittle.

"My mother taught me it was always advisable for a young woman to hesitate, lieutenant. Have you ever hesitated to reveal something?" Morgan flicked her cigarette ash into a mug on Lamar's desk. It was half full of yesterday's coffee, and the ash hissed.

"So tell me, Ms. Summers, or should I address you as Harriet Rankin, why did you falsify your auto registration? And why have you not come forward when your car was reduced to rubble? And tell me, please, who got killed in your car and why?"

"Am I under arrest Chief Detective? You haven't read me my rights. Don't you care about a citizen's rights?"

"Blanton, I do believe we need to go back to the precinct and pick up those arrest warrants. This is not a fit place for an interview." He stood, and Blanton jumped to his feet. With his hand on the doorknob, Cordell whirled around. "Ms. Summers, why were you that close—" he held up his hands like goal posts "—to your car when it exploded? And why haven't you sought to retrieve the green minivan also registered to Ms. Rankin, the one currently sitting in our impoundment lot since the day after the car bombing? Oh yes, we have a lot more to talk about. And we'll hold our next interview, Ms. Summers, at precinct headquarters." He almost slammed the door in his partner's face.

Lamar, grinning, walked into his office. "Well, I think you just might have pissed him off. What do you plan to do next, bite him on the neck?"

19

Immortal Beings, Eternal Rest
December 20

"In the long run we are all dead—unless you are a
vampire."

A Tract on Monetary Reform
by John Maynard Keynes, 1924 (as amended)

T he faint hum inside the GenLab cold room was
evanescent, like the ocean where it meets the distant
horizon on a fog-shrouded morning. Two gurneys had
been rolled into the middle of the room, flanked by wheeled racks
of vials against the walls. A reddish glow suffused the room,
enriched by the flickering light from two tower candles placed on
waist-high round tables that an hour earlier held profusions of fake
ivy. A rolling medical cart, the kind that normally held surgical
instruments, sat between the gurneys. But tonight, the

instruments placed on the white tablecloth covering the medical cart were radically different, for they were not meant to serve life but to end it.

Morgan looked down. Two sharpened Aspen stakes were wrapped in linen napkins. Between them was a ten-pound hand maul. Under the cart were two insulated carrying cases, already partially filled with dry ice. She studied the carbon dioxide laser unit beside the cart, along with the Medline surgical gown, cap, face mask, gloves, and goggles on the other side. A copy of *The Tibetan Book of the Dead,* bookmarked, lay on the cart as well.

She was alone, save the two entities that lay in torment on the gurneys, blood pulsing, eyes pleading, their feeble hearts still beating in time with the primordial rhythm of life.

Morgan donned the surgical apparel. She was ready. She began with the humming meditation she'd learned from Pythia, self-proclaimed descendant of the Oracle of Delphi.

Morgan's humming grew and surged like an ocean in its eternal quest for high tide, causing the candle flames to waver. When the meditation faded and sank beneath the surface, Morgan opened the book and began to read aloud.

"When karmic illusions dawn upon me and fear and terror grow within me, May I realize they are but reflections from within myself; May I realize they are a natural part of the Bardo of death; May I realize this moment as one of great opportunity; May I accept good and evil karmic illusions as my own."

Morgan selected and read two more passages. Then she leaned over each gurney in turn, speaking slowly and quietly in the ancient vampire tongue, the almost lost heritage from the Great Serpent of Charna who, it was thought, evolved from the coalesced fears and loathing of ancient men, yet lurked still on the dark periphery of the vampire realm. It was Charna's blessings she invoked. His acquiescence. For she knew that a vampire's journey unto death traversed a dismal plane, through dry and airless winds, past cathedrals of loss and wretchedness, long before the first faint light appeared, twinkling in the vast distance. Whether mirage or Holy Grail, only the most resolute on the journey would learn. It was called by vampires the "Voyage of the Great Serpent."

She heard the faint clicking sound they made in response, the last vestige of the voices they once had. Both were ready. Eager.

Morgan picked up the hand maul and unwrapped one of the aspen stakes. She held them high, seeking the blessings from the denizens of the four ordinal points: north, south, east, and west. She approached the male vampire first. Carefully placing the stake over his heart, which pulsed more rapidly now, she raised the maul and drove it down with all her force. What life remained in the desiccated creature fountained over her surgical gown, dripping back onto the punctured chest. Morgan felt horror, compassion, and sensual desire as she heard his long, guttural sigh signaling the vampire's death. His mate grunted her farewell.

Morgan quickly laid the maul aside and grasped the laser knife, activating the unit at full power. The vampire's throat tissues offered little resistance, and in less than a minute she had his head off and reverently placed into its container. She turned to the other gurney.

The female vampire raised one hand. A gold band circled the skeletal ring finger. The grunting increased as the figure on the second gurney pushed her left hand toward Morgan, who understood. Carefully, she slipped the ring off and placed it on her own ring finger. The grunting stopped, replaced by soft clicking.

"I shall wear your ring until the day I can return it to you, Rena." Morgan knew her name. It had been whispered on the winds. "Are you ready to begin your journey?" More soft clicking.

Morgan unwrapped the second stake, took hold of the maul, raised both for their blessing, and then paused to look at the vampire's eyes. Soft, warm light radiated from them. Morgan smiled then drove the stake through Rena's heart. Again, blood sprayed over Morgan, and again her emotions leaped like shadows from a fire in some pre-historic cave.

After Morgan had separated Rena's head and placed it in the remaining carrying case, she sang the ancient vampire *Song of the Vigil,* then quickly shed her clinical garb, stuffing it into the special processing box provided by the GenLab.

She stumbled to the door and collapsed into Lamar's arms.

20

The Mole
December 20

"Though in many of its aspects this visible world seems formed in love, the invisible spheres were formed in fright."

Moby Dick,
Herman Melville, page 42

Lawrence Ashton shrank down in a corner booth at the Sylphon Nymph. Why do people go to bars? he wondered. They're loud and filled with idiots who tell dirty jokes and try to pick up broads you would never invite to church or into your home. Not that he ever went to church. He sucked on the two straws and watched his second Pepsi diminish. Two dollars and fifty cents for a soft drink. They have to be making two forty in profit. He better slow down. The tab was already five bucks, and

Judeland hadn't even showed up yet. Why are women always late? The broad that works for Lamar, Jennifer, now I'd like to get a look up her skirt.

Wonder if Lamar has? Nah, he's got the hots for Morgan Summers. They try to be so cool, but I spotted it first thing.

Judeland's as ugly as a knothole in a rotten picket fence. A'course she probably doesn't think I'm any great shakes, either. But I've got something she wants. Access. Well, she has something I want. Money. She recently got a bundle from an uncle. Wish I had a rich relative keel over and leave me a bundle. One more semester and then finish my thesis. The thousand dollar "retainer" from Judeland allowed me to cut back my hours at the pharmacy and bear down on the thesis. If she was serious about another thousand, maybe I could make the down payment on a used car, one with high mileage but still runs good.

God, I hate it when she tries to get all lovie dovie. Women think all men can be led around by their schlongs. She'll soon find out I can't. She hasn't got the tits for that sort of stuff, anyway. She'll be asking me to insert a couple drops of whatever is in the vial she gives me into the stem cell cultures when the big boys start the resurrection program up again. To those PhDs I'm a lab rat, hardly one step above the janitor. But that's a good thing—they don't watch me. A thou here, a thou there, maybe I could go on for a PhD. I wonder how soon Heller and his gang plan to try it again?

Wish to hell I hadn't gone into the cold room. They got a couple of really scary dudes in there, all wired up to monitors and feed tubes, but their faces already look like they're half way to becoming skulls with a lot of gunk hanging off 'em. Make bitching Halloween masks. Maybe I can cop one of the photos they keep on taking. I guess they're still taking them. The cold room has been off limits the past three weeks except to Heller and a couple others. Yesterday I saw Bradford and Summers go in. How come they can go in? They're brand new lab rats. That just isn't right.

The GenLab is getting to look more like the dungeon of Dr. Frankenstein's castle every day. Wish I worked somewhere else, except for the extra money from Judeland's dead uncle. Lawrence finished his second Pepsi and looked up. Judeland was standing over him, smiling. His stomach suddenly felt gastric.

"Hello," she said, sliding into the booth and moving in close so their thighs were touching. "Have you eaten?"

"No." He thought about moving over but didn't. "What would you like? They have good sliders here."

"Yeah, that would be okay."

Judeland signaled a waitress. "Two orders of sliders with fries. Larry, do you want another Coke?"

"It's Lawrence, and I'll have another Pepsi." He jerked as Judeland's hand grasped his crotch, making his confined erection more painful. She had that effect on him, and he hated it. Sort of. Well, he might make an exception. Again. But only for today. He could always pretend it was Jennifer's hand.

Neither of them were paying the slightest attention to a man sitting at the bar. They didn't see him push a keypad button on a miniature directional voice receiver lying next to him, which looked exactly like a cell phone. The tiny red light winked out, replaced by a tiny green one.

The man ordered a Heineken and some wings.

"Father Hemming, please." Heller checked his watch. He was tense. What if Detective Peyton came back with a search warrant and barged into the cold room?

"Bless you for calling, Father Hemming here."

"Ed, this is Jamie Heller. How's everything in the hatch, match, and dispatch business?" He heard the man on the other end chuckle.

"Surely you are calling to arrange a confession, am I right? Haven't seen you in church since the waters receded from the ark." Heller could hear the mirth in Ed's reply.

"Guess I am rather overdue, my friend. I have a problem, and I need your help. It's kind of urgent. Any chance I could toddle over? It should take no more than thirty minutes max." There was a long pause. Only their breathing overlaid the electronic silence. Heller wondered if Ed was thinking back to the time he had saved Ed's buns, back when they were Harvard undergrads, and Ed had gotten involved with a stunning blonde—a real *Debbie Does Dallas* type. Jamie had lied when he provided Ed with an alibi, "proving" that Ed was with him during the night "Dallas" got smashed and totally indiscreet with Ed. And pregnant. Back before DNA paternity testing.

"I'll be waiting in my office, my old friend."

Jamie heard the disconnect. Well hell, Ed, I never, in all these years, called in the "my old friend" chip. Thanks for remembering.

Heller walked to Saint Paul Catholic Church in less than ten minutes, though he was huffing. He took the stairs two at a time, ignoring the eighty-eight year old architecture. Jamie had long thought the church looked more like a train station from the outside, though he admired the stately bell tower. He hurriedly passed through the arched front and into the familiar Romanesque church with its long aisles, vaulted ceiling, massive crucifix, imported German stained glass windows and statuary, pausing for a moment to look at the dark paneled vestibule, originally a wall dedicated to the Harvard men who died in World War One. He walked briskly through the connecting hall to the pastor's office in the administrative building adjoining the church.

Ed was waiting for him. They dispensed with the normal warm up as Ed poured them both a cup of coffee and sat back, raising his eyebrows.

"Ed, I need you to bury two bodies for me in your cemetery. As soon as possible."

Ed's mouth opened and he leaned forward. He shook his head as if to clear it. "A little mishap at the Genetics Lab, Jamie? You're sounding like Al Capone all of a sudden."

"Not exactly. We obtained two bodies—don't ask—which had special characteristics we needed to study. The study is complete. The problem is, I have reason to believe the Cambridge police are going to show up with a search warrant, and I don't want those bodies found in our cold room. Ed, if you have to have more detail, I'll read you in on this project. As you know, we do a lot of cutting edge research and have long partnered with the Department of Defense, so some of what we do is classified by DoD. Much of our other stuff is proprietary. The less you know, the better for both of us, but it's your call.

"Are you asking me to do something illegal?"

"No, Ed, I'm not. Burying dead bodies is an everyday occurrence."

"But *you* can't be seen to be involved with these two. And it has to be done by yesterday?"

"Yes to both." Jamie rubbed the back of his neck.

"I trust they come with death certificates?"

Jamie looked down.

"Jamie, I'm going to trust you on this, even if I have a squishy feeling about it."

"Your trust won't be misplaced, old buddy."

Father Hemming reached for the phone and dialed. Jamie listened as he made the arrangements. At one point Jamie got on the line to provide the exact pickup instructions. The bodies would be wrapped in funerary bindings and were not to be unwrapped. They were to be picked up this evening and held until the following day, when they would be buried in the plots designated by Father Hemming. All costs would be billed to the Church, but Jamie would cover those costs, of course. He would also order stone grave markers and schedule a secluded service for the two.

"That it, Jamie?"

"I think we've covered it. And I only ran over by, uh, six minutes."

"I think we're even now, my old friend." The father's voice was soft and flat.

"I hadn't thought of it that way, Ed."

Father Hemming stared at Jamie.

As Jamie walked back to the lab another thought hit him. Jesus, what about the heads?

Morgan got out of the taxi, paid the driver, and pulled two carrying cases from the back seat. She was walking up to the front door when she saw Lamar's car pull into the driveway. A young man approached her. He had sandy blonde hair, medium build, a scar across one cheek, wearing a jacket with a logo: *Monty's Auto Repair and Body Shop.*

"You Mrs. Bradford?"

"Yes." She was looking at the car, spotless and gleaming even in the dull sunlight. "The bill comes to nineteen fifty," Monty said.

"My husband won't be home for several hours. He writes all the checks."

"That's not what Mr. Roberts said. He told me to bring it right over, and he would pay me—in cash."

"Ah. I didn't know that. I'll go get him." Monty followed as she headed for the front door. She could feel his eyes and gave her hips a bit more lateral expression as she mounted the steps. Hooray for Dr. Chandless, best plastic surgeon east of the Mississippi.

Inside, she called Robert. When he appeared she told him Monty was outside waiting to be paid. She set the carrying cases in the hall, intending to discuss their content and placement with Robert, when the doorbell rang. Blast, couldn't Monty at least wait—

"Yes, madam?" she heard Robert inquire.

"Hi. My name is Jill Bonnet. I'm your new neighbor from down the street, and I wanted to introduce myself."

"I'm certain Mr. Bradford will be delighted to receive you, Ms. Bonnet. Unfortunately he is not here at the moment. Perhaps if you gave me your card?"

"How silly of me. I seem to have left them in my purse. I can go get one and return."

190

Morgan heard a loud brake squeal and peeked out of the front window lights to see a beat-up, old white Ford F-150 stop at the foot of the driveway behind Lamar's Jag. "Who is that?" Morgan asked Robert.

"I have no idea, madam."

Monty heard them. "That's Jake. He's my ride back to the shop."

"I have an envelope for you, Monty. Stay put, I'll be right back." Robert disappeared into the library. While Morgan waited for Robert to get rid of everybody, the new neighbor stepped into the hall.

"I see you've been hat shopping," she said.

Morgan flushed and stammered. "Uh, I guess you could say that."

"Don't worry, I won't say a word to Lamar."

"Lamar? Do you know him?"

"Well, not yet, other than by reputation."

"Reputation?" There was something about this woman she already didn't like. Several somethings, starting with her good figure, stylish clothes, and flawless complexion.

"Well, I feel a bit awkward discussing that here in the hall," the neighbor said.

Robert reappeared, carrying an envelope. He walked past the ladies and out to the porch where he handed it to Monty, who opened it and counted the money. Monty roared off in Jake's pickup, one that sounded like it needed a new muffler and a valve job. Robert hastily disappeared into the kitchen.

Morgan was taken aback when the visitor took off her winter coat and looked around for a place to hang it. "I won't stay a minute. I'm sure you are quite busy, and you probably want to go try on those new hats. I'd love to see them on you, if that would be okay."

"This is not a good time for me, Ms.—?"

"Oh, grief, I forgot you were not present when I introduced myself to Robert. It's Jill. Jill Bonnet."

Without warning Jill reached down and picked up one of the carry bags. "My, you must have chosen two rather heavy hats, Ms.—?"

"Call me Morgan." She reached for the "hat" Jill still held, picked up the other one, placed them in the hall closet, and shut the door.

"Okay. Morgan." Jill began to cough. "Could I have a glass of water before I go, please?"

Morgan stomped off to the kitchen and yanked open the refrigerator door. Something fell out at her feet. It was wrapped in a dirty undershirt. What the hell, she wondered, unwrapping it.

She jumped back, dropping it. A man's hand. Powder-burned, dirty fingernails, a ring with a silver skull embossed on onyx. Strands of gristle and bone protruded from its wrist.

"*Madam*?" Robert gaped at the hand as if it might begin crawling toward him.

At that moment, Jill screamed as if someone were cutting off her head. Morgan, in one motion, grabbed the hand, pitched it into the refrigerator, slammed the door, and ran back into the hall.

Shaking violently and screaming, Jill cowered in a corner, looking at the carrying cases she had pulled out of the closet, one lying on its side. A severed head, partially decomposed, had rolled out onto the hall floor. And it was staring at Jill.

Robert arrived, breath heaving, eyes riveted on the ghastly spectacle unfolding at Coleson Manor on Tory Row, in Cambridge's most exclusive Brattle Street District.

21

The Coffee Shop
December 20

"Who's watching the watchers?"

A common saying.

Blanton made the motion with his forefinger as if he were twirling a sparkler—a long-used signal to indicate a high priority interruption. Cordell looked up from the phone and shook his head in the negative. He scribbled one word on a pad, tore it off and held it up. The word was *Governor*. Cordell raked a forefinger across his neck, and Blanton stepped away and spoke into a cell phone.

"Look, Detective Peyton is on the phone with a VIP. Can he call you in a few minutes?

Hold it, lemme get a pen." Blanton copied the number. "He'll get right back to you, Mr. Bradford."

Five minutes later Cordell stood, head bowed and shoulders slumped, with sleeves rolled up to his elbows and his narrow tie pulled partway down his shirt front. Blanton walked over to Cordell's desk but didn't say anything. "Can't sit down for a week, Mac," the Chief Detective muttered. "Don't have any ass left. Guess I'll have to grow a new one. The Gov plans to burn down the precinct with me in it. Hell of a way to end a career."

"Maybe you don't want to take another call for awhile."

Cordell pulled out a pack of cigarettes that hadn't been opened and stared at it. "You got any idea how long I've had this pack? Carry it with me every day. Two years."

McConnell stuck out his hand. "You want me to carry it for you for the rest of the day?"

"Nope. The Gov can kiss my ass before I have one of those. Who called?"

"Lamar Bradford."

"Yeah? What did he want?"

"Wants to talk to you one-on-one, on neutral turf, no wires. Said he wanted to work something out. You up for that?"

"Sure. What have we got to lose? We can't find the kidnap victim, can't find the perps who stole the rescue vehicle unless it was the guys from the shootout, but the FD guys can't ID either body. Ballistics can't match the shell casings at the shootout to any piece in the database, the Bureau doesn't have anything on a gang with no nipples, apparently nobody saw anybody wiring the Rankin car, we have no idea who triggered the explosion or who got blown up. All the known bad guys in the area are accounted for, and we got no motive for anything that's happened other than speculation. And I just lost twenty pounds of ass." Cordell kicked his bottom desk drawer shut. "Would you believe now I got to report to the *man*—and everybody in the chain—every day except the weekends when he'll be fishing in Maine?"

At nine that night Cordell approached Simon's Coffee Emporium in the Porter Square neighborhood. Light from inside the coffee shop illuminated the softly falling snow outside, creating a Budweiser commercial without the Clydesdales. Long and narrow, the lighting inside was too bright, and the orange and yellow walls made the coffee shop look to Cordell like a kid's playpen. The patterned tin ceiling was probably left over from when Simon's had been an ice cream parlor. The sharp tang of coffee and cinnamon added to the ambience. Christmas decorations helped soften the glare and the garish colors. Brushing the snow off his overcoat, he looked around. The house cat watched him from a perch on the window ledge.

Lamar waved to him from a table against the back wall. Cordell ordered a coffee and joined him. Neither man spoke or offered to shake hands as the detective sat. Finally, Cordell said, "I believe it's your nickel."

"I trust this is off the record?" Lamar blew on his coffee and took a drink, his eyes never leaving Cordell's.

"I'm not wired, if that's your question."

Lamar glanced at the other two customers. Both young men appeared to be students buried in their notebooks. One waitress was cleaning table tops while the other was cleaning a coffee maker.

"I want to start by apologizing for Morgan's behavior yesterday. She is under a hell of a lot of stress. We want to cooperate with you. We're not the enemy."

"You sound like Richard Nixon."

Lamar ignored the remark. "You getting any breaks in your investigations?"

"I didn't agree to be interrogated, Bradford. The shoe is on the other foot. What's your relationship with Morgan Summers?"

"She's living with me, as I'm sure you already know. Look, Detective Peyton, you need to make some progress, and we need to be crossed off your suspects list. I'm willing to work a deal with you. I can get you started on a couple of lines of investigation. In return, you promise not to harass me and Ms. Summers and you drop the arrest and search warrants."

"Are you asking for immunity? Because—"

"No, I'm not. Neither of us has done anything for which we need immunity. If you don't find what I have to say interesting or useful, we both walk out of here, and this meeting never happened. If the reverse is true, we start meeting here and exchanging information. You can back out any time. But you show up with any warrants, and the spigot gets turned off. I'm asking you to trust me as I am trusting you about not wearing a wire."

Both stopped talking and watched one of the students walk to the window and look out, then pack his computer, put on his jacket, and leave. The waitress poured them a refill without asking.

Cordell groaned and stretched. It had been a long day. He didn't like Bradford. One of those Tory Row snobs living off inherited money, Harvard grad, driving a Jag, probably overpaid for a nothing job with a fancy title. But his intuition was whispering, and it was saying he should give Lamar a try.

"Okay, let's start. Why did Ms. Summers register two cars under the name Harriet Rankin? The *late*."

"She is afraid for her life. That car bomb was meant for her. And there have been three other attempts on her life in recent weeks. The guy that got killed in the blast was trying to steal Morgan's car. We saw that happen. We came within in a few seconds of both of us being taken out in that blast."

Cordell, who had rocked back in his chair, slammed it down and reached for his worn leather notebook and a ballpoint. He took a couple of cryptic notes and looked up. "Go on."

"Detective, you—*we*—are up against a ruthless international cartel. Morgan has outwitted them so far, but even a cat has only so many lives. I think I can give you the car thief for openers."

Cordell fixed Lamar with a laser stare. "How about telling me something a little higher up the food chain than a two-bit car thief?"

"Paula Bernard was an accident. She snitched a poisoned canapé meant for Morgan. Morgan thinks it was laced with calcium oxalate crystals, which induce a coma but can't be detected during most post mortem examinations."

"What? Your new girlfriend is a chemical engineer?"

Lamar ignored the question. "The cartel guys stole the rescue vehicle and carted off the unconscious waitress. No doubt, when they discovered their mistake they had to kill her and get rid of the body." Lamar pulled a small box out of his trench coat and handed it to Cordell.

"What's this?"

"One of the canapés that was meant for Morgan. Your lab boys should find it interesting."

Cordell put the box in a topcoat pocket.

"How did you know to come after Morgan?" Lamar asked.

"We recovered the VIN number off the Rankin car—the one that blew up."

"Hmmm. And how did you trace it to Morgan? She fed the DMV a dummy address."

I could use this guy in the department, Cordell thought. Oh, well, let's keep the ball in play. "We got an anonymous tip."

"Ah. Interesting. The cartel is trying to flush Morgan out of the protection offered by Dr. Heller and more recently by me. Even your investigation offers a small degree of protection. Cordell, I'm sure by now you suspect that the Bernard kidnapping, the shootout in the hotel, and the car bombing are pieces of the same mosaic, am I right?"

Cordell shrugged. "Keep going." But they were interrupted.

"Gentlemen, you may not have noticed, but it is snowing like mad out there. I already sent Beth home and asked the other kid to pack up and go, too. Now I'll have to ask you to call it a night so I can get home before the roads get any worse." Both men looked out the window and then thanked her, leaving a generous tip.

As they walked outside Cordell decided not to mention the gold band they found in the pocket of one of the shooting victims, the one with "Paula and Jeff 2010" inscribed on the inside. Staff Sergeant Jeffrey Green, USMC, had been killed in Afghanistan in June 2010.

"You said you could give me the car thief. How?"

"I've got part of him at home."

"Dr. Heller?" Lenore's voice was crisp, efficient. "Mr. Harold Stone is here. He apologizes for not having an appointment but says he needs to talk to you, briefly."

"Give me two minutes, then send him in." Heller asked his visitor if they could reconvene after lunch, shook his hand, and assured him he would carefully consider the matter as he walked him out of his office. "See Lenore and get booked on my schedule. I doubt it will take us more than another half hour, don't you agree?"

"Hal. Good to see you. We should have met at the club. I could use another dose of their Oysters Rockefeller. You coffee'd out yet?"

"Next time on the oysters, Jamie. I could do with another cuppa java, though." The always psychic Lenore appeared a moment later with a small tray, cups, and a fresh pot. When the door closed Hal began. "You have a mole, and I know who he is. Rather, there are likely two of them. You have a lab tech named Lawrence Ashton. He meets with Judeland Bundaeker.

"We had a guy nearby in the bar where they met who copied almost all of their conversation. She is paying him to sabotage at least some of your experiments. You can listen to the tape, but that's the bottom line. But there's more. We have reason to think that Bundaeker is working for a very mercurial organization, and we have reason to believe that the three recent crimes are connected and more than likely were carried out under the direction of that organization."

Heller whistled. "That absolute bastard! The pieces are starting to fall into place. That son-of-a-bitch Ashton probably buggered the stem cells. I guess it's time to call in the Cambridge police."

"No, I wouldn't do that. Not yet, anyway. It would be a setback to the bad guys, but they could recover and come after you again. We need to watch and wait. We need to get the big guns behind the street guys, so to speak. In the meantime, you could either transfer Ashton to some make-work job, or institute a two-man rule like the military has for launching nukes. I'd favor the latter. We'll wire Ashton's world so tight he can't even fart off the record."

"What about warning Flossie?"

"Probably not a good idea. We want her to act totally normal toward Judeland. We don't want to spook Judeland into bailing. We've done some checking and her bank account is bulging beyond her salary. Over the past several months a series of deposits, several hundred dollars each, in cash, can't be explained. She hasn't been receiving any overtime or special cash awards from the university and doesn't have a second job. I'd bet the rent money Judeland recruited this techno geek, Ashton. He may be a brilliant lab tech, but outside the lab a real zero. About to finish a masters and talking about going for a PhD—if the extra money from Judeland continues. He recently paid off a loan and quit his part-time job to work on his thesis. And he's been looking at used cars. Oh, and Judeland was playing footsie with him under the table."

Hal decided not to mention Lamar's meeting with Detective Peyton. He could run that operation better without Jamie in the mix. Lamar had played his role to perfection. Hal had listened to the tape twice and couldn't detect a single wrong move. The undergrad he'd hired to record the meet must have scarfed up twenty-five bucks worth of Simon's lattes, though. He would have to put him on a budget next time. Lamar dangled the bait and Peyton took it. Hal smiled.

"Jamie, one other thing. And this is going to sound weird. A couple of times Judeland and Lawrence lowered their voices almost to a whisper, but after we amped it up, it sounded like they were talking about vampires. Is that a project name you guys are using or maybe a password for one of your close-hold systems?"

Heller flinched before he could regain his composure.

"I must have stomped on a nerve. Care to elaborate?" Hal asked.

Jamie got what combat soldiers call "that thousand yard stare."

"You still in there?" Hal waved a hand in front of Jamie's face.

"Uh, yeah. I will, that is, I'll have to think about it."

"Seems to me you just did. It's hard to score when you're not all on the same team, Jamie. What else do I need to know?"

Jamie frowned as he made a snap decision. "Hal, you've spent most of your adult life keeping secrets. Have you got room for one more, and it's a monster?"

"I keep a little sign that hangs behind my desk: 'Secrets Are Us.' If you want me to take an oath, sign an indoctrination form, offer my first born in chattel to the Faculty of Arts and Sciences, I'm up for it."

Jamie stuck his head out of the door and asked Lenore when the last time his office had been swept electronically.

"Probably about three weeks ago if memory serves," she answered.

"Hal, let's go eat some Oysters Rockefeller and talk."

After lunch the chief of the campus police was almost convinced he'd uncovered a den of mad scientists in the middle of the oldest, most prestigious university in the nation. Hal was rattled. And he didn't rattle easily. At the Bureau he'd worked on Kennedy's assassination, the KAL 007 shoot down, 9/11, and a host of other flaps.

Hal could recognize an iceberg when he saw one. It would take him a lot of digging to learn what was below the water line.

22

From Stem Cells to Mortality
December 21

"There are more things in Heaven and Earth, Horatio,
than are dreamt of in your philosophy."

Shakespeare

Colonel Solento was in a black mood. Operations in North America had been one long string of disasters. Granted, one of those disasters had worked to his advantage. Cardinal Loconi had seen to his promotion to colonel and command of the Pontifical Swiss Guard. But the continued failures to bring home the heads of Summers and Bradford cast a dark shadow over his performance since he became the OVFS Acting Number Three.

What would prevent the cardinal from deciding to do away with me? Does this call for a preemptive strike? But then what would happen to the OVFS and the handsome stipend it pays? Ah well, Loconi ought to be pleased when he hears that we have planted another bomb, this time in Bradford's Jaguar, one that can be remotely detonated at a time and place of our choosing, certainly a time when both of our target vampires are in the car.

I shall contact a wax museum artist to fabricate their two heads for Loconi's collection. He spends too much time down in that vault, fondling all those locks of vampire hair. Celibacy must do strange things to the mind. Better to be a colonel than a cleric. Far better. Colonel Solento grinned.

He would visit Tanya tonight.

Dr. Heller looked at the indoctrination forms lying on the conference table. They bore three signatures: Lamar, Morgan, and Harold Stone. He looked up at the three and at Dr. Gibson, his Operations Officer for the Harvard Vampire Resurrection Project.

"You have read the indoctrination oath and signaled your willingness to abide by its provisions." Heller pointed to the forms. "I cannot stress forcefully enough the extreme vigilance each of you must bring to bear on everything related to the HVRP. Hal, thank you for getting this room electronically swept on such short notice.

"Once you've received Wally's briefing, there's no backing out, so if anybody has any reservations, any at all, let me hear them now." For a half-dozen pulse beats, the room was deadly quiet. "Right. Wally, I want you to focus on the *what* and skip over the *how*. Any questions before we start?"

Hal had one. "Who outside the GenLab knows of the existence of this project?"

"No one. Is that a problem for you?"

"No, I was only curious."

"Okay, let's begin," Heller said. "Our goal is to find and convert vampires into normal, mortal human beings. We have a competitor—the Order of the Vampire Final Solution, OVFS—a deeply hidden component of the Roman Catholic Church. I doubt the pope even knows of the existence of this group. Their goal is to find and kill vampires. One and probably two of their targets are sitting in this room."

Hal's head snapped up, and he looked at Heller, then at Morgan and Lamar. He shook his head and frowned deeply. "I, uh, don't know what to say. You look so, so—"

"Normal?" Morgan smiled and patted his hand.

"May we proceed, or do we need to process that, Hal?"

"Go on," Hal said. "This is going to be one hell of a ride." He began tapping his pen on the pad in front of him.

Heller continued. "We also have Chief Detective Cordell Peyton trying to solve the recent crimes, all perpetrated by the OVFS and all aimed at killing Morgan. We have already begun to help him with his investigations, but he knows nothing about the real mission of the GenLab, and we intend to keep it that way.

"Our first attempt to convert—I rather like the word 'resurrect'—two vampires was an abject failure, one we've spent countless hours trying to figure out. Hal put that piece in place for us yesterday. Hal, do you want to brief that part of the story?"

Hal shuffled through his notes and began. "We have cast iron evidence that the assistant to Harvard's Director of Human Relations, Ms. Judeland Bundaeker, is an OVFS agent and wants to destroy this project. To that end she has subverted one of your lab technicians, Mr. Lawrence Ashton."

Dr. Wallace Gibson half rose from his chair. "No! Oh, my God. That explains how... and we trusted him. He was the best lab tech we had. Jamie, he had access to all our stem cells—*by himself.*"

Heller responded. "Wally, get a grip. Now that we know why our first effort failed, and who caused that failure, we can correct the problem. Our next effort will be a success. And you will make that so."

Wally sat, shaking his head and muttering. "Where are we going to get more stem cells?"

Hal resumed speaking. "But we don't want either Judeland or Lawrence to become aware they have been uncovered. We need to find who is running the OVFS and neutralize them. I'd bet the ranch the Church would close them down immediately, especially if we use a bargaining chip: we won't go public if the pontiff disestablishes the OVFS and provides adequate proof of having done so."

"Good, Hal. Thank you. Let's move on, unless there are any questions." Heller glanced around the table.

"Jamie, what happened to the subjects of your first effort?" Hal asked.

The GenLab Director's face tightened. "Hal, they died, and we had them interred in sacred ground. It was tragic and caused a great deal of emotional tumult among the GenLab staff." Morgan had become rigid, and Lamar reached over and rubbed the back of her neck for a moment.

"Did you two know them?" Hal asked.

"Yes, to an extent," Lamar answered, too quickly.

"Folks, if we don't press on, we'll be here all day," Heller said. "Wallace, give us the fifty cent briefing on vampirism and our approach to curing it."

Dr. Gibson cleared his throat. "We must start with a basic understanding that DNA is the alpha and omega of all human life, health and the evolutionary process of the individual and the human race. It is the primary ingredient of our chromosomes and carries our genetic code—the instructions required to build and maintain the human body. While vastly complicated, our study of genetic sequencing is yielding a surprising array of data on how genes act, how disease is related to genetic malfunctions, and the flip side of that coin, how we might successfully intervene, through gene splicing—some now call it gene *editing*—and related therapies, such as targeted bacterial antibiotics that act to neutralize the genetic activators that appear to initiate vampirism and other diseases.

"Of late, however, the issues of law, privacy, and ethics have come into sharp focus. We are about to enter an era where the free and unfettered pursuit of the science of genetics will no longer be either free or unfettered. Our difficulty in replacing the lost stem cells is but one example of this issue."

Dr. Gibson looked at Heller with raised eyebrows. Heller signaled him to cut it short.

"With the stakes so high as regards the study of vampirism, we may need to find ways around the new limitations, at least until we've proven our system works. We, and every genetics lab worldwide, have been, until now, freely feeding off of the cells of a poor black woman from Baltimore, Ms. Henrietta Lacks, who died in 1951—"

"Wally, while that is fascinating history, would you step up the pace, please."

"Sorry, Jamie. Yes, well. Our approach is to grow healthy genes from embryonic stem cells, and when we get a good batch, to clone it. We then splice the good clones into a given individual's genomic sequence, at precisely the right place of course, after extracting the flawed or mutated gene that is responsible for causing a person to evolve into, or continue being, a vampire.

"Finding the trigger mechanism that activates the mutant gene is high on our priority list but is not yet fully resolved. That said, we achieved a breakthrough quite recently when we found that a colony of highly specialized bacteria may actually perform that function, as a result of either the introduction of a chemical substance or an external psychological stimulus. If we can develop an anti-bacterial agent that renders the bad bacteria cluster inert, we can inoculate members of a bloodline that contains latent vampire genes, such that their trigger mechanisms never fire.

"Bottom line for us is to resurrect existing vampires and make their descendants immune to active vampirism through inoculation. Similar to what was done with polio and smallpox, actually.

"But as sometimes occurs with organ transplants, we are at risk of experiencing rejection of the replacement genes. That can lead to genetic relapse, with the attendant resurgence of vampirism. We strongly suspect, however, that if we culture stem cells from the target individual, the probability of rejection decreases sharply. Whatever Lawrence did to our stem cell cultures caused catastrophic unwinding in the first two test subjects. Jamie, I fear that Lawrence polluted all our stem cell cultures. The only safe thing for us to do is assume that's the case." Wally raised his eyebrows at Jamie.

Heller nodded. "Point well taken, Wally. That will cost us time, but we really don't have a choice. Give me an estimate of how long it will take to recover. I'll have to do some fancy footwork with our grant people to keep their mother's milk flowing. We may need a couple more PhDs to add to the staff working on diseases other than vampirism to keep our cover intact."

"Dr. Heller," Morgan began, "I think I have a way to put some of that time you need to grow new stem cells to good use. At your convenience I'd like to brief you on my idea."

Heller looked at his watch. "Give me two minutes worth now, Morgan."

She looked at Lamar, who smiled his reassurance. "I'm convinced we need to develop a program that prepares volunteers for the radical change from immortality to mortality. The conversion process—resurrection as you call it—is not just about culturing stuff in a Petri dish. We have to treat the mind, the emotions, the fears; in short, the whole human complex. In effect, we need to create a protocol for psychological purification of the volunteer before he or she receives genetic plastic surgery."

Heller looked at Wally, who gave him a thumbs up. "Brilliant. Brilliant. As obvious as the nose on your face. Morgan, you have proved why scientists need to have non-scientists leaning over their shoulders. How soon can you brief us on your program?"

"This is Tuesday. How about Friday?"

"Done. Get Lenore to put you on my calendar. You're all invited to that briefing by the way. Anything else?"

Hal leaned forward. "I think we should put a security detail around these two. You said the OVFS has made how many— four?—attempts on Morgan. They obviously don't give up easily. And the GenLab itself should be under additional protection, along with cast iron surveillance of Lawrence and Judeland. We all understand this must be a covert op. If the OVFS discovers they are being watched, they will lay low for a long time."

"We've added a security surveillance detail around Coleson Manor," Lamar said, "but they can only provide surveillance and warning until sometime around mid-January when one of their contracts ends. Then we'll get perimeter guards as well. Let's talk about that after this meeting."

"Hal, how about you getting back to me in the next day or two with a full security plan including how we should handle Detective Peyton," Jamie said.

Hal agreed.

"Remember your oaths, everybody. Not a word to anyone outside the project."

They filed out of Heller's office and quietly closed his door. Jamie began pacing, his mind a thunderstorm of fears. Absently he picked up the security forms to straighten the pile before putting them in his safe. A small envelope fell out of the stack onto the floor. He picked it up. Odd, it wasn't sealed or addressed, and there was nothing inside. Then he spotted a note, penned in juvenile handwriting, on the inside of the flap:

"Daddy Dearest: You are being watched."

23

Things that Unravel in the Night
December 21

"The past is never dead. It's not even past."

1950 play, *Requiem for a Nun*
William Faulkner

Wind shrilled outside Simon's Coffee Emporium, the kind of wind that snaps at ears and nose, stiffens the face and aches the hands. The place was packed with customers thawing out over their lattes, a good half of them operating electronic devices. The rest were talking—nobody seemed to be listening. Even Cordell was on his cell when Lamar arrived. It took more than ten minutes for Lamar to get his coffee and squeeze back to Cordell's corner table.

"Bring your lunch?" Cordell asked looking at the faded and dented lunch box, circa the 1950s, with a picture of Roy Rogers on it. Lamar set it on the floor between his shoes.

"Not likely," Lamar replied, blowing on his hot coffee. His leather gloves still felt good. "Here's to Arctic air masses." He raised his coffee, and Cordell did likewise.

"You didn't show up at the lab or at my home. Thanks." Lamar had bought a couple of donuts and shoved one over to the man opposite him.

"You trying to be funny?"

"No, but I was hungry, and they're out of my favorite bagels."

"Besides your thanks and a donut, what else have you got for me? Let's talk about this cartel of yours."

Lamar hesitated, trying to assess where Cordell was coming from. "Okay. Get out your little notebook and pen."

"You really are a charming fellow for a Harvard guy, you know that?"

"If you can keep a lid on your anger we might make some progress, Detective. You—we— are up against a dangerous group. Call it a cartel if you want. What have we got, four bodies counting the waitress you haven't found yet, the two at the hotel, the car thief?"

"A great big X is on Morgan's back, no doubt one on mine, and possibly even yours. The bad guys may have bungled a handful of attempts on Morgan, but that doesn't mean they won't come after us again." Lamar took a large bite of his donut and swilled it down with some coffee.

"Tell me again why the cartel is so hot to off you two," Cordell said, blowing on his coffee.

"This is absolutely secret, Cordell. Morgan has volunteered to undergo a test, a procedure in the GenLab. If the outcome is what we hope, we may be able to defeat a host of major diseases like MS, Lupus, hemophilia, and possibly even AIDS. If this works, some of the mega pharmacies stand to lose millions. Some others will deposit that money. They have tried to penetrate the lab and subvert its work. We're ramping up our own security, but they may be better than we are.

"But the time has come for us to land some punches rather than sit back and wait for their next one." Lamar drained his mug but didn't break eye contact with Cordell.

Cordell squinted and looked off into the mid-distance. He took several deep breaths. "I'm still listening."

"This is speculation, but I'd put money on the notion that the two dead guys from the shootout were the ones that made off with Paula. Maybe wearing a disguise or something.

"When they reported to their boss, and he found out they'd offed the wrong gal, the shooting started. Did you notice whether either of the two dead shooters had their nipples shaved off?" Lamar asked.

"Yeah, one had. Why? What does that mean?"

"That's part of the initiation into the cartel. I'm surprised the Bureau came up empty on that. I suggest you ask them to look harder for the guys with no nipples."

"College boy, are you telling me how to run my investigation? And how the hell did you know the Bureau came up empty?" Cordell brushed powdered sugar off his tie.

"Cordell, do you think you're the only one with connections?" He wasn't going to mention that Hal Stone had two old friends still working for the Bureau.

Cordell changed the subject. "We retrieved a gold ring from the pocket of one of the dead shooters. It was inscribed 'Paula & Jeff, 2010.' Jeffrey Green, a Marine staff sergeant, was killed in Afghanistan in June 2010. His folks said he'd told them he was going to marry Paula when he returned."

"Interesting." Lamar rubbed his jaw. "But we still don't know where they dumped her."

"Not yet. Any chance you're going to show me what's in your lunch pail?"

"A piece of the guy that got blown up in Morgan's car. Might help you ID him."

Cordell frowned. "Is he a cartel member?"

"No idea. Just remember, Cordell, we're not the enemy. Morgan and I want to live our lives without having to look behind every tree. We want your help in getting the cartel off our backs. And I'm willing to do anything within reason to help you nail them. We don't have to like one another, but it would help a whole lot if we could develop a little more trust. I'm certain the cartel has Morgan and me under virtually continuous surveillance. Likely they have you under surveillance as well. Maybe if you could spot them, you could begin watching the watchers."

Too many surveillance types might become a problem, Lamar thought. With Stone's crew, the "lawn care" guys we hired, the OVFS and maybe a couple of Cordell's people, they're going to start crawling up each other's rectums. If nothing else, that might spook the OVFS into making a mistake, or at least make it harder for them to operate. On the other hand, they might go to ground.

Cordell sat back and pulled out his old pack of Marlboros. He looked at it, tapped it on the table top, and put it back in his coat pocket. "So what's your best guess at a starting point?"

"I think we ought to do some trolling." Lamar glanced at a Spandex blonde sitting next to them, pecking away at her laptop.

"Meaning what, exactly?"

"We pick a target person and send him on an errand. Your guys watch to see if anybody looks like a surveillance crew. If you can stay with them, we might find their headquarters."

"Who do you suggest we pick to be the troll?"

"Me."

Morgan's back ached. She got up and walked to her office window, idly watching the people in the Yard—a bees' nest. Refilling her coffee mug, she plopped on the sofa and set her mug on the end table. It was time to prepare her presentation on the program she'd recommended to Dr. Heller. It shouldn't be too hard; she'd been thinking about it for a long time. But this morning she awakened with a new idea, one that definitely deserved a place in her curriculum. She would make it the front-end piece, and it would not only solidify for the candidates the reasons why they had signed up for Resurrection, it would also fill a void for the scientists working on the project. She would answer the question: Why would a vampire seek to become a mortal?

She and Lamar had taken for granted that the value of Vampire Resurrection would be self-evident. And while for some vampires it would be, others would have to be shown the merits of giving up their special powers and their immortality. They must be shown that life in the vampire lane was not glamorous, not self-fulfilling, and not very user friendly.

Many vampires become mortally tired of running. Running from the madding crowd—peasants with flaming torches back in medieval times—and organizations like the OVFS in modern times. Tired of always having to move on when your acquaintances and few friends aged and you didn't. And the shame and dread of the killing, even when you killed animals. Killing people, while briefly exciting, was almost always repugnant when it was over. And there was no forgiveness other than one's own. For a vampire, there is no God, no angels, no heaven to look forward to. Morals, what few there may be in a vampire's life, were purely self-made.

Love was beyond a vampire's reach with but few exceptions. Yes, there was all the sex you could want and more, but it was mechanical and sterile. For Morgan it had been, at times, a source of income when she was destitute. Still, she had been taught enough about love from Blind Gretta, from age six to thirteen, that the desire for love hovered around her like an aura.

Hiding out from the medical community was another issue. You could hardly walk through a doctor's door before he or she wanted a blood sample. And vampire blood set off every code blue alarm in the hospital. Getting a job required references. Most of Morgan's best references were dead. Besides, she looked like she was in her early thirties.

Eating normal food was a problem for vampires. Nothing tasted like much unless, of course, it was bloody. And yet if a vampire went too long without eating, he/she would regress into "the hunting time." In that mode, anything on four legs—or two— began to look enticing.

There were other problems, but those were enough to get her point across. A very few vampires had become so depressed while trapped in their existence that they committed suicide with the help of other vampires. Morgan had assisted two vampire suicides in Paris in the mid-nineteenth century, administering the Vampire Death Rites. Well, that would suffice for lesson number one.

The other lessons would involve the renunciation of the dark arts, a briefing on the risks of resurrection, meeting a board to certify that the candidate had successfully fulfilled all the curriculum requirements, wearing the ring of renunciation ... there were others.

She opened a computer file and began to hammer away at her keyboard.

Morgan reached for her phone. "Lenore? This is Morgan. The boss told me to call and get on his schedule. Anything open? Eleven fifteen would work. We'll probably need about half an hour—maybe forty-five. Okay, see you then."

Maybe I'll go for a stroll in the Yard, she thought. I need some fresh air. She was pleased with the program outline she'd prepared and hoped Dr. H. would approve it. Her mind began to skip like a stone skimmed across a still pond.

The OVFS wouldn't take a shot at me in the Yard. Too crowded. I need to find a Christmas gift for Lamar—there's a first. That old car Robert bought is perfect. Looks like hell but runs like a Swiss watch. Monty did a great job on the Jag. You can't see one dent or scrape from the explosion. Too bad it has to stay in the garage. I wonder what Robert really thinks of me, of Lamar and me? Not a happy camper. He's had Lamar to himself for years. Back when Lamar used to be a wimp. That's one positive aspect of becoming a vampire. Lamar has done a one-eighty. He's become a real take-charge guy, now. Even in bed of late. She thought about the coming weekend and smiled, sensing the warmth spreading from down there. After sixty or so years of non-use—with the exception of a few business transactions—my *place* has seriously woken up. Guess it's like riding a bicycle. And ummm, what a ride it has been.

Now if I can only get Lamar's other organ to wake up.
His heart.

24

Robert
December 22

T he housecleaners are late, Robert fumed. He despaired of the younger generation. No work ethic at all. None. The door chimes echoed through the first floor. If we had some cannon, Coleson Manor's door chimes could sound like Overture 1812, Robert grumbled. He yanked opened the door and tapped on his pocket watch.

"Traffic was a snarl, Bob," the head cleaning lady said.

He glowered. *Bob*. He loathed and despised their insolence. "I will expect you to be extra diligent to make up for your tardiness." He counted five, including the one he hadn't seen before. They all smelled like detergent.

Robert wandered into the kitchen and looked at the compact freezer unit delivered earlier that morning. How would he, Lamar, and Morgan wrestle that thing down to the secret room? He hoped the ice he'd put in the two containers would hold up until Lamar and Morgan returned.

They told me to get the Jaguar repaired at a disreputable body shop, then buy a used clunker for them to drive to work, hire a security firm, oil the gun collection, and buy a freezer to keep two severed heads from rotting. Lamar's father, God rest his soul, must be spinning in his grave.

And, there is dinner to be reckoned with. Robert, who had once served as a professional chef, was disgusted over the Coleson Manor cuisine of late. What does she want to eat? Pizza. The refrigerator is filled with frozen dinners. Besides, she eats like a bird. And she has Lamar on the pointy end of a skewer from the sounds that emanate from the bedroom. The day will come when Lamar will give me notice. And then what? He can't change the trust fund that provides me a most comfortable living, but I've lived in Coleson Manor for a good thirty-six years. There is something about that woman. She belongs in the codex, not in Coleson Manor, but I still need to gain her confidence.

It was way too early, but he needed a drink. Robert walked briskly to the library. One of the cleaning ladies, the new one, jumped back from the desk. "Just what are you doing opening Mr. Bradford's desk, young lady?"

"The drawer was open. I was closing it, sir."

"Out. The library is not to be plundered."

"Yes, sir." She bolted for the door.

Robert looked down at the desk and found one drawer wedged open by the codex. He locked the library door and took the codex back to its original hiding place behind the encyclopedia. He would put it in the secret room as soon as they left. And call the cleaning service and ensure that woman never returned to Coleson Manor. Was her interest in the codex more than mere curiosity? He pulled out his key ring and walked to the gun locker behind a panel of fake books. The feel of the loaded Colt, snub-nose .38 revolver under his waistcoat provided a sense of renewed authority, even if it was contrived. He sighed as he pulled the check registry from its drawer in the desk. Good time to pay the bills.

But he found it hard to concentrate. *My sworn duty—sacred mission—is to protect Lamar from the scourge of his sickness, to the extent that's possible. Inserting the GPS chip in his watch had been a genuine inspiration. It certainly helped me find him in the alley the night he had his first vampire episode, though the watch was broken by the time I arrived.* He decided to call MaidPro Housecleaning before paying the bills. He would also confer with Nancy, head of the cleaning crew, about replacing the new girl.

Ah, Nancy. An unconscionable indiscretion. How could he have been so stupid? Now she calls me "Bob." It had been a long time though. He studied himself in the hall mirror. Not bad. Hard to tell he was eleven years older than Nancy, who was just forty-nine. He patted his tummy. Got to watch that. There was still a good draft in the old flue, he thought, smiling briefly as he recalled servicing Nancy. *Right and proper job of it, I must admit. And she said as much.* He turned his head one way and the other admiring the gray on the sides. Dignified. Just what the proper batman should have.

By mid-afternoon the cleaning crew had departed, he'd called MaidPro, his wonton soup and spring roll were finished, the dishes cleaned and put away. Ah, a bowl of pipe tobacco would be in order, he thought. And a glass of port. Where had he hidden that novel? Thankfully, Lamar had not discovered he was a closet Tom Clancy fan.

The hour spent reading, sipping his wine, puffing on his Dunhill bulldog, filled with his personal blend of Virginia Black Cavendish and burley, was exceptionally civilized. He breathed in the scent of old leather-bound books and pipe tobacco. Excellent. Calvin and Oxnard had squeezed into the bookshelves for a nap, and one of them was purring softly. He looked around. Coleson Manor's library would serve handsomely as a setting for a Sherlock Holmes mystery—or better yet, a Bella Lugosi horror film. His smile was sardonic. His thoughts drifted like the smoke from his pipe, and he dozed off.

Sometime later he was jolted awake, knocking his pipe onto the carpet. "Damn and blast." He picked up the pipe and slipped out of the library, his senses alert. Nothing. This would be a good time to take the codex down to the secret room. He retrieved it and a flashlight before opening the door behind the tall-case clock. Leaving the lights off, he closed the panel door after entering.

When he reached the room he flashed his light around. He tried to put the codex in the desk, but the desk drawer was too small. As he was scanning the room for an alternate place, he heard a noise. It sounded like the panel door opening. Listening intently, he pulled the .38 and aimed it at the opening along with the flashlight beam.

The flash preceded the report. The sound reached him a millisecond after the bullet. He pitched back, firing as he fell. His head bounced on the floor, and his reality dissolved into a black void.

Old Oxidation, as Morgan had named their backup car, pulled into the driveway. They were both tired after their workout at the Harvard fitness center. As they walked to the front door the automatic lights came on. "What's that?" Lamar asked, pointing.

"My God. It's the codex. And it's covered with blood," Morgan said, her voice rising.

"Robert," Lamar shouted, fumbling with the key. The front door was unlocked and swung open. Lamar called out again. "Search the library, and be careful. I'll take the kitchen." He had only run a few steps when he called Morgan back. "Look." He pointed to the secret door, which was partially open, smeared with a bloody hand print. Looking back, a trail of drops led over the Persian runner in the hall, all the way to the front door. Lamar ignored the familiar blood-induced sensations as he raced to the kitchen pantry where several flashlights were kept and grabbed two, handing one to Morgan.

"Go get a gun, Lamar."

Lamar dashed into the library, found his key to the gun case, opened the fake book panel and unlocked the case. The .38 Detective Special was gone. He grabbed his father's old Army Colt .45 semiautomatic, checked the magazine—it was full—and chambered a round, then ran back to Morgan. "Hear anything?"

"Nothing."

Using their flashlights, they walked down the passage, Lamar in the lead. The door to the secret room stood open. A dim streak from a flashlight lit an anemic swath across the floor.

Morgan found a lantern and lit it.

Robert lay on his back, the revolver still in his hand. His flashlight, nearly spent, had rolled a few feet to his left. Morgan felt for a pulse and leaned down to check his breathing. "Slow pulse but steady and reasonably strong," she said. Lamar unbuttoned Robert's vest and pulled up his shirt, exposing an entrance wound.

"Probably some internal bleeding, but if an artery had been severed he would likely be dead by now," Morgan said. "Look at his flashlight. This must have happened several hours ago." She examined the back of his head. "Just as I thought. He banged his head hard when he fell. Probably has a serious concussion. Maybe even a fractured skull. We have to get medical help fast. I don't know why he hasn't gone into shock yet."

Morgan grabbed her cell phone from its holster, but could get no signal. As she turned to run up the passage, Lamar grabbed her arm. "Wait. What about those?" He pointed to the two carrying cases jammed under the desk.

"Crap. I'll call 911. You add ice and put them in the Jag's trunk till we can think of a better place. We'll have to carry him upstairs and scrub the blood off the wall so the first responders won't learn about the secret room. I'll be right back." She ran up the passage as Lamar sprinted for the kitchen with the two heads.

Morgan and Lamar drove behind the ambulance to Mass General. The two hours they spent in the waiting room had been grueling. One family had been told their grade school son had an incurable disease. Another child, with her hand wrapped in a bloody T-shirt, howled continuously with pain and fright. A street person, probably drunk, snored through the bedlam. Finally a doctor, dressed in green surgical scrubs, came out.

"Are you related to Robert Diamond?" Both said yes.

"Walk with me down the hall. I can't compete with all that," he gestured at the waiting room. The doctor looked exhausted, his bedside manner totally abandoned. When they arrived at a window at the end of the hall, he stopped and faced them. "Diamond was shot with a .32 caliber weapon. The slug missed anything vital, but we had to go in and get it out and tidy up the wound. The surgery is not the problem. When he fell he landed hard on his head and has a fractured skull and a severe concussion. We've sedated him and plan to keep him under for a couple of days, maybe three, to allow the brain to recover slowly from the trauma. So he can't be visited, and he can't be interrogated by the police for at least three more days. He'll be in the hospital for about a week to ten days, possibly longer if he has any complications.

"Let's hope the knock on his head didn't erase some of his current memory. That's not too uncommon, although in many cases it gradually returns. Anyway, the bullet we dug out of him has to go to police ballistics. Any questions?"

"Did he say anything at all?" Lamar asked.

"He said something about *heads,* but it is common for someone who has suffered brain trauma to be inarticulate or even nonsensical."

"That's it—nothing else?" Lamar asked. The doctor shook his head.

"Will he recover?" Morgan asked.

"Yes, I think so. We should know more in a day or two."

"Thank you, doctor, for all you have done." Lamar shook his hand.

As he turned to walk away, the doctor added, "No sense to visit for the next two or three days unless it makes you feel better. He won't be communicating with anyone."

Morgan took hold of Lamar's forearm and steered him toward an exit. "We need to get home and clean the place before the police show up. And when did Heller say he was coming to look at the codex?"

"Maybe we should get Cordell and his lab techs in to get a sample of the shooter's blood before we scour it all away." Lamar hunched as the cold wind assaulted them.

"Better yet, let's get some samples and hold them as bargaining chips." Morgan opened the door to Old Oxidation and got behind the wheel. Lamar got in and sighed.

"We don't want the police rummaging around in the secret room," Morgan said.

"Just what we need. Another OVFS hit man. We have to figure out how he got in. Robert is scrupulous about keeping the doors locked, and when he's alone he usually keeps the alarm on," Lamar said.

"Who had access to the house today?" Morgan asked. "And why was Robert armed?"

"Let me see. The guys who delivered the freezer, I guess. Oh, and today is the regularly scheduled weekly house cleaning. Bunch of women. Been coming for years. Robert keeps an eye on them."

"My guess is that the assailant was wounded in an exchange of shots. You did notice that Robert had fired once?"

"Uh, I guess I was a tad preoccupied."

Morgan rolled her eyes. "Maybe Robert had decided to hide the codex in the secret room. Probably got the idea when we told him we would haul the freezer unit down there. By the way, Lamar, does the secret room have an electrical outlet?" Lamar shrugged. Morgan glared at him and continued. "The shooter must have followed him down. They exchanged shots, the wounded bad guy grabbed the codex and fled but was too badly hit to hang onto it. We should get Cordell to check all the hospitals and morgues."

"You'd make a good detective, Morgan. I'll call Cordell. Time we meet for some more coffee."

"I ought to rent some office space in this coffee shop," Cordell said as Lamar got to the table. "You always work this late?" He looked at his watch, which read ten forty-one.

"Did you get anything from the hand?" Lamar asked

"Yeah. Fingerprints. The guy was a two-bit car thief. Been in and out of detention for the past ten years. Too stupid to be one of your cartel guys."

Lamar shook his head as he draped his coat and scarf over an empty chair and sat down. "I was hoping the bad guys had lost their ace bomb maker. I guess the Bureau didn't get any hits on the cartel with no nipples?"

"Nothing worth writing home about, no."

"I have something new for you. The cartel sent someone to our house this afternoon. My butler, Robert Diamond, surprised the intruder, and they had a quick shootout."

Cordell was already writing in his notebook. He looked up. "Does your butler always carry a weapon while he's in the house?"

"Not normally. He must have heard something or become suspicious for some reason and pulled a revolver out of our gun case."

"You're gonna tell me all these guns are registered, right?" "Absolutely. The Bradfords have always been law-abiding citizens."

"But you hang around with some that aren't. Kind of makes you an accessory."

"The hit on Robert kind of makes me want to *kill* someone, Detective. Has your surveillance turned up anything? Ours hasn't."

"Yeah, another set of good guys doing surveillance. Your friendly campus cops. So now we're time sharing. You could have told me about them—what's all this big talk about trust mean?" Cordell shrugged into his topcoat, as did Lamar.

"Cordell, I'm not in the mood to spar with you. I just left Mass General where my valet had an operation to remove a bullet from his gut. He got off one shot and hit the assailant, who bled on the way out the door and all over the codex. He was apparently hit too bad to carry the codex, because we found it on the front porch. My man, Diamond, is heavily sedated." Lamar told Cordell everything the doctor had said as they walked to their cars.

"Has Mass General sent the slug to us yet?"

"How the hell should I know? Oh, I almost forgot. I brought you a sample of the assailant's blood. You didn't return my lunch box so it's wrapped in a Ziploc baggie." Lamar fished it out of his overcoat pocket and handed it to Cordell.

"Any sign of a break-in?"

"No, but maybe it was an inside job. That's what Morgan thinks. Could have been either one of the delivery guys or one of the cleaning girls that hid out till everybody was gone."

"Give me the names and organizations." Cordell stopped in front of his car, poised over his notebook.

"The two guys were from Sears. I'll phone you the order number on the freezer we had delivered. You can take it from there. The MaidPro Housecleaning Service has been sending a cleaning crew for years, since the early 1990s. They showed up today, as far as I know. On the rare occasions they can't make it they call to reschedule. Unfortunately, we can't ask Robert. Not for a few days, anyway. Maybe even a week or two, worst case."

"Have you talked to your lawn care surveillance guys? They should have picked up something."

Lamar shrugged. "Not yet."

Cordell's cell vibrated. "Peyton here. Yeah, where? Put a guard on the room. I'm on my way." He opened his car door.

Lamar raised his eyebrows.

"Mass General just took in a woman in her thirties with a gunshot wound. She's a bleeder. They've pumped in four pints so far."

"And?"

"She was wearing a MaidPro uniform."

25

Judeland
December 22

Lawrence blew out a breath and watched the gray "smoke" dissipate. He jammed his hands deeper in his jacket pockets. He hated the cold. Hated the sound of people a couple blocks away singing Christmas carols. But he hated Christmas even more. Growing up was the shits at Christmas, especially with an alcoholic mom. She got a bottle of gin to open on Christmas morning. Pop got a humidor filled with cheap cigars, which he chained smoked all day. I got a fruitcake, or the equivalent. One Christmas they forgot to get me anything at all. I was almost sixteen. So I took the TV apart and tried to put it back together. Lawrence chuckled. Took them two or three days to notice the TV wasn't working. They finally called somebody.

Boy was he baffled. That was some real grins.

"Where'd you buy this set?" the service tech asked my mom.

"How the hell should I know," she said and weaved into another room, reeking as usual.

But the day came when I could put one together from stuff I pilfered from parts bins and scavenged from landfills plus the one I stole. Two more blocks to Judeland's place; I better slow down some. Glad I left my wheels about six blocks back—I sure as hell don't want anybody to spot it anywhere near her place.

Never been in her condo. Why the hell couldn't she just hand me an envelope with the money, like the first time? She's got something up her sleeve—or up her panties. The thought was at once repulsive and exciting. "Crap," he said. Christmas lights were draped around bushes, doors, and the trees inside many of the houses he passed. Some were flashing on and off. Damn waste of electricity. He paused at her door. At least she doesn't have any colored lights hanging all over the place.

Lawrence—he never thought of himself as Larry and hated the nickname, especially when his mother used it—stood in front of her door. He breathed in, held it, then out, watching his breath. Maybe he'd buy a pair of gloves. And a hat. Gets too damn cold in Cambridge. The door opened before he could bring himself to knock.

"Come in young man, you'll freeze standing out there." She was wearing a purple satiny kind of thing with a sash around her waist and matching slippers. He'd never seen her hair down that way, and she had on eye shadow, lipstick, and perfume.

Enough to make a grown man puke, he thought. "I'll take your jacket and hang it in the closet."

"Oh, I don't want to take up too much of your time. If you want to hand me the envelope I could—"

"Nonsense. Your hands are like icicles. Besides, you need to relax. See, I've got the fireplace turned on. Sit while I go get some goodies."

She looks worse when she tries to smile. Bad teeth. Five minutes. Ten at the most.

As soon as she left he stood and wandered around, looking at things. He picked up a book from a side table next to a chair near the fireplace. *Midnight in the Garden of Good and Evil.* He didn't read stuff like that. Years ago he'd bought *Zen and the Art of Motorcycle Maintenance* but never got around to reading it. The other book on the reading stand was titled *Fore Play.* The jacket said it was "The best anthology of erotic romance in 2010." He wondered what foreplay was.

Judeland returned in a couple minutes with a platter of pigs in a blanket and a shaker of vodka martinis. When she bent over to place them on the coffee table he could see she wasn't wearing anything under the slinky purple thing. At least on top. And probably not the bottom either, he bet. Wish she had some cold beer. I don't like cocktails much. The martini tastes pretty good, though. Kind of limey. The pigs had some cheese and a drop of fancy mustard on 'em, and they were pretty good, too.

She sat on the sofa next to him and crossed her legs. Nice legs. She allowed the folds of her slinky thing to pull back even more. Sort of reminded him of the pole dancers he'd seen in Atlantic City at some dive he and his only high school buddy had gone to a few days after they graduated. I wouldn't call Judeland stacked by any means, but I wouldn't mind taking another look at her boobs, either.

This damn drink is making me light headed. Better slow down.

"Lawrence, do you like movies?"

"Yeah, I guess. I don't go to very many, though. I don't go out all that much." Not a lot of fun by yourself. Better to watch football on TV and scarf up a few beers. She walked over to the TV, which was set to play a DVD.

"Wow," he exclaimed. A woman named Bree Olson, clad in nothing but a G-string, filled the screen. The DVD, made by *Adam and Eve,* was called *Bree and Thee.* Within two minutes she was getting it on with some six-pack abs stud. Judeland untied her sash, snuggled over against him and began to rub his thigh. So he began to rub hers, and that's when the slinky thing pulled all the way back. Lawrence took a long swig of his drink, his eyes pin-balling between the action on the TV and Judeland's "charms," as his mom occasionally referred to a woman's female parts.

By the second scene, Judeland had his shirt and undershirt off, his belt open, button undone, and zipper down. He gasped as her hand slid beneath his underpants. By now, he was fully erect, and his attention was fixed on the woman beside him instead of the one on the big screen. She took his hand and guided it to her boobs, which seriously got his attention.

Lawrence was almost a virgin. He'd lost his cherry at a wild party he'd attended in an auto body shop over a year ago. The owner, a guy named Monty, had lined up some girls who were of "easy virtue," as his mom would say. He'd gotten laid twice that night with two different girls. Best damn party he'd ever been to. But when I stopped by the shop a week later, Monty had no idea who I was, and it was obvious he wasn't interested in finding out. A real creep.

"Bring your drink and follow me, Lawrence." By then she was only wearing her slippers; he still wore his white gym socks.

Wish I'd worn the pair that didn't have any holes.

"Put your drink on the night stand. Can I pour you another one?"

"No, thanks."

She patted the side of the bed. He sat and quickly pulled off his socks and pitched them some distance away so the holes wouldn't be so obvious. He was aware of an all music radio station, turned low, and the scent of lavender that was a bit too strong for his liking, but the thought was fleeting.

"I want you to give me a massage first." She indicated a bottle of massage oil on the opposite nightstand. She lay face down, head on a pillow, legs spread wide.

Damn, she doesn't have any hair *down there*. Wonder how you massage a girl? Still, how hard can it be? He smirked at his own pun and poured some oil on her back and started rubbing.

"Umm, that feels good. I'll bet you do this for all your girlfriends."

"Oh, yeah." He almost laughed. After her back he did her bottom and both legs, and with each stroke he came closer to her place. He was surprised when she rolled over.

"Now you can do the front side."

Lawrence was grinning like a kid at Christmas—any kid except himself. He noticed how her nipples got hard as he massaged her boobs. And how he got harder. And how she wiped oil off of her stomach and put it on his schlong.

"Now, Lawrence. Inside. Now."

He pushed into her and both of them groaned. He immediately started to plunge in and out.

"No," she gasped. "Slow down. Be still or you'll come too soon." She wrapped her arms and legs around him and held him tightly. "Breathe, Larry, my pet."

"I'm not *Larry,* and I'm not your damn pet." He resumed thrusting hard, hammering her, hearing her grunt each time he plunged in. He liked her grunting.

"You're hurting me. Be gentle. Stop. Stop it!"

"I'll teach you, you bitch." His thrusts became even more violent.

As he pulled back for another thrust, Judeland twisted with a surge of explosive strength. The two rolled off the bed, sweeping the lamp, an electric clock and two glasses of vodka onto the rug. The two landed hard on the tangled wreckage, Lawrence on the bottom. He screamed as shards of glass bit into his back. Reflexively, he arched his back to relieve the pain only to have more broken glass slice into his shoulders.

"Ahh. God dammit, get off," he yelled.

But Judeland's consciousness burst open, revealing a new world. She could taste his fear and pain, feel a surge of joy, blended with hate and anger. And lifelong abandonment. She wrenched the broken lamp base out from under him and smashed it on his forehead with all her newfound strength. Blood poured over his face and onto her hands and forearms. It was so warm, with a tang she'd never experienced. It felt rich and silky. Even in the dark she could tell his blood was beautiful. And delicious.

She bit into his forehead. All the rejection, all the loneliness, all the sexless nights, all the loss, all the disconnection from life engulfed her in a consuming rage.

Judeland died. But then who was left? She would have to find out.

"Jamie, dearest, wouldn't you like to know your own flesh and blood before she drinks yours?" she said. It was all right. No one could hear her. Not now.

Tonight. Ah tonight, she thought dreamily as she wandered into the kitchen for a butcher knife.

"911? Please send someone right away. Screaming. Something terrible is going on next door. I think she's being raped or killed. Hurry!" Judeland's next door neighbor raced back to the kitchen window, which was open just enough for her to hear.

26

Slaughter House
December 22

"Never in the Course of Vampire History has
so much blood been owed by so many to so few."

Winston Churchill
during World War II (as amended)

D etective Peyton? This is Charlie Poston at precinct. You weren't planning to spend Christmas with your family I don't suppose?"

"I already don't want to hear this, but go ahead."

"We got a slaughterhouse at a condo at 287 Harvard Street off the square. Your two detectives are already en route, along with the mobile crime lab and a photographer. One dead, all carved into pieces, blood everywhere and the perp no longer on the premises."

"Fuck. On my way."

"Cordell, not another one?" Barbara stood up, her face showing the pain of another beautiful evening ruined. It was Christmas week. The tree lights and a couple of candles cast a warm glow throughout their living room. Both boys were asleep. Two half-full glasses of wine on the coffee table marked the beginning of a special evening.

"I'll try to get back before the meat is burned," he said, shrugging into his topcoat.

"Here, at least take this." Barbara wound a muffler around his neck and kissed him. "I'll keep the meat warm." Her eyes were laughing as she said it. Cordell patted her bottom and grabbed his keys, wallet, and shoulder holster with his nine-millimeter Sig Sauer. He saw her wave as his tires screeched.

Flossie was on her second glass of wine and into her favorite show on Public Television, *Downton Abbey,* season two, when the doorbell rang. She was wearing a comfortable old terrycloth bathrobe and slippers, and looked disgusted as she muted the TV. "Who is it?" she called.

"Just Judeland." Her voice sounded as if she had been drinking.

Flossie unlocked the door and opened it. Her eyes widened. "*Judeland.* What's happened to you? Have you been in an accident? Come in quickly, don't stand out in the hall. How did this happen? Were you assaulted? Where's your coat?"

Judeland started to answer, and a trickle of blood dripped from her mouth to her chin and onto the carpet. "I think I have a problem." She swayed, and Flossie grabbed her. "Something strange has happened to me, and I didn't have anyone to turn to. I'm sorry."

"My God, Judeland. Come with me to the bathroom, and let's get you cleaned up. Are you injured anywhere? Your clothes are covered with—"

"No, I'm not injured." Flossie cringed at her hideous smile.

"Let's get you to the bathroom and out of these clothes and into the shower if you promise me you're not injured."

"No, I'm all right. Well, almost. I think. Maybe not so much."

Flossie got the shower going, helped Judeland undress and resisted the questions that frothed like boiling soup when she saw a multitude of bruises around her pubic area. "I've got another bathrobe. You stand under the shower and scrub hard with soap. I'll be right back."

"Campus Unit One to Control. Target entered 287 Harvard Street and did not come out. About fifty-seven minutes later a woman, possibly the owner of the condo, Judeland Bundaeker, exited. We tracked her to the residence of Ms. Florence Senger. Both remain in Ms. Senger's quarters. Suggest backup personnel enter Ms. Bundaeker's condo and investigate. Over."

"Stay fixed on the Senger quarters, and keep reporting at frequent intervals. Should they drive off, track 'em. Backup on the way to enter the Bundaeker residence. Out."

"George, get this message off to Stone on the double. He's at home. Read it back to me."

"*Urgent.* Target tracked to the Bundaeker residence. Hasn't come out, but owner has. Sound track badly garbled but suggests foul play. Owner has exited, and we tracked to a condo belonging to Ms. Florence Senger. Suggest you report to central ASAP. Out."

"Right. Go!"

Flossie bundled Judeland's blood-soaked housecoat and slippers into a garbage bag and placed it next to her washing machine. She grabbed two glasses, filled them with wine, found the other bathrobe and turned off the TV before Judeland finished her shower. She listened outside the bathroom door for a moment then slipped in and hung the bathrobe on the back of the door. Judeland was leaning against the shower stall, silhouetted in the steaming water.

"You okay, Jude?"

Judeland jerked away from the wall and turned the water off. "Do you have a spare toothbrush?"

"I'll leave one on the sink next to the toothpaste and mouthwash. I've got some wine poured for us. Are you woozy?"

"No. I'll be out in a few minutes."

Flossie closed the door and sat on the sofa. When Judeland appeared Flossie patted the sofa. "Sit. I have a blow dryer under the bathroom sink."

Judeland's hair was wet and stringy, though she had made a half-hearted effort to dry it with the towel. She reached for her glass and drained half of it. "Thank you, Flossie. You are being so kind. And I don't deserve it." Her head drooped.

"Of course you do. What are friends for?" The words sounded hollow as she said them.

240

Flossie had maintained a somewhat relaxed but formal distance from Judeland. Something about her always puts me on guard, she thought. Hiring her had been a special favor to Ed Hemming, a man she had dated when they were undergrads at Harvard. Pity he took the cloth. He had fallen from grace at least once while in divinity school. She smiled at the memory. Father Hemming was trying to lead Judeland back to the Church when he asked me to hire her.

"So. Why don't you start at the beginning." Flossie topped up Judeland's glass and sat back.

Tears glistened in Judeland's eyes. "That's the problem. I don't quite know what happened. Someone knocked on my door. I thought it was going to be some more Christmas carolers, but it wasn't." She gulped several swallows of wine.

"Best you slow down on the wine. I'll fix us something to eat after you finish telling me about tonight." Flossie adjusted her glasses and frowned at Judeland.

"He kind of pushed his way in."

"Is this someone you know?"

"We've met. He works for Dr. Heller."

"Can you tell me his name?"

"Um, I can't think of it right now. Maybe it will come to me later." She swallowed more wine. "I offered him coffee and snacks but told him I wasn't feeling well, and he'd have to leave. But he didn't."

This is turning into a fairy tale, Flossie thought. "So then what did he do?"

"He said he wanted to see the rest of my condo. I told him that would be okay if he came back some other time. Some other time, I told him. But he laughed and walked into the, into my bedroom." A tear trickled down her cheek, and she swiped at it with the back of her hand.

"Go on."

"I can't remember much else except that he hurt me. Hurt me a lot. I had to protect myself."

The phone in the kitchen rang and both women jumped. Flossie answered.

"Flossie? This is Hal Stone, Chief of Campus Police. Are you alone?"

"No."

"Is it Judeland?"

"Yes."

"We'll be knocking on your door shortly. We think she is completely unstable. Don't challenge her in any way. She may be dangerous."

Resisting the panic that surged through her, Flossie forced a smile. "Blanche, I appreciate your call, but I have company. Let's finish this conversation tomorrow, okay?"

"Well done, Flossie. See you in a few minutes." She hung up, smiled, and walked back to the sofa, her whole body tense. "That Blanche is a real talker. Now, where were we?"

"I need a few breaths of fresh air."

"I'm not surprised. Follow me. I have a small balcony that will serve, although it's a bit brisk out." Flossie started walking toward the sliding glass door. When she looked back she saw Judeland walk into the kitchen. Moments later she emerged with a butcher knife.

Flossie's eyes widened as Judeland walked toward her, lips pulled back, her face a grotesque mask. Flossie's hands closed around the back of a chair in the breakfast nook.

Judeland raised the butcher knife. Flossie screamed.

27

Butcher Knife
December 22

"The triumph of Evil is assured if good vampires do
nothing."

Author, October 7, 2014

Judeland's maniacal laugh almost punctured the surveillance man's eardrums, and he swept the headset off. "George, it's another killing. Get in there quick as you can."

George burst out of the van door and sprinted to the building entrance. The door required someone to answer the buzzer. He buzzed for the building manager but waited for no more than a few seconds before drawing his automatic. The surveillance operator in the van sent a red alert to the campus police headquarters: "Murder in progress. Need help fast. Unit Two."

Judeland was on a blood high and had reverted into the full vampire hunting mentality. In front of her stood another feast. As she lunged with the knife Flossie raised the chair, partially deflecting the blow, but it bit deeply into her forearm on the downward stroke. Flossie brought the chair down on Judeland's head with all her fear-driven strength. Her attacker fell and lay still as Flossie's blood pooled on the floor inches from the inert figure. She was hyperventilating and dizzy, and her ears felt like they were stuffed with cotton. She heard a man shouting, but he sounded so far away.

Judeland sprang at her as if fired from a circus cannon. The sound of gunfire—three quick shots—didn't distract either the vampire or her intended victim. Flossie backed into the balcony door knob. She turned and yanked the door open, slamming it in the vampire's face. Judeland rocked backward for a moment, the bloody knife still raised for another strike. Flossie grabbed a balcony chair and jammed it against the door, frantically looking for a weapon or a way out. The balcony was on the fourth floor.

Flossie grabbed the other chair as the vampire burst through the door and hurled it.

Judeland ducked, and it sailed over the railing, clattering when it hit the ground.

Judeland, her face a rictus of evil, eyes glowing, took two deliberate steps toward Flossie, who climbed over the railing, prepared to jump. Almost in slow motion she saw the knife raised to the highest arc of its intended strike. "*Dear God, receive me with grace,*" she implored a second before a shot pitched Judeland forward, the knife hurtling into the darkness.

Flossie lost her balance. She frantically grabbed for the railing, but her throbbing arm and numb fingers made the arm useless. George lunged for her, dropping his weapon as he pulled her over the railing and back onto the balcony. Half conscious, Flossie's legs buckled. She fell, her face inches from George's automatic. The smell of gunpowder acted as an astringent, and she reached for it, but another hand snatched it away.

Before Judeland could fire the weapon, George kicked it out of her hand. It slid under the railing to the edge, paused, and then disappeared. Judeland was off balance as George rammed into her like the Penn State lineman he had once been. She cartwheeled over the banister and fell.

"Ahhh." It was a short, sharp cry, followed by a thump. Then silence.

Breathing heavily, George turned to Flossie who sat back against the railing, her arm still bleeding profusely.

"My name's George."

"Oh, God, George," Flossie rasped before her eyes glazed, and she sagged onto the balcony floor.

George carried Flossie into the living room and put her on the sofa, using a dish towel as a tourniquet. As he tied off the tourniquet, George became aware of sirens that sounded as if they were converging from every point of the compass. Local, county, and state law enforcement officers ran into the condo. A SWAT team in full combat gear surrounded the building. Search lights illuminated the balcony and the bushes below it. George heard one officer say the 911 system had jammed, and that a hook and ladder truck couldn't get any closer than four blocks. The rescue squad vehicle got no closer than three.

Intense arguments over jurisdiction began to get ugly. Civilian dogs were barking by the score, while police dogs sniffed the grounds. Two TV crews frantically set up and began interviewing just outside the police-taped perimeter. Local news broadcasters were interrupted and handed new scripts.

It took Cordell twenty minutes to badger his way into Flossie's apartment. The crowd of onlookers doubled every five minutes, and nearly all of them had a phone with a camera. A teenager's video, showing a teetering Flossie and seconds later a body hurled off the balcony, was already going viral in Cambridge and would soon crisscross the nation.

Cordell, Hal Stone, the Cambridge chief of police, the fire chief, and others surrounded a beleaguered George, who was telling his story for the third time.

"She must have been wearing body armor 'cause I shot her in the back," George said, for the third or fourth time.

Flossie, sedated, was dimly aware that a first responder was working on her arm. He put something on it that burned like hell, but she didn't really care. She watched him disinfect and bind her wound to staunch the bleeding and wondered what all the commotion was about, moments before slipping into blissful oblivion.

Goddamn, he wanted a cigarette. Cordell poured another cup of stale coffee. Too tired to feel the caffeine jolt, his chin sagged onto his chest and his bloodshot eyes closed. He had talked to the governor at two a.m. and all but promised him they would find Judeland's body by the time he was having his ham and eggs. It was three thirty in the morning, and the police dogs still hadn't found it.

The nightly news was shrill: "Woman assaults her boss with a butcher knife for no apparent reason. Sources name the assailant as Judeland Bundaeker. Possibly high on PCP. Or had they quarreled? Had Ms. Senger fired her subordinate that morning? As they struggled, Harvard's Director of Human Resources was badly sliced by her knife-wielding assailant and may have nearly bled out as first responders shot their way into her apartment. One witness speculated that she might require stitches the whole length of her arm.

The gunfire terrified neighbors who called 911 by the score, jamming the local system. The two combatants spilled out onto the balcony, ten stories above the ground. As the assailant was about to pitch her boss over the railing, she was shot in the back by an armed member of Harvard's campus police, one George Henderson, a former Delta Force NCO, who has been on the campus police force for over five years and is licensed to carry a sidearm.

"The assailant then attacked and wounded Sergeant Henderson and disarmed him. Just as Ms. Bundaeker was about to throw Ms. Senger off the balcony Mr. Henderson pitched Ms. Bundaeker over the railing and grabbed Ms. Senger just before she would have fallen to her death.

"Yes, TV viewers, Cambridge has a new hero. But no one can find the assailant's body! Mr. Henderson's weapon was lost during the struggle and hasn't been found. Dr. Senger, Human Resources Director at Harvard had hired Ms. Bundaeker. Dr. Senger is in guarded but stable condition at an unidentified hospital. Flossie, as almost everyone calls her, lost copious quantities of blood during the fight, and is currently under police protection."

Cordell groaned, loud and long. For the hundred and thirty-seventh time the phone rang. "Cordell here." His voice was guttural. Forget the cigarette, he needed a large drink.

"Are you all right?" Barbara asked. "Can't you come home and get some sleep?"

"Hell, why not? They'll have my badge in a couple of days. Maybe I can get a job with the campus police. See you in thirty.

And have a very large glass of JD Black, lots of ice, no water, waiting outside the front door." He hung up and turned to Mac.

"I'm going home."

28

Trolling
December 2

"We have met the enemy, And they is us."

Pogo comic strip, circa 1950s

Calvin sat at the top of the stairs, growling. Oxnard was weaving between Lamar's legs, trying his best to trip his master, who waited impatiently for Morgan at the bottom of the stairs. It wasn't like her to be late for anything. He was about to shout for her to hurry up when she came bounding down, wearing her fanny pack.

"You're going armed?"

"If we're going trolling for bad guys don't you think that's a good idea? You should do the same."

"I still don't want you going with me. You're the most stubborn vampire I've ever met. This is supposed to be a surveillance run, not the invasion of Normandy."

Morgan grinned. "And how many vampires have you met? Lamar, I've been doing the back alley thing for over three hundred years. Now go get some artillery, and let's get going. We don't want to screw up the plan by being late to the rendezvous."

Lamar shook his head as he grumbled into the library, coming out with the .45 Colt. He would have rather had the .38 revolver, but that was in police custody, thanks to Robert's shootout. She'll be proud of me when I tell her I brought an extra magazine, he thought. She wasn't impressed.

"Just one?"

"Good grief. Should I go back for a tommy gun?"

Morgan ignored his retort. "It will be good to go in the Jag. The bad guys will probably be looking for Old Oxidation, and maybe we'll see them before they get a make on us. Besides, if we're going trolling we might as well do it in comfort." Morgan changed subjects. "Are the two carrying cases still in the trunk? Did you repack them with ice?"

"Yes and yes. Tomorrow we pick up the cornerstone at Woodlawn Memorial in Everett, transfer our friends into the cornerstone, seal it, and then deliver it to Father Hemming. He's supposed to have workmen standing by to cement it into the church's foundation, where the new Lady Chapel is to be built. A flawless plan, don't you think?"

"I've learned there's no such thing as a flawless plan. Does Father Hemming know about the two heads inside the cornerstone?"

"Dr. Heller was supposed to tell him, although I can't imagine the good father agreeing to that. Still, for total funding on the new chapel maybe he's prepared to look the other way. Don't say anything."

Morgan laughed and kissed him.

"What was that for?" Lamar was obviously startled.

"That was for last night."

"I'll never understand women, especially vampire women."

Morgan's smile faded. "What worries me is that Judeland is out there looking for another victim. She's likely still on the hunt. I'm glad Cordell moved Flossie to a safe house, but how safe is it? I'd give a lot to know who all is on Judeland's hit list. It has to include Heller and the two of us, not to mention the whole Genetics Lab."

Lamar motioned her to hurry. "Come on, we can talk in the car." They walked past the freezer, which was still in its crate.

Campus Police Chief Harold Stone reviewed his notes, the ones he would use when he briefed Jamie and his people that afternoon. He was pumped. In an hour the trolling operation would begin—a bit like the good old days. He was quietly proud of his department's two mobile intercept vans. They had proved beneficial for training a small squad of campus police officers as well as students in the university intelligence and security curricula. Now, they would have a new mission—the OVFS, although they would only know it as the cartel.

Hal frowned. He was overdue to brief Dr. Martin. Even though she has her hands full running the university, and has given me a pretty free rein, she didn't issue me a blank check. Still, she'll likely go along with the new security program after moaning about me turning Harvard into a police state. Especially if we help roll up the crew responsible for kidnapping, murder, car bombing, and other assaults. He'd bet the ranch that the woman wearing the Maid Pro uniform didn't die from her gunshot wound. With a jolt he realized he'd drifted off. Better get back to the briefing notes.

He would begin with the results of the trolling operation. Cordell and his team would man two unmarked cars. How could someone be shot in the back at point-blank range, then get tossed off a fourth floor balcony, and disappear without leaving a trace of blood anywhere? And, she probably collected George's automatic before disappearing. At least the police found the knife used to slice Flossie's arm. Judeland, even though wounded, is armed, and dangerous. He'd bet another ranch that she was somehow connected to all the other crimes over the past month.

The Bureau's lab guys had told him that Lawrence and Judeland had sex before she killed him in a grotesque way. They said Judeland had taken a bite out of the victim's forehead, and then she sliced and diced him. Alfred Hitchcock would have had a field day with Judeland.

Two OVFS footmen wearing painter's coveralls and caps sat in a windowless panel truck with an extension ladder secured to the roof. They were parked on Brattle Street near Coleson Manor. The logo on the side said, "Vision Painting Co., Commercial, Residential, Interior, Exterior." The man in the back tweaked the audio gain on his intercept equipment, checked the recorder, and scribbled notes on a pad. The voice-activated audio surveillance bugs planted in Coleson Manor by the OVFS agent who had traded shots with the butler were well placed and apparently well hidden, and they were state-of-the-art digitally encrypted transmitters. Number Two had ordered her execution. He knew it had to be done; the organization couldn't risk her being interrogated.

When Number Four read the message he turned to Jake. "The two vampires will leave Coleson Manor in fifteen minutes driving in the Jaguar. They expect to be shadowed by a friendly security detail, probably the campus police, but the city police might be part of the team. And they are armed. Their intent is to spot and track our surveillance vehicle back to its home base. What is the range of your detonator device?"

"Up to a quarter mile," Jake said.

"Where is it?"

"In a safe and easily accessible place."

"Where?"

"You don't need to know that."

Number Four gave Jake a hard look. "Get it and get in the van. We don't have time to argue."

"No, that would be too risky. I'll take the Chevy."

"That's been used too often. We think the female vampire would recognize it."

"You got another car?" Jake reached his arms up and arched his back as if it were the seventh inning at a baseball game, earning him another black look from Number Four.

"On our budget? Remember, we want to avoid collateral damage if at all possible. We especially don't want any police injured. Keep in touch with me throughout the operation. And don't forget to take photos, before and after."

"Trust me, okay? It wasn't my fault some stupid car thief blew the last mission." Number Four pulled the keys to the Chevy from a coat pocket and handed them to Jake.

"Try not to let the target identify you," Number Four said.

Jake grunted, zipped up his jacket, pulled his watch cap low over his forehead, and left.

He walked several blocks before getting into a silver Buick he'd rented from Budget without Number Four's knowledge. He checked his cell phone; it was fully charged. He did a quick communications check with Number Four then pulled the detonator from a leather carrying case and activated it in the test mode. The detonator, about the size of a bible, lay on the passenger seat, a green light blinking. He pumped his fist with satisfaction, flipped off the test mode and put on his dark glasses, even though it was heavily overcast. The morning weather report called for mixed snow and freezing rain, probably toward the end of the morning rush hour. He might have to abandon the car if he ran into a traffic scrum after the hit.

"See anybody?" Lamar asked as he slowly drove down Brattle Street.

"Lots of cars. Any one of them could be our guys or the OVFS. Both probably already have optics on us."

"Optics? You read spy novels?"

"Lamar, no more witty remarks, okay? Let's focus on staying alive. I have a prickly feeling, and prickly feelings have kept me alive for over three hundred years."

"Sorry. Won't happen again."

"If I tell you to 'bolt,' floorboard it, okay?"

"Right." Lamar's stomach began to tighten, and he could feel perspiration begin to form on his upper lip.

"Base to Juliette, over." Number Four took a drag on his cigarette and looked at the footman sitting next to him.

"J in position, over." Jake raised his high-powered telephoto lens and began scanning. As Brattle curved left onto Auburn he glimpsed two men in a black car. The passenger had binoculars and was scanning the cars behind him. "Shit on a stick," Jake swore, dropping the lens into his lap and devoutly hoping he hadn't been seen holding it to his eye.

As Auburn blended into Mass. Avenue, the black car sped up. That could mean only one thing: the cops had more than one surveillance car. He reached for his radio. "Juliette to Base, over."

"Base. Go ahead."

"Have identified one chase car, but he's disappeared. No doubt they have more than one. Is Tango Lima in place?" How clever of Number Four to name the other operative "Traffic Light."

The next intersection was Prospect Street. In a little over a half mile, when the target reached Vassar, Tango Lima would send a signal that would turn the light red in the target's direction. Jake reviewed the sequence one last time. He would hit the arming button, which would blink yellow for about four seconds. That would signal that the system was armed and ready for detonation. Jake could then push the final button, which would blink red. He reached over and grabbed the camera and screwed the telephoto lens onto it. He was passing Sydney Street. A quarter mile to go. The Jaguar was now three cars ahead of him. Click, click, click. He laid the camera back on the passenger seat next to the detonator and checked the time. Two more blocks.

Morgan twisted around and caught a glimpse through her binoculars of the driver three cars back holding something that seemed to be pointing toward them. "I don't like this," she murmured.

"What?"

"Just focus on driving."

"Time." Jake's voice was tight.

"Juliette, report."

"Not now," Jake yelled.

"Pictures?"

"Done."

"Armed?"

"Arming now. Out."

Jake pushed the yellow button in the middle. It began to blink.

The traffic light turned red, and Lamar stopped.

"Bolt right! Bolt right!" Morgan shouted.

Lamar jammed the gas pedal to the floorboard and yanked the wheel to the right. A car passing through the intersection careened left as the Jag screeched a line of paint off the side of the terrified driver's car, which smashed into another one in the Vassar Street left turn lane.

Jake mashed the blinking red button.

It turned solid red for one second.

29

And From a Cloud Gray and Dreary
December 23

"The body... lies here, food for worms, but the work
shall not be lost, for it will appear once more in a new
and more elegant edition, revised and corrected by the
Author."

Benjamin Franklin 1706-1790

The deafening explosion shook the Jaguar and its occupants. Morgan drew her weapon, prepared to return fire. A massive plume of dense white smoke billowed from under the Jag, obscuring everything.

"What the fuck," Jake yelled, watching the dense cloud engulf the target and everything around it.

"Juliet. Report," the radio squawked.

Jake glanced at the tracking readout for the Jag, but it was showing a null. The tracking device had obviously been disabled.

"*Report, Jul—*" Jake snapped off the radio. "Christ on a crutch, I gotta get out of here." He inched his way into the smoke that roiled through the intersection and turned left on Vassar. Once he cleared the expanding smoke he sped up but not for long. Sleet began bouncing off the windshield.

"That son-of-a-bitch sold me a dummy bomb," Jake yelled. A new thought tightened his gut. What if the guy was an FBI agent? I'm screwed. Everybody in the freaking world will be after me now. I've got to switch cars. He turned left on Broadway. It was sleeting harder. Traffic was crawling.

Number Four wiped his brow and lit another Fatima from the stub in the ash tray.

Something had gone terribly wrong. We are doing God's work, so why can't He cooperate for once? If the explosion had taken out Jake, it would have been on the news by now. He's too smart for that, though. Could the police have taken him? He's probably too smart for that, too. Having somehow screwed up the job, he's already following in Number Three's footsteps, and we'll never see or hear from him again either. And how will that sit with Number Two? At least we didn't pay him in advance.

Maybe I ought to start planning my own escape.

"Unit two to base," one of Hal's surveillance officers called.

"Go ahead, two."

"We've lost the troll and the stalker. There was some kind of explosion that produced a hell of a lot of smoke. When that finally cleared, they were nowhere in sight. Suggest we take Vassar west and unit three take Vassar east. The stalker is driving a late-model silver Buick rental. It drove into the smoke and disappeared. Now we got heavy sleet. Traffic is inching. Over."

"What the hell happened?" Lamar asked. Morgan was trying to get something on the radio.

"Whatever it was, it fried our radio," Morgan said. "Can't even get any static. I'd say we ought to double back to the command center. How's the car handling?"

"Oh, great. It's getting used to car bombs, side swipes, smoke bombs, and boltings. General Patton could have used one of these for his staff car."

Morgan grinned. "Turn right on River Street. We'd better stop for more dry ice. Next stoplight. *My God, Lamar.*" The car lost traction and began to skid.

"Crap." As the backend started to fishtail, they both stopped talking. Lamar steered into the slide, barely missing an oncoming UPS delivery van. When the car was under control again, Morgan continued.

"What if that smoke bomb had been like the one that blew up my car? Whoever put the smoke bomb on the Jag obviously meant for us to survive. They even made it easy to shake the OVFS tail because of the smoke screen." Morgan took a deep breath.

"How did you know to have us bolt right at Vassar?" Lamar asked, downshifting into second.

Morgan turned around, but the visibility was too poor for her to see more than two cars behind them.

"When you've been a vampire for three or four hundred years you'll understand. I can smell danger."

"There's a blessing." Lamar reached over and began rubbing her inner thigh.

"Pay attention to your driving or you'll have us in the Charles, and there won't be any vampire resurrections."

"That's not what you said last night."

"Lamar, it wasn't sleeting in our bedroom."

Hal tried to hide his disappointment about losing the hit man as he looked at the attendees. Dr. Heller sat at the end of the table, obviously downcast. Lamar and Morgan were on one side, both tense, with Cordell and Detective Sergeant Blanton McConnell on the other. Hal and George Henderson sat opposite Dr. Heller.

"Today was a downer," Hal began, "but there were some upsides. The cartel intentions went far beyond surveillance; they meant to kill Lamar and Morgan. We suspected they would try that."

Lamar leaned forward against the table, scowling. "You suspected—"

Hal continued. "My source at the Bureau briefed me on the sting they worked on a cartel agent who goes by the name of Jake. The Bureau had a guy posing as an international arms merchant. He sold Jake a smoke bomb dressed up as the real thing. Our intentions today were to wait until Jake detonated the fake bomb and follow him back to his headquarters. But he drove through the smoke screen and disappeared in the sleet storm. He was driving a rented Buick and carried the detonator package the Bureau's fake arms merchant trained him to use. They had planted a chip in the detonator so we could track them, but it went dead when Jake blew the smoke bomb.

"The up side is that Lamar and Morgan are unharmed. That was a gutsy piece of driving, Lamar. You might want to enter the next Indianapolis 500.

"Another plus is that we have a good description of our friend, Jake, and Cordell has the police looking for him," Hal said. "We found the Buick, which was, no surprise, wiped clean.

"We believe Jake has another set of wheels by now and is trying to get out of Dodge. The weather probably has Jake snarled, too, but we can't depend on that."

They were interrupted by a knock on the door. Jamie unlocked it and admitted Lenore with a cart of coffee and pastries. "Sorry to be late," she said. "Wouldn't you know our old coffeepot would pick today to go to the happy coffee grounds?" Everybody chuckled dutifully.

Jamie locked the door behind her, and Hal resumed briefing. "One of our intercepts suggested that the cartel has bugged Coleson Manor. I've ordered a sweep starting tomorrow morning at 0800, uh, that's eight a.m., assuming it's okay with you, Lamar.

Probably take about four hours. Sorry about it being Christmas Eve, but we can't have you giving away the farm any longer."

"Unless we want to use the bugs to plant some false information, or 'disinformation'," Morgan said.

Hal squinted at her. "I'm curious, Morgan, as to how you know about the use of disinformation."

"I read a lot," she said.

Hal looked at his notes. "We knew, of course, that the bomb the cartel agent hung under the Jag was a dud, but we didn't know it was a smoke screen bomb. My bureau contacts didn't tell us that, so we were as surprised as anybody when the smoke screen masked not only the two of you," he gestured at Morgan and Lamar, "but Jake and some of the friendly surveillance assets as well."

"Hal, ole buddy," Lamar began, his voice strained, "If I'm connecting the dots, you guys knew about the fake bomb and the bugs in Coleson Manor, but you didn't tell us. What kind of trust do you think that builds? Why the bloody hell didn't you tell us?"

Hal looked down at the pen he was absently tapping on the desk top. Tap, tap, tap, tap.

Morgan put a hand on Lamar's arm and squeezed. He didn't look at her.

"I don't mind taking risks, *Mr. Stone,* but I'd like to know all the bits and pieces ahead of time. Are we clear on that?"

"Clear. I may have made a bad call. My apologies." Hal's face showed how hard it was for him to say that.

"May have?"

"Let it go, Lamar," Morgan said quietly. "We've cleared the air now." Tap, tap, tap, tap.

Lamar, face flushed, sat back and crossed his arms, glaring at Hal.

"People, people, we're all on the same team. Nobody gets it right all the time," Jamie said. "Let's move on to the question of increasing our security. The bad guys are going to be enraged at yet another assassination attempt on you two going off the rails. And I, for one, would like to hear a little bit about how we can take a swing at them for a change." He relit his pipe and watched with satisfaction as everybody relaxed. Almost everybody.

"Okay, Hal, what else?" Jamie asked.

30

Confession
December 24

"The vampire's curse is to live an everlasting existence deprived of the essence of mortal life: love, hope, and death."

Attributed to Dr. Gene Claude Vompre
(a fictional character in this book)

The grisly part of the task had taken all morning. Lamar and Morgan drove a rental Ford F-350 to pick up the cornerstone and return with it to Coleson Manor, a distance of about twelve miles, through a wind-whipped rain storm. The weight of the granite stone, with its marble facing, changed the Ford's suspension, and the rain and wind didn't help.

They visited Robert at the hospital before leaving for the city of Everett and the Woodlawn Memorial, Inc. stoneworks. His recuperation was progressing more rapidly than predicted, and he had emerged with his memory intact except for the shooting and the first three days in the hospital. Cordell had been permitted to interview him but was disappointed that Robert couldn't identify his assailant. Cordell was bitter about the death of the MaidPro woman and was anxious to get the autopsy report, convinced that the cartel had silenced her.

The stone had been placed upside down and covered by a tarp. They had trouble forcing the two heads through the bottom hole, which was not as large as Lamar had expected.

Fortunately the heads had become more malleable, but the squeezing process made the grotesque expression on each face even worse, as it had taken brute strength and leverage to force both of them into the cornerstone.

"They led hard lives, endured hard deaths, and their reward is this final indignity," Morgan murmured. "How desperately sad they couldn't have gone into the ground with their heads and bodies intact." Lamar grunted as he forced a towel into the interior to block the view until it was sealed.

They had to return to Everett to get the hollow stone professionally sealed before driving to the church with their macabre cargo, and it was taking more time than they had estimated. Where is the OVFS now? Lamar wondered. Wish Hal or Cordell had a friendly tail on us.

Morgan made a face. "I almost gagged reading the inscription, Lamar: *Lady Chapel, Christmas 2011. May God place His soothing hand upon your brow.*" Her voice caught.

"Maybe he will," Lamar said.

"You've never mentioned God before. Are you a believer?"

Lamar shook his head. "I don't know what to believe. I've always thought the God stuff was unknowable and put it out of my mind. I believe in us, though. We're real." He reached over and cupped her left breast.

"Thank you, Lamar. That's the dearest thing you've ever said to me."

"Really? Well, I thought you knew how I felt. I've had more sex with you in the last few weeks than all the rest of my life put together." He wasn't about to mention that the only sex he'd ever had before Morgan was the pay-for-play kind. Well, there was Jennifer. . . .

"It doesn't work that way, my dear one."

How the hell should I know how it works? Lamar wondered. Morgan is the first person I've ever really trusted. And she's got to be the best bed partner on the planet. What else is there? We are committed to going through resurrection together. If that's not commitment I don't know what is. Besides, she's had over three hundred years to figure this stuff out—

"Hey, isn't that where we were supposed to turn left?"

"Crap."

The Kodak moment ended abruptly.

Father Hemming hung up the phone. The woman had sounded strange, and he wondered if she might be on drugs. He chided himself for being irritated that she had insisted on making her confession this afternoon, of all times. People would be showing up for Christmas mass all too soon. It was getting late, and he sighed as he went to the closet for his robe and clerical collar. Maybe he could finish his response to the building committee before she arrived.

Committees are the bane of my existence, he thought. Especially this one. And its chairman, Robert Shackleford, is a particular thorn. Together, they form a crown of thorns. Ed permitted himself a wry smile. The real problem was all the ducking and weaving he'd had to do over the "anonymous" funding of the Lady Chapel. He looked at his daytimer. Blast. Lamar and Morgan are due sometime this afternoon with the cornerstone. Why are they treating it like it was an NSA codebook or something? I ought to—

Father Hemming sensed a presence in the room. "Charlotte, is that you?" He recalled his secretary had asked to leave early and felt foolish. Getting up, he opened the office door and stepped out. Nothing. He walked across to the sanctuary. Quiet as a pyramid, though he could hear the faint patter of rain. As he walked back to his office, he checked his watch. He'd let the stone masons go almost an hour earlier. It's half past four, and she said she'd be here in ten minutes. Where the blazes—

As he reentered the office he was stunned. The lights were out and a single candle burned on his desk. Since the blinds were drawn the room was almost completely dark.

Standing in the doorway, he listened but could hear nothing.

"We can begin now." The female voice was deep and breathy.

Father Hemming jerked as if he'd touched a live wire. Then he became angry.

"If you've come for my help you're off to a bad start." He began to grope for the light switch.

"No light, Father. We do this my way."

Unaware of his reaction, his hands curled into fists. That voice was familiar, but who?

He needed to hear her speak again.

268

"There is a chair a few feet in front of you. Do sit down." Ed stood, listening hard, trying to place her.

"Sit!"

He sat, rigid, crossing his arms over his chest.

"Father, I have sinned, and I wish to confess those sins now."

"And you are?"

"That's not important."

"It is to God," Father Hemming said.

"That's why I'm here. Are you ready to listen?"

"I'm ready to turn on the light," Ed said, rising from the chair.

"You may, as you put it, turn on the light, Father, but not any artificial light. You see I have wired the lights in this room to a device that would cause substantial damage to Saint Paul if they were switched on."

She hasn't had time to do that. Has she? I've got a crazy on my hands, and it's someone I've met before. Probably trying to disguise her voice.

"I have killed someone," the woman said.

"Then you really need to speak with the police, madam. Murder is—"

"*Do not speak to me of the police.*" She slammed a hand down on his desk, making Ed jump. He peered hard at the silhouette that had risen from behind his desk.

"All right. Tell me all of your sins. When was the last time you made your confession?"

"I wouldn't expect you to remember."

The voice had suddenly become so soft he could barely understand her. More plaintive.

Girlish. So I've heard her confession before. "Tell me when you last confessed, my child."

Vic Brown

"You wanted me in your church, then. You pretended to care." The voice faded into a dreamy state. "But you don't really care. You never did. No one has ever really cared. But they will. Soon I will become Catholicism's worst nightmare. And Harvard's. In fact, I already am." Her laugh was a blend of anguish, arrogance, and insanity.

I've got to keep her talking. "You came to make your confession, and I am ready to hear it, as is your God."

"*My god?*" she shrieked. "If there really was a god there wouldn't be a *me*. Or should I say an us? Would the god you've conjured allow my kind to exist?" The candle flame wavered.

"God is the creator of all things in heaven and on earth. Tell me about your kind."

"Ah, so now I have earned your interest. Well, Father Hemming, we are the people of the dark. Have you never heard of the OVFS, a society of the Roman Church even more deeply hidden than Opus Dei?"

"No, I haven't. Is this to be part of your confession?"

"Oh, no. But it will be part of your confession—one day."

"You're talking in riddles, and it's getting us nowhere," Ed said, a note of anger etching his voice. "Either begin your confession, or we shall end this farce."

"Farce? *Farce?* Do you think the desecrated body of your secretary is a *farce*?" she screamed.

Ed hunched as if he'd taken a body blow. Steeling himself, his voice flat, he asked, "What can you tell me about my secretary?"

"Charlotte and Jude went up the hill to fetch a pale of wah—ter," she sang, her voice mincing. "Jude came down with blood on her crown, and wiped her chin, after committing a sin, leaving poor little Charlotte in ta—tters, not that it really ma—tters, for she'll never again see her kin."

270

A stab of fear coursed through Father Hemming as he pictured Charlotte being brutalized.

Judeland! The police have a massive manhunt looking for her, and she finds sanctuary in Saint Paul. He took a deep breath. Yea though I walk through the valley of the shadow of death, he recited to himself.

"Is this a dream, Judeland, or maybe some kind of fantasy?"

"No Father, it's quite real. Would you like to see her?" She could have been inviting him to share a cup of tea.

"Yes." He was glad it was dark, so she couldn't see him trembling.

"Walk slowly and make no sudden moves. I am armed and know how to use a gun. Open the door quietly and walk to the sanctuary. One false move, and I will end your masculinity. Do I make myself clear?"

"Quite clear."

"Then open the door."

"God, am I tired of lugging these heads around. But I'm sure by now Father Hemming has let his stone masons go. It's getting late, and it's Christmas Eve."

Morgan pursed her lips. "We're almost there. She snapped her fanny pack around her waist. "I'll bet the good Father Hemming will have some questions for us. It doesn't make sense to haul the cornerstone around in a rented truck rather than have Woodlawn Memorial deliver it, especially on Christmas Eve. And what earthly reason do we have for wanting it to be cemented in place as soon as it's delivered? *And,* if it's so damned important, how come Dr. Heller won't be there to make the grand presentation? He's got cold feet, that's why. He doesn't think his old friend buys the story, either. So we get hung out to dry."

"Well, we'll have to play it by ear," Lamar said, turning into the church parking lot. "Pray he doesn't ask too many questions while he's cashing Heller's checks. Only two cars in the parking lot. I think that one is Ed's. Obviously the workers have left. Oh well, the best laid plans." He wondered how they were going to unload the cornerstone without the workmen.

"What is gloomier than an empty church when it's raining?" Morgan asked.

"Charlotte," Father Hemming gasped. "My God, what have you done to her?"

His secretary hung from a seven-foot wooden cross. It was wedged between two chairs and leaning against a wall. Duct tape strapped her wrists and ankles to the cross, as well as several layers around her waist. Her chin was tucked against her chest, and her hair had been loosened and hung down almost to her breasts. She was nude. Blood trickled from a Jesus wound in her right side and puddled on the floor.

Ed groaned and raced to her. "Charlotte, Charlotte," he cried, unaware of the mindless cackle behind him. Ed whirled and faced the monster holding the gun. "So this is how you confess your sins? You destroy human lives and desecrate God's holy church? You will reap God's wrath and eternal damnation." His eyes narrowed and his fists whitened, as he quickly cast about for anything he could use as a weapon.

"I already have tasted his wrath and earned eternal damnation. I drank her blood, you know. That's what all vampires do. She isn't dead. Yet. In fact, she will nurse me with her blood. I shall have to cut off her nipples first, of course. And when I've had my fill, you shall have a turn. Have you ever nursed on Miss Charlotte before? No? Well now's your chance. Watch me and learn." With her free hand she withdrew a switchblade knife from her jacket pocket. "Lawrence won't be needing this anymore."

Ed stepped toward her. Judeland lowered her aim. "Don't sell your manhood now. You'll need it soon enough." Her eyes were blazing like sparks from a grindstone.

I have to keep her talking and pray for a miracle. "What exactly do you mean by me needing my manhood?"

"Oh, I have a nice surprise for you, Father Hemming. You are going to have sex with Miss Charlotte while I watch. Pity we can't videotape it for the subsequent pleasure of your congregation. Which shall we do first, *Ed?* Nursing or fucking? You choose." Judeland's twisted smile betrayed her twisted mind. "I'm looking forward to your performance, Ed. Do what I tell you, and I may spare both of you. So choose. Now."

Ed cleared his throat. "Judeland, in the name of God don't ..."

"Don't appeal to your so-called god," she screamed. "Do you think that centuries-old fable could possibly move me?" Her laugh reverberated throughout the sanctuary as if it had welled up from the Inferno, her face a maniacal mask.

"With her strapped to the cross, what you ask is physically impossible," he said, eyes downcast. God help me to keep her talking and to save this poor woman on the cross. Wasn't Jesus enough?

273

"You may unbind her. Clear the altar first. Use that for your conjugal couch."

"But fear prevents the necessary, uh, the required, uh changes I would need to, uh, do your bidding. Besides, I have been celibate for years. Stick a gun in any man's face and see if he can become ready."

"Ah, then, I shall have to provide you some help, won't I? Miss Charlotte, do your duty. Help him to become aroused. I want to watch him seed you."

"But Charlotte is unmarried. She may never have—"

"Bullshit! Stop stalling and get the duct tape off. Any more delay and I go for the nipples. If you do a good enough job rutting, I may even leave them on her."

After clearing the altar, Ed began unwinding the tape.

"Now undress, and be quick about it." Judeland motioned with her handgun.

Naked, Father Hemming stood in front of Charlotte, quivering, his emotions a kaleidoscope of shame, rage, and fear. He knew Judeland would not let them live after she had her way with them. Charlotte hung her head, mute, tears streaming down her face, one hand covering her genitals, the other arm across her breasts. Her feet were still partially numb, and she swayed.

"Stand closer together," Judeland said. "Miss Charlotte, you know what to do to make a man hard. So do it. Now!" Judeland made a pumping motion with one hand—her smile that of a gargoyle.

Charlotte looked up at her pastor, eyes glazed, shock etched deeply in her face. Slowly he put his arms around her, pulling her in close and bringing his lips to her right ear.

"That's more like it. Now grasp him Miss Charlotte, and start pumping."

Father Hemming whispered, "I am going to throw you to one side on the count of three. Ready?"

She nodded.

Judeland was moving sideways to get a better view and momentarily took her eyes off the naked couple standing in front of the altar.

"One, two, three." Ed heaved, and Charlotte did a racer's dive, landing hard. Ed lunged in the other direction, grabbing the cross Charlotte had hung on. He swung it with a strength he'd never had.

Judeland jumped backward and snapped off two shots. One embedded in the left arm of the cross, the other shattered Hemming's right hipbone, but he followed through with his swing, knocking the automatic from Judeland's hand. She leaped over the first pew and dove for the gun.

Hemming tried to go after her, taking one step before he crumpled, blood pouring from his hip. Judeland found the gun and searched for Hemming, who had crawled under a more distant pew.

She glanced at Charlotte's inert body before crouching down to search for Father Hemming. Finding a trail of blood, she followed it.

"Bolt right!" Morgan shouted. Lamar, who was hunched over and taking quick but silent steps down the main aisle, had reached the third pew from the altar. He dove to his right a second before Morgan fired four times. The rounds from her Browning .25

caliber automatic, with extended magazine, sliced off Judeland's left earlobe and formed a triangle on her chest.

Judeland staggered back but quickly regained her balance. She fired twice in Morgan's direction but couldn't see clearly in the dim light.

Lamar rose up and flung a large brass candlestick that had been on the altar, hitting Judeland and causing her to drop her weapon again. Leaping around the remaining pews, he launched himself at Judeland, his hands closing around her neck. But Judeland was stronger and threw him over her head. Lamar landed hard, his face in the puddle of Charlotte's blood beneath where the cross had been wedged.

As Judeland retrieved the gun once again, a hand from beneath the front pew grabbed her ankle. Judeland went down just as another fusillade from Morgan embedded in the altar.

Judeland rolled over and fired twice, but in that moment Hemming had rolled under a pew in the next row. The deranged vampire scrambled across the floor and yanked the gasping secretary upright, holding her as a shield.

"Drop your gun, or she dies," Judeland yelled.

"You only have one more round. Kill her and you seal your own fate," Morgan shouted back.

"My switchblade across her jugular would do the trick, don't you think?" Her laugh was short as she was still breathing hard. Judeland dragged Charlotte out through a side entrance and disappeared.

"Father Hemming? Where are you?" Morgan ran down the aisle.

"Here," he said, his voice weak.

"I have to pull you out into the aisle, Father." He cried out as she dragged him from under a pew.

Assessing his wound was easy, as he was naked. She tore off her scarf and folded it to make a compress. "Hold that on your wound, and press as hard as you can. I've got to call 911. I'll be right back."

Morgan dashed to the office and flipped on the light switch. She heard a muffled explosion and the sound of cascading glass. But there was no time to investigate. "911? Saint Paul Church. A lot of gunfire. Father Hemming is seriously wounded, and a bomb has been detonated. The church secretary has been kidnapped." She paused. "It doesn't matter who I am, just get here fast." She slammed the phone down. "Where the hell are you, Lamar?" she yelled.

"Lamar?" She found bloody handprints on the floor beside the altar and froze. He was gone. And her instincts told her why. He was on the hunt.

"Oh my God, I've got to find him."

God?

31

The Hunting
December 24

"Killing, the curse of the living dead, envelopes the
vampire like a shroud."

A quote from Gene Claude Vompre,
(a fictional character in this novel.)

Yellow police tape cordoned off the entire church. Cordell stepped over shards of stained glass and shattered saints. The smell of gunfire suffused the church. He looked down at the wood cross lying on the second pew, close to the aisle. The base and the end of one arm were shattered, and a bullet hole decorated the other arm. The whole front of the sanctuary appeared blood soaked. Outside, a colossal traffic jam was growing worse as parishioners were arriving and being turned away. He shook his head and pursed his lips and rubbed his eyes, resisting the urge to have a cigarette. "Okay, Mac, lay it on me. Merry fucking Christmas, by the way"

Mac grinned as he thumbed back two pages in his notebook and began. "A 911 call close to five o'clock reported a lot of gunfire in the church, with Father Hemming badly wounded.

"Caller also said the church secretary, a Ms. Charlotte Rhodes, was kidnapped, and a bomb had been detonated. I've heard the tape, and it sounds like Morgan Summers to me. When we got here, about fifteen minutes ago, nobody was here but Father Hemming, who was wounded and had lost a lot of blood. He did say Morgan had given him first aid. His car is in the parking lot, but Ms. Rhode's car is gone. Probably taken by the kidnapper. We got an APB out on it. Not another car in the lot."

"Somebody else must have been hit, 'cause we found a pool of blood with hand prints in it over there—" Detective Sergeant McConnell pointed. "We're still digging bullets out of the altar. A couple of the pews are shot up, along with the cross. And Charlie Poston, over there, says he found some small caliber holes. I'd guess the bigger ones are .40 cal, the smaller ones maybe .25s or .32s. The mobile lab should be here any minute along with the FD. I called in a bomb disposal guy, too. Porter thinks somebody triggered a small explosive that took out the stain glass window behind you."

Cordell squinted at the jagged shards of colored glass still remaining in the tall, narrow frame. In the gloomy twilight he could see a misting rain blowing into the church.

"Jesus. What the hell was this anyway, an Al Qaeda hit?" Cordell wanted a cigarette. Bad.

"More like the Gunfight at the Okay Parrish," Mac said.

"Very cute, Mac. Where are the Bobbsey Twins? I see their MO all over the place."

"No idea. I'll bet we're dealing with some of those cartel clowns who had their fingerprints surgically removed. And their tits."

"Jesus," Cordell muttered again. He looked at his watch. "This will make the late night news. That means our friendly governor will call me about oh-dark-thirty wanting to know if I'm planning to sell tickets to people who want to see the second coming of Sodom and Gomorrah."

"Have you put out an alert for Charlotte Rhodes?"

"Oh, yeah."

"Well let's find the Bobbsey Twins. They no doubt will have a lot to tell us."

"I'm on it, Chief."

Morgan was desperate as she drove the F-350 around the neighborhood. How long before the police find out that Lamar rented this beast? she wondered. Somehow I've got to find a place to park it. She peered through the back window and checked the tarp covering the cornerstone. If I get caught hauling around a couple of heads. . . . Damn, I'll never find Lamar in the dark. If the police take him when he's on the hunt, I'll never get him back, either. And he is the man with the key, the one I've been searching for the past three centuries.

She tromped on the accelerator and headed for Miss Lillian's.

Morgan slid to a stop; the downpour had changed to freezing rain. As quietly as possible she got out, selected a key from her key ring, and prayed to all the gods of the Universe. It fit. She heard a snap as the lock opened, and she lifted the garage door. It rumbled like all old garage doors, but then it probably dated back to the mid-thirties.

The porch light suddenly cast a hazy glow as she lowered the door. "Step forward," a voice commanded, "where I can see you." Morgan stepped closer, smiling.

"Morgan! My child. Oh, dear, forgive me." She tucked the .38 revolver in her belt. "Quick, come inside and have some wine," Miss Lillian said, her face a basket full of smiles. "I just knew you wouldn't forget me."

They hugged and swayed for a long moment. "I got your favorite, Gnarley Head. Been keeping this bottle of Merlot until you came back. Let me look at you. Um ummm. I never looked that good, even in my prime. I been reading all about you and watching the news.

"Let me think. You were in that church shootout they talked about on the TV. You're on the lam and need a place. Well, here it is." Miss Lillian hugged Morgan again when they were inside.

"The room on the first floor is vacant. Did you bring anything? All the guys upstairs are off to see a hockey game, so we have the place to ourselves." She poured the wine and handed a glass to Morgan. "Lordy me, I've been doing all the talking. Now sit down, and tell me everything that's happened since you drove off." She snapped her fingers. "I'll bet you're hungry, Luv. How about some of my homemade stew? I got plenty, and—"

"Miss Lillian, I love you." Tears glistened in Morgan's eyes. "Could I adopt you as my mother?"

"Lan' sakes, yes. All we need is the paperwork to make it legal. We've already done all the rest." She placed a bowl of stew and a couple of rolls with a pat of butter on the table in front of Morgan. "I could heat up a mess of beans if you'd..."

"No, no. This is great. I have to go back out in a few minutes." Strange, I don't think I've ever felt this hungry before, she thought.

"In this weather? With all the cops looking for you? No. I won't have it. You're safe here."

"I have to find a man. He's in trouble, and I'm the only one that can help him."

"Is he your man, Luv?"

Morgan put down her spoon and looked up at Miss Lillian. She started to speak but hesitated. "Pretty much. Yeah. He is. I think."

"But you're not absolutely sure."

"I know that if I don't find him, I'll lose him forever, and I'll lose myself, too."

"Then you better go after him. I'll wait up for you. He may need doctoring. Did you know I was once a nurse?"

"Oh, Miss Lillian, what would I do without you?"

"Well, what's a mother for?"

Morgan pulled away from the curb in Miss Lillian's thirteen-year-old Pontiac, wearing Miss Lillian's ancient yellow rain slicker and matching rain hat pulled low over her forehead. She had studied a map of the area and plotted a grid search. Her first priority was the Yard.

Lamar's heart raced. He felt surge after surge of heat course through his body and up to his neck and face. He was hungry. Even more, he was thirsty, but it was a special kind of hunger and thirst, one he'd never known. His sense of smell was point-of-a-dagger sharp, and his acute night vision took on a dull yellow-green hue. He felt strong, stronger than he'd ever been. How he would love to find Judeland and throw her around. Or Charlotte. He would finish the job left undone by that naked wimp, Father Hemming. Power surged through his groin. That part was ready, too. Absolutely ready. But not just anyone would do. He thought of Jennifer Marsh and wondered if she might be working late. He would find out.

Maybe they could take another shower. Only this time he would feast on Cricket first.

Spindly little bitch—all fur and eyeballs. The world would be the better if I snacked on that cat. Wouldn't take long. And who could stand against me?

Jennifer murmured and arched her back. She looked at the reports on her desk. What the hell am I doing here on Christmas Eve? Her head ached almost as much as her back. The pay raise had been marvelous, and they'd given her Lamar's old office, a private parking place, and an admin assistant, but the hours had left her drained. Her social life—after Lamar vanished into the GenLab—had disintegrated. She wondered how much longer she could keep up the pace.

I need a drink. And a roll in the hay, but not with some bar stud. I wonder what Lamar is doing tonight? I might call him. If that damn woman answers I can always hang up. She is a strange one. Maybe Lamar could use a hot shower and some company right about now.

Wouldn't hurt to call him. She pulled her cell phone out of her purse, which was sitting on top of the safe next to her desk, and smiled.

Lamar, unmindful of the cold, misting rain, was stalking across the Yard when his cell phone buzzed. Angry, he stopped, pulling it out of the pocket of his dark green rain jacket and punched a button.

"Yes."

"Lamar, is that you?"

"Yes. Who is this?"

"You sure know how to break a girl's heart. It's Jennifer. I'm calling to see how you are. You haven't called me in forever. Did I do something wrong?"

"Wrong? No. As a matter of fact, I was just thinking about you." The wind gusted, and Lamar pulled the hood up. "Where are you?"

"Still at the office. Your old office. I miss you. Could I buy you a drink?"

"I'm not far from University Hall. I'll drop in, and we can go from there."

"Marvelous. I'll lock up and be ready."

"You do that." He snapped his phone shut and shoved it in his jacket pocket. I seriously doubt you'll be ready for me, he thought, lengthening his strides. He walked past the bronze statue of John Harvard. On impulse he rubbed John's boots; everybody else did.

The guard, who had to be over sixty-five, was dozing as Lamar soundlessly walked past him.

Jennifer unlocked the door. "Well, Lamar, it's—" She stepped back as he shouldered his way in. Her eyes widened.

"My God, Lamar, have you been in a fight? Your face and hands are covered, uh covered...." She muttered. "Oh, lord. It seems that once again I need to get you cleaned up. My private bathroom, well, you remember. It was yours."

"Where's your cat? Cricket, right?"

"Cricket? Why would I bring her to the office?"

Lamar's eyes began searching the room until his phone buzzed again. "Where's the cat?" His voice was guttural.

"Uh, I think you should answer your phone. Then we can talk."

Lamar glared at the phone. "What do you want?" he shouted.

"Lamar, where are you? I need to talk to you."

"Why?"

"The police are looking for you. I have a place we can hide. Please tell me where you are."

"And spoil the feast?" His laugh rolled out from a dark cave, home to bats and gnomes. And vampires.

"Lamar, who is it?" Jennifer asked.

"Lamar, let me speak to that person. *Please*," Morgan pleaded. He shrugged and handed the phone to Jennifer. Jennifer's voice was calm, but her hands were shaking as she gently pulled the phone out of his hand. "Who am I speaking to?"

"Morgan Summers. Where are you, Jennifer?"

"In my office. His old one. I don't think he feels very well. Maybe he needs medical attention."

"Keep him there. I'm only ten minutes away. Keep him talking. Whatever you do, don't anger him."

285

"I already got that one sussed out. Hurry." She laid the phone on the coffee table. "Let's start with some coffee. I know I need some." She began making a pot, her back to Lamar.

His hands cupped her breasts and squeezed hard as he pinned her against the counter. "Sweetie, you're getting blood on my new dress. How about we wash you up before we find something more fun to do, okay?" Jennifer tried to turn around.

In one wrenching motion he tore open every button down the front of her dress, yanking it off her shoulders, and then pulling it out from under her feet.

"Lamar, your rough stuff is definitely not a turn-on. If you'll calm down, though, I think we can enjoy—" her voice faltered as he reached for her bra. She quickly unhooked it, pitching it on the dress near her feet. In two swift motions, she kicked off her shoes, leaving her in black stockings and matching panties.

"Almost ready," he rasped, kneading her breasts.

"Lamar, you're hurting me."

I've got to get there fast, Morgan thought. He's out of control. Deep into the hunting.

She parked, jumped out, slammed the car door and raced to the building entrance. "May I help you?" the sleepy old man at the front desk asked, rocking forward.

"I left my purse in the office. My ID card is in it. Won't take me a sec." She dashed to the stairs and began taking them two at a time.

"Hey, wait a minute. You can't just—"

As Morgan disappeared up the stairs the guard dialed a number. "This is Jeff at University Hall. Some gal rushed past me saying she had left her purse in her office. You want me to do anything?"

"Hang on a tic, Jeff; I'll check the video." A couple minutes later the guy on the other end came back to the phone. "I only got a glimpse of her, but I think that was the gal the police are looking for about the church shootout this afternoon. You stay put. I've already alerted the campus police. They should get there in a couple of minutes. And be careful, Jeff. Don't try to stop her. We think she's armed. Go get in a closet or under your desk. Let the pros handle it. Out."

"The pros? Get under my desk? Bull."

Morgan, breathing hard, burst into Jennifer's office. Jennifer was lying on the sofa in the fetal position, whimpering. Lamar had torn off her panties and pitched them on the floor. He was reaching for his belt when he became aware of Morgan and turned, eyes blazing, lips drawn back, spittle around his mouth.

"Why are *you* here?" he snarled.

"Because I want you. You're mine. Take me. Look." She had unbuttoned her blouse as she spoke, and she wasn't wearing a bra. "Look at me. Mine are bigger than hers. I can give you more pleasure."

Lamar lunged at her, crying out like an enraged animal.

"No! You must follow me to my lair. I don't want her to see us. She isn't worthy. Follow me." She turned and headed for the door, praying he would follow. She opened the door and quickly surveyed the hall. It was empty, and Lamar was at her back. "Now," she said and started to run, with Lamar trailing. She heard footsteps pounding up the stairs and grabbed Lamar's arm, jerking him into the women's restroom.

Three men ran past and down to the end of the hall.

"Cover me," one of them said as they burst into Jennifer's office.

A moment before the door slammed behind the campus police Morgan heard Jennifer shriek. "Now, Lamar. Run." The two raced down the stairwell to the east side of the building and through an alarmed door, triggering a raucous blaring. They raced across the Yard and the Plaza to the Science Center, passing only two students hunched under an umbrella. She knew the basement and first floor were open twenty-four hours a day. They headed for the GenLab, which was in the basement adjacent to a massive chilled water plant—and the cold room.

Morgan keyed the cipher lock, opened the GenLab door and dragged Lamar in behind her. Passing no one, they walked quickly to the cold room. She entered the cipher code and opened that door; they entered, and it closed automatically. Lamar's hands closed over her breasts. "By the balls of Beelzebub, Lamar, not *now*," she said, still breathing hard.

"Now!"

She looked at him, at the dried blood smeared on his face, hands, in his hair. Then she felt the heat. His and her own. In a flash she morphed from freezing to sweating. Her nipples were already erect, and her lubrication began to flow. Her mind turned dark red, lust building with every heartbeat.

"Yes, now," she said, leering at him. They circled like Sumo wrestlers, arms outstretched, searching for a handhold. Their bodies collided. Frenzied, they bit and kissed and sucked, pulling one another's hair, hands groping, both growling as if they were Adam and Eve discovering one another for the first time. She had tasted the blood on him and felt the hunting instinct cascade over her. She quivered. Her skin felt like it was on fire, super sensitive to his touch.

Their clothing lay around them, forming a crude circle, establishing the boundaries of a universe only they could occupy. At first she resisted, but he was too strong. He bore her down to the floor. It felt like a sheet of ice numbing her back, but only for a moment. He plunged into her, and she arched to meet him. He bellowed a cry of triumph, and she echoed it. Thrusting and plunging, devouring and pounding, they became a volcano, hot lava filling her, mind, body, and ... and the space in-between.

But that space was no longer a complete void. Something was there, something foreign that began to whisper to her, a calming, soothing voice. She went limp and felt tears streaking her face, as she looked into his eyes.

The fire was gone from them. He seemed to be studying her. "Morgan? Where are we? How did we get here?" He sounded hoarse. "God, it's cold in here."

"Not so cold as you might think, my love."

"What? What did you say?"

"We must dress quickly. We have to find the way out."

32

Judeland's Christmas Present
December 24

"It's always darkest just before it becomes pitch black."

Old Saying

I 'm so cold." Her voice was small, fearful and hopeless.

"Why, Miss Charlotte, I do declare. You are stark naked, and it's Christmas Eve. What on earth has happened to your clothes? I doubt Santa Claus is going to be very happy with you." Her laughter clattered like a string of tin cans behind a "Just Married" car. Judeland had parked in front of a vacant house with a For Sale sign on the lawn. Only one house in the neighborhood had outside Christmas lights turned on. A single streetlight, at a distant intersection, cast morbid shadows across the two women sitting in Charlotte's car. With the engine off the temperature was dropping.

"What do you want for Christmas, Miss Charlotte?"

"I want to go home."

"Home? *Home*? Do you know how many people there are tonight who have no home to go to? Right here in Cambridge, home of the mighty Harvard University? You could start with me. But *you* want to go home. Hmmm. Maybe that could be arranged. So, Miss Charlotte, if I were to give you home as a special Christmas gift, what gift would you give me in return?" She gave her passenger a leering smile, all the more sinister in the bleak light and hungry shadows. "Maybe a little kiss for a start. Isn't that a splendid idea?"

"Could, uh, could you turn the heater on, please?" Charlotte's teeth were chattering, and she was covered with goose bumps.

"Of course. What have you got to trade for a little heat?"

"I," she faltered, "I could promise not to tell anyone about all this." Charlotte blew on her hands and rubbed her arms, eyes downcast.

"Ah. I see. You would promise never to tell anyone ever?" Charlotte nodded.

"Never ever, ever, ever?" She nodded again.

"Well, then, we must seal our bargain with a kiss. Sit on your hands and lean toward me." As Charlotte leaned toward Judeland, eyes tight shut, she shuddered and drew back as Judeland pinched her nipples.

"They are quite cold, my dear, and hard as ten-penny nails. Come closer, and I will warm them up for you."

Charlotte sobbed.

"Here," Judeland said, "you can warm mine while I warm yours." She quickly unbuttoned her blouse and pulled her bra up over her breasts. "Isn't this what you used to do when you were making out with your high school boyfriend?"

291

Charlotte remained a statue, eyes cemented shut.

"Are you rejecting my Christmas present?" Judeland's voice turned harsh. Charlotte leaned over toward her captor but kept her eyes closed. She shuddered as Judeland pulled her nipples and massaged her breasts. As the other woman's lips pressed against hers, forcing hers open, she almost gagged at the rank odor: mildewed stew with heavy, coppery overtones. She felt one hand being pulled from under her and placed on a warm breast.

Charlotte's head opened like a clam shell, and her awareness drifted up. It bumped along the car's headliner, soft but firm. Then she emerged on a beach, lying on a blanket, with cloudless sunshine, gulls fussing, waves cascading over the shore, the high-pitched voices of children. It was warm and safe and so familiar. She wondered where Mrs. Corey, her sixth grade teacher, was. Maybe on the boardwalk.

She was ripped from her reverie by a hard slap across her face. In an instant she was naked, cold, violated, shaking, terrified. And her cheek was burning. "If you're going to kill me then do it," she screamed. The wound on her side, where Judeland had cut her, hurt like ice held too long against skin.

"Ah, so I've brought you back. You zoned out on me. Miss Charlotte, I am going to offer you a Christmas gift, the best one you have ever received or ever will receive. It is the gift of life. In return, you must pledge by all that is holy two gifts in return. First, you must not say a word about what happened to you today. Second, one day I will come back and ask you for a favor. And you will do me that favor, whatever it is and whenever I ask it. And always know that I will be watching you. Betray my trust, and it's back on the cross for you and off with those cold nipples. Do you understand all that I've said?"

"Yes," she said, her voice barely audible.

292

"And do you agree to our little exchange of gifts?"

"Yu, yu yes." Her lips were numb making it hard to speak.

"All right, my dear. I am going to drive around till I find the perfect place to release a naked lady. We don't want you to freeze to death on Christmas Eve do we?"

Charlotte shook her head.

Judeland started the car and pulled away from the curb.

"Why don't you sing us a Christmas carol, my dear?"

33

Escape
December 24

"I don't care what you do as long as you don't do it in
the street and frighten the vampires."

Mrs. Patrick Campbell, 1910 (as amended)

It wasn't much of a plan. No time for anything more elaborate.
The alternatives to getting out of the cold room were
hypothermia or being taken by law enforcement officers who,
no doubt, would soon be combing the building. They could only
hope that Jennifer had called the campus police and that Hal
would be able to intervene in their behalf. If Cordell got them
first, it would not go well. And Morgan was worried that Lamar
might lapse back into the hunt. If she were in the presence of a
hunting vampire too long, it could trigger a sympathetic response
in her, as it did after they ran over the cat—and their wild sex
just minutes ago.

And there was Judeland, who had survived multiple gunshots and a four-story fall, clear evidence she was a vampire.

It was time. Morgan looked at the alarm panel for the environmental control system that protected the GenLab's stem cell incubation process. An alarm would sound at the concierge desk, the Campus Police Command Center, and Dr. Heller's cell phone, as well as Thermotech, Inc., which had installed and maintained the system.

Morgan keyed in the access code. When the system cover plate unlocked, she raised the temperature setting to fifty degrees. A variety of lights began to flash, indicating that the alarm had been transmitted. They watched the panel as one by one, the lights stopped blinking, indicating the recipients had confirmed receipt. It took about a minute and a half for Heller's light to go solid, but he had no doubt been asleep.

Morgan shut and locked the cover. "Merry Christmas, Lamar."

"What? Oh. Yeah." He looked at his watch. "I guess it is. Merry Christmas to you." They hid in a small equipment storage area inside the cool room. When the police arrived they would find the door to the cold room ajar, the system still in the alarm mode, an internal horn blaring since the temperature had risen above the red line, and one of Morgan's shoes in the hall, near the stairwell. The duty officer in the command center would scan the GenLab emergency roster and contact the call-in designee, confirm that Thermotech had dispatched a system engineer, and call Dr. Heller with a status report.

Four minutes passed before two Cambridge police officers cautiously entered the cold room, guns drawn. Their eyes hadn't yet adjusted to the dim red light. After a cursory look, with the door ajar and the system failure horn blaring, they left. Another officer had discovered the shoe and yelled to his fellow officers that the perps were fleeing the building. Two minutes later they did.

Morgan started the Pontiac, and they pulled away, Lamar crouched in the back seat footwell under a blanket. A squad car pulled out and blocked their path.

"License and registration please," a very young Cambridge police officer asked. "Sorry, they're in my purse, which I left at the party. You could come with me," she said, unzipping her jacket and unbuttoning the top two buttons of her blouse. "It looks like I'm going to be very lonesome on Christmas Eve."

"Do you have some ID?"

"It's all in my purse, officer. We could get to the party in only a few minutes."

The officer sighed. "Some other time. I'm on duty."

"That's too bad, officer—"

"Uh, you could call me at the precinct. Ask for Bill Davies. What's your name?"

"Julie Mathews. I've never dated a police officer. What time do you get off?" she giggled. "I think you're cute. I think we could have a very Merry Christmas." She eased around the squad car. As they pulled out of the lot she saw him jotting something on a pad—her "name" and license plate number more than likely.

They would spend the night in Miss Lillian's vacant room. After Lamar insisted on paying for it, he and Miss Lillian became instant friends. She asked them to sit and talk to her for a few minutes, suggesting that Lamar add a couple of pieces to the fire. Miss Lillian opened a bottle of Sandeman Fine Tawny Port her late husband had bought for a special occasion. He had died in 1980 before they opened it. The three drank toasts to Christmas, the New Year, and Arthur, Lillian's late husband. She replaced the cork and said they would save the rest for breakfast. They shared a hearty laugh, and later, Miss Lillian rooted through her closet and presented Morgan with a pair of loafers.

"These are rather worn and probably a tad too big, but it beats going barefoot in the sleet." Lillian didn't ask why Morgan had hobbled in wearing only one shoe.

"I love you, Mom."

Tears glistened in Lillian's eyes. The light from the fireplace, two candles, and one string of blinking Christmas lights on a Charlie Brown-scrawny tree cast a soothing patina over them.

The arms of the sofa and both overstuffed chairs, no doubt from Goodwill, were covered with cheap doilies. Coasters tried, unsuccessfully, to hide all the rings on the much-abused coffee table. But it was a loving place. A place where anyone could have found respite in Miss Lillian's warm embrace.

Even two vampires.

34

Radical Unwinding
December 25

"It was a dark and stormy night"... or soon would be.

Edward Bulwer Lytton's
opening sentence in his 1830 novel,
Paul Clifford (as amended)

Christmas morning and deadly quiet. Jamie had given the Norwegian couple three days off. No tree, no decorations of any kind. Why bother? He sipped his coffee, now cold, and scowled at the cup as if it had betrayed him. He had to go down there, down to the basement to check on Jamie Junior— "JJ." Two days ago his son had experienced an episode of vampirism, the second such in ten days. Jamie wondered if the TV broadcasts of all the chaos in Cambridge had set him off. No way of knowing for sure. He would hunt up a pipe and boom up his coffee first. His hands trembled. "Dammit!"

Jamie scowled at the email, the only one in his inbox. Dr. Martin wanted to see him at eight o'clock tomorrow for an explanation of why the Cambridge Police were running wild through his office and the lab on Christmas Eve. Jamie ran a hand through his thinning, salt-and- pepper hair. He really didn't know what had happened and couldn't reach Detective Peyton, couldn't find Lamar and Morgan. Hal was out of touch, too, and Flossie was still recovering in the safe house. Hemming's secretary was under wraps in a psycho ward. Ed was scheduled for surgery in a few hours. He'd have to go visit him as soon as the docs allowed it. God. *If it wasn't for me the church wouldn't be all shot up along with Ed, and his secretary wouldn't be in a psycho ward.* He pursed his lips. He felt like he was in quicksand up to his armpits with no Tarzan to pull him out.

As he reached for his coffee in the microwave the phone rang.

Jamie started and sloshed coffee on his pants. "Jesus wept."

"This is Dr. Heller." His voice sounded angry. No answer. He could hear someone breathing. "*Merry Christmas to you, too,*" he said and was about to hang up when she spoke.

"Season's greetings, Daddy Dearest." Her tone was acid.

Jamie stiffened but modulated his voice. "Well. And whom do I have the pleasure—"

"Cut the crap, Daddy. You know who I am. I'm your little girl."

"If you are calling for a meeting I suggest you—"

"Oh, we shall meet, Father, but it will be at a time and place of my choosing. Let's make it a surprise."

"Madam, I am not easily intimidated; let me remind you I am a former Marine combat veteran."

"Oh, you remind me of quite a few things, Father, but now it's my turn to do the reminding. First, you begat me when you screwed Mary Engram your freshman year at Harvard. And I am, like your son, a third generation from a long blood line of polluted people named Heller. You abandoned us, Daddy Dearest. Mumsie was kicked out of school, disowned by her parents, and after I was born, she killed herself. All because of you." She stopped speaking.

Jamie was breathing with difficulty. After a long pause, she continued. "And now, you will pay and pay dearly, Daddy of mine. Most dearly indeed." Her voice had become quiet and deadly.

"First, JJ will become the father of a new coven of vampires under my control. We will destroy you. And the Genetics Lab. If you doubt my word, I suggest you talk to Charlotte before her mind disintegrates entirely and she kills herself like my mother did. Father Hemming will be defrocked. And all the cats will be eaten: Oxnard and Calvin and Cricket. Oh yes, we shall add Jennifer to our list. By the time we expose the GenLab your life will be in ruins. Then, *Dr. Heller,* we will mercifully end it with an aspen stake through your heart and, of course, decapitation. You will lie in state forever on our vampire altar." Her laugh sounded like a dolphin's underwater cry.

Jamie slammed the receiver into the cradle with such force that it separated from the wall. "My God," his voice cracked. The part about Mary getting pregnant and being kicked out of school was true, and her parents did disown her. I was going to help her out as soon as I got a job, but then she, she died. I had to finish my PhD and— "Oh, God, help me. I've brought *two* vampires into the world." But I can atone. I will atone. Vampire Resurrection can heal them, even Judeland if she will only, only….

Where the hell are Lamar and Morgan when I really need them? The ringing phone startled Jamie even worse the second time. He stared at it as if it were coiled, about to strike. And it was.

"Heller here."

"James, this is Robert Shackleford. From the church. What in God's name are you up to?" After a long pause he added, "Well?"

"Merry Christmas, Bob. I don't suppose you could be a bit more precise about the subject of your concern."

"Oh, you can count on that. I trust you've heard all about the debacle at Saint Paul. Our visiting committee is stretched thin with delegations dispatched to Father Hemming's bedside at Mass General and Charlotte Rhodes, who is sequestered in a psychiatric ward, not to mention those on our regular shut-in list. Oh, and our priest and his secretary are under police protection, as you may know. The police cordoned off our church *on Christmas Eve*, mind you, and the inside of it looks like a battlefield. Parishioners showed up in droves Christmas Eve, only to be turned away.

"The parking lot made Dunkirk look like an orderly withdrawal. You are responsible for turning Saint Paul into an insane asylum, and I want some answers. Our lawyer will want them as well." Robert was breathing hard.

"Yes, I have heard about all that. A dreadful state of affairs."

"Let's start with the two bodies Father Hemming recently interred at your expense. And you wouldn't happen to know the whereabouts of Mr. Bradford and Ms. Summers by any chance?"

"The whereabouts? It's Christmas, Bob. Have you tried Coleson Manor?"

"Nobody answers."

"And why do you wish to speak with them?" Jamie wasn't about to tell him that Robert was in the hospital with a gunshot wound.

"For openers, they were seen entering the church, and a bunch of shell casings indicates one of them fired a weapon, further defiling our sanctuary."

"Bob, it sounds like you should be talking to the police. Have you?"

"They won't talk to me."

"You might want to consider your blood pressure, Bob. I'm concerned you might have a heart attack or a stroke. I recall you took a shot across the bow only last year. I suggest you rely on the police to sort this all out. Get some rest. Play with the kids. And do have a Merry Christmas."

Gently, he replaced the receiver in the cradle that was barely hanging on the wall and shook his head. I need to find a screw driver to fix the phone. Phillips head or blade type?

No, he had to find Hal.

"Cordell, it's Lamar. We need to talk. Give me your word you won't haul me in for questioning, and I'll give you a total core dump on what happened. I'm sure you want to know everything before the governor calls you again, right?"

"Where are you?"

"We don't have time to play games. I hang up in twenty seconds so you don't get a make on my location. The coffee shop in twenty minutes. If I see any signs of a trap, you'll never learn the truth about the Saint Paul shootout."

Cordell paused.

"Ten seconds."

"Jesus, Mary, and Joseph and—okay, your rules. See you in twenty."

It hadn't occurred to either of them that Simon's Coffee Emporium would be closed on Christmas day. It was thirty-six degrees and cloudy; few people were on the streets. Cordell walked up to Lamar, who was leaning against a streetlight, deeply buried in a newspaper he'd fished out of a trash bin.

"It's closed," Cordell said.

"Yeah. What's open today, any idea?"

"Follow me. My car is a couple of blocks away." Cordell started off and then turned back. "You coming?"

"Yeah, just remember our deal."

Cordell pursed his lips as they walked to his unmarked sedan and got in. "We don't actually have to go anywhere. I'll start the car and warm it up. You talk."

Lamar told him almost everything, leaving out the part about him being a vampire and going into the hunting. He said that in the confusion, while Morgan was tending Father Hemming, he chased Judeland and the hapless Charlotte, and that's how he and Morgan had become separated. With the Campus Police closing in, he ran to his old office where he found Jennifer. Lamar fervently hoped she had covered for him.

"Jennifer said you were in your cups and tried to hit on her. You got a little pushy until she threatened to call the police. You beat it before the campus police got there. She was a bit disheveled and flustered they said. In fact, I don't think she gave us the straight skinny, old buddy. How did you avoid being found, by the way?"

"Morgan arrived as I was leaving Jennifer's office, and the two of us hid in the third floor women's restroom until the campus police officers went into Jennifer's office. When your guys showed up there was a lot of confusion, and we slipped out. We ran to the Science Center and hid in the GenLab cold room. Then we set off the alarm and snuck out."

"Where did you go?" Cordell popped a Halls into his mouth.

Lamar shook his head. "Who tipped you off that we were on campus?"

"The Campus Police command center duty officer called us."

Cordell finished taking notes and pocketed his old leather notebook. "Where's your boss, Lamar?"

"Hey, it's Christmas morning. How the hell should I know?"

"I called before leaving to meet you. Nobody answered. I just wondered if you might know. Oh, and how about you leave all the rest of the shooting to my guys?"

Lamar blew out a long breath. "I really hope so, Cordell, and you can take that to the bank."

35

The Reckoning
Monday December 26

The Vampire Marley: "You don't believe in me."

Scrooge: "I don't."

Marley: "What evidence would you have of my reality beyond that of your senses?"

Scrooge: "I don't know."

Marley: "Why do you doubt your senses?"

Scrooge: "Because a little thing affects them. A slight disorder of the stomach... You may be an undigested bit of beef, a blot of mustard... There's more of gravy than of grave about you... Humbug, I tell you; humbug!"

The vampire emits a frightful cry, causing Scrooge to fall to his knees and grip his chair to keep from swooning.

Scrooge: "Mercy! Dreadful vampire, why do you trouble me so?"

A Christmas Carol, Charles Dickens, Dec. 1843 (as amended)

I am the President of the oldest and most prestigious university in North America." Dr. Martin bestowed a withering look at each person seated around her conference table. "*I do not intend to preside over a madhouse.* You have been shielding me from the truth. And that truth can bring us down if we don't confront it and create a new reality—or recreate the old one. I am a pretty good judge of character. I picked all of you. We are supposed to be a team, but you aren't acting like one. Well, my friends and colleagues, no one leaves this room until I have, to borrow a hallowed phrase, 'the truth, the whole truth, and nothing but the truth.'"

Flossie appeared visibly shaken. Jamie looked tired—gaunt—but still hanging on. Hal, as always the consummate professional, looked inscrutable, unfazed.

"Jamie, you can smoke your goddamn pipe. I know you have it in your jacket pocket." Her voice turned soft. "Flossie, I know you've been through a terrible ordeal, and here I am making it tougher on you. But the future of Harvard may be hanging by a slender thread, so we all will just have to tough it out. You've been Director of Human Resources for a decade now."

"Nine years next month."

"Okay. You hired Judeland and Lamar and Morgan Summers. You were batting almost a thousand your first eight years. What happened? And don't sugar coat anything. I've turned my bullshit detector up to the max."

Flossie regarded her nails, straightened her posture and looked up. "Father Hemming called me and asked for a favor. He's been a great friend since our undergrad days at Harvard. He was trying to reclaim a troubled life and wanted me to take on Judeland Bundaeker. She is a Harvard grad with a good academic record and a recent convert to Catholicism. She had been an atheist, according to Father Hemming. I decided to keep her under my thumb and made her my administrative assistant. She was a quick read, extremely efficient and organized. For a long time I could find no fault with her other than that she was uptight and seemed to be devoid of humor."

"And then?"

"She became zealous in studying our personnel records, especially the new hires. I got the feeling she would have been a great addition to the Gestapo. I tried on several occasions to get her to lighten up, pointing out that it was *my* job to study the applicants. Undaunted, she began making more and more recommendations, always pointing out perceived weaknesses, to the point of suggesting that one or two of my hires presented a danger to the institution."

"Did her list include Bradford and Summers?"

Flossie looked down. "Mostly Summers."

"Do you have any idea as to why she would have killed one of Jamie's lab techs and attacked you with the same intention?"

"No. She was—is—obviously a dangerously obsessed person, but I have no idea what triggered the attacks."

"And Bradford and Summers?"

"I think I can speak to that," Jamie said, pulling out his pipe, tobacco pouch, tamper and lighter. His ritual all but brought the meeting to a standstill. As he lit up, the door opened and a young intern rolled in a cart with coffee, tea, and some danish. When she left, Jamie began.

"Let's start with Lamar." Jamie proceeded to praise his performance and his special contributions to the Faculty of Arts and Sciences. In turn, he addressed Morgan.

Dr. Martin listened attentively, sipping her coffee and nodding. Finally she spoke. "Jamie, that was textbook. Well rehearsed. Now how about we drill down to what you haven't told me."

Jamie leaned back in his chair, puffed his pipe back into full vigor, and regarded his boss the way a sniper assesses his target. "We are having to defend ourselves against an international threat from an organization in Europe that wants the GenLab to fail. Lamar and Morgan have been my sword and shield during our defense. The woman who was abducted from the Faculty Club was supposed to have been Morgan, but they got the wrong person. We will likely never know the ultimate fate of the waitress, Paula Bernard.

"The car that blew up just off campus belonged to Morgan. She was supposed to have been killed in that explosion. I am convinced that Judeland is a member of the secret organization— our enemy. They probably didn't know they had hired a loose cannon on deck, any more than Flossie did".

"Where the hell are the FBI and the CIA? Why are we having to defend against the John Dillinger gang without their help?"

"The FBI is working the case, or cases. So is your campus and Cambridge police departments," Hal said.

"Let me see if I can put some pieces together," Dr. Martin said. "We have kidnappings, murders, shootouts, attempted murders, a car bombing, a church desecration, the intention to destroy our Genetics Laboratory and God knows what else, and here I sit, having to drag it out of you?"

Abject silence. Pipe smoke drifted up through the air handlers.

"Do I have to subpoena each one of you to get to ground truth?" Her voice was stiletto.

"You have a university to run," Jamie said. "Things were happening rather fast. We discovered that the lab tech that Judeland killed was actually a mole on the payroll of this international cartel, and that he had actually sabotaged some of our work."

"Why the hell would Judeland kill her own man—or mole?" Dr. Martin scowled as she made a few notes.

"We are dealing with someone who is completely unbalanced," Jamie said. "As you know she also turned on her mentor, Flossie."

Dr. Martin looked up. "Does the FBI have any promising leads on all this?"

"They play their cards pretty tight, Dr. Martin," Hal said.

The door opened and the intern stuck her head in the conference room. "Sorry to interrupt, but Mr. and Mrs. 'Anonymous Donors' are waiting in your office, Dr. Martin. They didn't have an appointment. Just popped in. Shall I tell them you'll be a few more minutes?"

"No, I'll be right there. Thank you." The door closed. "Those two are going to build one of, if not *the*, biggest computer center on any campus in the country. We plan to ramp up our graduate degree program in computer science after we spend a double handful of their millions. Not a word of that outside this room. Class dismissed. But I want to hear the rest of the story, and I think there is one, so get on my calendar tomorrow." She glared at the three and left.

Flossie closed her eyes and trembled. Jamie slumped forward, running one hand through his hair. Hal pushed back from the table and stretched.

"Do either of you know what the OVFS is?" Flossie asked.

36

Flee the Dark Angel
Monday, December 26

"The vampire is genetically disposed to kill—be it animal or human. Vampirism is also soul destroying. Can the soul be restored? Ah, that falls into the province of the Church rather than to any scientific inquiry."

A quote from Gene Claude Vompre
(a fictional character in this novel).

She watched Heller drive off. Eight-oh-five and heavily overcast. Snowflakes zigzagged aimlessly in the cold, gusting wind. Ten minutes passed before the Norwegian couple arrived: Berjit and Hartvig Arensen. They were old and therefore quite expendable. It was shopping day, and Berjit would soon reemerge and drive to the grocery store. Their routine never changed. That would leave one old man upstairs and a young vampire in the basement. Soon, that vampire would be free. Soon he would enjoy his first hunting. Soon, she would initiate him into the vampire conjugal rites. Soon he would become her senior "footman," and later, her deputy. Together they would give birth to the ODA, the Order of the Dark Angels. In the fullness of time they would strike down the GenLab and its leader, Daddy Dearest. And they would blunt the "Terrible Swiss Sword" wielded by the Church.

She watched the old lady drive away, got out of her car, walked to the front door, and pressed the doorbell. Who would suspect a female officer of the Salvation Army? But she was there to collect far more than a few coins in a bright red kettle. She would collect a mortal soul and one not so mortal. She heard the door chime, soon followed by muffled footsteps.

"Yes?"

"We are collecting for the poor and needy people of Cambridge, sir. Would you have the heart to join with those generous spirits who provide some warmth and comfort for those less fortunate in our city?"

"Vell, of course, but you see I don't live here, I'm ust the—"

"Would you mind terribly if I stepped inside for a moment? My hands and feet are freezing. I won't take more than a minute of your time to warm up."

Hartvig frowned and stroked his chin. She knew he had strict instructions to let no one enter the house that hadn't been approved by Dr. Heller. But he finally shrugged and opened the door.

As Judeland entered she lunged for his throat, pivoting and slamming his head against the wall several times. He slid down the wall and folded over onto the rug. Judeland pulled a roll of duct tape from her satchel and quickly bound his hands behind him, then his ankles and mouth.

She stood and smiled. Rather portly. He would yield a feast, one quite fitting for JJ's first. The thought sent quivering sensations between her legs. She would conduct her first initiation, and it would be her most memorable. There would be many to follow, of course.

"JJ," she crooned, as she closed the front door and headed for the basement stairs. She was shocked to find a key pad at the door to the stairs. "Help me, oh Dark One. I call upon thee, Great Overlord of Charna, to remove all obstacles before your anointed one." She felt a surge of strength, of raw power. Her mind focused as if it were a laser beam. She pulled the door handle out, reached through for a handhold, and slowly tore the door from its hinges, quite enjoying the rending sounds of metal and splintering wood.

"Dad? What's that? What's happening?" Judeland heard the young man's alarm.

"Patience, my young one. You are soon to be free." She seemed to float down to the basement.

"Who are you? Where is my father? I have never had a visitor before. Where are Berjit and Hartvig?" He stood looking through the bars.

"Ah, JJ, you have a new life before you now. Stand back while I unhinge the final obstacle to a world filled with promise, excitement, blood, and sex."

"Does my father know you're here?"

"I am here to take you away to safety." She twisted the lock on his cell door until it snapped and fell in pieces. The door swung open. "You see how simple life can be for our kind? Come," she reached for his hand. "Upstairs."

"First we shall feast and then we shall fuck."

JJ's eyes widened and his breath quickened. "Surely my father would never allow—"

"Shhh, my dear one. I speak for your father now. Come quickly. Time is fleeting." Upstairs she handed him the knife. "Slit his throat." Hartvig's eyes bulged with terror, and he mumphed through the tape as he struggled.

Pale and shuddering, JJ stepped back and reached for the wall as if he might collapse.

"Like this." Judeland snatched the knife from him and slashed it across the older man's throat. Blood spurted over her arm. She wiped some of it on JJ's cheeks as the fire in her began to build. Hartvig's legs kicked several times before he lay still. At first the blood spurted, then flowed and finally seeped from the severed throat. JJ's eyes darkened, and he sank to his knees and bent over the lifeless body of the man who had been his only friend for over two years. The hunting was upon him, and he reveled in it.

After he had reached his surfeit, Judeland led him up the stairs to the master bedroom, where she undressed him. She could smell their father on the sheets. "Oh, Daddy Dearest, if you could only be here to watch," she cried out with joyful abandon, as she stripped off her clothes.

She pulled JJ on top of her. He was already hard, his face bloody, eyes glittering, lips pulled back in demonic glee. She noted with satisfaction that they were spreading blood on Daddy Dearest's sheets and knew that soon they would add his son's semen to the bloodstains. Oh, what a splendid Christmas present they would leave. She had become a mistress of vampire initiation—a dark angel. Soon she would create and rule a vampire nation. But for the moment, she reveled at the realization that she was being fucked by her own brother.

While they showered and dressed, he was as obedient as a well-trained dog, showing her where to find his father's cash, spare credit cards. and other valuables, which she placed in the Salvation Army satchel she had left by the door. She wrote a note in blood:

> *Jamie Dearest,*
>
> *I have need of your son. He is quite masterful as a swordsman, by the way. And he enjoyed the feast provided by our host, Mr. Arensen. We found your bed much to our liking. You have good taste in beds, Daddy Dearest. We must depart now. But fear not, for like that famous general said, I shall return.*
>
> *Jude*

And then they left.

37

Litany of Infamy
Monday Night, December 26

"There is no medicine to be found for a life which has
fled."

Ibycus, Ancient Greek lyric poet, 580 B.C.

Cordell watched the FBI crime photographer as she took pictures of the bedroom. She'd already finished with the body. Dr. Heller was in the dining room, sobbing intermittently. The sedative he had taken earlier had worn off, and he had taken something stronger—his favorite, a gin martini. Lamar and Morgan were with him, trying with little success to provide some comfort. Dr. Martin had come and stayed awhile, along with Dr. Wallace Gibson, but she'd ordered Flossie to stay home. All the visitors except Harvard's president knew the real implications. JJ had been taken and was on the hunt. He had to be found, and quickly.

This time Lamar and Morgan had an airtight alibi, Cordell thought. They had been attending a meeting with Dr. Martin when Mr. Arensen was killed. Someone tore up the house freeing JJ. Probably that Judeland woman and maybe a couple big guys with crowbars. Nobody has the faintest idea where either of them have gone. Dr. Martin had handled it surprisingly well, at least so far. Cordell admired her quiet, empathetic demeanor. He could use a little more of that, something his wife mentioned from time to time.

When the late news gets this, God help us all. Another murder, another kidnapping. Any more of this shit, and the pillars of Harvard could crumble. Cordell looked in the Heller living room at the knot of dark blue suits and FBI windbreaker jackets muttering and speaking in quiet, clipped tones into their cell phones. They had finally taken total control of the "Cambridge Crisis," as the *Globe* now called it. Cordell felt listless, empty, but secretly delighted to have been relieved. This is one case where the crap is going to flow uphill, he thought. Lord, what a blessing. This is way over my pay grade. Still, he had half the local police force combing the area for Judeland and JJ. They probably won't find them, but at least they are putting on a good show. Time to put the squeeze on Lamar. Time for some more coffee at Simons.

WCVB's Brady Duncan had her game face on as she began. "This morning, while Dr. James R. Heller, Dean of Harvard's Faculty of Arts and Sciences and Director of its Genetics

Laboratory, was meeting with President Martin, his home was being ransacked, his housekeeper killed and gutted like a river trout, and his son kidnapped. Welcome to the new Cambridge, one now resembling Chicago when it was ruled by Al Capone's gangsters. We have yet to emerge from *Bloody December,* with its litany of infamy. Our local police have been overwhelmed, and the FBI has taken over the investigations. Unsolved assaults, murders, a shootout, a car bombing, a church desecration, and multiple kidnappings have spread a dark pall over the celebration of Harvard's three hundred seventy-fifth anniversary and the holiday season. The formerly quiet collegiate town of Cambridge, home of America's oldest and most...."

Simon's Coffee Emporium was unusually quiet. The sunrise looked like an overturned sponge cake. Cold, gusty wind blew trash and a few leaves down the street. Inside, an old man chewed on an unlit cigar and shuffled the New York Times. Two teens, their heads snugged together, sat across from a frat boy sleeping off a hangover. Lamar sat at "their" table. Cordell didn't even make eye contact as he dropped his overcoat and battle-stained fedora on an empty chair and sank down. He sipped his coffee and finally looked at Lamar, who looked like he'd pulled an all-nighter.

"So, what have you got for me?"

Lamar slowly emerged from his stupor. "I heard the FBI pushed you aside, Cordell. I'm sorry. Really sorry."

"They probably won't play nice the way I have." Cordell pulled out his pack of cigarettes and tapped it on the table.

Both men stared at the creased but still unopened pack.

"Don't quit on us, Cordell. This is your town. What do you think would happen to Harvard if we don't stop Judeland and the others?"

"I know," Cordell said. "The late night talk shows would have another blast at our expense. Heads would roll. Good heads."

"And the best families would send their kids to Yale," Lamar added. "And the GenLab might be shut down leaving all those people the world over who are suffering from diseases we were on the verge of curing out in the cold."

"What do you propose we do?" Cordell asked. Before Lamar could answer they heard his cell phone buzz. "Cordell here." He listened for about a minute."

"I'll meet you back at Precinct in thirty minutes." He snapped the phone shut.

"Merry Christmas. I think we got a new lead. Seems when the shop was servicing one of our unmarked sedans they found a beacon transmitter somebody attached under it. They traced it back and found out where and when it was purchased. Boston, first week in December. My guess is that your cartel guys attached it sometime before our trolling exercise. I suggest we get with Hal and see if he has any way to backtrack to the place where it was being monitored.

"Likely that's the cartel's safe house or headquarters. Maybe we could take them out of the game. And we might find a lead to where Judeland has gone to ground."

"I'll set up the meeting with Hal," Lamar said. "You and McConnell, Hal, Morgan, and me. No more." Lamar pulled out his cell phone and in five minutes had arranged the meeting at Hal's command center.

"Our two mobile vans are tuned to the frequency of the tracking device they planted. When we activate it, the base station—the bad guys—will begin monitoring it out of curiosity about how and why it went active. Then we ping them."

"Hal, can we cut all the communications lingo and run that one again in English?" Cordell asked.

"Yeah. Sorry. We can get what's called a triangulation on the bad guys." He drew a crude map showing the command center and its two mobile outstations. "The point where the three vectors intersect should be the location of the cartel monitoring station—their safe house."

"How soon can you set that up?" Cordell asked.

"A couple of hours, max." Hal was already reaching for his cell phone. "Can you have a squad of your guys ready to take them down?"

"Absolutely."

"Cordell, you going to cut in the FBI?" Lamar asked.

"Hell, no."

"Stay under the blanket, Jamie," Judeland said. "I'll go in and make the arrangements. We need another vehicle, because they're looking for this one." Jamie's answer was muffled.

The outside was unimposing. Cinderblock covered with white paint, it looked like something out of the twenties. Monty had "paved" one end of the alley with gravel. It was half filled with cars, some of which were rusted out. His customers were welcomed by a handmade "No Trespassing" sign. Big black letters on the building proclaimed: Monty's Auto Repair and Body Shop. Both repair bay doors were shut, as was the office door. The window glass looked like it hadn't been cleaned since the Johnstown flood, and several panes were cracked. The alley was silent and deserted. Judeland turned the office doorknob and smiled. It was unlocked.

"Anybody home?" She rang a corroded miniature cow bell sitting on the counter.

A forty-something guy walked in from the repair bay wiping his hands on a rag. "Yeah?"

"Are you Monty?"

"Who wants to know?" His voice was surly.

"I'm Judeland. I need a car. One without a VIN number. Number Three told me about you."

Monty frowned and looked out the window at her car. "You know where Number Three is?"

"No. Is that important?"

"Cash. I do a cash business."

"We can work that out. That and a lot more. Is it safe to talk here?"

"I'm the only one here."

Not any more, Judeland thought.

"Mobile One in place and ready." It was parked on Tory Row, near Coleson Manor. "Mobile Two in position and ready." They were northeast of the Harvard Yard.

"Hit it," Hal said to his operator who switched the unit to transmit and keyed a signal. It connected with the transponder, a device similar to the World War II IFF—Identification Friend or Foe—which had been placed in Lamar's garage.

A red light began to flash on the control unit located in the OVFS monitoring center, located inside a parts room off one of Monty's two repair bays. "What the hell," Monty said. He leaned over the bench and read the LED output. "That's got to be Bradford's place. Why would the unit light up now?"

He quickly transmitted a signal. "It's not moving." His face darkened. He sent another signal, one designed to turn off the transponder. "Damn, that wasn't the unit we put on Bradford's Jag, it's the one on that detective's unmarked wheels. That's odd. Too odd.

"Any chance you were followed, lady?"

"No, I wasn't followed. I drove a break tail pattern before coming here."

"You got any electronic stuff on that car you're driving?"

"No."

"Bingo!" Hal shouted. "We got 'em." He pointed to the giant wall map. "Right there, Amherst and Danfort, a stone's throw from the Harvard Bridge. Cordell, get the east end of that bridge blocked off quick as you can. I have half a dozen guys as backup for you."

"Right. Your guys should cover both ends of Harvard Bridge. My guys will block Memorial Drive both east and west, plus one here, at Amesbury and Vassar, and we put one at Mass. Avenue north. Any questions?"

"Be careful, Cordell," Morgan said. "Judeland's got JJ. She may try to use him as a shield."

"Right. Blanton, get everything we have moving."

Detective Sergeant McConnell already had Precinct Dispatch on the line. He fed the instructions in crisp, police style, making the dispatcher repeat each one. Hal was doing the same with his people.

"Maybe I should go," Morgan said. "I can talk her language."

Cordell and Hal both nodded, and Lamar and Morgan raced for Miss Lillian's Pontiac.

The light was fading fast.

Monty grabbed his jacket, a holstered automatic with two extra magazines, the electronic device off the bench, some cash out of a drawer, and shoved it all in a laundry bag. He grabbed a set of keys hanging from a key board and started for the repair bay.

"Hey, where're you going?" Judeland's voice was edged with panic.

"I don't know about you, but I'm getting the hell out of this place."

Judeland stood, rooted, as she heard the growl of his pickup truck engine and a grinding of gears. In a moment Monty's became so silent she could hear the neon bulb overhead. Then she bolted for the alley, jumped in the car, and started it. When she reached the alley entrance she saw a Cambridge squad car racing down Amherst, lights flashing, no siren.

"Scheisse!" She backed up—all the way into the junk yard parking area. "JJ. Quickly. We must flee." No answer. She twisted and reached into the back seat, pulling up the blanket. He was gone. "Charna, why hast thou forsaken me?" she implored as she opened the door and slipped out into the gloom around Monty's auto body shop.

Darkness was ever her friend.

38

Vampire Resurrections
December

When a vampire takes "The Road Less Traveled."

From the title of a book by M. Scott Peck
(as amended)

D r. Heller sat in his dining room, disconsolate, stirring the potato leek soup prepared for him by the equally inconsolable Berjit Arensen, who burst into tears on the hour and on the half hour with the regularity of Big Ben. The chairman of Saint Paul's visitation committee and his wife had just left. They had been no help. Nor had the Ativan he'd taken. Nor had the two very dry Tanqueray martinis. He wished he could talk to Ed Hemming, although Ed probably couldn't offer any hope either. The doorbell rang. Jamie didn't even raise his eyes from his soup. He heard Berjit pad to the door and open it but couldn't understand what was said. Berjit still wasn't all that conversant in English; she had relied on her husband too much for that.

"Excuse me for interrupting your dinner, sir, but I got a cab out there," the cabbie gestured, "with a young man who can't pay for the ride but said you would. Comes to $21.50."

Jamie looked up at the man without the slightest comprehension, staring at his ancient leather flight jacket crisscrossed with cracks that looked as if they had been created by a surgeon's deft hand.

"Just outside sir. Won't you come take a look? He probably needs a bit of help to get going."

Jamie stood, slowly, and looked at the man through narrowed eyes. What was he saying? Why was he here? Especially now. He cleared his throat, which felt raw. "You must have made some mistake," he began.

"You are Dr. Heller, the guy they been talking about on radio and TV? This guy, the one out in my cab, says he belongs here. Come on, Dr. Heller, and I'll introduce you." The cabbie took Jamie by the hand and led him out the door, treating him as if he were a patient in an Alzheimer's ward.

Jamie stopped on the front porch. "It's cold out," Jamie said. "Look at all the stars. You don't see stars very much anymore. Too much smog, I guess."

"You should have a jacket, Dr. Heller, but this oughtn't to take a minute." He led Jamie to the cab and opened the back door. A figure shrank into the shadows. "I got to remember to get that inside light replaced," the cabbie mumbled.

"Father?"

The world stopped dead. Time quit—not another tick. Sound vanished. Light swirled into a black hole, somewhere out in space. Heller never felt the ground yank him down. Never heard the unintelligible lamentations of the Norwegian woman. Never felt his cell phone buzzing. He was only aware that he wasn't aware of a single thing.

Judeland crawled out of the trunk of a rusted-out 1993 Plymouth. The police were finally gone. She ached all over from being confined for so long, and she was hungry. She wondered if any stray cats were around. A place like this ought to have one or two, she thought.

Startled by the light inside Monty's office, she crept to the door and looked inside. A middle-age man sat, head on a curled arm, dozing on Monty's desk, a copy of *Penthouse* lying on the floor beside him. Probably an off-duty cop serving as a guard. Some guard. She found a fairly large rock and slipped in, walking silently around the sleeper, then slammed it on the back of his head. Taking his gun, holster, cash, and keys, she tied him up with lengths of chain she found in one of the repair bays. The keys to a beat-up white pickup truck parked in the other bay hung from the key board in Monty's office.

She turned left out of the alley.

Two sofas formed a right angle in the living room. Jamie Senior lay on one, JJ sat on the other. The cabbie had been paid a hundred dollars and had gone straight to WCVB to be interviewed in his old Korean War flight jacket. Morgan and Lamar applied cold compresses to Jamie, tucked in blankets, provided hot toddies, and struggled with their emotions. Cordell stood back and shook his head. The FBI hadn't even arrived yet, but it wouldn't be long.

Heller the younger had been found walking on the railroad tracks that paralleled the Charles River. Two young boys, brothers, had befriended him and taken him to their home. Their parents had called a cab after feeding JJ a hot meal. They had written down Dr. Heller's address and given it to the cabbie, telling him to bring him back if it was the wrong address. All that and more would fill the morning papers.

Monty must have somehow slipped through the blockade, Cordell thought. And Judeland must know how to become invisible. Cordell chuckled out loud as he thought about the confrontation with Wilson Jarboe, the FBI Special Agent in Charge. Wilson was livid that the Cambridge Police, along with some of Harvard's campus police, had conducted an operation not authorized or controlled by the Bureau. Cordell had told Wilson that it all happened too fast to bring in the Bureau, which was absolute bullshit, and Wilson knew it.

Colonel Johann Solento sat stiff-necked in the dark confessional. Sweat soaked his starched uniform shirt and slid down his flanks. He glared at his watch, barely able to read it. He'd been waiting for over fifteen minutes. God rot the man even if he is a cardinal. His lips moved silently, and his eyes stung. The air had become stale, and he began to slump. The door to the adjoining compartment opened and closed almost noiselessly, and the Colonel stiffened again. He paused a moment before saying, "Cardinal, I have sinned twice."

"We can skip the code words," Cardinal Manlocara said. "I watched you enter the confessional."

"You watched me—"

"The OVFS is at grave risk. All of our operatives in North America are either dead or in hiding, both from us and from the FBI. It is time for a total cleansing. The two of us must become invisible. So must Cardinal Loconis, but he must be silenced for the remainder of eternity. Do I make myself clear?"

"Perfectly clear." Johann found it difficult to speak as his throat had nearly closed tight.

"This must be done to perfection, and it must be finished not later than tomorrow night.

There will be an investigation. The books will be audited, but the auditors will find nothing amiss. You will insure they find nothing else that condemns either of us. Our mission is not over, Colonel. We will go into remission. We will wander in the desert for forty days, but we will emerge stronger, more resourceful, and better led. I will be Number One. You will be Number Two—if you carry out the cleansing, the purification, completely and quickly. We will continue to rid the world of its insidious cancer. For those who do God's work in this great cause, there will be substantial rewards. Do you understand all that I've said?"

Although stunned by his words, Johann murmured, "I do. And it shall be done, Your Eminence."

Silence consumed the confessional. Only faint breathing. The other door clicked softly as it shut. The Colonel counted to a hundred and departed, trying to erase the vestiges of a smile. He could have served as a model for Michelangelo.

Vic Brown

Johann knew his victim's habits. Soon, his target would disappear into the necropolis passageways beneath the Vatican and find his way to the secret vault, where he would study the codex, run his pudgy fingers over the locks of hair, peer upon the rows of heads, and be moved to tears that God had chosen him—Cardinal Alfonso Loconis—to be his terrible Swiss sword. And so it came to pass, a scant six hours after Johann's trip to the confessional.

Alfonso had been in the vault for twenty minutes when Johann opened a bucket of quick-drying cement and troweled shut the brick that activated the door. He worked feverishly to add a layer of ancient brick in front of the door. Alfonso usually remained in the room for about an hour. Johann finished his work with ten minutes to spare. He would dispose of the nearly empty bucket, trowel and gloves in an ancient cistern at the far end of the corridor. Even if found, they would bear no fingerprints. The tools and cement had been bought by a nameless urchin who had no clue as to the Colonel's real identity. He had worn gloves, of course.

Johann smiled and stretched. He had spent a king's ransom on a bottle of vintage claret as his reward for this night's work. Tanya would help him drink it. He had arranged to have dinner brought into the nondescript hotel several blocks outside of Vatican City. Soon, he would own a new car, but it couldn't be too expensive. It would have to be affordable on a colonel's pay. Almost.

Earlier, Johann had removed the portable secure voice system and hidden it in the safe house he maintained. He would scan the Cardinal's files and select any that needed to be destroyed or removed. But tonight was his to enjoy to the utmost. He wondered, idly, how long the good Cardinal Loconi would last. In desperation, he might drink some of the Egyptian emulsion—the

330

"brine of antiquity" Loconi had called it—that had been used to preserve the heads.

A ghastly thought.

Dr. Heller sat at his desk in the GenLab, beaming. Chugs of pipe smoke rose as he spoke to those present: Dr. Wallace Gibson, Morgan, Lamar, and Flossie, who had received her indoctrination and signed the security clearance oaths, as well as received an initial operational briefing the previous day. She was focused, but her face revealed a twinge of bewilderment, having been fire-hosed into a whole new reality. Flossie's entry into the vampire fraternity resulted from her giving the OVFS Watch List, which she had found in Judeland's files, to Dr. Heller. Morgan conveyed their heartfelt thanks to Flossie. The watch list would form the basis of their search for possible vampires who might want to be resurrected to mortal life.

Wallace Gibson had a surprise for them. In 2010 he had provided a few productive stem cells, therapeutically cloned from the original batch, to a friend and fellow scientist in Heidelberg, Germany. Upon learning of the compromise of all of their currently active genetic material, Wallace had contacted his friend and secured a return set of fertile stem cells that had originally been harvested from DNA contributions from Dr. Heller.

"The odds of genetic rejection go way up if the stem cell donor is not also to be the recipient. In this case, however, the father-son relationship provides favorable odds against rejection," Wallace said. "We have agreed to accept the slight risk of rejection in our next implant, that of Dr. Heller's son. Meanwhile, we are culturing stem cells for Ms. Summers and Mr. Bradford, and they should be ready in early March of 2012. Are there any questions?"

"I have one," Jamie said. "Morgan has developed a course of preparation for resurrection therapy, and my son hasn't had time to go through it. Shouldn't we delay his treatment until he completes that program?"

"Let me speak to that," Morgan said. "From the earliest days of the discovery of your son's, uh, condition, you have kept him confined. He experienced only two recent bouts of depression, a precursor to going into the hunting. And, sadly, one experience of hunting, which lasted only a short time. That he flipped out of the hunting so fast is a good sign. While he is at the entry point of active vampirism, the adolescent stage if you will, the first two vampires, victims of Judeland's treachery, were old vampires—like I am. And you didn't know as much about the metabolism of rejection when you conducted resurrection therapy on them. With Jamie Junior, his mindset—the level of his desire as well as his inexperience as a vampire—is the key to success. Those who follow us will have to go through the whole program, the one I have developed and will conduct as we find new members who wish to become mortal."

Heller sat back, looking at Wallace, who was chewing a thumb nail. "Okay, that's settled. Anyone else? Good. We take a break for New Year's Eve and let's target Wednesday the fourth. I'll coordinate security arrangements with Hal. Morgan, are you sure it's a good idea to have my son move to Coleson Manor and live with you?"

"Yes. We need to give him a few days of freedom from the confines of your basement. He needs a few walks in the park, so to speak, to clear his mind. I think we can rely on Hal plus the new people we have hired from Watts Security."

"Well done. Superb job, Wally. I won't forget what you've accomplished to keep our program on track," Heller said. "Now, everybody go home and rest. Decompress. Have an adult beverage of choice to celebrate."

January

Dr. Gibson banned Dr. Heller and Lamar from the operating room. Morgan, who was a trained nurse, was allowed to observe and assist. The process took a bit over four hours. Hal had almost forcibly taken Jamie to the club for some Oysters Rockefeller during JJ's operation, although both ate sparingly. Back in his office, Jamie forced himself to read and approve a couple of monographs on the prospects of genetic alteration of blood disorders like lupus and hemophilia. He had sadly neglected the "open side" of his responsibility as Dean. Jamie wondered if others would think he had atrophied on the job.

His cell buzzed. "Jamie, it's Wally. Can you come over to the lab?"

"On my way. How did it go?"

"Come see for yourself."

Jamie snapped his phone shut and raced for the Science Center.

March

The months had passed slowly, but at times it felt to Morgan like she and Lamar were in warp drive. Late March in Cambridge was a fickle maiden. Hints of spring intermingled with frequent haunting recollections of winter. A light jacket would freeze a person; a heavy one would become suffocating. Like the weather, much had changed in Cambridge.

The trauma factor had dropped to zero. No more murders or kidnappings. The media chalked that up to the persistent presence of the FBI. The GenLab had regained its stability after Judeland and Lawrence were gone.

JJ hadn't changed so much physically, although his initial sense of gratefulness was almost overpowering. Morgan believed he hadn't been afflicted by active vampirism long enough to have suffered much of the soul corrosion that older vampires endured, although Morgan seemed to be an exception. She had developed a personal power strong enough to fight off the duality of vampirism—depression and manic highs. She had subdued or even eliminated most episodes of hunting over the past two centuries. Somehow she had managed to hang on to shards of her soul and was ready for resurrection without requiring any special preparation. She had guided Lamar through his early exposure to vampirism such that he required relatively little tuning up. Both eagerly awaited their genetic rebirths—their resurrections.

According to Dr. Gibson their stem cells would be ready for transplant in about a week.

Most of the smaller loose ends had been handled. Miss Lillian's Pontiac had been returned. The freezer had been sent back to Sears. The new Lady Chapel at Saint Paul was half finished, the cornerstone securely in place. A proper burial service in Saint Paul's Cemetery had been conducted for the two headless bodies and handsome headstones erected.

Robert was back and had reestablished order at Coleson Manor, although it was more a fortress now, having been ringed with security guards. He was looking forward to stocking the fish pond when the weather warmed up. Father Hemming was off to the Vatican, intent on seeing that the OVFS was permanently disestablished. Judeland, Monty, and Jake had apparently vanished from Cambridge. OVFS communications ceased on the twenty-seventh of December and had not reappeared. FBI agents had interrogated everyone associated with the "Harvard Crime Wave" from Dr. Martin down to the sous chefs at the Faculty Club.

But miraculously, not a hint of Vampire Resurrection leaked.

39

Prelude to the Afternoon of a Fawn
June

"For since by man came death, by man came also the
resurrection of the dead."

I Corinthians 24

A late spring sun lit the breakfast nook at Coleson Manor.
Outside, wrens flitted from branch to branch; their
squabbling added a cheery note to a tense quiet,
punctuated only by the occasional clink of a silver spoon in a
porridge bowl or coffee cup. Robert's tight face was mirrored by
those of Lamar, Morgan, and JJ. It was the Ides of June, the day
of resurrection for Lamar and Morgan. Their procedures would
begin at eleven a.m. Robert would have much preferred to send his
charges out into the mortal world filled with his signature Eggs
Benedict, but no one seemed hungry. Dr. Gibson had directed that

they have only a light breakfast—nothing after eight o' clock and nothing more substantial than toast and juice.

Morgan, no matter how hard she tried, could not banish the images of Rena and her husband, nor forget the agony she experienced as she drove the stakes into their hearts, and then removed their heads. Who would do that for us, she wondered? She had left detailed instructions sealed in the desk in the secret room. JJ had been initiated into the "Secret Room Society" and knew that if something went terribly wrong today, he was to open and read the instructions and then carry them out. If all went well, the four of them, even Robert, would burn the letter in the library fireplace while toasting to one another's good health and impermanent longevity.

But that wasn't all that burdened her as she stared at her meager breakfast. How would Lamar act after the resurrection? He was the man with the key to her salvation, as foretold by Pythia so long ago, but he had become more than that. Although mortal love was still something of a mystery, one awaiting her on the "other side," she couldn't predict what resurrection would mean to Lamar. She knew he valued her friendship, companionship and especially their sex, but all that was no more than a *Prelude to the Afternoon of a Fawn*. Morgan wanted Lamar to love her the way she had read about in poetry and novels, watched in plays and movies, and observed in real life, especially during World War II. She knew that real love transcended what they had already created. Though she longed to be mortal, she wanted to be a *loving* mortal ... and a loved one.

"May it please all the gods of the Universe, make him come to me as a loving mortal." With closed eyes she murmured the prayer. When she opened them, the others were staring at her.

Jamie Senior hugged Morgan, who was wearing a hospital gown and slippers, which failed to hide her centerfold features. "Break a leg, kid," Dr. Heller said, his voice husky.

She hugged JJ as well and smiled as he took a quick peek at her breasts. Robert had given her his warmest wishes for success before they left Coleson Manor. She had received a phone call from Hal earlier. Flossie had taken her out for a quick glass of wine the previous night, and she had visited Miss Lillian.

Wally entered Jamie's office quietly and smiled at Morgan. She would go first. It was time. She would say goodbye to 327 years of membership in the fraternity of the living dead. What would she say to Lamar, who waited to walk her down to the operating room? They had experienced peak sex last night—twice—as vampires. That will never happen again, she devoutly hoped.

"Lamar, if anything goes wrong, don't go through with it," she whispered, squeezing his hand.

"Nothing will go wrong, Dear Heart," he said. "And nothing will keep me from following in your footprints. We are in this together, ever since that night at the Faculty Club. You are my woman. Our journey is only beginning."

Then he kissed her. But he didn't say he loved her.

Her eyes opened abruptly. He was standing over her, wearing one of those ridiculous hospital gowns, with a mask, and he was smiling. She could tell by his eyes.

"How do you feel, mortal lady?"

"I don't know." Her voice sounded raspy. She glanced at the various monitors around her bed and noted the wires and tubes but quickly dismissed them. "I'm so tired." Her eyes closed but opened again. "Lamar, I want you to wear this." She tried to raise her left hand but couldn't. "The ring. Take it. Rena gave it to me. It was her wedding ring, the one she would wear—" Morgan couldn't finish.

Lamar slipped the ring off her ring finger and put it on his little finger. "Break a leg, my Dearest Heart," Morgan said, as her eyes fluttered and closed.

40

Mortality for the Damned
June

Now JJ was supposed to eat and drink of the body set before him. The long hall was filled with demons in black cloaks, eyes red, all focused on him. Rush lights burned in sconces around the room, producing acrid smoke. Tallow candles added their pungent aroma, but all of that quailed in contrast to the smell of the drawn and quartered wretch laid out on the table. Pale bone and entrails, still warm, were his and his alone. A silver chalice filled with the man's blood rested beside the severed head. Hartvig's look of terror frozen on the face of the severed head, elicited ribald comment from JJ's companions, all of whom were urging him with their shouts, whistling, and banging of their pewter mugs on the trestle tables.

No few were female. And though they wore the same black cloaks, theirs were pinned back to reveal prodigious breasts, their large nipples rouged. They were making lewd gestures, inviting him to impregnate them on the table, in front of the horde of creatures whose raucous choruses of derision and encouragement swept over him and bounded off the damp stone walls.

JJ was startled as two cats—Calvin and Oxnard—leapt upon the table and started to fight over a piece of intestine. Flying claws, hissing, and angry growls delighted the demons, who stood up on the benches, the better to see. The demon sitting to his right reached over and pushed JJ's face into the offal and held it, to the great delight of his fellows. JJ began to retch while all around him laughed and redoubled their chants for him to eat and drink and fornicate. The cats turned from their feasting and attacked JJ's hair.

He launched back from the table, screaming.

JJ's eyes snapped open. He was shaking, and sweat trickled down from his hair. The sheets were twisted around him as if they were living tendrils. Calvin meowed. Oxnard answered. Both watched him as if he were a mouse.

The sob that tore through him scattered the cats and ended in a choking cough. He had killed his only friend and then eaten him. And drank his blood. All the resurrections in the world couldn't change that. He wasn't fit to live in the world of normal mortals, and he could do nothing about that, either.

Well, maybe one thing.

41

Welcome Home, Vampires
August

"Vampire history just isn't what it used to be."

The author of VR

T he Jag purred as if it was in the jungle instead of speeding northeast on Route 128, the Yankee Division Highway, bound for the town of Rockport on Cape Ann's Sandy Bay. The day was perfect, embellished by small bunches of random clouds, ocean scented winds, the evocative sounds of Baroque music, and a grumbling Calvin in his carrying case on the back seat.

So much had happened in the past two months. Morgan smiled thinking of the top secret banquet at Coleson Manor for all those who were cleared and indoctrinated for the Harvard Vampire Resurrection Project, even Robert. The event had included Harvard's President, who had barely survived the realization that

Harvard had become the nation's first vampire reclamation center. She had quoted from her long-deceased mother: "I don't know whether to kiss you or kill you."

After being briefed on all the positive genetic research, with its strong potential for curing and preventing many diseases, including AIDS, she decided to substantially plus up the "open" side of the work of the GenLab, and to treat the Vampire Resurrection wing with the same secrecy as the Manhattan Project during World War II. At best, she viewed vampire resurrection as an inoperable tumor on one of Harvard's primary organs. She buried those feelings, however, and provided all who were connected with "Project Resurrection"—she had purged the word "vampire"—a substantial bonus. Morgan rejoiced as she was finally able to pay off the last of her credit card debt.

She was concerned about JJ, however. He was moody and quiet—probably flirting with depression. He had no friends his own age, nor had he applied to Harvard. JJ was all but housebound at Coleson Manor. He read and re-read the codex, spending too much time in the secret room by himself. And Morgan was convinced the psychologist he was seeing wasn't helping him.

Calvin was another of Morgan's worries. He'd begun to age, had lost weight, his appetite swinging like a pendulum, he slept even more and no longer jumped up on furniture with the ease and grace of the previous three plus centuries. Was losing Calvin one of the prices she must pay for mortality? And Lamar? An icy tide surged through her. So far, being mortal for Morgan amounted to being poised, observant, patient … and prayerful. She lived on bated breath.

Dr. Gibson was writing furiously and would publish a genetics blockbuster by year's end.

A separate paper would document every aspect of "Project Resurrection," but it would be restricted to those who were cleared and indoctrinated for the project.

The OVFS Watch List had quickly proven itself a gold nugget resource. Three vampires had been found and enrolled in the first of Morgan's classes, and all three were showing a strong sense of dedication. A fourth, a rather mercurial sort, had somehow found his own way to the project. Morgan was developing a psychological profile to help in assessing a vampire's potential for success, in addition to her classroom instruction. She had already proved to be a natural behind the lectern.

She read extensively in the field of genetics and asked Dr. Wally and the other members of his staff endless questions. What troubled her was the possibility of "clinical recidivism." Was it possible for a graduate to slip back into vampirism? Would former vampires have to undergo periodic treatment similar to taking a yearly flu shot? That remained to be determined, and she watched Lamar and JJ for any symptoms.

Poor Father Hemming, she thought. He had come home from the Vatican almost empty handed. They had white-washed the OVFS. It never happened. They had patted him on the head, suggested he might want to consult a psychologist, provided a substantial contribution to Saint Paul's building fund, and invited him to become a consultant during the drafting of a new encyclical. He had returned, disappointed, angry, and embarrassed. Still, he believed the OVFS had been expunged—a major victory for the Church, although the participants were neither exposed nor censured.

"Tell me about where we're going, Lamar. I like surprises, but since we're almost there you could at least tell me the name."

Lamar chuckled and reached over to rub the back of her neck. "What's happened to your vaunted delayed gratification?"

She stuck her tongue out at him, and he chuckled again.

"We, my mortal maiden, are going to a Victorian hideaway called the Pleasant Street Inn. It is a grand old B & B, perched on a hill overlooking Rockport. Been there since you were only a couple hundred years old. The owners, Jerry and Tom Rogers, seem like really nice folks. I've talked to them on the phone and exchanged a couple emails. I asked them if they had any prejudice against housing vampires and told them we had to sleep during daylight hours—"

Morgan poked him in the ribs. "I think I liked you better as a vampire."

"Well, how do you know I really took the cure? You were asleep."

"I definitely liked you better as a vampire."

"Okay, we're on Mt. Pleasant Street. Be looking for Spring Lane. It should be a couple of blocks or so after that."

"Is everything going to be 'pleasant' at the Pleasant Street Inn, Lamar?" Morgan giggled.

Calvin growled.

42

The DNA of Love
August

"Out beyond the idea of wrong doing and right doing
there is a field. I'll meet you there."

Rumi, Medieval Persian Sufi Poet

Morgan walked slowly back to their beach umbrella, conscious of the warm sand scrunching beneath her bare feet. In one hand she held her flip flops; in the other she held Lamar's hand. She was momentarily aware of Rena's gold ring—his now—on his little finger. They had both worn it during their resurrections. Now they were faced with another, equally important resurrection: the building of a mortal life together. She wasn't quite sure how to do that.

The afternoon sun was dazzling, but the cool bay breeze made them feel alive. And mortal. She pulled a beach towel around her as they sat under a brightly colored umbrella, reading cozy beach novels. She shook her head, remembering the British Penny Dreadfuls from the nineteenth century. The one in her lap wasn't much better. She wondered if her memories of the distant past would fade, maybe even disappear. She hoped not. For good or ill, they were part of who she was—had been.

"Let's go in. I'm getting cool, and I need a shower before dinner," Morgan said.

"I think I like you hot and sweaty," Lamar said.

Morgan squinted behind her bizarre, oversized sun glasses, one of Lamar's beach gifts to her, along with the alligator claw flip flops. She didn't often wear sun glasses now that both her eyes were green. "That sounds like a line out of *Penthouse*."

"Did I mention how fantastic you look?"

Morgan smiled at her cheap beach watch, with its garish-colored band, another of Lamar's gifts. "I'd say it's been a good forty-five minutes. You don't look so bad yourself. I used to think all those workouts were just excuses to ogle Jennifer Marsh and watch *her* get all hot and sweaty."

Lamar stood and stretched. "Okay, I'm ready."

"Lamar, whenever you're really ready, come to *me*."

"Love is a lot more than just the sex, you know," Lamar said, watching a sand crab skitter sideways.

"What? Say that again."

"Oh, it's just something I read recently."

Morgan threw her book at him.

He laughed and pulled her up and into an embrace.

As they walked in, Jerry waved them over to the desk. "I got a call for you from a gentleman named Robert Diamond. He needs to talk you as soon as possible. Says it's urgent. Didn't leave a number."

Lamar and Morgan frowned at one another. "Thanks, Jerry." They hurried up the stairs to their room on the second floor.

"Robert, Lamar here. What's happened?" In the long pause that followed Morgan watched his face with a growing sense of dread.

"Oh, God, *no*. When?" Lamar sagged into a caned, barrel-back chair, his face ashen. Morgan covered her mouth with prayerful hands, fear and dread cascading through her. Her intuition was screaming. JJ!

Lamar pursed his lips and held his breath, then blew it out as if it were his last breath. "We'll start packing and get there as quick as we can." His cell phone dropped onto the shag carpet.

Finally, he looked up at Morgan.

"JJ is dead. Shot himself in the secret room about two hours ago."

Morgan screamed and began flailing her fists onto Lamar's chest, tears pouring down her cheeks. "*I killed him. I killed him.* I put him through resurrection, and he wasn't ready. I left him when he needed me most. Oh God, Lamar, I never did anything so horrible in all the years I was a vampire. Maybe I still am a vampire. Maybe it didn't take on me." She crumpled into his arms.

"We all thought he was ready, even Jamie." Lamar held her in a crushing grip until her shaking subsided, but her knees buckled, and he lowered her onto the bed. Her head twisted from side to side until her eyes glazed and she became pale. And still. And cold. Her breathing shallow and too fast. As if she were surrendering her newly won mortality. Lamar failed to register that one of her eyes had turned brown. Or the faint scent of absinthe.

He heard the light knocking on the door, followed by Jerry's voice. "Mr. Bradford, is everything all right? Can I help you?"

"Call 911, my wife has gone into shock."

Wife? At the fringe of consciousness, Morgan paused to savor that word for a moment before crossing the fringe into the dark.

They arrived at Coleson Manor after midnight, having barely spoken on the way home. A very somber Robert met them in the front hall, his voice subdued. The body had been collected by Keefe Funeral Home. Robert had delivered the devastating news to Flossie, who delivered it in person to Jamie after alerting Dr. Martin and Dr. Gibson. Both arrived at Jamie's residence soon after Flossie, who stayed the night.

Morgan and Lamar arrived just after 12:30 am, but Lamar insisted they sleep at Coleson Manor that night. The next morning they returned early. Morgan, eyes dark, shoulders slumped, could barely speak as she and Jamie clung to one another and swayed. No words were possible or necessary.

But Lamar did hear her say, "We will be your children now, Jamie. Lamar and me." He couldn't hear Jamie's reply, but it sounded like he had accepted her offer.

Epilogue
August

Father Hemming paused before beginning the graveside service and looked at the small gathering assembled to render a last farewell to JJ. Outside the tent that covered the gravesite a warm, breathy wind pulled at the tent flaps that were fastened around stakes driven in the soft, green turf. Clouds raced across the sky, causing alternating shadow and brilliance, as if a camera shutter were intermittently clicking on and off. He knew most of the attendees; the others he had met before the late morning service in the church.

Jamie Heller stood, head bowed, eyes closed, lost in darkness. He was flanked by Lamar and Morgan, who held his arms. Robert stood behind them. Nancy from MaidPro stood a discreet distance from Robert. Dr. Martin, Flossie, and Harold Stone stood behind Morgan. JJ's high school principal and Dr. Heller's secretary, stood behind Lamar. On the other side of the grave seven of Jamie's colleagues from the GenLab, headed by Wally Gibson, stood in somber ranks, along with Cordell Peyton and Blanton McConnell. Nineteen in all.

The grave marker was simple: "JJ Heller, Beloved Son of Jamie and Jennette. Eternal Peace at Last. 1992-2012."

Father Hemming drew a deep breath and began. "We come together in a timeless ritual, one that raises our eyes and our thoughts above the flotsam and jetsam of our daily lives. For we are here to affirm the eternal truths that love replaces fear, that letting go replaces continual remorse, that resurrection of spirit fills the void, and that friendship is the fuel for the lamp of truth and light. And so on this day of farewell, I want you to…."

His words faded. JJ, I'm so sorry, Morgan thought. But I will make you proud of me. I will prepare those who follow so they can walk the full path of their newfound mortality. You will serve as a beacon to them—and to me. You have not left me. Us. The veil between us is no more than a gossamer wing. She was aware of a mockingbird singing with abandon.

"Thank you, JJ," she murmured.

Just outside the tent, not visible to those within, stood Alden Hebbda. At least that's what it said on his nametag. He leaned on the shovel he had driven into the ground. And waited. He could afford to wait. Alden pulled out a gold-plated pocket watch and opened the back, looking at the engraving: "Gene Claude Vompre, 1893." He smiled and replaced the watch in the pocket of his coveralls.

He had all the time in the world.

September

It was nearly dark. A few lightning bugs were blinking around the back patio, and the crickets were warming up. The sound of water from the fountain in the center of the new fish pond was soothing. Lamar had stocked it with a variety of brightly-colored gold fish. Morgan and Lamar held one another in the quiet gloaming. They were healing, but their path to becoming normal humans was fraught with the huge hole created by JJ's death, along with the normal roadblocks and detours life presents.

After standing silently for a long time Lamar spoke, his voice quiet, introspective. "Your brown eye is almost green again."

Morgan squeezed his hand. "You have been magnificent. I don't know how I could have made it without you. You have shown me what love really means, and in doing so you filled the place inside me that remained a void even after resurrection. Now it's filled with love."

"I love you, Morgan. With all my heart. And soul." He kissed her.

She kissed him back, tears from her green eyes gracing both of their cheeks.

The next morning Morgan leaped out of their bed and barely made it to the bathroom before she was sick.

What was that for? she wondered. I don't have a fever. I only had two glasses of wine last night. In fact, I've never felt better in my—

Oh. My. God.

THE END
(OF THE BEGINNING)

Vampire Resurrection Characters
Major Characters

Lamar Bradford	Wealthy owner of Coleson Manor.
Morgan Summers	325-year-old vampire born in Old Salem Village.
Robert Diamond	Gentleman's Gentleman to Lamar Bradford at Coleson Manor.
Dr. James R. Heller	Dean of Harvard's Faculty of Arts and Sciences and Director of Harvard's Genetics Laboratory.
Dr. Florence Senger	Called "Flossie," Director of Human Resources at Harvard University.
Ms. Judeland Bundaeker	Flossie Senger's office manager.
Jennifer Marsh	Lamar's administrative assistant.
Dr. Wallace Gibson	("Wally") Director of Operations at Harvard's Genetic Laboratory.
Cordell Peyton	Chief Special Detective for Cambridge Police.
Lieutenant Colonel/Colonel Johann Solento	Deputy/later Commander of the Pontifical Swiss Guard at the Vatican.
Cardinal Alfonso Loconi	President of the Vatican's Fabbrica and head of the secret OVFS— Order of the Vampire Final Solution.
Cardinal Santoro Manlocara	Vatican Treasurer and financier for the OVFS.
Father Ed Hemming:	Catholic Priest at Saint Paul Catholic Church.
Harold Stone:	Chief of Harvard's Campus Police Department.
Charlotte Rhodes:	Saint Paul Catholic Church secretary.

Minor Characters

Miss Lillian	Special friend of Morgan Summers.
Dr. Glenn Ellen Martin	President of Harvard University.
Jim Larkness	Special Detective, subordinate of Cordell Peyton.
Blanton McConnell	Special Detective, subordinate of Cordell Peyton.
Paula Bernard	Waitress at the Harvard Faculty Club.
Jake (no last name)	Bomb maker for the OVFS.
Lawrence Ashton	Lab Technician at Harvard's Genetics Lab.
George Henderson	One of Harold Stone's surveillance operatives.
Monty (no last name)	Auto mechanic; member of the OVFS.
Gretta (no last name)	Gretta the Blind - Woman who raised Morgan Summers in Old Salem after Morgan's mother was pressed to death.
Dr. Gene Claude Vompre	19^{T}-20TH century genetic scientist.
Dr. Archibald E. Garrod	The Father of Genetics. (A real person who died in 1936.)
Lenore (no last name)	Dr. Heller's Administrative Assistant.
Coleson B. Bradford	Lamar's father.
Jill Bonnet	OVFS agent.
Imre Sandar (also known as **"Number Three"**)	OVFS agent.
Rena (no last name)	Female vampire killed by Morgan.
Nancy (No last name)	Senior cleaning lady of MaidPro Housecleaning and Maid Service.
Robert Shackleford	Chairman of Saint Paul's Building Committee.

Acknowledgments

This is really *our* book. Jenny, my wife, not only kept me fed during the months of literary gestation, she served as a talented research assistant and hawk-eyed editor.

The late Professor of English Libuse ("Libby") Reed, Ohio Wesleyan University, spilled gallons of red ink on my compositions as she hammered into me the concepts of good writing. I can still feel her proverbial ruler on my knuckles. And throughout the decades she continued to correct my writing, at one point asking me if I "owned a cliché machine or was I making all of them up myself."

Mary Bargteil was the first teacher and evaluator of my fiction. She convinced me I could write a novel.

All the members of a string of critique groups worked to herd me down the *write* path. This is especially true with fellow writers in the *Novel Experience* and *Wren Writers* groups.

My three writing partners who have dissected me with a surgeon's skill: CJ Cooper, Cindy Young-Turner, and Cyndy Kelly.

Tj Turner, consummate writer, warrior (three deployments to Afghanistan as an Air Force officer), patriot, and good friend. We've traded war stories and manuscripts. Good therapy that.

Jeanne Johansen, at High Tide Publications, Inc. Fixer of all problems, morale builder par excellence, developer of really cool Web sites, pure grace under fire, marketeer—she does it all.

For what success I can bring to the table, all my mentors must share in the feast. Where I have stumbled, the faults are all of my own making. And at the end of the day—my very most favorite cliché—everyone who has ever stomped or flitted through my life has left a residue, one I have collected into many characters that whisper to me from these and the pages of other books yet to grace the shelves at B & N.

Dare I leave out the Muse?

Hardly.

About the Author

Born in Washington, D.C., Charles V. Brown wrote his first fiction short story in the fifth grade. He still has it; in fact, it is reproduced in his as-yet-to-be-published memoir, *Sleeve an' Me*.

For years a dabbler in fiction, he allowed a thirty year Air Force career and an advanced degree, along with raising two daughters, three horses, breeding English Setters, playing innumerable Dixieland Jazz gigs, and a tour in Nam to get in the way of writing.

His second novel, *Viking Lady,* won grand prize in the Maryland Writer's Association's annual novel contest, and then he got serious about writing.

After seventy-two years as a Marylander, Vic and Jenny moved to Williamsburg, Virginia, and rescued a cat—*Crickett* (with two ts!).

Vic still plays jazz and writes and critiques and basks in the warmth of a mighty-nice place to live: Windsor Meade.

www.ingramcontent.com/pod-product-compliance
Lightning Source LLC
Chambersburg PA
CBHW071514260626
47170CB00002B/364